I0674336

The Determined Woman

M.L. Lexi

Titles by M.L. Lexi

The Blind Woman
The Deceitful Woman
The Forgiving Woman
The Grieving Woman
The Guilty Woman
The Loyal Woman
The Noble Woman
The Resolute Woman
The Unfaithful Woman

The Farfalla Family Saga

The Determined Woman
The Persevering Woman
The Invincible Woman

The Fearless Woman Series

The Fearless Woman
The Naïve Woman

Copyright

To my readers, for your support in helping
to make my writing dream a reality.
Thank you! Thank you! Thank you!

Nothing is impossible to a determined woman.

—Louise May Alcott

Prologue

THAT ONE ACT set everything in motion, and the consequences were still reverberating all these years later. Now, things Isabella thought would remain inside her forever had to be told.

On a long breath, she dropped her weary body into the plush leather of the Kensington recliner. The golden liquid in her glass sloshed dangerously close to the rim. Resting her head against the chair, she squeezed her eyes shut and struggled for calm.

Isabella wasn't under the delusion this moment would never come. She only hoped it wouldn't, but the repercussions of a single vile act could go on and on for years and touch many lives. As hard as Isabella tried to keep the painful experience from reaching her family, the time had come when it would.

Isabella's expression shifted as her daughter's angrily lobbed questions came to her—again.

How could you do this to me, to daddy?

How could you lie all these years, and with such ease, Mother? What else have you been lying about?

Do you know how betrayed and broken I feel knowing the person I love and trust most in this world has lied to me my entire life?

My whole life has been a lie.

The anger hot and pulsing in Bianca's voice as she came at Isabella with the questions, accusations, and hate, her response was to run away—far away from her daughter. Escaping, shrouding herself from everything and everyone was what she needed, and in the darkness of night, Isabella made the two-hour drive to her northern retreat.

No matter how long Isabella had mentally prepared for when the moment came, when it did, it felt like a detonating hand grenade to her system. The shameful, ugly secret she'd kept buried in the deep recesses of her mind for the twenty-three years of her daughter's life, her entire married life now had to be told.

Isabella was bone-tired, but as much as she needed to lay her head down, her racing mind wouldn't allow sleep to come. She did the next best thing. Isabella fueled herself with the remaining brandy in her glass.

Swooping to the bar, she slopped brandy into her glass then crossed to the window. The first light from a rising sun peeked from between the treetops. Isabella cast eyes to the natural, unspoiled surroundings of Lake Rosseau. Spring was beginning to show her face in the small Canadian town, and fields and forests framing the lake were steeped in the budding green heralding the season. Canada geese migrating from their winter sojourn filled a vivid blue sky.

In the deafening silence, her father's words rushed at her.

Secrets are like walls, Isabella. They will protect you and those around you from the pain they can inflict and the harm they can spawn, but only temporarily because no matter how shocking or terrible those secrets are, eventually, they always come out.

Hers now had.

The warmth of the living room suddenly felt stifling, and Isabella stepped out onto the terrace. The air against her face, cool and moist, carried the pungent peaty smell of damp earth and dew from the previous week's rains. The sounds of dawn were all around. Within the shelter of trees that sprang up majestically toward the sky, a soft wind rustled through their leaves. Birds joined in the chorus of birdsong, and creatures stirred.

The soothing and utopian panorama she escaped to when she needed recharging from her busy life today did nothing to calm her restless mind. Today, her heart ached too much. It ached for her daughter and her unsuspecting family. Resurrecting the long-hidden event from her past was going to cause deep hurt.

She prayed her daughter, husband, and son would understand and forgive her. At the thought, they may not, a frightful chill cut deep, and Isabella wrapped her hands around her shivering body.

"How could I have been so careless?" she thought, eyeing the envelope—the cause of all her problems—sitting on the coffee table. Twice she'd attempted to read its contents but hadn't found the courage to do so.

She should have locked the goddamn thing in her office safe when her assistant handed it to her, but there were so many distractions. The ringing telephone, the tantrum from her Vice-President of Sales complaining about late shipments, and her secretary's urging words to get to the boardroom for the meeting she was running late for had her dismissing the envelope. Although Isabella thrived on such chaos, the contents of the envelope, which was about to change her family's life, had her mind distracted, and she rushed off to her meeting, leaving it on her desk for Bianca to find.

Isabella couldn't fault her daughter for the screaming match she'd incited or the accusatory and hurtful words

Bianca hurled when she so much as handed her the DNA report she'd requested without her knowledge.

Guilt compressed in a tight ball in the pit of Isabella's stomach.

The should-haves whirled in Isabella's head. She should have done this or that, but it was too little too late, and her impulse was to run to avoid Bianca's demands for answers, for the truth.

Not that she blamed her daughter. If she were in Bianca's shoes, she too would have demanded an explanation, answers. She, also, would have flung the hateful words Bianca hurled like daggers aimed to wound because she and her daughter were alike. The thought, however, didn't lessen the fact Bianca's hurtful words cut Isabella deeply.

You're my mother, the person I trust unconditionally, and now you're nothing but a lying, deceiving— I will never trust you again, Mom, and I couldn't hate you more right now if I wanted to. I hate you. I hate you. I hate you.

Isabella hadn't known a hurt like that of a child telling their mother she hated her.

Her daughter's words echoing in her ears with the intensity they were meant to, Isabella imagined the depth of Bianca's pain, the feeling of betrayal when she read the report.

No one escaped the past, Isabella thought. A shiver cut through her like a serrated knife, and she wrapped her arms around her body for warmth. Closing her eyes, she opened herself to the memories and the lie at the heart of it all.

Part I

Resolve

When you come to the end of your rope
tie a knot and hang on.

—Franklin D. Roosevelt

Chapter 1

January 1982

THE STOMACH CANCER detected during the routine check-up seven months ago had metastasized. It was a word Isabella didn't fully understand its implications but sensed it wasn't an outcome her father deserved.

Six weeks from the diagnosis, with his wife, Maria, and daughter, Isabella, by his side, Angelo Farfalla drew his last breath. He was forty-one. As painful as it was to watch her father die, seeing him at peace and pain-free was soberly gratifying.

On a February winter day, under a dark sky with a cold, howling wind seeping deep into your bones, Angelo was laid to rest. Isabella and Maria flanked by Angelo's brother Gianni, his wife Nina, and their daughter Michaela filled the front row as Father Lenny recited prayers. Looking solemn and respectful, friends and neighbours gathered around the family.

Angelo Farfalla was a loving husband, father, good brother, and caring friend. He and Isabella made so many plans. They were going to visit the major fashion houses in Italy, Paris, and New York. They planned to attend every major fashion show, and when the time came, they'd work together to turn the modest tailor shop that bore Angelo's name into a renowned fashion house.

Growing up watching her father work in his small tailor shop gave Isabella a taste of tailoring. With a strong taste in her system, Isabella knew what she wanted for herself at a young age.

A mixture of love and pride illuminated Angelo's face when she told him she wanted to follow in his footsteps and learn all she could from him. From that moment, her father centred his dreams and hopes on Isabella, but she didn't mind. She wanted to take over the business and carry his legacy as much as he wanted her to.

Isabella was nine when she became his apprentice. Every day after school, she rushed to her father's tailor shop and, like a sponge, soaked every detail of what he taught her. She hung onto every word he uttered. Isabella couldn't have asked for a better teacher or mentor, and he couldn't have asked for a better student.

Angelo taught Isabella about textiles, fabric grains, and bias. He tutored her on running, basting, buttonhole, and every type of stitch there was. Angelo taught Isabella everything he knew about the craft of tailoring. Intently, she watched her father trace the lines onto the fabric with the tailor's beeswax, which turned into the patterns he'd assemble into the custom-made suits he proudly tagged with a FARFALLA TAILORS label.

"Sewing is one of the most ancient of the textile arts," Angelo told Isabella. "Beautiful things can come from a bolt of fabric. Let your imagination flow, Isabella."

Those words set Isabella's mind rolling. She didn't just want to make beautiful clothes. Isabella wanted to create garments that made women feel feminine, extraordinary. To design clothes, women sought out and bragged about wearing. Isabella wanted to become a household name.

"And one day, you will, Isabella. You're very talented," Angelo assured.

"When will that be, Daddy?"

"I'll let you know, princess. Until then, everything that's in me will be yours. You will be bigger and better than I could ever be because you're smarter than I am. You've inherited the entrepreneurial gene and an aptitude for business from your old man."

They had so many plans, but as fate would have it, at the age of twenty-two, Isabella watched her father's casket lowered into a darkness he'd never come back from.

After the funeral, people filed to pay their last respects. Many commented on how beautiful the service was and offered words of sympathy and unconditional support.

Until that moment, Isabella hadn't felt more alone.

FROM THE SHELTER OF TREES A pair of eyes fixated on Isabella. Firing up a cigarette, they watched her every move, studied her, and surveyed her face. It had been months since they'd come upon her, but she looked as beautiful as always.

Eyes the colour of aged bourbon were sad and solemn today. Her mouth was wide and full. Her long dark hair tumbled in waves around an unpainted face as delicate as silk. She wasn't one to flaunt her striking beauty, but she didn't have to, he thought approvingly.

A warmth came over him when he watched Isabella gnaw that lovely lower lip in the way she tended to do when she was nervous or deep in thought. She'd done that since he could remember.

For a moment, he thought Isabella flicked wary eyes in his direction, but with a tug of relief, dismissed the notion when her cousin Michaela reached for her hand and walked her to the car.

He pitched the cigarette at the grass and hid from view. Isabella never saw or sensed the eyes that remained on her until she left for home.

Chapter 2

ISABELLA'S EYES ROLLED over the stack of overdue bills, then flicked to the bankbook balance. The $59.25 wasn't going to cut it, and she pushed the bankbook and bills aside when the sense of helplessness overtook her.

As much as Isabella wanted to save the shop, she couldn't hold on to it much longer. The mounting bills and debt collectors were more than she could deal with. She had no option but to close the doors to her father's tailor shop and give up her dream. Struggling against twin urges of defeat and failure, every bone in her body felt weighted by the most dreadful fatigue.

Isabella looked around the small shop, borne out of her father's sweat and sacrifice. Stacked on the wood shelves bought at the Goodwill were dozens of neatly folded bolts of fabric ready to be shaped into beautiful garments. The second-hand sewing machine sat idle and tape measures, scissors, rulers, and iron, cluttered the workbench. Linoleum grayed from use matched the wall colour. It wasn't much, but it was her father's life work, and she hoped it would be his legacy.

Angelo had worked hard, sacrificed, and given so much of himself to his business, hoping one day it would fulfill Isabella's long-sought dream of becoming the next Versace or Chanel. After years of sweat and sacrifice, it came down to one option, shutting the shop and her dream down.

It wasn't fair.

Life wasn't fair.

Isabella lay her head down on crossed arms and let the tears of despair flow.

"What have I told you about crying?"

Isabella knuckled tears from her eyes to clear her vision. "Daddy?" She closed her eyes, opened them. There he was. "Jesus, I need to get some sleep."

"You do, princess. You're looking tired and thin. I want you to take care of yourself. You're all your mother has. Promise me you will, Isabella." Smoke flowed from the cigarette in Angelo's mouth upward in a lazy curl.

Isabella stared at her father. He looked real and healthy. His eyes were the sapphire-blue she remembered from his healthy days and full of life.

"It's me, princess." Angelo walked toward Isabella, bringing with him the smell of Old Spice and cigarette smoke. "Promise me, Isabella, you'll look after yourself. You're mother needs you."

"That's rich coming from you. You know those things killed you. How many times did we beg you to stop smoking?" Isabella tossed back with the bottled-up anger she'd carried since burying him.

"I deserve that."

"It's too late for that now," she said when he moved to crush out the cigarette. "I don't think they can kill you again."

Angelo let out a booming laugh. "I always did appreciate your sense of humour."

"I miss you, Daddy."

"I miss you too, princess. I'm sorry for leaving you and your mother. I should have taken better care of myself."

"Yes, you should have."

"You want to take the shop over and make it your own as we planned."

"I do, but…" Isabella let the sentence hang. She couldn't tell him the shop he'd worked so hard to establish was on the verge of bankruptcy. Isabella wouldn't tell him the mounds of bills made it so most days she felt like a salmon swimming upstream through a current of despair.

"No excuses. Don't be afraid to reach for the stars, princess. You have your dream to fulfill. One we planned for since you were a little girl." Angelo held up a cigarette. When Isabella shrugged her shoulders, he lit it with the Bic lighter he dug from his pants pocket.

"But, Daddy…"

"Reach for the stars, princess. Fulfill your vision, but do it for yourself, not me."

Isabella rolled teary eyes to her father. "I can't do this for you or me."

"Of course you can, and you will make a name for yourself, not for me." Gazing into Isabella's eyes, Angelo plugged the cigarette into his mouth, inhaled. "What is it?"

"We're broke, Daddy," Isabella reluctantly admitted.

"Princess, we've always been broke." Angelo exhaled a long plume of white smoke, watched it curl upward until it faded. "You're too young to be taking on so much responsibility, but you're way more clever and capable than I was. You have brains and talent, Isabella. You can do this. Believe in yourself, and everything will fall in place."

"Hello." The man's voice brought Isabella out of her slumber.

"Can't you see the closed sign on the door?" Isabella groggily shot out with a mixture of irritation and annoyance.

"I'm sorry to bother you."

"Well, you are, and I said we're closed," Isabella barked before her angry tone waned.

His eyes were the colour of the sea and sky with long, thick lashes. His hair, peppered with snowflakes, was a mane of jet-black waves that framed a compelling face with a wide mouth curved into a warm smile. A fashionable stubble added a sexy touch, and aside from the slightly crooked nose, he was perfect.

"My name is Antonio Sabatini. I'm your landlord."

His allure faded. "If you're looking for money, take a number, Mr. Saba-whatever." Isabella's rasping tone netted a raised brow.

The irritated eyes that stared at him were hazel, flecked with specks of orange. Sexy, he thought. "Antonio works. May I speak to Mrs. Farfalla?"

"No. Talk to me." Isabella snarled, unable to control the bitter edge to her tone.

She was a cranky one, but easy on the eyes, Antonio thought. Hair, the colour of mink, was smoothly pulled back to accent a delicate face devoid of make-up—as he liked his women. Her mouth was full and pink. She was five or six inches shorter than his six-foot frame, and although she wore a baggy sweatshirt and sweat pants, he figured the body beneath it was lean and curvy. He wondered how she'd escaped his attention until then.

"I wanted to talk to you about…"

"I know what you want to talk to me about. We owe you back rent. And like I said, take a number." Isabella's voice punched like a fist. Whether he heard it or not, he took no notice. The anger lighting the large, hazel eyes had him entranced.

"Not having a good day?" Antonio's dimples flashed with charm.

"Pfft, a day I can handle. I'm not having a good life," Isabella said with a sarcastic half-laugh as he sized the full bottom lip and determined it was perfect for nibbling. "Stop staring at me," she snapped.

"I'm sorry I didn't mean to make you uncomfortable," Antonio said when he saw her nervous hand move closer to the iron, which he didn't doubt she wouldn't hesitate to lob at him. Fire and beauty, with an indefinable hint of sensuality in a woman, were admirable qualities in his book. "And I'm sorry about not having a good life, but I promise you it does get better."

The kind-hearted flow of his words pulled at Isabella. "It's me who's sorry. Mrs. Farfalla is my mom. I'm Isabella."

"It's nice to meet you, Isabella." Antonio took the offered hand to pump and held it for longer than he should when his heart bumped and hammered hard at her touch.

"How can I help you?" Isabella said, prying her hand free.

"I did want to talk to you about the rent."

The knot in Isabella's stomach knit tight. "I don't have your money right now."

"I'm not here to collect." Isabella kept puzzled eyes levelled on the spellbinding blue ones. "I know you're going through a difficult time, and I stopped in to tell you not to worry about the rent. You can take all the time you need." Antonio watched her raise a quizzical brow. "I've been in your shoes, and I know right now, you don't need the additional pressure of making rent."

Something powerful and raw in his tone, in the eyes so compassionately gazing at her, made it difficult for Isabella to hold her composure. To his utter terror, she let the tears flow.

"I'm sorry. I … didn't mean to… Oh, jeez. I didn't mean to upset you. Honestly," Antonio stammered with the panicked feeling that consumes a man at the sight of a crying woman. Her heart-wrenching tears pulled at his heartstrings, and he wound his way around the table to wrap arms around her. "Please, please don't cry."

"I'm sorry." Isabella pulled loose from his hold.

"Do you feel better?" Antonio's fingers skimmed over her cheeks to dry tears. "My mom always said a good cry made her feel better."

"Yes, thank you." Feeling conscious of their closeness, Isabella took a few steps back. "I'm so embarrassed."

"If anyone should be embarrassed, it's me. My charismatic personality is supposed to appeal to your female sensibilities, not have you in tears."

Isabella smiled at that. "Your charismatic personality doesn't need fine-tuning. It's that out of everyone who's offered a helping hand, you're the only one who's meant it."

Her vulnerability, her softness, the teary eyes tugged at Antonio. He slid his fingers under her chin, lifted her face to meet his. "And I mean it. You take as long as you need."

The gesture spoke volumes, and the hopelessness and misery that filled Isabella for months faded. The stranger she'd just met with a simple act of kindness, restored her faith in humanity. "Thank you."

"Your father was a good man. He was always kind to me, and I'd like to repay the favour. If you or your mother needs anything, you come to see me. Day or night, you can find me at The Café."

"Thank you, and I'll have your money to you as soon as possible."

"I know you will. In case you don't, I know where you live." Antonio's comment netted him a brittle smile. "That's better. I guess it's been a rough few months for you." She nodded, tucking the errant strand of hair behind her ear, and as hard as Antonio tried not to stare, he found he couldn't take his eyes off her. "It'll get better."

When? Isabella wondered, giving him a faint smile and a nod.

Antonio scanned his watch. "I'm sorry, but I need to get back to the cafe. Here's where you can reach me." He penned his number on a piece of paper. "And, Isabella, keep smiling. You look great when you do."

Chapter 3

IN HER FIFTH floor office of the Hart Designs building, Isabella studied her charcoaled sketch one last time. Deciding the fitted plaid jacket's fluid lines and complementing gray, low-rise pants were perfect, she set her pencil down and turned her focus out the wide, square window.

To the east, old and new buildings of architectural beauty populating the downtown core stretched high to the sky. Straight ahead, Lake Ontario spread to the horizon under a staggering blue sky. The hustle and bustle of people with rushed lives packed sidewalks and bumper-to-bumper traffic crawled along Lake Shore Boulevard. Isabella loved the view she'd earned during the past three years at Hart Designs.

Graduating top of her class, Mr. Hart was relentless in his pursuit to bring Isabella on board as a junior designer. Isabella accepted Mr. Hart's offer after her father convinced her the experience she'd gain at the reputable fashion house would be invaluable.

Now, Isabella wondered if she'd ever put the knowledge she'd learned to use. Launching her fashion house would take effort and energy. That she had lots of, but starting your own business took money, which she didn't have.

But she was her father's daughter, and like him, had the entrepreneurial itch to satisfy. How she'd do it five years ahead of schedule, without her father or a penny to her name, was a detail she had to work out? Very soon.

"It's a great view." The voice drifted in from the doorway, and Isabella swivelled her chair to face the tall, willowy Gail Williams.

"I haven't seen much of you lately," Isabella said, studying her exotic looking friend who always looked as if cut from the pages of Vogue.

Today she wore a coral flare-sleeved jacket over a cream silk shirt. Her russet skirt rode shorter than it should for an office setting, but Gail's mission was flaunting toned legs. The waterfall of brown hair fell in layers of tight curls around a heart-shaped face with large saucer-round eyes. Her skin was the colour of midnight and as smooth as an opal.

"The move is keeping me busy. I have to start saying no to that man. That old coot has this crazy notion I'm at his beck and call to do with me as he wishes." Gail ranted of Mr. Hart. "I'm his assistant, not his office manager or babysitter or personal shopper or…"

"Breathe, Gail." Isabella prompted. "Remember your blood pressure."

Gail held up a hand, palm out, to silence Isabella. "I'm not done, and I sure as hell shouldn't have to deal with the relocation of our design division from Toronto to New York. So many personalities, so much attitude. You want to see grown men and women turn into children? Have them move. It's taken all my strength not to bang their heads together to knock sense into them."

"Is that coffee for me?" Isabella said when Gail stopped for breath.

"It is." Gail jiggled the cup off the tray and handed it to Isabella.

Folding the tab and locking it in place, Isabella took a long, satisfying sip. "You're officially my best friend."

Gail flashed Isabella a dimpled smile. "How are you doing, honey?"

"I'm getting there. I'm just happy Mr. Hart spared me from making the move to New York and allowed me to stay put. With just having buried my dad, I couldn't leave my mother."

"I know, honey." Sipping coffee, Gail slid a look over the sketches on the drafting table. "Next winter's line?"

"Yep, just finished the last sketch. I managed to come up with ten designs in two weeks." Gail set her cup down, flipped through the sketches. "They're rough drafts. Mr. Hart and Fizz rushed me to get them done," Isabella told Gail when she cocked a thin, dark brow.

There was such artistry, such ingenuity and imagination in the sketches, Gail thought. Having no artistic talent herself, she appreciated the artistry in Isabella's designs. Isabella's eye for fashion was one that couldn't be taught, Gail thought. You were either born with the creative gene or not, and Isabella was.

"Mr. Hart and Fizz will select six from the ten if not all. They should net the company five million dollars in sales." Isabella drained more coffee from her cup.

"Both you and I know it will be Mr. Hart doing the selecting because Fizz, simply put, is the useless, untalented daughter latching on to daddy until he's six feet under. The girl wouldn't know fashion if it hit her in that lipo-sucked ass of hers."

There was anger in Gail's tone and fire in her eyes, but Isabella couldn't help but snort a giggle. "You shouldn't hold back, Gail."

"I only tells the truth, honey, and speaking of, these are amazing, Isabella."

"You think so? I still have a lot to learn." Isabella watched Gail slide her lean frame into the guest chairs.

"You don't give yourself enough credit. I've been here for ten years. I've seen designers come and go, and I'll tell you, Isabella, you have a special talent." Gail crossed a long, toned leg over another.

"That means a lot to me, Gail." Isabella's eyes flicked out the window and followed the flock of Harlequin ducks sweeping across the sky, then seamlessly glide on calm water.

"Have Mr. Hart and Fizz seen the sketches yet?"

"No. We're supposed to meet this Friday when they get back from their New York trip to go over them."

There was a stretch of silence, as Gail considered. "I'm going to tell you something, Isabella, and it has to remain between us," Gail said, deciding to break confidentiality she swore to uphold as Mr. Hart's assistant.

"It will." Isabella turned the key on a pursed mouth.

"The reason Mr. Hart and Fizz rushed you to complete the sketches is that they wanted them before they…." Gail hesitated.

The clicking from the photocopy machine spitting copies when Amy, receptionist, and gossip extraordinaire, pressed START, filled the silence in Isabella's office.

"To what, Gail?" Isabella watched Gail walk to the door and slam it on Amy's snooping ears.

"Fire you."

A cold chill shot up Isabella's spine. "What are you talking about? You're mistaken. They promised me a bonus and a promotion with a salary increase. It's why I'm in this office."

"I'm sorry to be setting this minefield off, especially now, but none of that is going to happen."

Shoulders slumped, Isabella sunk to the depths of her chair. "I never got the impression they wanted me gone. Mr. Hart and Fizz have repeatedly told me how pleased they are with my work. They were good to me when I asked them if I could stay behind with the Canadian division after my father's death." Isabella's mind worked quickly now.

"Mr. Hart is very pleased with your work, but Fizz, well, you know she has him wrapped around her finger. Before their New York trip, I overheard a conversation between them. Fizz talked Mr. Hart into making her the Vice-President of Design, and you know you're bound to upstage her. She won't let that happen."

Isabella's throat constricted without warning. "I need this job. Now more than ever, and they know it. I was planning to play catch-up with the shop's bills with my next paycheque and bonus," she said, the quiver of distress in her words.

Isabella begged, degraded herself, worked her fingers to the bone, and she hadn't cared as long as she remained on the payroll.

"I know, honey. I'm so sorry." Gail's eyes followed Amy as she walked past Isabella's office, heading back to her desk.

"Are you sure, Gail? You're sure what you heard?"

"I'm sorry, honey."

"How can they do this to me now?" Isabella nervously paced her office. "Jesus, the time I've dedicated, the money my designs have generated for them, my loyalty to this company. Doesn't any of that mean anything to them?" Isabella lifted her hands to her temples, massaged in a circular motion. "I'm broke now as is. Without this job, I'll be this close to becoming destitute."

"I'm sorry I've upset you, honey, but I thought you should know what's coming because I don't think you should let them have these designs. They sure as hell don't deserve them."

"Oh, God, what am I going to do?" The sick ball at the pit of Isabella's stomach twined tightly as her mind raced.

How was she going to keep up with the shop's bills that never stopped coming? She owed back rent, and utilities were on the third past-due notice. They could survive without a telephone. How were she and her mother to survive without heat through the winter months? How were they going to survive, period?

"Calm down, Isabella. I know this comes as a shock, but you can find a job anywhere. You're extremely talented, and our competitors are bound to snap you up as soon as they find out you're looking. I can put some feelers out with my contacts."

Nerves bouncing, Isabella paced. "Yeah, so they can pull the same stunt after draining me of my energy and dignity." Isabella let raw temper carry her into an oath-laced rant with the sharp stab of anger and resentment racing over her.

"You let it out, girl," Gail said, impressed by her prim friend's extensive knowledge of the vulgar language.

"I gave that sonofabitch twelve-hour days, weekends, holidays, all without pay because I love what I do. Because I thought they would follow through with the bonus, advancement. And this is how they repay me?"

"I'm sorry, honey." Gail's eyes flashed sympathy.

"They have to be taught a lesson."

Brows drew together to form that vertical crease between them, Gail called her intellectual line. "What are you going to do, Isabella? Don't do anything you'll regret."

Isabella lifted a brow. "That ship's sailed. I'm so regretting everything I've done for this company, for Mr. Hart."

"You can make your point, even be vengeful in a sophisticated way."

"Yeah, you're right." Isabella set her mind to think mode.

Gail's dark chocolate eyes went baleful when she recognized the scheming look in Isabella's eyes. "Isabella, what are you planning to do?"

"A pinch of mystery always adds lustre to an artist's aura," Isabella said, thinking it best Gail remained in the dark.

"All right. Just promise me you won't do anything crazy."

"I promise." The distressed look had left Isabella's face, and settling in at her drafting table, with great positiveness, added, "Thank you for telling me. One day I'll return the favour. Now, I gotta get to work." Isabella tied her hair back with a clip and picked up the four-B graphite pencil.

Chapter 4

ISABELLA LOWERED THE toothbrush and stared at herself in the mirror. She was about to take a significant step, and she hoped it paid off. She had a lot to do this morning, and she was ready for it. Rinsing her mouth, Isabella walked back to her room and picked up the telephone.

"Hi, Gail... Yeah, I know the meeting is about to start... Yes, I figured you've been trying to find me. I'm not in the office... No. I'm fine. Everything's fine. I just wanted you to tell Mr. Hart I won't be making it in for the meeting... Everything's fine, but I do need a favour." Isabella swung the closet door open, selected a white cotton shirt, shrugged into it.

"Anything you need, honey. I'm your girl." Gail's sympathetic voice flowed over the telephone.

"In my office, you'll find the sketches and my letter of resignation." Isabella searched for the least worn pair of jeans. She would have preferred to shrug herself into a black Chanel suit against a rose, silk blouse, but a polyester shirt tucked into jeans would have to do. "I want you to turn both over to Fizz. Not Mr. Hart, Gail, Fizz."

Gail's gasped breath followed with a brief moment of silence. "I didn't mean for you to take such drastic measures. Are you sure about this, honey?"

Isabella cradled the telephone on her shoulder as she slipped faded jeans over her hips. "I desperately need the money, but I've never been more sure about anything.

Leaving Hart's is the right decision. The best one I've made in a long time." It was the first time Isabella voiced the thought aloud, and the tight ball in her belly loosened, and the butterflies flew free.

"But maybe I was wrong. Maybe there's more to what I overheard. Maybe you could have talked them out of asking for your resignation if it did come to that." Gail whispered voice came over the telephone line.

"What you heard was right. I've sensed I was on my way out since the day Fizz set foot in the company. You just put it into perspective for me. I could probably talk them into keeping me on, but I don't want to work for someone who puts me in a situation where I need to beg for my job. I've contributed enough to Mr. Hart and his company's bottom line to expect better. I'm not giving them any more of my time or energy, my loyalty, the long hours to an ungrateful employer so his undeserving spawn can profit."

"I hear you, and I'm in complete agreement, but why are you," Gail's voice shifted to a dull whisper, "giving them the sketches?"

"Fair is fair. They've paid me for that work." Tucking her shirt into her jeans, Isabella slanted a look at herself in the dresser mirror and pinched her cheeks for colour. "Trust me on this, Gail."

"But…"

"You've been an absolute doll." Isabella cut Gail off. "And, Gail, I meant it when I say I'll return the favour."

"Don't worry about that, honey. I want you to be okay."

The smile Isabella gave her reflection was full of sureness. "I will be. This is what I need to do." Isabella finger-combed her hair and slid her feet into flats. "It's time to flesh out the idea that has been brewing in my head for years but that I haven't dared pursue. I needed that kick in the butt, and I'm grateful to you for giving it. Now, remember, turn resignation letter and sketches over to Fizz, and don't mention anything about them to Mr. Hart. Talk to you soon," Isabella said, hanging up and crossing CALL GAIL off a long To-Do list that ended with OWN HART DESIGNS.

Chapter 5

ARCHED IN THE doorway, Isabella scanned The Café crowded with the lunch crowd. Chatty diners and couples, their heads closed together in intimate conversation, filled every table. Stools at the bar were full, and a long line of caffeine-craving customers waited to be served. The aroma of ground beans and brewed coffee drifting in the air was nothing short of heavenly.

The Café was four the size of her father's store with a European flair. Framed cafe related images hung on tan washed walls. There was a giant dancing coffee bean sporting a sombrero on his head. Next to it, a steaming coffee cup, the words ESPRESSO emblazoned below its thick rim. There was a cartoonish looking barista serving coffee to smiling customers. Two industrial-size coffee machines hummed behind the bar as they poured steaming espressos and steamed milk for cappuccinos.

Isabella's eyes landed on Antonio behind the counter. He was in his element, engaging customers in casual banter. She watched him pour cup after coffee cup. Her mouth bowed when he burst into joyful laughter along with the heavyset man whose cigarette bobbed from the corner of his mouth in sync with his enormous jelly-like belly.

Isabella felt an extraordinary liquid warmth spread when she saw Antonio's face brighten the moment he saw her.

"Hi," Antonio mouthed, waving her in.

"I'm sorry to bother you. Can you spare me a few minutes?" Isabella called out over the din.

"I can. Marco take over for me," Antonio called out.

When Marco flashed a raised thumb, Antonio tossed the dishtowel draped on his shoulder and the black barista apron around his waist onto the counter. Stepping out from behind the bar, he led her to the table vacated by the young couple.

"I was about to grab some lunch. Will you join me?" Antonio pulled the out chair for Isabella.

"Just coffee for me."

"I don't think so. You're going to eat a meal." Antonio's voice was more firm than he meant it to be, but Isabella looked too thin to be passing the offer of food.

Isabella opened her mouth to apprise him that she wasn't a helpless little girl and could think for herself but closed it when she remembered why she was there. Control Isabella, she told herself, inhaling the good and exhaling the bad. On her exhaled breath, she opened her eyes to Levi's on a tight butt when Antonio spun around to wave Marco over. Her eyes fixed on the tight butt you could bounce a quarter and see it spring back, her temper petered out.

"Now, I'm all yours." Antonio slid into the chair across her. "What did you want to speak to me about?"

"I, that is my mother, and I would like to know if you're okay with us moving out of the upstairs apartment and downstairs to the back of the store."

"To live?"

Misunderstanding his reaction as derision, Isabella lunged into defence mode. "We can't afford to pay rent on the store and the upstairs apartment. I realize it's short notice, and it's a lot to ask since the store is not zoned for residential use, but it will be a great help in reducing my expenses."

"But there's no shower downstairs or a decent bathroom, not to mention the lack of a kitchen or bedroom."

"With your permission, I can make the necessary plumbing adjustment, at my expense, of course. We'll improvise a kitchen and sleeping quarters at the back of the store." Begging was a humbling experience.

"What does your mother think about this arrangement?" When she remained silent, Antonio said, "She doesn't know about these plans."

"Not yet, but…"

"I'm going to say no."

Her mouth tightened into a harsh, bitter line. "What do you mean, you're saying no?"

The disappointment at his empty offer for help sparked a flash of anger in Isabella. She believed, trusted him enough to come to him on bended knees asking for help, but he was like everyone else, offering platitudes. She didn't need platitudes. She had enough of that from everyone around her.

"You told me I could come to you for help. 'You've only to call me. You can turn to me for help anytime,'" she mimicked. "Now that I come to you for a simple favour, which won't cost you anything, and this is what I get." Her voice ice over steel, Isabella lobbed angry words from between gritted teeth.

A firecracker, Antonio thought, staring at the brown eyes going deeper in colour. Deciding it best to let her get her pent up anger out of her system, Antonio leaned back in his chair and watched the blazing eyes, the flailing hands, and the flash of temper as she snapped at him like a German Shepard. From time to time, he'd toss the random nod, the "I understand," or "I'm sorry" to keep his end of the conversation.

Women were unpredictable creatures at the best of times, and he'd learned long ago a compassionate expression accompanied by an "I understand"—although men rarely did—went a long way when dealing with an angry woman.

"Don't patronize me with that understanding nod because you don't. Otherwise, you'd be more helpful. Thanks for nothing." Isabella bolted to her feet.

Antonio loved fire in a woman, and on her, it looked great. "That's not going to happen because I'm not going to have you and your mother living under substandard conditions. You're staying put in the apartment," Antonio said, as she was about to storm away.

Isabella's angry expression withered into a sheepish one. "But we can't afford it."

"I told you you don't have to worry about the rent," Antonio assured, waving a hand to silence her when she opened her mouth. "No arguments. I'm standing firm. "Now, please sit back down." Resting his hand on hers, a flash of heat shot down to his loin and stayed long after she plopped down in her chair and yanked her hand free.

"You know I won't be able to pay the rent for a few months. I need the money to…" Isabella went silent when Marco appeared with coffees and pressed paninis with a side order of salad.

"You have plans," Antonio said when Marco moved on to the next table. "I'm a good listener." Antonio took a generous bite of panino, never leaving the tawny eyes lost in the dark liquid of her coffee cup as she debated whether to tell him.

"I want to take over the tailor shop." Isabella absently picked at her sandwich. "Open it under a new name, a new concept."

"I see." Antonio chased panino with coffee.

"I've given this a lot of thought, and it's what I want to do." There was an odd pleasure at saying the words aloud with such confidence. Moving forward with her life, without regret or a backward glance, was the right decision.

Isabella told Antonio of the plans she'd made with her father to take over the business as her own. She told Antonio that although Mr. Hart and Fizz's plan to oust her drove her to her decision to do it now, it was her dream all along. Isabella told Antonio things she hadn't told her mother. She wasn't sure why she had, but it felt great.

"It's a huge undertaking. Running your own business is not as glamourous as it sounds. It's long hours, stressful days. It's worries of where your next dollar to pay the bills comes from."

"How's that different from my everyday life."

His lips stretched out in a soft smile. "You feel up to the challenge?"

"I do. I really do." There was something solid and reassuring about feeling confident for the first time in a long while. "The store is there now, and my father has an existing clientele I can tap into. There are inventory and equipment I can use." In her momentary silence, the din of conversation, customers placing orders, the ding of the cash registers, and the brewing coffee machines became voluble.

"I think it's a great idea."

The words of encouragement she needed made her eyes glint with confidence. "I have the contacts and the necessary connections, which I've forged over the three years at Hart Designs. I know they will support me." Isabella held back, telling him she got busy penning contact, customer, and supplier information from Hart Designs' files since her talk with Gail.

"Sounds as if you have it all worked out." Antonio chased the last bite of his sandwich with the remnants of his coffee. "Have you thought about how you're going to finance your venture?"

"I have a few thoughts." She shared them.

Entranced with her, he listened, biting back the urge to offer her financial help. Isabella Farfalla was her own woman, and he was sure she wouldn't accept the handout. He offered the next best thing once she went silent. "I'll help you put a financial plan together. You know for Mrs. Johnstone, the bank manager at the Imperial Bank. You are planning to talk to her into financing your venture."

Isabella's enthusiasm waned. "I was, but I need a financial plan?"

Antonio nodded. "You need to present your financial objective and the long-term goals for your business. Mrs. Johnstone's a stickler for details. She'll want to see an overview of projected earnings, cost runs, dollar outlay, and your expected future returns when you ask for the financing you require to set your plan in motion."

Isabella's thin shoulders hunched over. "I, ah, don't know anything about what you said." Numbers were her kryptonite.

"No worries. I'll help you put together a professional proposal to present."

"I don't want to impose."

"No imposition. Round up invoices, bank statements, all the paperwork you can get your hands on, and meet me back here in three hours." Antonio reached for her hand when she started to rise from the table. "Not before you eat up. I have no interest in having my temperamental chef grill me on why the pretty woman having lunch with me left a masterpiece like that on her plate."

Antonio considered it a small victory when she gave him a dimpled smile and reached for the panino.

Chapter 6

DRAWING THE BLINDS to his apartment window open, Isabella saw the moon cresting on the horizon. Buildings and trees were caped in white. Burning streetlamps pooled light over snow-covered sidewalks, and rush hour traffic-clogged the streets.

"I didn't realize how late it was. I'm sorry I've taken so much of your time." Isabella gathered her paperwork off the kitchen table.

"It's only five-thirty, and stop apologizing and thanking me. It may sound odd to someone who thinks numbers are the spawn of the devil, but I enjoy working with them. I am a chartered accountant." Antonio poked his head in the refrigerator, chose the bottle of Zinfandel he thought she'd like, and held it up for her assessment. "Will you join me?" When she nodded, he peeled the seal and uncorked it.

"You have no idea how foreign that sounds. I've always hated numbers, can't seem to make heads or tails of them, especially not when you're putting them into a financial plan as you've done. That takes talent." Isabella sank her tired body into the soft leather of his living room couch, and for the first time, noticed how stylish his apartment was.

Italian sofas, upholstered in a creamy leather, dark wood, and glass-filled the loft-style apartment. A second story bedroom accessed by a winding wrought-iron staircase looked out over the living room, which crossed into the kitchen. Polished oak floors and large picture windows brightened the open space. Abstract paintings blotted with vibrant greens, reds, and orange hung on olive-green walls. It was a man's apartment with a touch of modern sophistication.

"Then, I'll have to take on the role of your accountant." Antonio waved down the oncoming argument. "No, buts."

"I can't afford to pay you. Not right now, anyway."

Antonio handed her the glass of wine before sinking his tall frame next to her. "You will eventually. I, like your father, believe you're destined for great things." His comment elicited a surprised look. "He told me your entrepreneurial talent exceeded his. After this afternoon, I can see what he meant."

Isabella felt her chest constrict. "When did he say this to you?"

"Often enough. He sensed you're destined for greatness. Ask anyone in the cafe."

"He talked to you, to people, about me?"

"He did. He was proud of you."

"Thank you for telling me. It means a lot."

"You're very welcome. Will you stay for dinner?"

"I'd love to, but after this glass of wine, I really should get going. My mother is probably wondering where I've gotten to. Rain cheque?"

"Of course," he said, surprised at the disappointment that squeezed at him.

"I'll go to see Mrs. Johnstone tomorrow."

Antonio watched Isabella take the last of her wine. "Stick to the script we discussed, and you'll do fine."

"Got it right here." Isabella patted the file folder where she'd stored the notes of questions Antonio thought she should ask to appear business minded.

"I'd say good luck, but I'm sure that once she sees the brilliant business plan your accountant's put together, you're a shoo-in."

Isabella's lips stretched out in a smile. "I don't need luck. What I need is a miracle."

"I feel a miracle coming on," Antonio said, making a mental note to call Mrs. Johnstone first thing in the morning.

FROM THE SHADOWS, A POOL OF crushed out cigarettes on the ground, eyes gazed up at Antonio's apartment window, wondering what he and Isabella were doing for over three hours.

Sighing in cigarette smoke, pleasure filled The Eyes when Isabella stepped out of Antonio's apartment and saw no affectionate exchange. There wasn't a peck on the cheek or a friendly embrace. The pleased smile on The Eyes' face quickly evaporated when Antonio leaned against the doorjamb and set tender eyes to Isabella walk away.

Seeing the emotion flowing from Antonio's eyes, a tight, angry fist lodged in The Eyes' chest. Hot rage on top of cold fury had The Eyes' mind raced to plot its revenge.

Chapter 7

WALKING THROUGH THE doors of the Imperial Bank, Isabella's stomach muscles knotted. Telephones shrilled, and calculators clicked. Customers lined the long counter while others queued for their turn.

Isabella hoped she didn't look as tired as she felt. She'd stayed up all night, perfecting her pitch, going over the notes to ensure she had everything Antonio laid out memorized. She had one chance at this and needed to do it right. Her mother's and her life depended on it.

Drawing in a breath, Isabella walked up to the receptionist. "I'm here to see Mrs. Johnstone."

The young girl with the waterfall of honey-blonde hair behind the desk looked up with angelic blue-eyes. "Do you have an appointment?"

"No, but I need to see her." Isabella's tone was flat and final as Antonio told her it should be. "Please, I need to see her."

Scrutinizing blue eyes held, a moment, two. "All right, I'll see if she's available." Blue Eyes rose and disappeared into the corner office. Moments later, she returned and said, "Mrs. Johnstone will see you, Miss…"

"Isabella. Thank you, Kathleen," she said, angling eyes toward the nameplate all the while wondering why the modelesque beauty she pinned at seventeen sat behind a receptionist desk rather than in front of a camera.

"You're welcome. Have a seat, Isabella." Kathleen waved a slim hand toward the vinyl guest chairs lined against the wall. "I'll call you when she's ready."

"Hi, Isabella." The familiar voice had Isabella whirling to face her cousin Michaela sauntering toward her.

In a red, Chanel tapered jacket and pencil skirt Michaela looked stunning. At the end of long legs, she wore black Valentino pumps. Her honey-blonde hair floated in shining waves around an oval face.

"Fancy meeting you here." Michaela's Cherry-red painted lips and crowned with heavily mascaraed lashes, curved into a smile.

"I thought you were off weekends." Isabella returned the peck on the cheek.

"Supposed to be, but I'm now the Loans Officer and super busy," Michaela said. Isabella missed the thin blonde brow that shot up above Kathleen's round eye. "I'm sorry I haven't been by since your dad's funeral, but I've been a bit busy."

"I know all about life, keeping you busy. It's been keeping me on my toes."

"You here to see Mrs. Johnstone?" At Isabella's nod, Michaela glided into the chair next to her. "A word of advice. You don't have to make good on your father's debt. It's under his name, and if there's no money in the estate…"

"Not a penny to my name."

"Well, then, you don't have to assume it. The bank will swallow the debt. It won't look good on Mrs. Johnstone, but thirty thousand dollars is nothing to a bank this size."

Isabella's eyes popped wide. "Thirty thousand dollars? How do you know?"

"Loans Officer, remember? I have access to files."

"Jesus, how am I supposed to pay back that kind of money?" Nerves bouncing, Isabella rose to pace.

"I told you. You don't have to."

"I do because…"

"Because why, Isabella? Sit down, talk to me." Michaela's eyes followed Isabella. "You used to tell me everything,"

Isabella used to. She'd confided every thought, secret, and dream to the girl she thought of as the sister she never had until the change.

Although Michaela was older than Isabella was, they'd shared the same interests, the same circle of friends, and together did what young girls loved to do. That is, until their junior year of high school when the momentous occasion when a girl crosses into womanhood transformed Michaela's five-six beanpole body into a sultry, curvy woman.

Everything once plain no longer was. The flat chest bloomed into large, firm orbs that swelled over low-cut sweaters. Her pimply complexion turned ivory smooth, and the platinum blonde hair miraculously became shiny with just the right hint of wave.

A stunning beauty, Michaela became the talk of Thornhill High. Every boy desired her, every girl despised her, and she couldn't have been more in her element. Michaela's dating calendar overflowed, and her focus turned away from Isabella to the boys that kept her social life eventful.

It wasn't long before the gossip and rumours swirled, and boys were lining up to cross into manhood with backseat-Michaela. When the stories reached Isabella's ears, she shared her concerns with Michaela. An indignant Michaela denied everything and claimed the underdeveloped Isabella was envious of her popularity.

The cousins drifted apart, but it wasn't until the Clooney-Esque Joe Smith infused himself between them that they went their separate way.

A senior, Joe's eyes were the colour of a midnight sky. His hair was dark and thick. His dimpled cheeks could liquefy your insides. Joe was the popular jock, every girl's desire, and Tad Smith's—proprietor of Smith Home Builders—son. Joe had all the qualities Michaela admired: looks, popularity, and lots of money. When Michaela decided Joe would be hers, he didn't stand a chance because what Michaela wanted Michaela got.

Like a spider spinning her web to trap its victim, Michaela set her plan to ensnare Joe into her net. It wasn't long before Michaela was introducing Joe Smith as her boyfriend, and Isabella became a distant memory. From that moment, Isabella realized ties of blood did not assure allegiance or love.

"I would never betray your confidence, Isabella." Michaela waved to Mrs. White, who queued behind Mr. Romano for a teller. "If I know you, you've come prepared, but a heads up. Mrs. Johnstone is demanding. She guards the bank's money as if it was her own."

"That's what Antonio said."

Michaela didn't miss the subtle smile that lifted the corner of Michaela's mouth. "Antonio, huh?"

"From The Café. Do you know him?"

"Who doesn't?" Michaela grinned when she saw the exasperated expression on Rosie's face as she endured Mrs. Jackson's story on the feats of her one-year-old grandson's accomplishments during his weekend visit. Having experienced those long-winded, boring stories herself, Michaela empathized with Rosie. The occupational hazards of a teller, Michaela thought.

"As it turns out, Antonio junior, not senior, is my landlord. He helped me prepare for today and helped put my financial proposal and presentation together."

A brow raised in interest, "Do I sense more than a professional interest in Antonio?"

The thought of Antonio and her together brought Isabella a surprising secret pleasure. "No. Maybe. No, he's just my landlord. Well, I guess a friend now."

"Sure, a friend." Michaela's shoulder bumped companionably against Isabella.

"I don't have time for men, dating, or relationships."

"All right, if you say so."

"I do. Right now, I need to focus on getting my business off the ground. That's why I need to see Mrs. Johnstone." Isabella went on to tell Michaela about Mr. Hart and Fizz's plan to fire her.

"I'm sorry, Isabella." Michaela rested a comforting hand on her cousin's. "Employers nowadays have no regard for their employees. As I see it, it's their loss. I'll see what I can do to help you out with Mrs. Johnstone. You know I have a talent for sweet-talking people. After your meeting, let me know how your talk with Mrs. Johnstone went, and I'll have a chat with her. I'll sing your praises and prod her along." Michaela brushed the spill of long, golden hair back. There was an undeniably feminine touch to the gesture, which was invariably a part of Michaela's genetic makeup. It was why men lined up for Michaela and not for her, Isabella thought. It was why at twenty-two, she was still a virgin.

"I'd appreciate that, Michaela." Isabella smiled, feeling a rewind to their younger days when they turned to one another for support.

"No matter what, we're family. I think Mrs. Johnstone is ready for you. Fingers and toes crossed." Michaela did as they had so many times in their youth.

Chapter 8

THE DAYS THAT followed Isabella's meeting with Mrs. Johnstone was one of those rare times in her life in which everything came together.

Approved for the necessary financing, planning and designing the store consumed her days. As much as she hated to change her father's store, updating and modernizing to depict the tone for the exclusive clientele, she sought to attract was what had to be done.

Isabella ordered a new sign to replace the dated one. It read ISABELLA FARFALLA FASHION in gold, flowing script, against a black background. A butterfly design—the English translation of Farfalla—she intended to brand as her logo accompanied the name.

The interior of the store was transformed into a sophisticated shopping oasis. Chocolate-brown wood floors replaced worn linoleum. White sconces glowed on cream splashed walls. Mirror tiles in the shape of a butterfly that covered the east wall gave the illusion of space. Two glass display cases built to Isabella's specifications stood in the middle of the room.

Alongside her mother, Isabella spent countless hours stitching the two dozen original designs she planned to display on opening day. After giving a lot of thought to how best to display them, the idea came to her. She'd have a live model wear the garments as she mingled amongst customers.

Isabella made a note to talk to Kathleen on her To-Do list. Kathleen had the perfect body for her designs. The best part was that as a novice model, she could talk the young receptionist into the modelling job without putting a huge dent in her limited budget.

As crowded as Isabella's mind was, Antonio, popped into it—often. She hadn't seen him since they'd worked on her business proposal, and she had yet to thank him for his help. As much as agreeing to assume her father's debt played in Isabella's favour, she was sure that were it not for Antonio and Michaela's words of support, Mrs. Johnstone wouldn't have approved the much-needed financing.

As soon as she could surface for air, Isabella planned to pop in at The Café. Antonio deserved a face-to-face thank you. For now, getting her business going to generate income was her primary focus, Isabella decided as she rounded King and Queen Street and set eyes on Textile Depot.

Mrs. Rita Cropper, the sole owner of Textile Depot, inherited her husband's failing business after his unexpected heart attack ten years ago. At the age of fifty-six, Mrs. Cropper took on a business she knew little about and was heavily in debt.

In the first few years, the struggles to keep the business afloat were many. In the end, Mrs. Cropper endured and turned Textile Depot into a countrywide fabric supplier. Not bad for a nearly failed business, Isabella thought.

PERSEVERANCE AND DEDICATION GOT ME HERE. SERVICE AND SELECTION KEEP YOU COMING BACK said the sign above the entrance. Rows of pendant lamps hung from steel beams on a high ceiling. Floors were gray concrete, and the walls were red brick. The smell of fabric and the sight of stacks of neatly folded bolts in every imaginable colour begging to be constructed into fashionable apparel had Isabella's mind weaving designs in her head.

Of the cream viscose bolt, Isabella envisioned a knee-length, flared silhouette dress with delicate bodice stitching. She pictured an off-the-shoulder dress with a flowing skirt for the black, cotton fabric. The ribbed, russet fabric was perfect for a body-hugging mini dress with a chain-link bodice.

"Allo, luv," Mrs. Cropper called out, in her east London cockney accent.

In a white cotton shirt, sleeves rolled up, faded Levi's, and comfortable loafers, Mrs. Cropper carried herself with understated elegance. A short gray-streaked, wavy bob framed a face devoid of the roadmap of the struggles she'd faced. Her charcoal-black eyes were powerful, her gaze confident. At sixty-six, Mrs. Cropper looked the picture of beauty and health.

"Good morning." Isabella leaned in for a hug.

"I was just about to have a cupper. Will you join me?" Mrs. Cropper said, wrapping a motherly arm around Isabella's shoulder.

"I'd love to. I'm that parched," Isabella said, to Mrs. Cropper's amusement.

"Aye, a good Britt ye are. Let's go to my office." Mrs. Cropper led Isabella up the steel staircase and down the short corridor.

"I see it's as organized as always." Isabella eyed the desk piled high with invoices, catalogues, correspondence, and the day's newspaper. Stacks of bolts covered the two guest chairs and filing cabinets propped against the wall. In the ten years since her father introduced Isabella to Mrs. Cropper, she'd never known the office to be anything but a cluttered mess.

"It's an organized mess, luv." Mrs. Cropper cleared a chair and signalled Isabella to sit as she took the chair behind the desk. Reaching for the telephone, she eventually located under the stack of invoices Mrs. Cropper instructed her assistant to bring a tea tray to her office. "My condolences, luv," she said, returning the handset to its cradle.

"Thank you, but it's me who should be apologizing. I should have called you sooner, but there was the funeral and…"

Isabella broke off when Mrs. Cropper waved a dismissive hand. "No need for apologies. I suspected there was something wrong when I didn't hear from you in weeks. How are you faring?"

"All right." Isabella left it that.

She didn't see the point in telling Mrs. Cropper how much she missed her father or that there were days she cried herself to sleep. Isabella definitely wouldn't mention she spoke to Angelo often as if he were there with her. She hadn't even shared that bit with her mother.

"Be patient, luv. It'll take time. Right now, keeping busy is key. It's why I took on this failing business after my Edward left me. He was an exasperating man, stubborn, with a poor head for business. Worse, he wouldn't listen to reason, but he was mine, and after thirty-seven years of marriage, I missed him terribly. I still do. This business is what helped me get through the days." Mrs. Cropper waved in the freckled face girl arched in the doorway with the silver tray. "Set it here,

Daphne, luv." She motioned to the corner she cleared on the cluttered desk. "Milk and sugar?"

"Both, please." Isabella took the offered cup. "I don't know if you know, but I left Hart Designs."

Mrs. Cropper nodded. "Mr. Hart's inept daughter, who introduced herself as Ms. Hart, Director of something-or-other," she mimicked in a haughty voice, "told me she'd taken over when she called in an order a couple of weeks ago." Mrs. Cropper set down the spoon with a clunk after stirring the sugar in her cup. "You know she messed the order up three times. The girl is as dense as a post, with an attitude the size of Jupiter. I told her next time she pulled a similar stunt, I'd charge for delivery."

Isabella's lips curved and then proceeded to tell Mrs. Cropper her reason for leaving down to the last sordid detail.

At the end of Isabella's account, Mrs. Cropper blew out a breath of anger. "Wanker. I knew Julius Hart was a ruthless man without principles, but I never imagined he was stupid enough to mistreat a star employee. What are you planning to do now, luv?"

"Bring down Hart Designs, and buy them out at five cents on the dollar." Isabella contemplated aloud.

There was such conviction in Isabella's tone Mrs. Cropper could only say, "Blimey, don't want to cross you."

Isabella's eyes lit with a smile, but Mrs. Cropper thought she saw something more—Hate? Anger? Resentment?—behind them.

"It's only on my wish list. For now, I plan to take over my father's business."

"Good for you. Between you and me, I always thought you had far too much talent to waste fulfilling someone else's dream."

"I'm glad to hear you say that because I need your help." Isabella waved the offer of scones. Her knotted stomach couldn't take food.

"I'll help you where I can, luv." Mrs. Cropper spread a generous dollop of butter on the scone she cut in half.

"I'm going to be completely honest."

"I wouldn't want it any other way." She bit into a scone.

"My father didn't leave much in the way of money as much as he did in debt. I've paid off some suppliers and negotiated payment terms with those willing to work with me. Today, I want to clear the three thousand dollars debt with you."

"Good plan so far." Mrs. Cropper topped their cups.

"I hoped in return you'd extend me a twenty thousand dollar line of credit." Isabella spewed out the ambitious request in a calm, firm voice. Since perceiving her appeals not as plead for help but as business negotiations, it became easier to make demands.

"Blimey, you don't ask for much." Mrs. Cropper's incredulous expression withered into admiration.

Mrs. Cropper recognized the flicker of fire that burned in the young girl's eyes, the eagerness to burst from her cocoon and transform herself into a colourful butterfly. She knew first-hand Isabella's desperation fuelled her ambition, her drive, and her need to succeed. In Isabella, Mrs. Cropper saw so much of the woman who took over a failing business ten years ago. Isabella mirrored the desperation she felt ten years ago when she took over a failing business she knew nothing about.

Isabella was too young and green, but the expertise she lacked she made up in youthful energy. Raising steepled fingers to her lips, Mrs. Cropper fell into deep thought, keeping Isabella on pins and needles for longer than she cared.

"I know exactly what you're going through, and as much as I want to help you, luv, I have to protect me interest." The words came down on Isabella like a sledgehammer. Sensing the uneasiness she'd caused, Mrs. Cropper corrected herself. "What I meant is I have a proposal for you. I'll meet your terms with a stipulation."

Tit for tat, something Isabella was learning was part of the business world. "Which are?"

"One, I become your mentor."

Isabella's smile brightened, "I wouldn't have it any other way."

"Holy Cross High, the all-girl private school, is looking for a new uniform manufacturer. They're not happy with their current supplier. I'd like you and me to bid on the contract, you as the manufacturer and me as the fabric supplier. I'd contemplated partnering with Hart Designs, but I quashed the idea when I found out you'd left. You couldn't pay me enough money to deal with that daft, arrogant, rude, cow…"

Isabella cut off the oath laced rant. "I don't mean to interrupt, Mrs. Cropper, but you were saying."

"I'm sorry, luv. Thinking of Fizz gets my panties in a bunch. Anyways, as I was saying, I owe you for bringing me on as Hart's supplier when you started working there, and I'd like us to collaborate on this contract. It'll be a challenge. You'll have to…"

"I'll do it." Isabella cut in.

"Luv, you have to think about this carefully. It's dealing with ungrateful, demanding parents, and impossible teenagers, which I wouldn't wish on me worst enemy and not the clientele you're aiming for." When Isabella opened her mouth to cut her off, Mrs. Cropper waved a finger to convey she wasn't finished. "The contract is not a hugely profitable one, but it will guarantee you steady work and revenue, and me my investment, if you decide to proceed."

"I'll do it." The gleam of hope was back in Isabella's eyes.

"Are you sure?"

"I'll take any business that comes my way, but how do you know you can secure the deal. Doesn't tender mean several bidders?"

"It does, but I'll be your fabric supplier, and I, my luv, am the best textile buyer in town." She gave Isabella a wink.

"I have no doubt. When do we begin partner?" Isabella eagerly pumped Mrs. Cropper's hand while wondering how she'd fulfill her end of the bargain.

Chapter 9

A CRESCENT MOON hung bright in a sky bursting with stars. A cool March air with the teasing scents of the incoming spring blew when Isabella, with a smile on her face, made her way from Textile Depot to the King subway station.

The platform was crowded with homebound riders. It wasn't long before the northbound train rolled into the station with a gust of wind and screeched to a stop. Stepping on, Isabella sat next to the woman in a blue, gabardine, ill-fitting pantsuit that screamed masculinity.

Reaching into her vinyl tote, she took out the notebook. Isabella made a notation to work on a collection of professional feminine wear. Hers would offer more than the traditional black and blue boardroom colours. After some thought, she decided to call the line Farfalla Femme Carriere.

Isabella let her eyes wander, analyzing what women wore. She studied the accessories at their neck, ears, and arms, their sense of style. From the best to the worst dressed, young to old, and everything in between, she made notes.

What a difference a day made, she thought. Days ago, life grabbed her by the throat and squeezed tight. Today she felt as if she could conquer the world, and she had Antonio to thank. Because of him, Isabella was able to get a step up in life. It was inconsiderate of her not to contact him and express her gratitude. But in the past few days, life was taking her in every direction. Still, he deserved a face-to-face thank you.

It was late, and she was dead on her feet. She had days of sleep to catch up on. She hadn't eaten anything all day. She should head home, grab a bite, soak in the tub, and jump into bed. Maybe tonight, for the first time, she'd get in more than four hours of sleep. With that in mind, Isabella exited at the next stop and walked the block to The Café.

Storefronts and lampposts blazed gold with light as Isabella wound her way past thronged sidewalks. She stepped aside to give way to the mother with the baby carriage while meeting the cherubic child's smile. Isabella waved at Mr. Masselli arched in the doorway of his bakery, taking a cigarette break, a flour-dusted apron around his ample waist.

Minutes from The Café, the scent of coffee slid into Isabella, and thoughts of Antonio came to her. It wasn't so much she wanted to see Antonio. That wasn't it at all. She just wanted to thank him. She'd postponed it long enough to verge on rude, or so she told herself. The man affected her life as no one had and didn't deserve to be ignored as long as she had, she reasoned, dismissing the prickle of heat in her belly at the thought of seeing him.

As if sensing Isabella's presence, Antonio's head whipped up the moment she walked in. His wide, dimpled smile sent Isabella's heart fluttering.

"Take a seat. I'll be right there," Antonio mouthed, pointing to the empty table by the window.

Isabella did as told as Elton John's voice floated from the recently installed jukebox.

"Thought you'd like an espresso." Antonio set two cups on the table.

"Thank you," Isabella said, although she didn't think her bladder could handle any more liquid after the three teacups she had at Mrs. Cropper's. "I'm sorry I haven't been by sooner. I've been swamped."

Antonio scraped back the chair next to her, sat.

"Well, I'm glad you're here now." His laser-focus on her made her cheeks deepen in colour.

"I wanted to let you know that thanks to you, it went well with Mrs. Johnstone. She gave me the financing without making me beg, not much anyway. Seeing your name on my proposal saved me from the degrading task."

"I doubt that, but I'm glad it worked out."

"And I have more good news, but I haven't told anyone yet, not even Mama." Isabella's rich-brandy eyes radiated excitement.

"I swear to say nothing." Antonio crossed his heart.

With intoxicating enthusiasm, she told him about the uniform deal. Hands gesturing flamboyantly, Isabella described the effort it would take, but she felt confident she could do it. Throughout it all, the smile that lit her face never left.

He toasted with his coffee cup. "Congratulations, it sounds as if you're having a better life. This calls for a celebration. Will you join me for dinner? Nothing fancy. I can whip up a quick spaghetti dish."

For a moment, her mind went blank.

Dinner in his apartment, alone with him, she rolled that in her brain when it sprouted back to life. Was it a date? What would he expect of her? She had pressing issues to focus on, and getting involved with him would be a distraction she couldn't afford. As always, she over-analyzed and reminded herself it was dinner.

"I'd like that," she said, deciding to step off that over-analytical cliff without looking down.

"Great, let me tell Marco I'm stepping away," he said, and doing so, led her upstairs to his apartment.

While Antonio poured wine into two glasses, Isabella called her mother to apprise her of the change of dinner plans. When she hung up, she slid onto a stool at the kitchen bar.

"Dinner will be ready in fifteen minutes." Antonio handed her the glass of wine and turned the kitchen radio on.

"You seem to have many talents." Sipping on wine, Isabella watched Antonio expertly mince garlic, dice tomatoes, chop anchovies, olives, and capers.

"You can thank my mother for that. I subbed for the daughter she never had, so she taught me how to cook, clean, and do laundry. You know all those fun domestic things." Antonio added the freshly made pasta his chef insisted he use into boiling water.

"A smart woman," she said, as Kenny Rogers' whiskey-soaked voice floated from the radio.

"She was. She passed away eight years ago. I was eighteen, and yes, we were close." Antonio stirred the pasta.

"I'm sorry. I didn't know." Isabella watched him add garlic to hot oil. Its flavorful aroma instantly filled the room.

"I miss her, but I also like to think that her death wasn't in vain." He set the wooden spoon down, picked up his wine.

"How do you mean?"

"My father and I grew closer after her death. Our relationship was rocky for most of my life. You know son and father dynamics. Anyway, after Mom's death, we became the best of friends." Antonio added all the ingredients to the sautéed garlic and stirred.

"Sounds to me as if she had a hand in it."

Antonio smiled up at Isabella thinking his mother would like her. "I thought the same." Antonio lowered the flame on the sauce. "Anyway, after graduation, I took over The Café, and Dad decided to spend more time in Italy. He loves Sicily. We have tons of relatives, and the warmer weather is more suitable for his aching bones." Antonio transferred al dente pasta from boiling water to the sauce and stirred. "Dinner is served."

As the evening rolled on, they ate, drank more wine, and talked—mainly Isabella did—and Antonio listened intently. It was easy to embrace him as a friend, which she decided was the tone the evening took in the end.

Maybe the wine had gone to her head, but she felt she could tell him anything and did. Isabella told Antonio of Mr. Hart and Fizz's plans to take her designs then cut her loose. When she saw his face flush with anger, she assured him it was the best thing that happened. Isabella told Antonio her goals and dreams and how she planned to realize them with her father.

Isabella's pained expression made Antonio's chest tighten, and he said, "Well, I'm happy to help you any way I can." He was smart enough to add, "Only if you need it," in case she misinterpreted his offer as pity.

"Thank you." Something reached deep into her soul, and Isabella felt a connection with him. Whether friendship or more, she wasn't sure. All that mattered was that she trusted him implicitly. But now, feeling as she did, she wasn't sure she trusted herself with him.

Antonio gathered the dirty dishes when the silence lingered. "I hoped you liked dinner."

"Yes, it was delicious." Isabella turned to wipe the table clean to keep her hands busy. "I'll wash."

"You're my guest."

"You cooked. It's the least I can do."

"I'll wash, you dry." Antonio handed her the dishtowel.

"All right."

Standing side by side, performing the homey task filled them with a comfortable familiarity they liked.

"It's getting late. I should get going," she said when the last dish was dried and stored.

Antonio watched her cross to the couch to pick up her jean jacket. "All right. I'll drive you home."

"That's not necessary. I can walk home." She shrugged into her jacket, then slid her purse crossways over her body.

"It is necessary," Antonio said because he didn't want the night to end.

It was nine, and traffic was light. Out of the car window, Isabella watched strolling couples. Some stopped to peek into the window displays. Late-night joggers in shorts and windbreakers took advantage of the uncrowded sidewalk. Other nightwalkers were out with leashed dogs.

Ten minutes later, Antonio pulled the sleek Corvette in front of her apartment as Foreigner's Waiting For A Girl Like You drifted dreamily from the car radio.

"Here we are." The sweet smell of her shampoo, in the confines of his car, drove him crazy, and he itched to brush lips over hers. "I had a nice time tonight."

"Me too, and thank you for letting me talk your ear off," Isabella said.

"Anytime."

"Thank you for everything." Isabella hesitated for a moment, and deciding there would be no harm in it, she leaned in and kissed him on the cheek.

It was a two-second, friendly kiss, but she made his stomach knot tight. She was in his blood, and he knew the feeling wasn't going anywhere any time soon.

ISABELLA AND ANTONIO DIDN'T MARK THE tailing car. They never saw it pull into the parking spot on the opposite side of the road. They never thought to suspect the wild, begrudging eyes watching their every move for the past few hours meant to harm.

Although *The Eyes* was only able to see their shadowed figures through the curtained apartment window, it hadn't painted a pleasant picture.

A simmering rage had *The Eyes* clenching and unclenching fists when they perceived Antonio and Isabella locked lips. Unable to watch any longer, *The Eyes* pulled out of the parking space with a squeal. White-knuckled hands wrapped on the wheel, *The Eyes* formulated the plan to stop their blossoming romance.

Chapter 10

SALVATORE MESI FLARED up the brass Zippo and touched it to the tip of his cigarette. Drawing a mouthful of smoke, Salvatore immediately felt the pang of regret as he often did at the gratification the nicotine imparted on his nervous system. He'd tried to quit the nasty habit for months, but his dependence was stronger than his resolve.

Dismissing the thought, Salvatore plugged the cigarette into his mouth and inhaled deeply. Draping an arm on the back of the bench, he peeled eyes on Isabella again.

In the past two hour hours of watching her, she hadn't stopped for a breather. The wonders of youthful energy, Salvatore thought. He watched Isabella tap her bottom lip in thought when the workmen slapped the first coat of paint on the wall. Bobbing her head from shoulder to shoulder like a metronome, it took her fifteen minutes to give her nod of approval.

Salvatore watched Isabella supervise, scrutinize, and analyze every aspect of the renovation to ensure it met the sketch she often referenced. A couple of times, Salvatore watched the frustrated workmen step outside to get a lungful of air to regain their composure. He snickered, thinking it was the cost of dealing with a perfectionist.

Taking a draw from his cigarette, Salvatore's eyes darted up to the men on the cherry picker erecting the new sign. Large, gold letters against a black background read

Isabella Farfalla. Beneath, Fashion Company appeared in a smaller font.

He liked the gold butterfly with an I between its wings set to the left of her name. Salvatore deduced the I represented Isabella's initial and the butterfly to be the translation of her last name. Salvatore assumed the butterfly logo was her brand. Artistic and innovative, he mused, but then from what he'd been told, he didn't expect anything but the epitome of creativity from Isabella.

And Isabella's creativity shone in the renovation. With limited funds, she'd transformed the tired, dated space into contemporary-chic. Dark wood floors replaced faded linoleum. Mirrors gave the illusion of height and space, and wall sconces provided romance lighting and a touch of elegance.

It was some time before Isabella stepped outside. Breathing in afternoon air laced with the scents of baked bread and pizza, she took the seat next to Salvatore on the bench. Toeing off her flats, she flexed her feet before looking up to give her sign the once-over. From the expression on her face, Salvatore deduced she was pleased with what she saw.

"It catch the eye, si?" Salvatore's comment, made with a charming Italian accent, made Isabella swivel to the complementing stranger.

"You think so?"

Salvatore took the glasses perched on the end of his Romanesque nose, polished the lenses and set them back. "To me, it look classy and elegant,"

Pride flared in Isabella. "That's what I was going for." The excitement radiating from the brandy-brown eyes made Salvatore smile.

Salvatore lit the umpteen cigarette of the day and proceeded to take a long drag. "Then, you've hit the nail on the noggin." Salvatore made Isabella laugh and saw so much of her mother.

Isabella was inches taller than Maria was, but there was no mistaking the mink coloured hair, and the flawless olive skin were traits handed down by her mother. There was fatigue in the intelligent hazel eyes that gazed at him, but they were a reflection of Maria. Isabella fit the description given to him, beautiful, smart, and ambitious to a T.

He crushed his cigarette underfoot. "I am Salvatore Mesi."

Sizing him up, Isabella took the offered hand. "Nice to meet you, Mr. Mesi. I'm Isabella Farfalla."

He was medium height and impeccably dressed in a three-piece suit. Italian silk, she concluded. He had friendly, brown eyes, a shock of short silver hair smoothly combed back, and the deepest cleft chin she'd ever seen. Isabella put him in his early fifties.

"You are the owner of this fine establishment?" Salvatore's gaze flipped to the workmen who waved at Isabella.

"See you tomorrow, and thank you for your patience," Isabella called out, waving back. "God, I hope they come back. I was a bit hard on them today," she muttered, making Salvatore's mouth twitch. "To answer your question, Mr. Mesi, yes, I'm the owner."

"You have a fine store, Miss Farfalla." Salvatore's cigarette bobbed with his words.

"It'll look much better when it's finished," Isabella said, with a bubbly smile Salvatore thought was another one of the many traits inherited from her mother.

"Presentation is everything in retail." Salvatore took a drag of his cigarette.

"My father says the same thing." Isabella watched him expel a funnel-shaped cloud of white smoke into the air and bit back the comment on the dangers of smoking at the tip of her tongue.

"He is a smart man."

"He ... was. He's no longer with us." The pained look in Isabella's eyes made his heart clench.

"I'm sorry for your loss." Salvatore let a short stretch of silence hang because they both needed a moment. "Was this his business?"

Isabella nodded. "I'm taking it over. I want to carry on my father's legacy and fulfill my dream. I'm a designer aiming to offer custom-made garments to women. I want to manufacture my line of Farfalla branded couture," Isabella said, with confidence and an inexplicable willingness to share with the stranger she felt a familiarity with. "Have we met before, Mr. Mesi?"

Salvatore's eyes flickered to the flock of pigeons that landed at his feet, cooing, bobbing heads as they pecked the ground. "No, we haven't."

"Funny, I have this odd feeling we have."

"I have a common face." Isabella smiled at that, although she thought he was anything but ordinary. "The butterfly on your sign is a creative touch. It's your name, isn't it?" Salvatore said to divert the staring eyes.

Isabella's eyes rose to her sign. "One day, that butterfly is going to become a highly sought out brand."

"I don't doubt it."

Isabella watched Salvatore swallow smoke as if it was his last breath. "Those things killed my father," she exclaimed, waving her hand at the thin white cloud that drifted toward her. "And they're going to kill you."

"I'm sorry." Salvatore stubbed the cigarette out with his heel.

"No, I'm sorry," she said, flushed with guilt.

"Don't be. You're right. I've been trying to quit for a long time."

"How's that going?"

Salvatore met her smile, Maria's smile. "By chance, would you be looking to hire a tailor?"

Isabella's face held just the right amount of curiosity and interest. "I am. You know someone?"

"Me."

"You?" Isabella pasted a polite but suspicious smile on her face. It all felt too coincidental and set off warning bells.

"I noticed the renovations going on in your store and figured there might be a small chance you may be looking for an experienced tailor." He hoped the fabricated explanation allayed the apprehension he saw in her eyes.

"Tell me more about yourself," she said when she concluded the explanation plausible.

"Happy to. Talking about myself is one of my favourite hobbies. I'm from Italy. My tailoring expertise began thirty years ago under the tutelage of a man I considered the master of his craft. He taught me everything about tailoring. After my apprenticeship ended, family responsibility derailed me, but I eventually opened my tailor shop, which I've owned since then. I custom craft my patterns and have experience with designing and sewing both male and female—come si dice?—apparel." Absently Salvatore continuously flipped the Zippo's lid to keep his cigarette-free hand busy.

"Is your store still in operation?"

"Yes, but for now, it's in the hands of," my only son, he wanted to tell her, but said, "My sister." It wasn't as if he was lying, as much as he was bending the truth. "Have you lived here long?"

Salvatore shook his head. "I've only been in town for a few weeks. A friend wrote to me a few months ago asking for my help, and here I am." Salvatore fell silent as the wave of memory from the unexpected letter hit him.

When the letter landed on his desk, Salvatore set it aside. A few days later, when he got around to open it, the content of the letter rocked him to the core, stirred emotions and memories decades old, which for the longest time, Salvatore fought to compartmentalize.

Now, being there and seeing Isabella and Maria felt surreal.

After receiving the letter, Salvatore felt as he was floating on cloud nine. Other days, the fear of facing the unknown was insurmountable, but he'd been given a second chance at the love he left behind decades ago, and he couldn't, wouldn't, let it slip away—not again.

He'd waited so long for this moment, sacrificed much, and needed to find out the truth. Life was giving him a precious second chance to recapture the happiness he once had and rekindle the love he once felt. Opportunities like these didn't come often, and he wasn't going to let it slip away.

"Does your friend live in the area, Mr. Mesi?" Isabella's eyes cut to her window display and decided her exhibit would feature a spring theme and incorporate her butterfly logo floating from the ceiling. She'd line the base of the three mannequins, which would don Farfalla originals, with potted tulips bursting with colour.

"Please call me Sal, as my friend Antonio insists on calling me."

A smile spread over Isabella's face. "You're a friend of Antonio Sabatini?"

"Si, Antonio Sabatini from The Café. You know him?" When she nodded, Salvatore's hands gestured flamboyantly. "It seems everyone know Antonio. Then, he can be my reference."

Isabella hadn't banked on that, and her decision came quickly. "If you're a friend of Antonio's, that's good enough for me. Welcome on board, Mr. Mesi. That is if you want the job. I mean, I can't pay much, and I'm not sure how much work I'll have. I am just starting, and…"

Salvatore waved her silent. "Call me Sal, and money is no important, and everything else we work out. I would love to work for you. When do you want me to start, boss?"

"It's Isabella, and how does nine o'clock Monday sound?"

"Monday, I'll be there with my bell on."

Isabella laughed heartily and locked hands with Salvatore to seal the deal. "We don't open for another two weeks, but I think it would be a good idea to start sooner than later. That'll allow us to get to know each other and strategize."

"Sounds like we have a plan."

"Good. See you then." Isabella started to walk away, then stopped. "By the way, Sal, do you have any objections to working alongside three women? I've brought on two seamstresses from my ex-employer."

A bitterness Salvatore didn't think Isabella possessed flashed into her eyes for a mere few seconds before it withered into a smile. "I enjoy to work with women. Who's the third?"

"My mom. I'm not so much worried about the seamstresses working with you as I am about my mother. She's the head seamstress, and she's only ever worked alongside my father. Working with a stranger may…"

"Be difficult for her." Salvatore finished. "It's understandable. I will do my best not to get in her way," he said, to alleviate her concerns.

"She's a formidable woman, Sal."

"Don't worry, Isabella, I have very thick skin," Salvatore said, although he suspected Maria wasn't going to be as accommodating.

The thought of facing Maria terrified him, but he'd made a promise, and there was no going back now. He only hoped he'd be forgiven and welcomed after the Pandora's Box he was about to unleash.

Chapter 11

AT THE BREAKFAST table, Isabella reviewed her To-Do list. She crossed out completed tasks and added new ones. Beneath the *Hire Hart Designs' Seamstresses* bullet point, Isabella drew a line through *Hire Tailor* and debated how to tell her mother about Salvatore Mesi.

Although less frequent now, there were still nights Isabella heard her mother crying herself to sleep. Last night was one of those nights. The smile that always adorned Maria's face was gone, and it broke Isabella's heart.

Isabella needed to introduce Salvatore in a calculated way. In Maria's fragile state, she'd see Salvatore as her father's replacement. Isabella hoped her mother understood that wasn't the case because her father could never be replaced.

"Mama, I need to speak to you." Isabella's anxious expression led Maria to assume the worst.

"What is it, honey? Are you okay?"

"I'm fine, Mama. It's about the store."

With an exhaled breath, Maria said, "It's looking great, honey. You've done a wonderful job," and proceeded to gather the breakfast dishes to set in soapy water.

"You know that sooner or later, we need to hire a tailor."

"We do, but that will come in due time, honey." Maria wiped the table clean then draped the damp cloth on the stove handle.

"I, ah, met someone that would be a perfect fit." Isabella's stomach knotted. "I'd like to hire him. Actually, I've…"

"We don't need anyone right now. We can manage on our own." Maria picked up the coffee pot from the stove and walked it to the table.

"We need an experienced tailor, Mama. I'm not capable of…"

"You have me. I can handle a sewing machine." Maria poured coffee into their cups.

"You can, but Sal is very experienced. Way overqualified for the job if you ask me, and he'll be a great mentor."

"You've already hired him, haven't you?" Silence fell. "Isabella."

"He starts Monday."

"Why would you hire him without consulting me first, Isabella? When did this happen?" Maria hissed the words with impatience.

Isabella rolled hazel eyes from her mother to the brown liquid in her cup. "Yesterday."

With a huffed breath, Maria fell into her chair. "Where did you find this, Sal?"

"He was sitting outside, on the bench, in front of the store." Isabella heard the words that slid out of her mouth. Did they sound as ridiculous as she thought?

"What do you mean sitting outside on the bench?" Maria's eyes lifted to her daughter, who had sense enough to remain silent this time. "Isabella, what do you mean sitting outside on the bench?"

"He was watching the sign going up," Isabella got to her feet, crossed over to the sink with the empty cup and saucer.

"Are you telling me you started a conversation with a stranger you met sitting on a bench, watching a sign going up and hired him on the spot?"

In that context, it sounded even more ridiculous. "You're becoming agitated, Mama." Filling a glass with water, Isabella walked it to the table. "Sal's a friend of Antonio's."

"That doesn't give you a pass to hire him on the spot, Isabella. You're too young to be making these decisions on your own." Maria's chiding words came out harsher than she meant them to.

"My gut feeling tells me he's the perfect fit for us." Isabella held back, telling her mother about the comfortable familiarity she felt with him. Her mother wouldn't understand that. She didn't understand it. "How about if I stop by The Café this morning before I set off to see Mrs. Cropper and ask Antonio about Sal. Hopefully, he'll dispel any reservations you have." Isabella threw her mother a smile, which didn't have the effect she intended.

"How's speaking to Antonio after the fact going to help? You've already hired the man. Really, Isabella, I think you're making rash decisions because we're cutting it close to opening day, and this is certainly one of them."

"Maybe, but I can just as easily rescind the offer if Antonio doesn't vouch for him. I will." Isabella cut her mother off when she started to speak. "I didn't want to risk losing Sal. Mama, I know this is difficult for you, but it's what we need to do. Sooner or later, we have to hire an experienced tailor." Isabella rested a hand on her mother's. "Daddy is not coming back, Mama."

"I know." Hearing the tears in her voice, Maria cleared her throat to disguise them. "You know there are still times I see him walking into the kitchen asking for breakfast or his favourite dish," Maria said, feeling the loneliness crashing down.

It was a loneliness that filled her every minute of every day. The nights were the worst. Maria missed Angelo's warm body next to hers in bed. She missed his arms around her. Many were the nights she held on to his pillow and filled herself with its scent as he cried the night away.

Isabella's heart bounded hard in her throat, and she bent down to peck her mother on the cheek. "I miss Daddy too. Sometimes I see him walking around the apartment. The other night I thought I saw him sitting at the edge of my bed, smiling down at me. A few times, I've had conversations with him."

"I know. I've heard you." Maria's admission surprised Isabella.

"You never said anything."

"Because it's normal, honey. It's a helpful way of dealing with grief. It's your way of dealing with grief."

"I see him. I feel his presence. I smell those nasty cigarettes when he's around. He's helped me make decisions. Launching the store was his idea."

"If you're comforted by his guidance and the choices you make, there's no harm in that." Maria didn't see the point in telling her daughter the decisions were all her that she'd turned to a hallucination of her father for reassurance and encouragement at a vulnerable time in her life.

"Then, you know daddy would support me in hiring Sal."

Sighing, Maria pressed her fingers against her eyes. "Change is… It's all so hard."

"I know, Mama, but you understand that it's what we need to do."

This time Maria looked up at her daughter with understanding in her eyes. "Yes. I want to meet Sal before he starts working for us."

She regarded her mother calmly. "All right, Mama. I'll arrange a meeting. I'm sorry for the way I went about this."

Maria shook her head. "You did nothing wrong, honey. You have to give me some time to get used to … everything."

Chapter 12

PUTTING THE FINAL touches on the fabric display, Isabella took a step back. Satisfied with how the colourful selection of charmeuse, crepe, and chiffon bolts of fabric flowed like soft air on the display case, Isabella picked up her purse and jacket and headed out for the four-block walk to The Café.

A morning sun washed down out of a cloudless sky. The melody from fluttering birds happy spring was in the air wafted above her. Streets were coming alive, and the stores were opening their doors.

Her eyes drifted to the stores that lined the streets of Little Italy. There were pizzerias and restaurants that dished out authentic Italian dishes and cafes that offered a European flair and gave residents a taste of home. There was Enzo's Hardware, two supermarkets, a salon, and a barbershop. Her store soon would become a part of the landscape—a landmark.

Walking past Mama's Pizza, Isabella caught sight of her reflection on the storefront window. She'd have to shed the cotton T-shirt, worn jacket, and jeans look and replace it with a chic, sophisticated one. What she wore and how she presented herself had to reflect the concept she set out to promote.

Taking in a big breath of crisp morning air scented with the aroma of freshly baked bread she'd never tire of, she picked up her pace. Before she knew it, she stood in front of The Café. Arched in the doorway, Isabella scanned the crowded room for Antonio when his head rose from behind the counter. Isabella only had to look at the warm blue eyes and the shaggy mass of dark hair to get the tugs pulling in her belly.

His gaze met hers, and the smile he gave her said, I was thinking about you. The flush of heat she felt at her belly rushed up to her cheeks.

Why did he have to be so cute and appealing? She didn't have time for men or a relationship. She had bigger fish to fry. She had her dream to pursue, a legacy to carry. She had her mother's and her survival to consider.

She stopped her mind from over analyzing when Antonio's hand rose above the crowd, pointed to the table by the corner wall.

"Hi." His voice flowed musically when he sidled up to the table.

"Do you have a minute?"

"For you, I have all the time you need." Antonio waved Marco over. "You're up bright and early."

"What'll it be, boss?" Marco wiped the table clean, then slung the dishtowel over his shoulder.

"Two espressos, please and…" Antonio turned to Isabella.

"Just coffee, Marco. Thank you." Isabella waited until Marco walked back to the bar. "I'm in a bit of a rush. I still have so much to do to get the place ready for the grand opening." The words tumbled out with exhilarated excitement.

"You need to relax. Take a breath."

"I will once I've put the store opening behind me."

"No, you won't. Relaxation is not in your DNA." Antonio tilted his chin in greeting at the men who walked in as Marvin Gaye's voice shot out from the jukebox for everyone to get it on. Turning his attention to her, he said. "I haven't seen you in a few days. You look tired."

And she thought she'd dabbed enough foundation under her shadowed eyes. "You certainly know how to flatter a girl."

"It looks good on you."

Isabella arched a dark brow. "Smooth save, but you're right. I'm barely getting four hours of sleep. I have a thousand little worries…"

"That you could brush aside and that you shouldn't let yourself get twisted inside out over." Antonio took the coffees from Marco.

"I open in less than three weeks, and I still have so much to do."

"You're not going to be good to anyone if you take sick. You need to slow down." He added sugar to their coffees.

"Kettle, pot." Isabella lifted her cup in a half-salute.

Antonio's dimples flashed. "Point taken. I want to come by to see what you've done with your store. That is if I'm allowed. I know you're keeping it cloaked under a veil of mystery until the opening."

"All right, only if you swear not to divulge any of my secrets before opening day." Isabella smiled when Antonio locked his lips and threw the imaginary key away.

"How about I come by Saturday, early evening? I'll bring dinner. Something simple," he added before Isabella could protest.

"All right." Isabella caved in under the hypnotic blue eyes. "Oh, I almost forgot the reason for my visit. Do you know Salvatore Mesi? I ran into him yesterday, and we got to talking. Next thing, I'm hiring him as my tailor."

She watched Marco exchange a flirtatious look with the two women at the bar as he turned over their cafe lattes. "He claims to be a friend of yours."

Antonio nodded. "He stopped off here for dinner after your talk. He's happy to be working with you and your mom. He's qualified for the job." Antonio pointed out.

"I sense he's overqualified, and I wondered why he'd be interested in taking on such a menial role." Isabella reached for the sugar. When her hand accidentally touched his, he floated with the electric feeling that flared up in him.

"He's here on a personal matter."

"Sal mentioned something about that in passing."

"He'll be a great addition to your team. Are you having doubts about him?"

Isabella shook her head. "Mama is. Her reaction when I told her I hired Sal made me second-guess myself." She stared down into her knitted hands. "She sees him as Daddy's replacement."

"How do you see it?"

"It's strictly business for me. Anyway, Mama wants to meet with Sal before he starts to work with us."

"Would you like me to call him to set it up?"

"Would you? In the excitement of the moment, ditzy me didn't get his contact info."

Drowning in the hazel eyes, he'd agree to anything. "No problem. I'll set it up for this afternoon."

"I'm going to be tied up for most of the day at Textile Depot, and for Sal's sake, I'd rather be there as a buffer, but time is of the essence. This afternoon it is. I appreciate your help." Isabella hesitated for a moment. "You know it's the oddest thing, but I felt a familiarity with Sal when we first met. It was as if I already knew him."

"Interesting." Antonio's eyes focused beyond her.

"I thought so too. Anyway, I'm sorry, but I have to run."

"All right. By the way, do you know Joe Smith?" Antonio asked in passing.

"I knew a Joe Smith in high school, but I haven't seen him since I graduated. Why do you ask?" Isabella drank the last of her coffee.

"No reason." Antonio shook his head dismissively, but Isabella saw something deep in his eyes that called for further questioning.

She'd have to leave the conversation for another day Mrs. Cropper was expecting her in forty-five minutes.

Part II

Discovery

Every new day opens a portal to self-discovery,
to experiences that shape us, makes us
the person we become.

—M.L. Lexi

Chapter 13

LATE AFTERNOON SALVATORE Mesi took a seat at the slotted bench. Eyes fixed on Isabella's store, he flipped the Zippo open, running his thumb against the flint wheel until he got it to flare up. Touching flame to cigarette, Salvatore inhaled deeply and waited for the nicotine to weave its way into his system. He desperately needed its nerve-calming effect.

Since his telephone conversation with Antonio, Salvatore had struggled with how to tackle his meeting with Maria. Maria was bound to become anxious when they came face to face.

Two decades had passed since they'd seen each other. Aside from a few extra pounds and the lines etched around his eyes—that, in his opinion, made him look distinguished—there wasn't a significant change that made him unrecognizable.

Although Salvatore never stopped thinking of Maria, he'd given up hope of seeing her again. Never in a million years did Salvatore imagine this day would come to pass. Even after the letter came, disbelief had Salvatore dismissing the letter's authenticity. When he finally accepted the letter as genuine, it took weeks to prepare for today emotionally. Now that the moment was here, Salvatore's stomach twisted into a mass of knots, and his mind circled between fleeing and facing Maria.

It was a mistake to romanticize a rewind of the past, he decided. Salvatore travelled thousands of miles, he'd waited so long for this moment to come, but the idea of coming face to face with Maria unleashed a storm of emotions. God knew what Maria would say and do what she was going to feel when she saw him because no one escaped their past. Your past was a burden you carried with you—always.

Nerves overtook Salvatore, and he rose to leave.

"Sal?" Maria's voice floated into him, and the tidal wave of memories rushed at him. Like a movie set on rewind, he saw and felt.

"I'm sorry I have to go," he said, his mind dancing in all kinds of direction, his heart tightening.

"Antonio called to let me know you'd be by, and when I saw you sitting here, I assumed... I'm Maria Farfalla, Isabella's mother." Maria heard him suck in his breath before whirling to meet her piercing gaze.

Time had been kind to her, Salvatore thought. She looked as beautiful now as she did on that spring day twenty-three years ago. The exquisite face that captivated him then hypnotized him now. Maria's olive skin was silk-smooth. The Rich golden-brown eyes under slashing dark brows sat above high rosy cheeks. Maria wore her sable-brown hair tied back in a loose braid that trailed down her back, a look reminiscent of her youth. Petite and slim, she looked like the same woman he'd met on that memorable day.

Salvatore felt the clock turn back in time, and the stir of emotions that gripped him all those years ago flooded him now. He wanted to chain his arms around her and hold her as he had all those years ago. Salvatore wanted to brush his lips to hers to taste her.

There was now a larger, tighter knot at the pit of his stomach and taking a quick swallow, he said, "Yes, I'm Sal."

"Isabella mentioned you'd be working with us, and I thought it would be a good idea to meet. To see if we were a good fit before we got in deeper." Sizing him up, she felt a sense of familiarity with the brown eyes that stared at her. "Would you like to come inside?"

"It's a warm spring day. We can talk right here." Although sunlight filtered through bad-tempered clouds and the threat of rain hovered over them, the open public space, he decided, was the better option for their talk. When Maria lifted her eyes to the darkening sky, he said, "The rain won't come for a while yet. Please have a seat."

Making herself smile, she sat at the bench, and Salvatore followed suit. "I'm afraid my daughter can be quite impulsive at times, and I wanted to ensure this wasn't one of those instances."

Salvatore's eyes caught sight of her wedding band, and a sharp pain cut into his heart. "I can assure you she's made a rational decision. I have nothing but her best interest at heart."

Maria's brow arched high. "That's very kind of you, but I'm curious why you'd be so invested in my daughter's interest when you've just met her."

"You'll have to trust me." Salvatore's soft melodic voice stirred Maria's memory.

"I'm sorry, but have we met before?" Staring hard into his brown eyes, the jolt of recognition hit her with force, and the long-forgotten memories resurrected in her mind from depths unknown. Maria's shoulders tensed as the shock reverberated deep and strong. The tightness in her chest became suffocating.

His hair was now a cap of steel-gray around a face marginally lined with the map of his life, and the once carefree, brown eyes had a wiser depth to them. There was no denying it was him. Maria's white-knuckled fingers clutched the arm of the bench.

"Salvatore?"

"It's been a long time, Maria."

For a spell, the shocked silence fell heavy between them.

"How? What are you doing here?" she said when she found her voice.

"I'm here to see you." God, he craved a shot of nicotine.

Old wounds, she'd buried long ago, surfaced swift and raw. "I want nothing to do with you. So, you can go right back to wherever you've been hiding all these years." Maria's voice was clipped and edgy.

"I'm sorry, Maria," was all Salvatore thought to say.

The swell of anger bubbling inside her for two decades burst from her, and she barked, "After all these years, after what you did to me, that's all you can say? You appear out of the blue at my doorstep and expect me to accept a paltry apology. I guess you'd also like me to welcome you with open arms." Maria's tone was as frigid as the arctic air.

"I know it's not much, but I am sorry, Maria. All I ask is that you allow me to explain." Absently Salvatore reached for her hand, but she pulled away.

"That's not going to happen. I want you to leave right now. I want you to leave Isabella alone, and I want you to leave me alone." Her face flushed with fury, she shot to her feet. Getting far away from him was all she wanted.

"You're even more beautiful today than the woman I met all those years ago." Salvatore's voice trailed behind her.

Maria whipped dark, injured eyes at Salvatore. "You think I can easily be swayed by flattery? I want you to crawl back under the rock you came from. I want you to disappear from my life just as you did twenty-three years ago."

The angry words lobbed with conviction squeezed his heart, but he couldn't leave. He wouldn't not until she got the explanation she deserved. "I've waited a very long time for this moment, Maria. I've thought of you every day, every waking minute of my life. I never thought this moment would ever come my way. Please, Maria, give me a chance to explain. It's all I ask. Please."

His pleading tone rather than his words broke her, and she melted into the bench. "Why now, Salvatore?" Her eyes welled up.

That he was the cause of her tears stabbed Salvatore at the center of his chest. "Please don't cry, Maria. I don't want to upset you. I just want to talk to you, Maria. Just talk. I want you to allow me to explain, to apologize. I know this is difficult for you. It's difficult for me."

"Your chance for an apology came and went long ago." Maria trembled with the fury that sprang hot in her. "You do remember just leaving me without as much as a goodbye."

"I never meant to leave you, Maria. I never meant for what happened to happen. I want you to know I've never stopped thinking of you or loving you. Not a day has gone by when thoughts of you didn't fill me."

Maria snatched a tissue from her sweater pocket, dabbed at her eyes. "When all's said and done, the fact is you left. You disappeared without a trace. I heard nothing from you as days turned into weeks, weeks into months. I needed you. I needed to talk to you, Salvatore."

"It was never my intention to leave you, to leave us, the way I did. I had to leave when I did." There was despair in his voice. "Please believe me when I tell you I didn't leave because I wanted to. I had to leave town then."

Maria gazed at him with unforgiving eyes. "Save your self-serving words, Salvatore. You're deluded if you think I'll ever trust you again."

"It breaks my heart to see you this way, and I don't want to upset you any further, but if you can't do this for me, do it for Isabella. I can help her, Maria. I can teach her and mentor her. I can make her dream a reality."

Nerves frayed, she barked, "What do you know about Isabella?"

"Antonio…"

"He had a hand in this." Maria cut him off, her face flushed with fury. "So, you've known Isabella was my daughter this whole time. You didn't accidentally run into Isabella, and getting her to hire you was a carefully concocted scheme to sidle up to us. Well, I've managed all these years without you, and I certainly don't need your help now. I don't need you in my life, and I want nothing to do with you." Her words cut deep.

"None of this is concocted. Not in the way you think, and I mean it when I tell you I can make Isabella's dream a reality, and I want to do just that for her." Salvatore's words weakened her guard.

On a long shuddering breath, she stopped dead in her tracks. The need to help her daughter was greater than the need to safeguard her broken heart. Turning toward

Salvatore, Maria scrutinized him with cautious eyes for a long while before she sat back down.

"Although our path crossing now was not coincidental, Antonio was an innocent bystander." Salvatore hesitated for a moment, "There's no good way to tell you this, so I'll just let you read for yourself." Salvatore took out the envelope from his left breast pocket and handed it to Maria. "Please read this," he pressed when she refused to take the envelope.

After giving it some consideration, she ripped the envelope from Salvatore's, slid the letter out.

> Mr. Mesi,
>
> I want you to understand from the onset, I write this letter to you at a time of desperation and as my last resort.
>
> My name is Angelo Farfalla. We have never met, but we have one person who weaves our lives together. Her name is Maria Farfalla. You know her as Maria Falco.

Maria's face paled white. Her eyes fixed wide in shock, she threw Salvatore a look of utter disbelief, and he motioned for her to continue reading.

> Maria is the love of my life. Always has been, always will be.

She's brought unimaginable joy to me—so very much joy.

She's been a devoted wife and a loving, caring mother. She bestowed me the privilege of being a father (and a proud father I am) to Isabella, a beautiful, intelligent, and compassionate person. You could say mother and daughter are cut from the same cloth.

And my Maria is so beautiful. She's more beautiful today than the first day I laid eyes on her. There hasn't been a day I haven't been proud to be by her side. I've loved her as much as a man can love a woman.

My love for her prompts me to write you this letter. I'm dying. Doctors say I have weeks before leaving this earth before leaving my beautiful wife and wonderful daughter on their own.

I write you this letter not to ask for pity, for I have no regrets. I've had a wonderful life because of them. I'm a better man for having had them in my life. However, I believe that in the *overall scheme of things, the sum of one's life is no more than a series of overlapping stories, which define us, make us who we are, who we become.*

My story, although ending much too soon, is as fulfilled and complete as it could be. My story, however, is coming to an end, and yours will now begin.

As good as our years together have been, I've always known Maria's heart belongs to you.

Maria felt something inside of her break; something she knew would never heal. Knowing Angelo suspected all these years, how she felt broke her heart. She buried her face in her hands and cried tears of guilt, remorse, and regret. The silence stretched before she mustered the courage to continue reading.

I've been fortunate for the circumstances that allowed me to pursue my story of love. You must now let Maria write hers by taking care of her and Isabella by becoming a part of her life. I want you'll take care of my family after I'm gone.

In the beginning, Maria will push you away and possibly resent your intrusion into her life, but in time, she will let you in and tell you what needs to be said.

Everything will make sense when the time is right.

Sincerely,

Angelo Farfalla

Maria felt her throat slam shut, but she read the letter a second and third time. Each time she read more slowly, focused on every word, every sentiment, giving weight to every word. She'd never felt so loved, and her heart swelled with love for Angelo.

Maria tipped her head back just as the first droplets of rain broke from dark clouds. Rain and tears mingled on her cheeks as she thought of the courage Angelo showed through his months of suffering. She marvelled at his compassion and kindness that coursed through him at the worst time in his life, and her heart bloomed with love for him.

"He was near death when he wrote this letter," Maria said, scanning the postmark on the envelope and thought she didn't deserve such a wonderful, selfless man.

"Everyone faces death in their way."

"And he spent it worrying over Isabella's and my welfare."

"He sounds like a good man."

"He is—was."

Silently, Salvatore watched her fold the letter as if it was a long lost treasure. "You keep it," he said when she turned it over.

"Thank you." Maria thought how sobering it was that the sum of such a wonderful man's life fit into a few pages. "Isabella must never see this letter. She must never be told of its contents."

Salvatore's response was an unequivocal nod of understanding.

"We'll work together under the guise of having just met." She lifted a finger when Salvatore began to speak. "For Isabella and to fulfill a noble man's wish."

Again, Salvatore gave her a silent nod.

Chapter 14

STREAKS OF LIGHTNING flashed across a velvet-black sky, and the explosion of thunder followed close behind. The rain that began to drizzle late that afternoon was coming down harder now as Antonio grabbed the bags and exited his car.

Walking through the front door of Isabella's store, he found her tapping her chin, hemming, and hawing as she walked around the faceless mannequin draped in a short, black dress. Running his hand through the damp hair, Antonio silently watched Isabella. As if performing an ancient ritual, she circled the mannequin, eyeing it with scrutinizing eyes, pinning and unpinning, tucking and untucking.

With her last walk-around, Isabella's eyes widened as the idea came to her. Stepping back, Isabella murmured, "Perfect." The half-inch tuck of fabric at the neckline transformed the dress.

"Agreed," Antonio said with a nod.

A startled Isabella whirled to him. "How long have you been there?"

"A couple of minutes." Antonio set the bags in his hand down to shrug out of the damp leather jacket. "You were deep in thought, and I didn't want to break your trance. I'm glad I didn't. Whatever you did made the dress look that much more sensual. I guess that's the right word."

"It is. It's what I was going for."

"As a staunch heterosexual, I'd give a second, possibly a third look to the woman wearing that dress," Antonio said, all the while wondering how the short, black number would cling on the curvy body concealed under a burgundy cowl neck sweater and jeans.

Isabella smiled at that. "As a staunch heterosexual, you would, would you?"

Antonio moved closer to the mannequin, circled it. "If it looks great on this headless thing, I can only imagine how it would look on a woman with curves and other ... assets."

"Enhance curves and assets is what it's supposed to do."

"As a staunch heterosexual, I thank you for creating such an asset enhancing dress."

"You're welcome," Isabella said, for the first time noticing the rain damped hair clinging to his neck and the scent of soap and man lingering in the air. For the third time—she was keeping count—she felt the long-dormant fire in her burning hot. Dazed by the feeling, Isabella took a quiet breath and planted a smile on her face. "Is that dinner?"

"I hope you're hungry. My chef whipped up his specialty, lasagna, with side orders of Caesar salad and garlic bread. And I'm pretty sure he threw in a bottle of red."

Isabella's mouth watered. "That's going to hit the spot. I've only had a piece of toast today."

"What have I told you about not eating?"

"I know, I know, but I still have so much to do. Sal's been an absolute angel. He's been giving me pointers on how to improve the look of my designs. And man, does he have an eye for this."

"Don't sell yourself short. So do you."

"Thank you, but Sal knows his stuff. I have a suspicion he was born with a needle in his hand. And oh, my God, does he know the finer points of pattern making, and..." Isabella rambled on and sharing in her contagious enthusiasm, he let her.

"No coffee for you tonight."

She flashed a smile. "Are you okay if we set the food up on the display case?"

"Sure." Where they ate was of no consequence to Antonio. He'd been looking forward to tonight for the past fifty-six hours twenty-two minutes and forty-five seconds.

Isabella slanted a look over her shoulder. "Grab the two folding chairs from the back while I lock the front door."

"You've done a great job with the place. This doesn't look a bit like the store you started with." Setting the chairs down, Antonio scanned the space. Brass, glass, and cocoa-brown floors gave the space a chic look, like something out of a magazine.

"I'm glad you like it." Isabella spread a towel over the case.

"I do. It's amazing what you've done with the limited budget you had." Antonio dug out the bottle of wine from the bag, uncorked it. "Maybe I should hire you to do the interior design at The Café. It needs sprucing up, especially now that it's going to be in league with your store."

"I'd love to help you spruce up. I enjoyed designing this space. I'm not sure the workmen would share in the sentiment, but I've enjoyed every minute of the process." Isabella spread the meal before them. The scent of garlic and tomato that wafted from the unlidded containers made her mouth water.

"Let me know when you have the time. Between you and me, I've been toying with the idea of franchising The Café, and I'll need to give the space, my staff, and my sign an updated marketable look." Antonio poured Merlot into plastic glasses.

"That sounds exciting. I'll put together a few designs for you in a few weeks. Once I get the opening over and done with this Monday, I should have more time to spare." Rain pattered on the window, soothing drumming. "I love the smell and sound of rain. Do you mind if I turn these lights off and leave only the backlight on? That way, I can roll the shade up on the display window and still keep any possible gawkers at bay." Isabella flicked the lights off at Antonio's nod and rolled the shade up on the display window just enough to cast the room in shadows.

"Did you also design the window display?"

Isabella nodded. "Down to the last detail. It's a spring motif: new beginnings."

Lightning lanced the sky, turning the room silver. Through the rumble of thunder that followed, the rain lashed torrential and unforgiving.

"It's very artistic. You have a talent and an eye for colour and detail." Antonio raised his glass in a toast. "To new beginnings."

"To new beginnings." Isabella echoed, touching plastic to his.

The wind whipped rain against the front window, its drumming in the silence relentless as Isabella and Antonio's eyes met and held. The intensity in the deep, blue eyes that gazed down at her echoed his feelings.

Watching him through long, thick lashes, she hoped he could see the same in her eyes.

When Antonio stepped closer, Isabella heard his quickened breathing. She wondered if he could hear her pounding heart. Face to face, his eyes were riveted on her. Inches from Isabella, Antonio's burning need to take her into that deep kiss he'd fantasized about flowed like liquid heat through his veins. After a quick internal debate, he took gentle fingers down her cheek. The tender touch of his fingers against her skin left her tingling.

Antonio's lips hovering so close to tasting, he breathed her scent until he could taste her. His breath caught, released when the wave of want and need sucker-punched punched him. It staggered and frightened him. Never had he wanted a woman as much as he wanted her then.

Taking a long deep swallow, Antonio wrapped strong, large hands around her waist, pulled her in. Locked together, the heat between them stoked the fire inside her, making her already dizzy head spin faster.

Antonio tucked a strand of hair behind her ear. "I want to kiss you."

She laid a hand on the one floating in her hair, wrapped her fingers around it. "What are you waiting for?"

With the flash of heat, need, and want rippling in him, Antonio crushed his mouth to hers. His mouth locked on hers, his tongue tangled with hers, tasted, and explored.

Antonio made everything inside her body pulsed to a wonderful beat. "I've wanted you to kiss me all these months," Isabella said.

"Then, I have some catching up to do," he said before his mouth back on hers.

He made her breathless, drove molten heat in her that reached out to every nerve cell in her body, and unleashed the feral woman in her she didn't know existed. But she'd never been kissed with such intensity, need, or want.

Isabella was a plea away from begging him to take her on the wood floor there and then. If he kissed this great, she imagined what he would do to her craving, aching body when she heard the swell of a symphony flowing around them.

The crescendo rising in her head, she murmured, "Did you hear that?"

"Hear what?" Antonio's mind reeled from the hold she'd taken on him.

"Never mind," Isabella said, crushing her mouth to his.

With the rush of blood pounding in his head, Antonio took Isabella's mouth harder. His moist tongue parting the velvety soft lips to tangle with hers, he swallowed every soft, throaty moan that escaped her.

Tongues joined in a rhythmic dance, the kiss was sweet and magical, and both knew the memory of that moment would stay with them forever.

He looked into the eyes of the woman who made him restless, achy, and filled his thought—day and night. "I've wanted to do that for a long time."

The taste of him deliciously floating in her, her smile spread sweetly. "What took you so long?"

"I was scared you wouldn't let me." He hadn't figured out when, why, or how she'd gotten so deep under his skin that it thwarted his confidence.

Any other woman he would have already charmed her with his trademark smile into bed. She wasn't any woman, and sex wouldn't suffice. Thoughts of her rolled in his brain when he was awake. She kept him awake at night. None of the women he'd taken to bed since Isabella came into his life satisfied him or filled the void he felt inside of him.

It scared him to feel this way.

"I never pegged you for the insecure type." She looked him in the eye. "You've left me to wonder all this time how you felt. It's been three months that I've waited for you to kiss me."

Before she could get another word out, Antonio pulled her in, fused his mouth to hers. Hungry and frantic, she met his demands, equalled his emotions. Something shifted inside of him, something fast, unexpected, and inevitable. Antonio knew then, his feelings for her took a tumbling roll into uncharted territory.

UNDER THE POURING RAIN, A POOL of crushed out cigarettes on the ground, The Eyes watched the shadows beyond the display window. Fury pulsed hot when Isabella and Antonio locked lips for what seemed like an eternity.

The time had come to set the plan in motion. Harm would come soon.

Chapter 15

LESS THAN AN hour before opening, the shop looked perfect, welcoming, bright, and chic, but Isabella made another walkthrough. She had supervised every step of its creation. Still, Isabella checked and rechecked every detail down to the distance between hangers-on rods one more time.

From Mrs. Cropper's collection, bolts of fabric in every colour and texture were neatly stacked in display cases and shelves. Garments Isabella sketched on paper, and Maria and Salvatore stitched, hung on black hangers—precisely two fingers apart. The thigh-high black dress with the seductive low front and sequined waist draped the mannequin at the entrance. A ploy to ensure the design bearing Isabella's name on the label caught the attention of every customer walking through her door.

The adjacent mannequin displayed a champagne silk, floor-length strapless with a sweetheart neckline and black rhinestones embroidered at its bodice. Both dresses were the perfect addition to any girl's wardrobe and ideal for the upcoming prom season. Two other mannequins aimed to seduce the professional woman's eye donned a stylish pinstriped gabardine suit and a black tapered jacket with white piping over skinny pants. Kathleen would wear the remaining original designs as she mingled with customers.

Isabella herself looked casually professional but stylish in a black silk dress that flowed as fluid as water over her body. The tailored dress made her look taller and enhanced her cup size—not an easy feat.

Isabella hadn't expected to be as nervous as she was, but suddenly the nerves, doubts, and fears she'd shelved during the harried few weeks of preparation leading to today surfaced. Now, she wondered if they would come.

Would they come?

She didn't doubt the snoopers and gossipers would come to gawk and shoot a curious look to the girl whose father's death pushed her to take on so much at such a young age. She'd already heard the rumblings in the neighbourhood. Isabella wouldn't let it affect her today. The store launch wasn't just a dream, it was her survival plan, and she wasn't going to fail. No way, no how, was she going to fail.

Skin clammy, stomach rolling, she told herself to get a grip. The people who mattered would come.

"You haven't come this far and worked so hard to collapse at this stage."

Isabella turned to face her father perched on the workbench, a smoking cigarette at his lips. "I won't, Daddy."

"Good because you did well, Isabella. This place looks great, and your designs are smart and stylish."

"You think so, Daddy."

Angelo nodded. "I knew you were talented, but I never imagined you'd be such a shrewd businesswoman. You negotiated with creditors, you figured out how to deal with Mrs. Johnstone, and you managed to get Mrs. Cropper to supply you with the fabric. I couldn't have done better."

"I learned everything from you." Isabella wafted smoke out of her face. "Daddy, please put that thing out."

"You're never going to stop nagging me about this, are you?" Angelo said, stubbing his cigarette out.

"I only wish I'd done it when you were alive. You might still be here."

"Don't blame yourself for my early departure. It's on me. I'm the grown-up. I should have known better." Angelo let the silence she fell in to hang for a moment.

"Daddy, are you okay with me hiring Sal?" Isabella glanced sideways at him, then away.

"I am, princess. He's a great asset to you, and I am confident he has your best interest at heart." Angelo heaved himself off the table and ran a finger over the wood he'd worked on for so many years.

"I had the workmen sand the table down. It was getting splintery." Isabella put the tailor's beeswax, scissors, and the pin box into the carousel. "I only wished mama was as accepting of Sal. She tries to shroud her animosity for him in politeness, but anyone can see in her eyes. She sees Sal as your replacement."

Angelo rounded the table to stand behind it, let the memories drift. "The table needed a good sanding. As for your mother, she'll come to accept Sal."

"I'm sorry, but I had to move a few things around to make space for the retail floor," Isabella said when Angelo's eyes scanned the cutting room.

"It's a much more efficient layout." Angelo ran his fingers over the rulers hanging on the wall, making them swing like a pendulum. "How about this fellow Antonio?"

Isabella's cheeks tinged red. "You know about him?"

"I know everything. Just like I know, he sent you those." Angelo's eyes turned to the two vases on the display cases, each spilling with tulips.

"He did. He's been very nice, helpful, and a good friend."

"You like him as more than a friend."

"I have layers of complications that need nursing right now without adding a man to it."

"We all have layers of complications to deal with, and a good person by your side makes the journey much less complicated. I've known Antonio since he was a child. He wasn't always the upstanding man he is today, but every boy goes through the trials and tribulations he did on his way to manhood. He's smart, and as long as you let him, he'll be there for you as a friend, and hopefully, more. I hope both because you deserve a good man in your life."

"I'm glad you think so because I think I like him as more than a friend." Isabella fessed up.

Angelo smiled at his daughter. "Good. You need a good man in your life, one who will take care of you. You deserve to be happy, princess. Are you happy?"

"I'd be happier if you were here with me today."

"Today is your day, and you don't need me anymore. I'm very proud of you. You're going to be very successful, princess. You have great people around you. They will support you and be by your side at every turn."

At the realization of what he was saying, big, silent tears coursed down Isabella's face. "You're not going away, are you, Daddy?"

"I am. You've shown me you can stand on your own two feet and handle whatever comes your way. I'm very proud of you, Isabella. Our lives take many forms. Each one has its root and unfolds into a story, your story. Make it count, and never forget I love you. I always will."

Isabella's felt as if a boulder pressed down on her chest as she watched Angelo vanish before her eyes. "I love you too, Daddy."

Chapter 16

TO ISABELLA'S DELIGHT, from the moment the doors to the Isabella Farfalla Fashion Company opened, there was a steady stream of customers. The resident busybodies came in droves to placate their curiosity, but many were long-time customers of her father's. Regardless of their reasons, everyone who walked through the door would spread the word, and Isabella welcomed every patron with the same enthusiasm.

Mrs. Johnstone dropped in to check up on her investment. In the few minutes she was there, Isabella talked her into placing an order for two sleek, feminine pantsuits to replace the dull, manly, uniform looking ones she wore. Mrs. Johnstone didn't flinch at the steep price tag for the plum and mustard-yellow one-button jacket with gathered sleeves and slim-fitting pants.

On her way out of the store, whether by design or as a matter of conversation, Mrs. Johnstone told everyone of her purchase. Soon after, the orders started to roll in, filling the first two pages of Isabella's order book.

Valerie Leone, local braggadocio, scooped up the little black dress off the mannequin. With prom around the corner, that word-of-mouth advertising was invaluable and worth the fifteen percent discount, Isabella offered Valerie as an incentive to reach into her wallet.

It was late afternoon when Mrs. Cropper walked into the store. Tall and willowy in a white suit, her sandy-blonde hair tucked into an elegant updo, she moved fluidly across the store toward Isabella.

"Is that you, Mrs. Cropper? You look amazing."

A smile of satisfaction spread across Mrs. Cropper's face. "You didn't think I owned anything other than jeans and cotton shirts."

"No, well, yes, sort of. Anyway, you look great. Armani, right?" Isabella leaned in for a hug.

"Soon to be replaced by an Isabella Farfalla." Mrs. Cropper surveyed Isabella's handy work, watched browsing customers eyeing the garments on hangers. Women milled at the display cases admiring fabrics or the pencilled sketches Isabella laid out for perusing eyes. Some eyed themselves in the full-length mirrors on the change room doors. "You've done a wonderful job with this place."

Isabella's lips curved. "I'm glad you like it."

"And if those garments," Mrs. Cropper's gaze cut to the mannequins, "are any indication of what you're offering your customers, you're heading for great success. They're fetching, Isabella."

"Too right." Gail's voice had Isabella and Mrs. Cropper whirling. Bouncing glossy mink curls haloed her face, and her dark skin looked radiant against a lemon-yellow blouse and short, pleated skirt. "Aren't you glad I talked you into not leaving your designs behind for those vultures? They look great on your mannequins and hangers."

"I've already sold four of those designs." Grinning, Isabella leaned into Gail for a hug. "Mrs. Cropper, I'd like you to meet a dear friend."

"If not her only, Gail Williams, pleasure." Gail's eyes smiled as she offered Mrs. Cropper her hand.

"Gail's Mr. Hart's assistant," Isabella offered when it looked as if Mrs. Cropper was trying to place Gail in her memory.

At Mrs. Cropper's abject expression, Gail said, "That's how I feel Monday through Friday. Oh, shit. This isn't going to be good for anybody." The women's eyes followed Gail's gaze when it slid to the front door.

"I thought you were sick, Gail. Don't bother." Fizz waved a silencing hand when Gail started to speak. "Nice place you have here, Isabella. It's just too bad our lawyers will have it shut down by the end of the week. What are you staring at?" Fizz snapped at Mrs. Cropper through the haze of cigarette smoke.

"You're a nasty, rude one." Mrs. Cropper plucked the cigarette from Frizz's mouth, tossed it out the door. "This is a no-smoking area."

"Old lady, you have no right to do that." Fizz dug into her tote for the pack of cigarettes.

Mrs. Cropper snatched the pack from Fizz's hand. "One, who are you calling old? Two, darling, you need to put some effort into your pursuit to bulldoze Isabella's success. That is what you're trying to do by purposely spewing filthy cigarette smoke in her store." Mrs. Cropper turned over the crumpled cigarette pack to Fizz. "Once in a while, you need to get the hamster in there to power the wheel," Mrs. Cropper said, tapping Fizz's temple.

Fizz's eyes spit fire at the snorted giggles that followed. "Listen, old lady."

"Let's step into the back room, ladies." Isabella offered when customer's ears spun in their direction.

"I don't need to step anywhere. I just came to tell you you're in violation of your employment contract, which stipulates…"

"That I can't work for your competition for a year after leaving Hart Designs, and as you can see, I'm not. This is my store. Meaning I'm working for myself." Isabella pointed out with conviction.

"Isabella's one hundred percent right." Gail jumped in to defend.

"Shut up, Gail, and you can consider yourself fired." Fizz's tone was steel.

"You can't fire me. I don't report to you. I report to your father, and I'd like you to deliver him a message. Tell him I quit because the last thing I want is to work alongside a bitch like you. Secondly, you don't have a leg to stand on where Isabella's contract is concerned, and your father knows it because he has a functioning brain." Gail's last two words came out slowly.

Rage had Fizz's blood boiling and the colour flooding her face. "You're done at Hart Designs, and I'll make sure no one in our business ever hires you."

"Oh my God, I am so never going to be employed by the one person who'll take your call. If you think you have the ear of your colleagues in the business, think again, Fizz. They all think you're a rude, talentless, spoiled brat whose only talent is to sponge off daddy." Gail's face inches from Fizz drove a shiver down her back, but she refused to show it.

Whispers from the crowd gathered around them had Gail kicking Fizz's ego and ass hands down.

"Please, ladies, let's continue this discussion in the back room." Isabella encouraged to the crowd's disappointment.

With a huff, Fizz turned from Gail to Isabella. "I'll make it my life's mission to destroy you and your bosom buddy here," she said, turning to make her dramatic exit.

"Don't let the doorknob wedge between your lipo-sucked ass on the way out," Gail called after Fizz. The snickers that followed her out the door added to her humiliation and fueled her seething anger. "She's such a twit. Don't worry about her."

"I don't know about that. She looked pretty pissed." Isabella put in.

"She'll simmer down. The only reason she's so pissed is that Macy's threatened Hart Designs with a lawsuit for plagiarizing their line of two winters ago when she presented your designs. Word got around like wildfire, and her reputation and that of Hart Designs is now in tatters."

Isabella rolled her big, brown eyes. "Imagine that."

"Yes, imagine that. You pirated the designs and counted on Fizz to sign her name to them and present them as her own. It's why you insisted I give them to her and not Mr. Hart." Gail watched Isabella innocently bite on her bottom lip. "Girl, I couldn't be more proud of you."

"You are full of surprises, Isabella. I didn't think you had such a devious streak in you." Mrs. Cropper's lips turned into a wide grin. "I said it once before, and I'll say it again, better not cross this girl."

"I don't know what either of you is talking about." Isabella turned to Gail. "And I guess as of tomorrow, you're working with me."

"I appreciate your offer, honey, but I'm not about to become a financial drain. I can get a job anywhere." Gail's eyes turned to the tall, handsome male form with the black curls and the misty lake coloured eyes walking in. "Sweet Jesus, that is delicious."

Mrs. Cropper followed Gail's gaze. "You're not wrong about that, luv," she hummed, eyes wide in appreciation.

"I'll make it work, Gail. Be here tomorrow at nine. Now, if you wouldn't mind entertaining yourselves for a bit, I have customers to tend to." Isabella turned to make her way to Antonio.

"God, the things I could do with that gorgeous specimen of a man." A wicked gleam flicked in Gail's eyes.

"Me too, luv." Mrs. Cropper sighed along with Gail.

"You look … umm, yeah, stunning." Antonio stammered.

In the curve-hugging dress that rode high enough on the toned, never-ending legs on three-inch black stilettos, Isabella made the sexual ache beat thick in Antonio. The fountain of long chestnut waves spilling over her shoulders made him want to tangle his hands through it, but it was the luscious, cherry-red painted lips that drove the jolt of heat to spread.

"Thank you." Isabella's soft smile sent his heart doing a quick gallop. "And thank you for the flowers."

"I'm glad you liked them. I thought tulips, as in the first blooms of spring. You know new beginnings."

"Tulips for new beginnings," she hummed. That he'd put so much thought had her heart fluttering.

"You have quite the turnout." Antonio ran the back of his hand down Isabella's arm making her tingling all over.

"I've had a lot more traffic than I imagined. I think I've already taken enough orders to cover half of the back rent I owe you. Did you hear what I said?"

"Sure, something, money. I had a wonderful time, Saturday." He reached for her hand, gave it an intimate squeeze.

The move took Isabella by surprise. "You're not listening."

"We should do it again soon."

"I'd like that, but..." Isabella's brain seemed to disconnect when she felt him trace his thumb along the back of her hand.

"How does tonight sound?" Antonio was close enough that she could feel his hot breath on her face.

She felt the clutch in her throat. "I can't. I don't close until nine, and then I'll probably be dead on my feet."

"I'll massage them."

The tug, the pull when the image flashed in her mind, came fast. "As intriguing as that sounds, I have tons to do, and I've told you..."

"This is a lovely place you have here, Isabella." Mrs. Byrd broke in on her way out the door.

"Thank you for coming by, Mrs. Byrd. Hope to see you again."

"You will. I have to rush off to pick up Junior from school, but I'll be back. You have a couple of things I'd like to try on. Gotta rush out, hon."

"As I was saying before, I was interrupted. I have the taste of you in me, and I'm desperate for more." Antonio's smile was curved just enough to have his dimples flickering, and she thought her knees buckled.

"You're a bad influence. I need to get back to work."

Antonio flashed Isabella a mischievous smile. "You're a great influence. I'll call you."

"I'll call you."

"Promise."

This time she leaned into him and breathed into his ear. "I need to get back to work."

No woman kept him speculating or on his toes, as she did. "I'll be waiting by the telephone, and I pledge not to add a layer of strain to your demanding life. You won't even know I'm around."

"Hi, Isabella." Michaela's voice cut into the intimate moment. "Aren't those flowers beautiful?" She nestled the Dior sunglasses into the platinum-blonde hair.

Isabella's eyes flashed to her cousin. In a polka dot blouse over a high waist pencil skirt, gold hoops at her ears, and the golden hair tumbling in waves around her face, she looked her usual stunning self. "They're from Antonio. This is my cousin Michaela. Michaela, Antonio."

"Nice to meet you," Antonio's eyes never left Isabella as he shook Michaela's outstretched hand. "I need to get back to the cafe." Antonio took the hand Michaela held tight back.

"Please don't leave on my account," Michaela said, batting heavily mascaraed lashes.

"I'm a man short, and I told Marco I wouldn't be gone for long. I'll have lunch for you and your staff dropped off shortly." Antonio tenderly brushed his lips over Isabella's cheek with Michaela watching on.

"I didn't even think about food. Thank you."

"See how well we work together," he said, with Isabella's and Michaela's eyes following him out the door.

"I believe you're smitten, cousin."

"We're just friends."

"I've never seen anyone eye a friend with such puppy dog eyes. Spill." Michaela nudged Isabella with her shoulders, and Isabella did. She told her cousin about their kiss.

"The moment our lips came together, I thought I heard a symphony floating all around us."

"That good, huh?" Lost in the memory of the kiss, Isabella nodded. "I need to start talking to you more, live vicariously through you, especially now that I'm going to be permanently chained down." Michaela extended a ringed hand to Isabella.

"You're engaged. That's great news. Jesus, that's huge and gorgeous." Isabella brought Michaela's ringed hand for closer inspection.

"It's a two-carat, round cut, solitaire, set in platinum."

"It's stunning. Who's the lucky guy?"

"Joe Smith, of course." When Isabella stayed silent, Michaela said, "I know you don't like him much because he came between us in high school, but things are going to change. I'd like them to, Isabella. We're not kids anymore. We're grown, women. I'm about to be married, and you're launching your own business and have a love interest."

"That all sounds so mature, and Antonio's not my love interest. We're…"

"Yeah, I know, friends. You can always be friends with benefits, and I'm guessing with that smouldering sexuality, he exudes that there will be benefits soon. I bet you he looks great naked."

"Jesus, Michaela, you haven't changed." Isabella snorted a giggle. "You think he looks good naked?"

"Oh, I know so. Look how fine he looks in those tight jeans." Michaela winked, and both cousins broke into laughter. "And he wants you. I saw it in his eyes. It makes me green with envy. Now, let's talk about me. I'm getting married this November. It's not a lot of time." Michaela spent the better part of the next ten minutes telling Isabella every aspect of her wedding plans.

"I'll make your wedding dress. It will be Mama's and my wedding gift."

"I couldn't have you do that."

"I want to."

"I'm warning you. I'm very much a bridezilla, and you know the wedding gown is the most important aspect of the wedding, so I'm bound to go nutty."

"I'm willing to take on the challenge. Besides, I'm not totally selfless. You'll be promoting my brand and the store by wearing an Isabella Farfalla original to all your ritzy friends."

"You're not wrong there. Joe's mother plans to invite everyone from the mayor to the police chief to prominent business leaders and their wives. If you think women whose pastime is spending their husband's money will benefit you." Michaela gave Isabella a teasing smile.

"Are you kidding me?" Isabella's mind raced at the possibilities.

"All right then, it's a deal. There he is." Michaela shifted her gaze to the front of the store. "Over here, babe. Isabella, you know my fiancé Joe, don't you?"

Isabella's body instinctively tensed. "Yes, of course. Hello, Joe."

"It's been a long time, Isabella. It's great to see you again." Joe offered his hand, held it out until Isabella took it. Pumping it, she felt his thumb intimately trace the contours of her hand. The gesture made knots of tension tighten in her stomach.

Isabella thought she'd left Joe Smith behind in high school, but here he was inches from her, making her revisit a past she didn't want to revive. She didn't want the fear or helplessness Joe had triggered for most of her high school years to find a place to live in her again.

Isabella didn't want to rekindle the feelings of vulnerability and defenselessness Joe provoked when he refused to accept her rejections. She didn't want to revive what he'd perceived as nothing more than a hard-to-get game when she'd scorned his advances. Isabella didn't want the anxious feelings Joe had filled her then with each of his coincidental encounters that happened too often to be unintentional.

To Isabella's relief, the encounters stopped, but only when Joe and Michaela became a couple. With Michaela demanding Joe's complete attention, he didn't have time to focus on her, although there were many times she sensed his presence around her.

Isabella debated telling Michaela about her unwelcomed encounters with Joe, but she opted against it in the end. Joe's good looks, popularity, and wealth blinded Michaela, and she'd dismiss Isabella's warning as the rants of a jealous woman.

Distancing herself from Michaela was her only option. To Isabella's relief, Michaela saved her the trouble when she cast her aside for Joe, and the once inseparable cousins drifted apart—far apart.

"Congratulations on your engagement." Isabella tugged her hand free from Joe's grip.

"Congratulations on your store opening." Joe looked around the crowded store. "You're a hit. If this keeps up, you'll have to expand soon. If you need help with construction work, call me. I'm sure I can work something out for you."

"Isn't he just a prince?" Michaela linked a possessive arm around Joe. "Babe, Isabella's offered to design my wedding dress as a wedding gift."

"Thank you, Isabella, but that's not necessary," Joe said.

"But, baby, Isabella was going to make me an original, and in return, I was going to promote it for her."

"You can have your original dress, but Isabella is just starting out. I'll pay for it." Joe held up a hand to silence Isabella's oncoming refusal. "No arguments. Give Michaela anything she wants. Money's no object."

Michaela rested her head on Joe's shoulder. "And this is why I love this man."

"I'll have sketches for you to review in a few days. I'll call you when they're ready."

"All right. Joe and I will be sure to make ourselves available whenever you call. Won't we, baby?"

"It's not necessary to inconvenience Joe, Michaela." Isabella was quick to throw out. The last thing she wanted was to be in the same room with him.

"It's no inconvenience, Isabella." Joe aimed a look that sent a shiver down Isabella's spine.

Chapter 17

ONE HOUR PAST closing time, Isabella walked the last customer to the door and flipped the lights off. "I know I'm taking a risk by offering to work on Michaela's wedding dress, but you know I love a challenge." Isabella dropped back onto the chair. "My feet are killing me."

"Wearing those stilettos for the entire day will do that." Maria slid off the tape measure around her neck and set it on the workbench. "I know you enjoy a challenge, but a wedding dress is a monumental task."

"I know, but Sal told me he's had experience with wedding gowns and will help me." Isabella toed her shoes off and heaved a satisfying sigh.

"You enjoy working with Salvatore, don't you?" Maria's eyes stayed on Isabella.

"I do. In the short time, I've worked with him, I've learned tons." Isabella walked to the window display, turned the spotlights on. "He's way more knowledgeable than he lets on."

"Yes, I sense that as well." Maria watched Isabella move to slide clothes back on the hangers.

"I'll draft some sketches, and Sal will work with you and me on constructing it." Isabella immediately picked up on the distress that came over Maria at the mention of Salvatore's name. "Mama, are you okay with Sal being here?"

There was the briefest pause as Maria considered her response. In the end, she said, "I am."

"If you're not comfortable working with him, I can ask him to leave. I don't want you to be on edge, which is how I sense you are when he's around. I want you to be happy, Mama."

Nervous energy had Maria turning to straighten the bolts that didn't need it. The reality was she wanted Salvatore out of their lives, but that wasn't in the cards. Isabella needed his help, and Angelo's wish was that he give it to her.

Salvatore wasn't lying when he'd told Maria he could make Isabella's dream a reality. Working with him the past couple of weeks had Maria appreciating his tailoring skills. From designing to pattern making and garment construction, the man was talented and artistic. Salvatore had the expertise to mentor Isabella and steered her in the right direction.

Maria would sacrifice everything to ensure it happened for Isabella.

"Mama, talk to me."

"I'm fine with Salvatore working here." Maria's fingers tightened around the bolt of fabric in her hands.

"The truth, Mama."

"I need some time to get used to not having your father around. That's not too much to ask."

"Of course not."

"Good, then, that's that." Maria stacked the bolt in place. "I'll head upstairs and heat the leftovers from lunch for dinner. Antonio sent enough food to feed a small army."

Isabella followed her mother to the backroom, and together, they bagged the containers of untouched meatball sandwiches and salad. "What do you think of Antonio, Mama?"

"He seems like a polite, thoughtful young man. I can see why your father liked him. And he's certainly smitten with you."

"No, he's not." Isabella stopped bagging. "You think so?"

Maria nodded, reaching for the two bottles of unopened pop. "His face lights up when you're around, and so does yours. I think you're as smitten with him. Are you?"

"I think so, maybe. I'm not sure. I don't know if it's because he's brought such normalcy into my life when I needed it or if it's because he's been so nice, or..."

Maria touched a hand to Isabella's arm. "Stop over-analyzing. You can't do that with matters of the heart, Isabella. Enjoy his friendship, your time together, and if it was meant to be, it will be."

"He wants us to get together."

"Do you?" Maria stopped wiping the round lunch table, which doubled as Isabella's desk.

"I do, but I'm not sure it's the best time to delve into anything like that now. I have so much going on."

"Honey, you're not marrying the boy. You're not, are you?"

Isabella was pleased to hear her mother's playful jab. "Of course not."

"Then, stop making excuses and have some fun. It never ceases to amaze me how you can make difficult business decisions on the spot, but when it comes to your wellbeing, you think everything to death." Maria scraped two chairs closer to the table and signalled for Isabella to do the same with the two closest to her.

"I know, but..."

"No buts. Do something for yourself for once. You need happiness in your life, Isabella. You've had more than your share of sadness these past few months. More than anyone of your young age should experience." Maria leaned in to peck Isabella on the cheek. "I want you to enjoy yourself. Youth comes once in a lifetime."

Isabella followed Maria out to the retail floor. "I'll finish closing up. Mama? Thank you for your support for everything."

Maria locked eyes with those so much like hers. "I'm proud of you, Isabella, and your father was right. You clearly have the knack for," she looked around the room, "this. And I know Angelo is looking down on you with a huge grin as he marvels at what his little girl accomplished today."

"That means a lot, and you know this is only the beginning. I have so many plans."

"I know, and I was wrong to try to stop you. You fulfill your dreams, honey. I'll be by your side every step of the way." Maria closed the store door behind her, praying Isabella would one day forgive her.

ALONE IN HER STORE, ISABELLA'S LIPS curved into a smile as she looked around and relished in her success. It was the first day, and there were more barriers to overcome, hundreds of challenges to face, but her newfound confidence gave her the courage to tackle anything that came her way.

With the glow of delight on Isabella's face, she made her way to the back of the store. Her eyes came to rest on the framed picture of her father hanging above the workbench. She hoped he was pleased with today. This was his dream as much as it was hers. It was early days, but she'd never felt better than she had today. After a moment of contemplation, she turned the remaining lights off.

In the room plunged in shadows, Isabella made her way to the front of the store. She felt the warning glints of panic pressing down on her chest the moment she saw him. Undesirable memories stirred in her, and she froze in her tracks.

Joe's eyes were glassy, his hair dishevelled, and he swayed unsteadily on his feet. The smell of alcohol radiated from his breath and every pore of his body.

Isabella jerked back when Joe attempted to take a step toward her. She found comfort that he couldn't manage the step and instead fell against the wall for balance and caught his breath. Isabella watched Joe's eyes wander the room, whether because he was disoriented or to make sure they were alone, she wasn't sure. Afraid to trigger a reaction, Isabella remained as still as a statue.

How a human being sank to such depths was beyond Isabella? Joe had looks, money and was in line to take over his father's multi-million dollar construction business. She wondered what drove a man who had so much to the broken man before her. One thing she knew was that she wasn't the scared girl she once was, and she wouldn't allow Joe to instill the fear in her he once had.

"Get out of my store, Joe."

Joe threw her an absent-minded half-smile. "I'm sorry I couldn't stay longer when I came in earlier, Isabella. But you know when Michaela starts droning on about the fucking wedding and her goddamn dress, she…" His mind wandered, and he forced himself to think. "Yeah, that fucking wedding, blah, blah, blah. I want to put a goddamn bullet in my head when she goes off." His angry words slurred.

The panic spread through Isabella, but she held her composure. "You're drunk, and I'm closed. My mother will be down if I don't head upstairs for dinner now," Isabella said, the first thing that came to her panicked mind.

"You look really good, Isabella. Really, really good. That dress suits your curvy body." Joe mumbled incoherently.

There was something so chilling in the eyes that scanned her from head to toe. Fear washing over her, Isabella cast her eyes out the window. She pressed a hand to her stomach when she caught sight of the empty sidewalk.

"Leave, Joe. I have to finish closing up."

Joe held his arm out to block Isabella from taking a step. "You know I was at the cemetery when they buried your father. I was watching you from a distance. It was the first time I'd seen you since graduation. I thought you looked better than you did in high school." Joe's glazed eyes bore into Isabella. When he took a step toward her, she put space between them. "Don't be scared of me, Isabella."

Masking the flicks of fear engulfing her with every appearance of calm, Isabella said, "I'm not scared of you, Joe. I want you out of my store. Now."

Unsteady on his feet, Joe stumbled backward. "Don't be like that, Isabella. I would never hurt you. I just want to talk to you."

"You're drunk, Joe. Leave now, or I'll call the police." Isabella's tone was cool and deliberate. Mustering her unsteady legs to move, she walked to the telephone, picked it up, and dialled.

"All right, I'm going, but I have to tell you, Isabella, you look hot."

"You come around here again, Joe, and I'll get the police after you," she called after him as he staggered out the store.

FROM A SAFE DISTANCE, EYES CURVED into a smile as they watched a terrified Isabella bolt to the door to slide the lock in place. Watching Isabella fall back against the wall and wrap arms around herself to stop from shaking, *The Eyes'* smile widened.

Tapping away cigarette ash, *The Eyes* thought how well the plan was working. Isabella would learn what it felt like to be crossed.

Chapter 18

"ISABELLA TO EARTH. Come in, Isabella." Gail's voice shook Isabella out of her reverie.

"Sorry, I was miles away,"

"I've meant to ask. What's that bell thingy above the door all about?" Gail walked the coffee pot to the table, poured steaming coffee into two cups.

"Good customer service. It announces the arrival of every customer, so I can pounce on them the moment they walk in." Isabella hoped that sounded logical enough because telling Gail—telling anyone—about her run-in with Joe wasn't an option. Word would reach her mother's ears and burden her with unnecessary worry.

Joe hadn't been by in the weeks since their confrontation, and Isabella put the encounter down as a one-off lapse in judgment on Joe's part. Still, she took every possible precaution to avoid a second incident.

"For the record, I think that bell is annoying. Refill, boss? For—what?—the third cup of the morning." Gail grinned when Isabella's expression went sheepish.

"Stop calling me, boss."

"But you are my boss, boss." Gail teased.

"Stop it." Isabella held her cup out. "Pour."

"See, you're subconsciously treating me as your peon." Smirking, Gail poured coffee into Isabella's cup, topped hers. "When are you going to stop this nonsense? You're my boss; own it, girl." She spooned sugar into both cups.

Isabella leaned back in her chair. "When I can begin to pay you what you're worth." Isabella wrapped her hands around the hot cup.

"How many times have I told you you're paying me enough?"

"That's why you moved back home with your mother, right?"

"I've already explained this to you. She's getting old and needs me to take care of her." Gail raised a hand to silence Isabella when she opened her mouth. "No more discussion on this. Now, let's get to work so we can get this company of yours making money. The first point of order, I need a raise." When Isabella winged a brow, Gail said, "Joking."

"Let's get started on reviewing today's To-Do list before Mama, Sal, and the seamstresses get in."

"All right. The first point of order is mmm-hmm will be my catchphrase and shall remain as such." Gail's eyebrows shot up, and both women burst out laughing before they got to prioritize the issues requiring attention.

Dealing with rising issues head-on before they snowballed into complications was how Gail thought Isabella should start her day. That type of proactive thinking led Isabella to rely on Gail to deal with the daily minutiae that greased her business's wheels. Minutiae Isabella hadn't the time nor the patience to deal with and was happy to leave that part of the business in Gail's trustworthy hands.

"And today, I'll finish mailing out the last of the notices advising parents of our discounted price if they place their order by the end of this month. That should get pre-orders on the book, which will keep the seamstresses and Maria busy. The best part is it will get cash flowing in now. Discounting pre-orders is a great idea you came up with."

"We'll barely be breaking even by offering the discount, but it's our first uniform contract, and we need to ingratiate ourselves to the parents. Once in the door, we'll have them eating out of our hands and seal the contract for years."

Gail traded pen for coffee cup. "Everyone is on board with doing anything necessary to schmooze the parents. We're not going to lose the contract as the last supplier did because of poor customer service."

"Good. For a while, I was worried. I mean, Mrs. Cropper hadn't heard from the school board, and I'd hired the two seamstresses away from Hart's." Isabella absently played with the tip of duct tape that came loose on the chair's armrest. "I'll admit now I lost a lot of sleep during the weeks we were waiting on the school board's decision."

"Well, that's resolved now."

"Temporarily anyway. Mrs. Cropper talked them into giving us the contract on trial run until September when they'll make their final decision." Isabella picked up her pen, clicked it a few times. "With us being a new manufacturer, they didn't want to seal the deal so quickly. Mrs. Cropper went out on a limb for us on this."

"And we'll do right by her. I sense there's something else on your mind," Gail said when Isabella's eyes turned pensive. "You know you're supposed to tell your consigliere your innermost secrets."

"So now you're my consigliere?"

"Consider me your Tom Hagen. Now, tell Tommy what's bothering you." The statement delivered in a Godfather's voice made the bubble of laughter burst from

Isabella. She could always count on Gail to infuse levity into any situation.

Isabella kicked back in her chair. "I'm thinking of how we haven't heard from Fizz or Hart Designs. This may be the calm before the storm."

"Is that what's been bothering you these past few days?" Gail slid the pen into the spiral spine of her book.

"Aside from walking out with my designs, I took their contact information, and I'm doing business with many of them, particularly Mrs. Cropper. God bless that woman. The business's couture side is doing okay, but it's not enough to carry the store. If it wasn't for the uniform contract, a contract meant for Hart Designs, none of us would be here."

Gail closed her minute book, crossed one slender leg over another. "For one, it was Mrs. Cropper's option as to who she partnered with, and she chose you. With good reason, and two, fuck 'em. Fuck Fizz and fuck Mr. Hart. They got what they deserved. It's called Karma."

Despite herself, Isabella snorted a laugh. "You are poetic."

"I am that. Now, stop feeling guilty about doing what you have to do to survive. As far as Fizz and Mr. Hart coming after you, don't waste your energy on a what-if, besides Tom Hagen is on your side." Gail stared at Isabella fixedly. "He's not the one they took out on the lake, is he?"

"That was Fredo, and you're probably right. I need to stop wasting my energy on a what-if." Isabella watched Gail move past Isabella to the coffee maker.

"You're right. It was Fredo. Fredo was weak, and of course, I'm right." Gail measured coffee into a filter dropped it in place.

"And modest." Isabella watched Gail pour water into the reservoir and flick the on button.

"Now, one last question before we close this meeting. What time is Blue Eyes picking you up tonight?"

"That's tonight? I forgot about it." The coffee machine spurted the first drops of coffee and filled the back room with its aroma. "I don't have time for this right now. I have too much to do. What was I thinking? I'll cancel."

"No, you're not. You've been postponing for two months. I'm surprised Blue-Eyes is still sniffing around you after you've put him off so many times."

Isabella's eyes rose to Gail over the rim of her cup. "Don't make me feel worse than I already do. It's just not a good time. I have way too much to do right now."

"Is that the sole reason you've been putting gorgeous off?"

Isabella reached for Gail's empty cup and walked it to the sink. "What other reason could there be?"

The fear he won't be as crazy in love with you as you are with him sat on the tip of Gail's tongue. "Well, you're not putting Blue Eyes off. Tonight you're going to put on that cherry-red lipstick he likes. Please, even a blind person can see how fixated he gets on your lips when painted that harlot red. And I want you to make sure you wear something that tells him how much you want to tangle in the sheets with him."

Isabella let out a howling laugh. "Jesus, Gail, you really should get a filter."

"You want to tell me you haven't once thought how capable he might be in the boudoir?"

Isabella choked on a laugh. "Boudoir, really, Gail?"

"Yes, boudoir, and if you're about to tell me, you haven't thought of him in that way, save your breath because I won't believe you. I've thought of him in that way on your behalf, and my money says he can go on for hours and give you, at minimum, a three orgasm, toe-curling experience every time," she said, with a wicked wiggle of eyebrows.

"Filter, Gail."

"Give me your word you'll doll yourself up tonight and be done with this already because if you're considering postponing Blue-Eyes again, I'm moving in on him."

Isabella's eyes lit with laughter. "All right, all right. I'll go out with Antonio tonight,"

With a shake of her head, Gail looked up at Isabela. "I better not find out Monday you didn't. I do, and he becomes a free agent, and talent recruiter Gail Williams will round him up to play on her team." Gail stepped out of the backroom with a reproving finger, leaving Isabella pondering what the night held in store.

Chapter 19

THE SHORT, POMEGRANATE-RED, satin dress Isabella treated herself to from her collection, hung low on her back, and its thin straps left creamy shoulders exposed. She'd left her dark hair tumbling in loose waves. At her ears, glittery columns of plated gold danced. Her lips were painted red. Gail wasn't the only one who'd noticed Antonio's fixation with her lips when they were—as Gail so eloquently put it—traced in harlot red.

Isabella was checking herself in the mirror for the umpteenth time when she heard Antonio making small talk with Maria. Taking one last look at herself in the mirror, Isabella fluffed her hair, and breathing in deep, made her way to the living room.

Antonio's eyes aimed straight for her when she walked into the room. Eyes following her every step as she walked to him, his heart took one hard leap into his throat. His long two-month wait was so worth it, he thought. Etching her into his memory, he filed it away to dip into whenever he thought of her, which now was more often than he cared to admit.

"You look wonderful, honey. Doesn't she look great, Antonio?" Maria turned to Antonio, who said nothing, but he didn't need to. All his thoughts were there to read on his face. "Well, enjoy your dinner, children." Maria made herself scarce when she became invisible.

"Hi." Antonio's lips brushed over Isabella's once and again when his system hungered for a deeper taste.

"Hi, back."

"You look, umm, yeah." He exhaled a breath.

"Thank you. You clean up nicely too," she said, eyeing the freshly trimmed stubble, the flowing dark mane, and the white silk against sinewy arms and shoulders. His slacks were black, pleated, and snug enough for her liking.

"Where are we going?" Isabella flicked eyes dusted in bronze when she slid into the leather seat of Antonio's car.

"It's a surprise." A boyish smirk twisted his lips.

"A man of mystery."

Antonio steered the sleek convertible into the flow of traffic. "Tell me how the past two months have been?"

A glint of guilt flashed in Isabella's eyes. "I'm sorry I've only spoken to you in rushed sentences over the telephone. And I'm sorry I've postponed tonight for so long," she offered, now wondering why she had.

"You have nothing to apologize for. I know how draining, and all-consuming a business can be. The important thing is you're here now. Catch me up on what's been happening." He rolled to a stop at the red light.

Isabella's guilt eased, she went into an animated account that lasted for the entire drive. Eyes beaming, she told Antonio how she'd taken a gamble by up charging for her exclusive designs, but that it was paying off. Her face was luminous when she outlined her solution for keeping her couture and uniform business from clashing.

Animatedly, Isabella recounted how she and Salvatore trekked to her haute couture clientele's homes to maintain the allure of exclusivity. The individual attention her customers received in the comfort of their home, she told him, was a hit. Having her elite clients place their orders, have their fittings, and take final delivery of their garment from their living room's comfort gave them a sense of exclusivity. With unbridled enthusiasm, she told him that the personal service allowed her to charge obscene prices.

A brow of admiration rose. "Sounds like a perfect solution and a wise business decision that will net a nice profit margin."

"It's a lot of extra work. The travelling takes a chunk of my day, which I have to make up after hours, but it has to be done. At least until I can afford to rent other premises to separate the uniform business from the couture side."

"I can help you with that. I have a building on that block coming available at the end of the month you can have at the very reasonable price of whatever-you-can-pay."

That he wouldn't think twice to offer her help made Isabella's heart melt. "That's very generous, but I'm not there yet, and I want to do this on my own."

"All right, but it's there for the taking when you want it." When Isabella's eyes became thoughtful, Antonio reached for her hand and was pleased when she enveloped it around his. "What's on your mind? Spill."

"I have my eye on the two buildings adjacent to my store. If the couture side of the business keeps up at the current momentum, it stands to reason it will do well enough to invest in the additional space." Talking with Antonio, leaning on him for ideas and support, felt natural, and Isabella didn't hesitate to tell him her thoughts.

"Planning an expansion already, that's ambitious." Antonio gently traced his thumb over her hand. The roughness of his skin against hers sent her stomach fluttering like a hummingbird's wings.

"I know it's still early days, but I'd like to start working out the numbers to plan the expansion phase. You know the early bird and all that."

When Antonio came to a full stop on red again, he swivelled blue eyes to her. There was nothing more attractive than a driven, ambitious woman talking his language, he thought. "I think it's good to plan, and you can never go wrong investing in real estate. Why don't I run some numbers for you?"

Isabella breathed a sigh of relief. "I was hoping you'd say that. You know how good I am with anything accounting related."

After allowing pedestrians to cross, Antonio made a left on Front. "All you had to do was ask."

"I know, but…" Isabella hesitated.

"Isabella, there's no shame in asking for help. Besides, seeing as you can't string two numbers together, I thought I was officially your numbers, man." Humour danced in his eyes when her fire-red mouth opened in a stunned O.

"Well, you are, Mr. Smartie-Pants, but seeing as I can't afford to pay you yet, and I still owe you one month of back rent, I don't want to impose."

"You're not imposing. I'm running a tab, which I'll present to you as soon as you start making a profit." His remark got him a jab to the ribs. "Here we are." Antonio killed the engine.

A warm July breeze fluttering off Lake Ontario carried the scent of summer and water. The area bristled with a mix of tourists and locals in search of entertainment. The Human League's Don't You Want Me rang out from the speakers of a nearby patio bar above the chatter of diners. Couples window-shopped or made their way to dinner. A group of teenagers debated whether to get a bite to eat before heading out for a night of dancing.

"I've never been up there." Isabella craned her neck up at the illuminated CN tower that stretched five football fields high into a black sky.

"We're going up to the restaurant at the very top." Antonio pointed skyward. "Did you know the restaurant completes a full rotation every ninety minutes giving you a panoramic view of the city and lake?"

Isabella's face lit with a childlike wonder that reached deep within him. "That sounds exciting."

"It does," Antonio said. Although he'd been there many times, sharing in the moment with her made it feel like a new experience.

BOARDING THE CROWDED TOWER ELEVATOR ISABELLA'S eyes fixed out the glass doors. Back pressed against Antonio, she watched the city skyline's panoramic view studded in bright lights come into view as the elevator floated to the top. The elevator climbing higher, the sprinkling of stars and a white moon in a blackened sky came closer. She felt as if she could reach for them.

The moment the elevator doors opened, Isabella and Antonio were escorted into the dining room dimly lit under the warm glow of soft light. Floor to ceiling windows heightened the view as the restaurant spun in slow motion. Fresh carnations speared from porcelain vases, and white candles flickered on tables covered in blush-coloured linen.

Isabella's face lit in wonder when she caught sight of City Hall as it came into view. Against a dark sky, its twin concave towers were brightly lit in vibrant colour. From her vantage point, she caught sight of the ant-size people milling about its square or sitting around the square reflecting pool, spouting water like long thin fingers reaching for the sky.

"I hope you like champagne," Antonio said when the waiter approached their table with the pre-ordered bottle.

"My palate hasn't experienced anything that sophisticated," Isabella confessed with unabashed honesty.

"Then, you're in for a treat." Passing Antonio's taste-test, the waiter poured two flutes and informed them their meal would be out shortly.

Tilting back her glass, she drained half in one swallow. "This is wonderful."

"I'm glad you like it, but unless you want to be carried home, I'd drink it slower." Antonio topped her glass.

"I'd heard about this place, but I never imagined it to be so grand. I like it."

Antonio tapped his flute to hers and smiled when she took a delicate sip. "I'm glad you're enjoying yourself."

"I am. God, that's deelish," she said with a cluck of her tongue. The display of innocence added a sexy appeal he liked. "Thank you for everything, for tonight, for this."

Antonio held the bottle up, and when Isabella nodded, topped her glass. "Wait until you taste the food, which I took the liberty of pre-ordering. I hope you don't mind."

"Not at all. My days are spent making decisions. I welcome someone else taking charge for once, but only for tonight," she added with a warning look.

Antonio's lips curved. "Only for tonight, scouts honour."

Their lobster and steak dinner was delicious, and conversation flowed easily. There was a pleasant familiarity and comfort as they spoke about everything and anything with ease.

"I hope you have room for dessert. It's a Grand Marnier chocolate tower," Antonio told her when the server set what looked like a culinary masterpiece.

Taking a spoonful of cake, Isabella let it roll on her tongue, hummed with pure sensory pleasure. "Oh. My. God. This is to die for."

Leaning back in his chair, Antonio watched her over the flicker of candlelight. Her smile lit the room brightly. Her wide-eyed innocence took hold of him in a way no other woman had. He wasn't entirely sure what he was experiencing, but being with her felt right and perfect.

He wondered where tonight was taking them. Not just in the next few hours, but in the days and months to come because he didn't want it to end.

Antonio leaned forward to skim his thumb over her cheek. "Chocolate."

Inhibition floating with her third glass of champagne, Isabella snorted a laugh. "Guess I should act more ladylike."

"Not on my account. I think chocolate looks good on you." He reached to wipe the chocolate streak she dabbed over her other cheek. "You're feeling way too happy. We need to get coffee in you."

"But that'll just kill this wonderful buzz I have going."

Jesus! Her mother was going to kill him.

At the fretful look in his eye, she reached for his hand, gave it a quick squeeze. "I'm joking. I'm not drunk. I'm just having a great time."

"So am I. I almost forgot. I have something for you." Antonio set the black velvet box on the table. "Go on, open it."

Flipping the lid open, her eyes widened at the butterfly wings cast in solid gold gleaming against black velvet. The I between the wings was a row of diamonds, and the chain was gold.

"It's my butterfly logo." Isabella's voice came out a loud squeak making several of the diners turn.

"You like it?" Antonio slid the chain around her neck.

"It's beautiful and so perfect." Her heart bloomed with emotion, and appreciation and affection came through in her voice.

Trailing fingers over the pendant, she held it for a long while as if connecting with it. It was the most thoughtful and perfect gift anyone had given her.

IT WAS ELEVEN WHEN ANTONIO OPENED the door to The Café. The room was cast in shadows. Chairs were stacked on tables, and in the silence, the steady hum of the refrigerated cases was the only sound in the room.

"Take a seat while I get the coffee machine to heat up." His hand reaching for the light switch, Isabella wrapped hers around his.

"Leave them off."

"Would you like pop or orange juice? I don't think you should have any more wine. Your mother will kill me if I bring you home sloshed." Her scent, hovering around him, clawed at him.

"I'm not sloshed, and I don't want anything to drink." Isabella twined her fingers with his. "I want you to take me upstairs." Her lips stretched out in a smile, she took a grip of his hand and led him up to his apartment.

In the gentle hue of moonlight streaming through the unblinded window, Isabella leaned into Antonio, moved her lips over his. Antonio tasted Cristal on them. Developing a taste for her, wanting more, he crushed his mouth to hers, plundered, and drowned himself in the taste of her.

Her scent, sweet and intoxicating, lingered even after he pulled back. His need for her was all-consuming, new to him. It left him feeling defenceless.

"From the day you fell into my arms, you've filled my dreams in sleep and my thoughts when awake." Emotion, honest, and real filled the eyes that met hers. When all Isabella did was smile, Antonio wasn't sure how to interpret that, and he said the first thing that came to his muddled brain, "I have a bottle of Zinfandel in the fridge."

"I don't want anything to drink. Right now, what I want is you. I want you to touch me." Never breaking her gaze on him, she reached behind to unzip her dress.

His breath caught in his throat, and his heart skipped a beat when she brushed the straps off her shoulders, and red satin glided down her body to pool at her feet. He revelled in the rich-brown rainfall of hair that tumbled over bare shoulders and the red lace bra and panties that were a stark contrast against the creamy skin.

Antonio's eyes roamed over curves down to long legs, which rode to spiked heels. None of the fantasies he'd conjured, the longing that had speared through him was as powerful as what he felt for her then.

"You're stunning." His heart pulsing in his chest like a jackhammer, Antonio glided his mouth over her lips. Skimming moist, warm lips down her neck, over her shoulders, his hands busied themselves over lace to cup her breasts and play with her nipples until she shivered.

Burning for the feel of his skin beneath her hands, Isabella unbuttoned his shirt and slid it off the broad shoulders. "I've wanted to touch you for so long."

It was a man's body under her touch when she took her hands over the hard chest curves, the muscled arms. She breathed a man's scent when her mouth roamed over his neck and shoulders.

"I've wanted to see you for so long," she whispered, unhooking his slacks and letting them slide over his hips. Her breath hitched at the sight of the naked body ready for her.

She didn't laugh this time. She giggled.

He said nothing to that. Jesus, what could he say?

"I'm sorry. I didn't mean that. I'm just so nervous," she said when she saw the injured expression on his face.

"You started this."

"I know, but... I don't... I think, the Cristal, I got ahead of myself. I'm sorry."

Antonio grabbed her hand as she started to walk away, pressed it to his chest. "Touch me, Isabella."

Guiding her, she skimmed curious fingers over the chest as hard as steel. Her fingertips traced over the childhood scar from when he fell off the maple tree in his backyard.

Her fingers continued their exploration down his belly, rounding to his back. Walking around him, she took him in with an appreciative eye. The muscles on his back and shoulders rippled. Olive skin, slender hips, long legs, he was beautiful.

Her hands on him drove the blood to pound in his head, his throbbing loins to scream, but he reined in the urge to rush through the moment. He wouldn't devour her, as he wanted to. Tonight he'd savour and love, as he never had.

Lowering his mouth to hers, he kissed her tenderly, seductively. Antonio took his mouth slowly down Isabella's neck, to her breasts. Her skin was hot and as fragrant as flowers in spring.

His hands and mouth explored. Taking gentle nibbles, agonizing her with long, caressing, tender strokes, he drove her body to float and tremble. It put a fire in her stomach, and she wondered how she'd lived without this for so long.

When he lowered his mouth to the swells of her breast, down to the lace-covered nipples, it sent her head spinning.

No way, no how would she live without this anymore.

Expert hands seamlessly unhooked her bra and slid it off. A fresh wave of shocking delight flared through her when his demanding mouth swallowed her breasts.

Her breath came faster when he clenched her nipples between his teeth. Eyes glazed over as he tugged and rolled his moist tongue over them.

"Oh my, God, that feels so incredibly good," she cried out on a shuddering moan.

"It's just the start." Antonio scooped her into his arms and carried her to his bed.

His gaze never leaving her, he inched his naked body close to her. Her skin was soft as silk, his body solid as steel. Bodies pressed together, she felt him against her leg. She couldn't help but smile at the thought she was the cause, and lying next to him felt as perfect and as right as she imagined it would.

"I hope my naked body isn't what's making you smile."

"Uh-uh." Isabella casually wound her finger through dark chest hair. "I think it's a very sexy body. I've pictured you naked many times and never imagined you looked this good. I mean it. I…"

He brought her finger to his lips, kissed it. "My ego, thanks you." He trailed lazy kisses over her face, eyes, and mouth, made her shudder when he nipped on her ear lobe.

"Oh, God, that feels amazing." She moaned long and deep when his tongue teasingly skimmed down her belly.

"I want to do to you wonderful things that will make you cry out and shudder." He glided his lips over hers.

Gripped by the dreamlike words full of promise, everything throbbed at once. The thought of his hands, mouth, and tongue claiming every part of her body had her shivering in anticipation. "Make my body come alive."

"Your wish is my command."

Slowly he traced a finger along the edge of lace that covered her. Her whimpers became more vocal when she felt him slide her panties off, and his fingers dived into the wet heat. With a slow and deliberate motion, he detonated dormant sensations that stirred her body to life.

Her alone me-time would never do again.

The man was skilled. God was he skilled. He could do whatever he was doing to her forever.

When his mouth and tongue replaced fingers, he set off a grenade of unimaginable pleasure she never thought possible. It thrilled her, made her body burst to life.

After this, her alone me-time would never do.

It wasn't long before the orgasm burst like a long-dormant volcano, and she cried out unrestrained, delighted sounds that had been waiting to escape for years. Years of sexual drought dissolved, and it felt so good, so right.

Her body felt alive, satiated, but he didn't stop there. He didn't stop when the second orgasm had her shuddering and humming his name like a prayer. It wasn't until the third tidal wave of unbridled eruption that drove her hard over the edge that he stopped.

She tried to catch her breath. "Dear God, that was stupendous." Her voice sounded throaty, breathy.

Straddling her, he looked her in the eyes. "That's a ten?"

Slumberous eyes looked up to him. His body glowed under a thin layer of sweat. She breathed in the muskiness of man, the subtle scent of his cologne. "It's a solid eleven. Do you always make it feel this good?"

Brushing the wild mane of hair from her face, he shook his head. "I'm that much better because I enjoy being with you, pleasing you."

Eye to eye and mouth to mouth, she felt the heat of his breath on her face. Feeling loved, she joined her mouth to his and almost blurted out what she'd wanted to say for months, but instead said, "Take me into your heart. Make me feel more special than you already have. Make me yours."

Blue eyes burning with need and the ripple of lust swimming straight to his loins, he drove himself into her fast and hard. She was hot, wet, and tight. So deliciously tight, he thought. The blood humming in his head, pounding at his loins, he thrust himself with reckless abandon.

When he saw the tears spilling down her cheeks, he panicked, pulled himself out of her. "I'm sorry, Isabella."

"Don't stop now," she said, even as the tears rolled down her cheeks.

"I'm hurting you. I don't want to hurt you." Stomach twisting in knots, he raked fingers through his hair. "Although I'm not sure why I did, I mean, it's not as if I haven't done this before." He sat at the edge of the bed.

"It's just a little pain," she murmured, although it was more like an electric shock to the system. "You're not denying me this. Put it back in."

He wasn't sure whether to laugh or brand her crazy. "I'm not hurting you. It's not supposed to hurt. I mean, I've never made anyone…" The light bulb lit brightly. "Jesus, Isabella, are you a virgin?" Isabella's cheeks flushed a warm pink. "God, Isabella, I didn't know."

"I said, put it back in."

"You should've told me." He stalked around the room. He'd driven into her like a wrecking ball, a thoughtless, hormonal possessed man. "Goddamn it, Isabella. I was so rough on you. I'm sorry."

"It's me who should be apologizing."

That she'd find the need to apologize to a baboon like him who'd had no regard for her surprised him. "You have nothing to apologize for."

"I don't have the experience to know how to … physically satisfy you like I imagined the women you've been with can."

Sitting beside her, he brushed the hair from her face. "Physical satisfaction can be honed with practice through communication. The emotional happiness you fill me with can't be, which's more important to me than the physical. And that you'd want to give yourself to me makes my heart swell so big it feels as if it's bursting through my chest." He slowly traced his fingers over her cheeks. "I'm sorry I was so rough, but I've, well, I've waited for you for months. You know I had a lot of pent up energy," he stammered.

"You've waited for me?" Isabella secretly grinned.

"Mmm-hmm." Antonio stroked his hand down her hair. "Five months seventy-two hours forty-five gruelling minutes. I'd wait longer if necessary."

Isabella rested her hand on his cheek and looked deep into his eyes. "Make love with me." When he started to open his mouth, she joined lips with him. "I want you to be my first. I want you to make it memorable. I want to remember tonight forever. I want you to make me yours."

His stomach twisted in knots of pure love he got on top of her. "It's a lot of wants. I'll try to fulfill them."

"I think you could."

"Look into my eyes. Focus on me," he said, and as Isabella did, he slid into her.

This time his strokes were slow and gentle. This time there was no pain, just an incredible feeling of togetherness that filled her heart to brimming.

Hot flesh on flesh, naked bodies melded into one. Together they moved in the slow seductive dance of lovers. Through it all, with a tender voice, he patiently guided her. It wasn't long before it felt as if they'd been doing this all their lives.

The sounds that escaped him were purely male, purely primal. His breaths coming short and ragged, his heart bursting with love, he filled her with all he had.

She was his, and he was hers.

EYES FIRMLY FIXED AT ANTONIO'S APARTMENT window, they watched the silhouetted shadows embracing, kissing. The screams in *The Eyes'* head felt almost unearthly when they watched Antonio scoop Isabella into his arms and disappear from view.

The thought of what he was doing to her, with her, made the anger burn hot. Why should Isabella have everything handed to her? The cheating, lying, scheming bitch's time would come, and when it did, *The Eyes* would make sure to leave a mark in Isabella's life she wouldn't soon forget.

Chapter 20

SALVATORE BREATHED ON his glasses gave them a quick polish with his handkerchief. Holding them up to a hot August sun, he inspected them for smears before sliding them onto his nose. Taking a seat at the bench, he closed his eyes and willed for calm.

Maria's temper leaped and bit when the mood struck, and today it hit and bit hard—for no reason. After each unprovoked attack, Salvatore gave her the space she needed. Most days, watching the world go by, he'd timeout at the bench. During those times, he wished he hadn't promised Isabella he'd give up smoking because, God, he needed a cigarette.

At every turn, he went out of his way to give Maria the distance she needed. Still, she never failed to find fault for everything he did or didn't do, for what he said. Salvatore didn't provoke the outbursts or did anything to deserve it, yet Maria found a reason to lash out.

Isabella overheard the arguments, watched the one-sided exchange feeling helpless. Any calming attempt resulted in Maria huffing an exasperated breath and storming out of the store. It was easier than offering explanations or apologies.

Maria had nothing to apologize for, and Salvatore understood that. She was projecting the pain and heartache he inflicted years ago and carried all this time. Salvatore imagined the feeling of rejection she'd felt all these years had amplified with time.

All he could do now was apologize, but she wouldn't hear it. Every time he'd start to explain his reason for leaving, Maria walked away. But he wasn't about to give up any time soon. He'd searched for her for years, and now that he'd found her, he wouldn't give in so easily.

Taking the seat on the bench next to Salvatore, Isabella felt the August sun heat on her face. "I can't say I'm sorry enough. These outbursts are so out of character for Mama."

"Your mother is still grieving. You need to give her time." Salvatore absently reached for the phantom cigarette between his lips and made Isabella smile.

He'd smoked his last cigarette days ago when she plucked the one dangling from his mouth, and stabbing it out, told him she wanted him to be with them for a long time. To her surprise, he threw the pack out and hadn't smoked since then.

"She's usually pleasant and easy-going. I know you've done everything to make her feel at ease." Isabella followed the scream of crows overhead. "I like to thank you, Sal. I haven't said it often enough, but only because a thank you isn't enough for everything you've done for Mama and me. I don't know what I, we, would have done without you."

He wished Maria could be as accepting of him as Isabella was. "It's me who should be thanking you for taking me in as you have."

Isabella could counter his statement with so many examples. Salvatore was the perfect mentor, skilled and talented, with invaluable knowledge he shared with her. Besides his artistic talent, they shared a love for fashion the business, and he was easy to talk to. She was where she was because of Salvatore.

"You're interested in those buildings?" Salvatore asked when Isabella's eyes darted to the for sale sign.

"It's early days, but the uniform sales have been steady, and Mrs. Cropper tells me the school board is pleased with our price and the exceptional service. Thanks to Mama's excellent customer service, parents are singing their praise to the school board." Isabella pointed out to shine a positive light on Maria. "Mrs. Cropper's contact told her the school board is ready to commit to a five-year contract with us to supply all the schools," she said, over the din of late-day traffic.

Roads and sidewalks were thronged with people homebound. Outside the IGA, shoppers sorted through fresh vegetables and fruits stacked on the outside display stands. The aroma of baked bread, cakes, and oven-baked pizza perfumed the air.

"So, you'll need the additional space." Salvatore draped his arms on the back of the bench.

"The couture side is doing well, and with the growth in uniform business, I'll need the existing space."

"What does Maria think?" Salvatore watched Isabella bite on her bottom lip as her mother did in her younger years.

Isabella shook her head. "Mama is…"

"Conservative in her thinking," Salvatore finished.

"I was thinking more, not as business-minded. She hates debt, but the reality is that it's unavoidable when you're in business. The trick is staying ahead of it."

"Agreed. What's your plan?" Salvatore asked, and Isabella willingly told the man who understood her as well as her father had her plans.

"I want those buildings to house the couture business. Our time is getting tight, and home visits are becoming unmanageable. Expansion, in the next twelve months, is inevitable." Isabella's voice brimmed with confidence.

Seeing her rationale, Salvatore said, "Real estate is always a sound investment, and it sounds as if you have all your sheep in a row. What's holding you back?"

Biting back a smile, she thought of correcting him, but gaffes like that were part of his charm. "The asking price for those two buildings exceeds my financial reach," she said candidly, to the man she fell into easy conversation.

"May I offer a word of advice?"

"I'd like you to."

"Never underestimate the bank's willingness to lend money to a savvy entrepreneur, which you are. What you need is a good business proposal, and you can get Antonio to help you with that."

Antonio's name set images of their night together to flash in Isabella's mind. As much as she craved to see him, and her body his touch, the business consumed her time. It had been four weeks since their night together, and she made a mental note to make time for a repeat night soon.

"The second thing you need is confidence, which you have." Salvatore's words left Isabella considering. "You're the type of entrepreneur investors take notice of. As much as the bank asks for all sorts of nonsense, I guarantee you they won't turn you down because what they're investing in is you."

"Thank you for that." Isabella edged forward, pecked him on the cheek. The unexpected gesture left Salvatore staring. "And I'll have a word with Mama."

"No need for that, love. You have enough on your plate. Besides, I have a feeling things will work out soon enough," Salvatore assured, watching Maria pop her head from behind the display window to watch them.

Since his relationship with Isabella blossomed, he often caught her watching them. The fact she did from afar without coming between them was proof enough for him that the wall Maria erected was crumbling—admittedly one brick at a time. It was a matter of time before it collapsed, and when it did, he was ready to walk over those bricks and straight into her heart.

Chapter 21

ISABELLA'S LIPS CURVED when she saw the long line of coffee lovers queued for their daily dose. Since implementing her interior design, Antonio's business saw a fifteen percent increase, and he projected an additional ten in the next six months.

Isabella scanned the room transformed with inexpensive changes from dated to chic. Wood floors were stained a rich coffee-brown. Ivory painted walls combined with soft lighting gave the cafe a warm, modern sophistication. Dated frames on the wall were replaced with the modernized design of The Café logo. The new fire-red logo, strategically positioned on every wall, was in clear sight of every patron regardless of where they stood. Brand recognition was imperative, and customers should leave with the logo etched in their mind, Isabella reasoned.

Along with the room décor, the staff was fitted with a new uniform. The red on beige, chef-style jacket with a striped waist-high apron promoted a European flair.

Isabella was happy to see Antonio traded up from the plain Styrofoam to the paper coffee cups with The Café logo she recommended. He'd also changed the bland descriptive names on the menu board for Italian terms adding to the European sophistication. Those minor changes were already drawing a young, trendier crowd, making The Café the place to be seen.

As if sensing Isabella's presence, Antonio's eyes rolled to the front door. Eyes filled with delight, and lips curved into a smile the moment he saw her.

Dark hair rained down to her shoulders, and she wore a cream silk shirt and ankle-length slim pants. The thick, red leather belt at her waist matched the patent slingbacks. A pair of dark Ray-Ban sunglasses topped the stylish look. Isabella looked confident, poised, and ready to seize the world. This, Antonio thought, was the same teary-eyed woman who'd fallen into his arm.

Isabella tipped her glasses down, tossed Antonio an easy grin. "Hi," she said, over the din of conversation, coffee grinders, and spurting espresso machines.

"Hi. You look like you're ready to burst." Antonio leaned in to glide lips over the glossed lips. No matter how often he did, the connection always triggered a tug-of-war at the pit of his stomach.

"The school board committed to a five-year contract." Isabella's excitement was contagious.

"Congratulation, you deserve it," Marco commented with a wink as he walked by. "Take a seat, and I'll bring over celebratory espressos."

Isabella met Marco's smile as Antonio took her hand and led her to the empty table. "I think he's smitten with you, and I knew you'd get it."

"This one is on Mama. Parents who sit on the school board were so happy with her service they insisted the contract be awarded to us for the next five years. The best part is Mrs. Cropper got a price increase. Meaning in a year, we'll become profitable." The excitement added sparkle to her brown eyes.

"I've made a million plans. I'm going to need you to help me draft a proper business plan for Mrs. Johnstone because I'm buying the two buildings I've had my eyes on. I'm going to house the uniform division in the existing building, your building, and..." Excitedly, Isabella prattled on, her hands gesturing flamboyantly.

There was something sexy in a soft, feminine woman oozing with drive and towering ambition, Antonio thought. Yessiree Bob, there sure was.

"I've missed seeing you these past few weeks," Antonio murmured when Isabella finally ran out of things to say.

"I'm sorry, but I've been so busy." Her hectic schedule had kept them apart for too long. When Isabella had time to spare, her tired mind and body craved sleep, and a short telephone conversation with Antonio was the best she could offer.

Antonio reached for her hand. "I just wanted to let you know I've missed you."

"Are you busy tonight?" Isabella saw Antonio's smile deepen. "So we could go over my financial proposal. I want to meet with Mrs. Johnstone in the next few days. I brought all my documents with me." She watched the smiling lips curve into a pout.

"All right, I'll have the chef whip something up for dinner. You will stay for dinner."

Isabella watched Marco set coffees on the table. She was pleased to see the miniature biscotto next to her coffee cup—one of her many suggestions, but a simple touch that separated The Café from all others.

"Thank you, Marco, and to answer your question, I'd love to stay for dinner. By my calculation, if you're not cooking dinner, that'll free up thirty minutes."

Antonio's smile deepening, he skimmed a finger over the back of her hand. "What did you have in mind?"

"Working on my proposal before dinner," she said. It took him a beat to realize she was teasing. "I've missed you too, and we have some catching up to do. After working on my proposal, what do you say we do some serious catching up?"

Dimples winked out. "I think I could be persuaded."

A FEW TABLES AWAY, MICHAELA'S EYES were cast on Isabella and Antonio, debating whether she was as smitten as he was. In Michaela's eyes, men's make-up was primarily hormonal. As much as Michaela appreciated that singular fact, Isabella was a novice at relationships and men.

Since Michaela could remember, to open her own design company was Isabella's sole focus, and her cousin could be tenacious. Men in Isabella's mind were a useless distraction. She'd shunned them and dating to spend time with her father. Not that it had been difficult to do. Isabella never garnered the attention of the male species, as Michaela did.

As much as Antonio was a catch, Michaela hoped Isabella wasn't interested in anything other than her business. Isabella was on her way to achieving her dream, and Michaela hoped Antonio wasn't derailing her cousin.

"Do you think Antonio is in love with Isabella or using her for sex?" Michaela smiled when she saw Antonio seamlessly twine fingers with Isabella, and she pushed his hand away.

"I don't know, and I don't care." As much as Joe didn't appreciate Antonio's emotional display, the cheek caressing, hand-holding, and finger twinning with Isabella, he'd be damned if he'd let Michaela know. Joe wasn't about to fuel Michaela's misguided notion that he was in love with Isabella.

Isabella did look good, though, Joe thought, eyeing her from the corner of his eyes. Her skin was made to be covered in silk. The shirt buttoned down to the swells of her breast was proof. He appreciated the skin-tight pants hugging curvy hips, riding over long legs.

Joe couldn't help but to worshipfully eye her.

She was beautiful and intelligent, with a dose of refined femininity. Her drive and ambitious nature threatened insecure men, but Joe found those qualities alluring.

He couldn't understand what Isabella saw in that pantywaist Antonio. If Isabella gave Joe a chance, he'd prove to her that he had far more to offer than that pansy. But Isabella never gave him a second look, not in high school, not afterward, not now.

But rejection only made a woman that much more desirable.

"Antonio probably thinks because he's loaded, he can have anyone he wants." Michaela went thoughtful. "Hmmm, maybe he's lured her to his bed, and she's finally given in to temptation. If that's the case, I say, good for her. It's about time she gave her innocence away. She's twenty-two, for God's sake."

Egging some more, Joe thought. Well, two could play at that game. "If she is a virgin, Antonio will treasure and cherish her that much more. For a woman to give a man, such a coveted gift is unheard of today." That would drive his point home to Michaela, who'd slept her way through her senior year by the time he got to her.

Michaela's back went up, and the coffee cup in her hand went down with a thud. "Why do you so often feel the need to bring up my past?"

"I'm sorry," he said, in the grovelling tone he used to avoid the oncoming argument.

"I'm devoted to you, baby. You know that."

"Yes, I know." Not as much as you are to my trust fund, he added to himself.

Michaela loved money. Not that Joe faulted her because who didn't. Neither did he care that she'd slept with half of the senior class and a handful of teachers. After all, he was reaping the benefits of her sexual expertise.

Michaela was an untameable tigress in bed and so very adventurous. Her willingness to try anything, anytime, anywhere, made it easy to overlook her prostituting herself to the highest bidder. If he couldn't have someone as wholesome and pure as Isabella, the next best thing was her opposite, Joe reasoned.

"I never wear underwear," Michaela told him the first time he took her in the backseat of his Camaro when he slid his hand under the short skirt and looked at her with wondrous eyes. "Easier access, anytime any place," she added, guiding his fingers into the damp heat.

What man didn't appreciate an adventurous, beautiful woman? And head-turning beautiful she was. Waves of honey-blonde hair, a wide, luscious mouth, and heaving D-cups were enough to have him forget Isabella. And that body of hers was made to please a man. It was a man's wet dream and never failed to get him iron-hard no matter his mood.

Joe knew Michaela played her beauty to his male vulnerabilities. Women like her were skilled at turning men into their lapdogs. Joe didn't care as long as Michaela gave him what he wanted, as he was about to ask her to do so in the men's bathroom. The thought of her spread eagle on the bathroom counter while he did to her whatever came to mind had him thrumming between the legs.

Feeling himself go hard drove home why he stuck it out with Michaela and why she stuck it out with him. He was in the relationship for sex, she for his money. A fair trade-off, Joe concluded. In life, you took the good with the bad.

Joe's gaze whipped up to Michaela. "Prove to me how devoted. Meet me in the bathroom. Now," he ordered with urgency pushing to his feet.

Michaela's face went bright with smiles and her tone sugar sweet when she caught sight of the hard bulge against denim. "It'll be my pleasure to take care of lollipop, baby," she said, taking pleasure in the flowing dampness and throbbing between her legs.

THE EXPRESSION ON ANTONIO'S FACE TURNED to concern when Isabella's back stiffened. "Are you all right?"

"Yeah, I'm fine," she said, masking her anxiety.

"What's wrong, Isabella?" He followed her eyes but could only catch a back view of the man that disappeared into the men's washroom.

"Nothing," Isabella said, looking into the wary eyes. "I have a lot on my mind." Her expression was neutral, and her voice calm, but her eyes said otherwise.

IN THE BRIGHT STRIPES OF LIGHT leaking through the louvred blind of Antonio's apartment, *The Eyes* watched him and Isabella wishing for a more unobstructed view.

Both had worked at the dinner table since heading upstairs. They worked for one hour and stopped to share a pizza and a bottle of wine when Marco brought it up. Once finished, they went back to work.

All indications led *The Eyes* to believe they were working on something relating to Isabella's business. It was growing by leaps and bounds, and she was already planning on expanding.

The Eyes made sure to be well informed on everything about Isabella's business. It was critical to planning what would befall her. *The Eyes* hadn't eliminated the idea of physical harm. For now, fear tactics were working just fine. One thing was sure. *The Eyes* was going to cash out on Isabella's windfall and make her never forget the hurt she'd inflicted.

Chapter 22

FALL WAS ON the brink of winter, but its biting cold already stung the air, and the falling rain wasn't helping. Walking into the bank for her monthly meeting with Mrs. Johnstone, Isabella stomped her shoes dry and dusted her snowy shoulders.

The monthly meetings weren't standard procedure, but Mrs. Johnstone insisted on the face-to-face reviews for Isabella's benefit. A young entrepreneur could use a seasoned business professional's guidance and financial expertise, Mrs. Johnstone told Isabella. To Mrs. Johnstone's surprise, Isabella concurred, but then, her mind was logical and direct. Ambition didn't translate into success. Learning from seasoned professionals did.

It was early morning, but the bank already bristled with customers. The air was crowded with chatter, tapping calculators, closing file drawers, and the thump of stamps.

Kat looked up from her keyboard with a welcoming smile. "Good morning, Isabella. You're ten minutes early for your meeting." In the discount-bin red cowl neck sweater and black polyester pants, Isabella thought Kat looked stunning.

"I wanted to find out if you've had a chance to contact my friend Elsa from the Sutherland Modelling Agency." Isabella waved at Mrs. Byrd, waiting in line for an available teller. She looked stunning in the lavender pantsuit she'd bought from Isabella weeks earlier.

"I did." When it became apparent Kat wasn't going to elaborate, Isabella made a rolling hand gesture to spur Kat along. "She wants to sign me on."

"That's fantastic news." Isabella waited while Kat took an incoming call, transferred it, and returned the cradle's handset.

"It is." Kat fell into a lengthy silence.

"I sense a but coming."

"She says I have the potential to make it into the big league."

"Those were her exact words, Kat?" Isabella watched Kat nod, then hold up a finger when her phone rang. "That's fantastic news. When do you start working with Elsa?" Isabella asked when Kat set the telephone down.

An uncomfortable smile exposed dimples in blushed cheeks. "I need to come up with the money for my training. Elsa is willing to pick up the portfolio's expense and travel to auditions, but she won't pay for anything else. Not that I expect her to, but…"

"But what, Kat? This is an excellent opportunity for you." Isabella refrained from blowing out an exasperated breath. Talking to Kat sometimes felt like a visit to the dentist.

A slow deeper flush worked its way up Kat's throat to her cheeks. "I can't afford it. See, it's just me, and my mom and every penny we earn goes to rent and…"

Isabella jumped in. "I'm sorry, Kat. I should have been more thoughtful." Isabella went silent when Kat turned over the green folder to the approaching teller.

"Mr. Forrester's account history and contact information are in there," Kat told the teller before turning to Isabella. "I'm sorry to let you down."

"You haven't let me down, and I don't want you giving up on such a fantastic opportunity." An idea began to take root in Isabella's head. "Do you want to become a model, Kat?"

"I do. I mean, I like working here, but I'd like to get past living paycheque to paycheque. Elsa said I could draw a decent salary modelling." Kat absently reached for the discarded coffee cup, sipped. "Sorry, I should have offered you a coffee. I think there's a fresh pot brewing."

Isabella waved the offer down. "Elsa explained it will be a lot of hard work, long hours, and require a lot of dedication."

"I have no problem with that. I've been working since I was seven. My mom couldn't afford a babysitter then, and she'd take me along to her cleaning jobs, and I'd help her."

That was what Isabella wanted to hear, and she said, "I'll pay for your training." It would require tossing numbers around with Antonio to see how to come up with the money. Isabella could already hear the grunts and lecture on the evils of tossing good money away when she was getting off the ground, but she was confident her plan would pay off.

"I don't know, Isabella."

"Hear me out." Isabella held up a silencing hand when she saw Kat's doubtful expression. "I'll pay for everything if you commit to doing my four-yearly modelling shows for the next five years."

Kat's brows creased. "I'd do that for you anyway."

Kat didn't see the potential in herself, but Isabella did. Kat had the indefinable look designers wanted to flash their garments on the runway or in glossy magazines. Kat's refined good looks were lens perfect. At five-eleven with a body that suited the most rudimentary garments, Kat was supermodel material. Isabella predicted Kat would garner the eye of worldwide designers.

"Then agree to my terms, and I'll finance it. Do we have a deal?" Isabella held out her hand, and Kat didn't meet it.

"No, Isabella. That's not enough." Kat watched Isabella's hand go limp. "What I meant is five years is not enough. Ten is more reasonable." With a dimpled smile, Isabella pumped Kat's hand. "I won't let you down, Isabella. Can we keep this between us?" she said on Michaela's approach.

"Mums the word. I'll call Elsa to make the arrangements."

"You two look like you're up to no good." Michaela's voice cut into Isabella and Kat's conversation.

"Nothing of interest." Kat looked at Michaela with a brimming smile.

"Mmm-hmm." Barbie was lying, but Michaela didn't care. The girl was batshit crazy at the best of times. "Are we still on for tonight, Isabella?"

Isabella nodded. "Your wedding dress is ready for pick-up. I'm thrilled at the way it turned out. You're going to be the most beautiful bride your guests have ever seen."

"I do look good in it, don't I?" Michaela caught Kat giggling to herself. Bat-shit crazy.

"Every woman in the church is going to be green with envy when they see you walk down the aisle." Isabella watched Mrs. Rossi break away from the teller's desk mid-way through her transaction to chase after four-year-old Josie, making a mad dash out the front door when the peppered haired man held it open for the older woman by his side.

"Mrs. Rossi will catch up to her. The kid does it all the time. Now, back to me. I like the sound of walking down the aisle and having every woman eye me with envy. And you better not forget the favour I'm doing for you by promoting your dress. As Joe's wife, to uphold the Smith image will become a full-time job. They're an influential family with a wealthy circle of friends. Meaning I'll need a wardrobe update, and I want to stock it with Isabella Farfalla designs. And I expect a family discount." This time Michaela caught Kat's full eye roll over Isabella's shoulder.

Michaela was about to toss a sneering look Kat's way when Isabella jumped in with, "I won't forget, and I'd love the opportunity to design for you again."

"Wonderful, I'll come to see you after my honeymoon. We're going to tour Italy for three glorious weeks. I can't wait." Michaela's eyes shone with excitement. "Do you believe it? My wedding's just a couple of weeks away." Michaela and Isabella watched a red-faced Mrs. Rossi drag the rebellious Josie through the front door. "Told you. That kid is a nightmare. Ugh, thank God, I'm never having one of those. Joe had better not expect otherwise. By the way, is Antonio your plus one?"

Isabella's stunned look lingered for a moment. How Michaela could flip from a monumental comment to idle chat bewildered her. "He is."

"Maybe he'll get inspired at the wedding."

"He's my plus one, and that's it. I have way too much going on in my life right now to consider delving into something as serious as a relationship, let alone marriage."

"But you wouldn't be opposed to it." Michaela watched Isabella considering.

"I don't know. I never thought that far ahead. I mean, we barely get the time to see each other."

"How's he in bed? Is he as good as I told you he'd be?"

"Jesus, Michaela." Isabella's beet-red face spoke volumes.

"So, he made you hear the swell of a symphony then too?" Michaela let out a playful laugh.

"I think Mrs. Johnstone is ready for me." Isabella sidestepped the question.

"I'll get an answer from you yet," Michaela called out to Isabella as she wound her way to Mrs. Johnstone's office. "What's she here to see Mrs. Johnstone about?" Michaela croaked at Kat. She wasn't sure why, but the girl irked her just by breathing.

Feeling Michaela's burning gaze on her, Kat kept her eyes focused on her keyboard. "I don't know. I don't," she repeated when Michaela's stare became intense.

"You better be telling the truth." Michaela's irk-meter teetered on high.

"I'm the receptionist at the bottom of the food chain. No one tells me anything."

"Mmm-hmm. So, what's this about you becoming a model? Yeah, I hear everything." Michaela's biting tone led Kat to determine she'd snap her head off at the truth, and the last thing she wanted, was the wrath of Michaela on her. The woman was a relentless bitch to her.

"She wants me to walk her clothes through the store. You know, the same way I did at her grand opening. I'm sure she'd ask you to do it, but it's beneath someone of your stature." Kat was relieved when Michaela's lips curved approvingly.

"You're so right." With that, Michaela turned on her heels and sauntered back to her station.

Chapter 23

IT WAS A perfect day for a wedding. A bright November sun angled high in blue skies. Birds, as if knowing about the special event to take place, flitted happily in song. Inside St. Michael's Church, the sun streamed through the colourful stained glass, and the air was painted with the fragrance of the red roses spearing from tall vases. White rose petals were scattered on the red aisle carpet, and cascading bouquets with flashes of scarlet hung from pew ends.

Regardless of Joe's imperfections, he looked handsome in a black tuxedo against a champagne silk shirt and tie. In his sober state, he looked like the man Isabella remembered from days long gone.

Bach's Pachelbel Canon rang out from the pipe organ, and all heads turned. Lips curved, and the awws followed when the two flower girls in organza pink dresses with tulip skirts and waist sashes twisted into a bow—an Isabella original—led the procession down the aisle.

Close behind, five-year-old Tommy, carrying a heart-shaped pillow with two rings, zigzagged his way down the white carpet. Eight bridesmaids, their arms linked with groomsmen in black tails, made their way to the altar.

The women looked extraordinary in Isabella's hand-stitched long, flowing skirt with a hand-beaded bodice. The maid of honour, who trailed behind them, wore a similar dress in pomegranate-red.

The organ music got resoundingly louder as the Bridal Chorus burst from its pipes. The air brimmed with anticipation as Joe and everyone in the church waited to get a glimpse of Michaela in the ten thousand dollar wedding gown she'd bragged about to anyone who'd listen.

Hundreds of eyes darted to Michaela when she started down the aisle with her father by her side. Michaela looked the most beautiful Isabella had seen her. Her platinum blonde hair swept up into a braided chignon was topped with the Swarovski pink crystal tiara, which, thanks to Salvatore's schooling, Isabella crafted by hand.

Michaela's eyes sparkled when every woman oohed and aahed as she sashayed her way down the aisle slowly enough for everyone to catch a glimpse. As the flashing lights from hundreds of cameras clicked from every angle, Michaela was in her element.

Isabella heard the murmur of voices using adjectives such as breathtaking, spectacular, and stunning to describe the yards of white silk with sparkling crystals that clung to Michaela's curves. Women floated names such as Carolina Herrera, Oscar de la Renta, and Priscilla of Boston as the designer's name.

Vows exchanged, and rings slid on fingers, Michaela and Joe exchanged their first kiss as husband and wife.

A Cinderella carriage drawn by two white horses carted the newlyweds off to the reception venue, a European-style castle, with five acres of picturesque gardens overflowing with fall colours. The site was a grand structure, steeped in history, but no one expected any less from Michaela.

Isabella and Antonio, along with Salvatore and an irate Maria, wended their way through the crowd of silk draped women and tuxedo-clad men to their table. Perfume and cologne scented the air, and over the speakers drifted, Diana Ross and Lionel Richie pledging their endless love.

"Not telling your mother you invited Sal as her plus one was bound to have consequences." Antonio slid the chair out for Isabella. "And by the way, you look great." He cast eyes on the short, fuchsia strapless enveloping shapely curves and exposing the miles-long legs that drove him to insanity.

"I know, but there's no undoing it now. At least Sal seems excited to be here." Isabella angled her gaze to the handsome face with the lake-blue eyes, dark flowing hair, and fashionable stubble. "You look great too. I'm thinking of having you wear a tuxedo every day."

His dimples flashed with charm. "What do I get in return if I do?"

"I'll show you later."

"I can't wait." Antonio reached for the bottle at the center of the table and poured wine into two glasses. "But back to Sal and your Mother. What you're trying to pull off is tantamount to suicide. For your sake, I hope this reconciliation game works in your favour." He turned a glass over to Isabella.

"You know as well as I do if I'd told Mama Sal was going to be here, she wouldn't have shown up. I'd hoped the festive setting would set her in a better mood and allow her to get to know him better. Although my mother denies it, there's tension between them, but it's mainly coming from her, and I don't understand why. Sal's been nothing but helpful. He's taken me under his wing and taught me so much. I don't know that I'd be where I am without him."

"Still, don't try to fit a square peg into a round hole."

Antonio was right, Isabella thought, watching Maria push away the glass of wine Salvatore poured for her. Springing Salvatore on her mother wasn't her brightest idea, but her mother left her no choice.

From the moment Salvatore stepped into the store, Maria had been aloof and hostile to the man. No matter how pleasant he was or how many times Isabella assured Maria Salvatore wasn't there to replace her father, she never had a kind word or pleasantry to exchange.

Forcing her mother into a friendship, she wasn't ready for was the wrong approach. She had to let fate take its course and allow things between Maria and Salvatore to evolve—or not—on its own. After tonight, Isabella vowed to back away and let the chips fall where they may.

Chubby Checker urging to twist faded and segued into Etta James' bluesy voice claiming she'd finally found love.

"Stop worrying about Sal and your mother and dance with me." Antonio took Isabella's hand, and she rose with him.

"I don't know if leaving mama alone with Sal is a wise idea. There are knives on the table."

"They're dull." Antonio joked, and when for one heady moment, Isabella considered turning around, in a gesture of pure tenderness, he brushed a strand of hair from her face. "I need to get my arms around you," he said with the look that caused that flip-flop thing in her stomach, and she let him lead her into the music.

On the dance floor, Antonio's arms urged her close. Bodies pressed tightly together, his brain staggered under the scent of her perfume.

Swamped with the need for the taste of her, his mouth found hers. The heat of her breath, the feel of her lips on his, had Antonio's head swimming. His arms wrapped tight around her waist, he urged her up to her toes, took sweetly and tenderly.

"People are watching," she whispered, pulling back.

"Let them. I want everyone to know I'm with the woman I love," he said, the words he'd ached to say for so long.

Her head and heart took a hard bump. For a long moment, robbed of speech, while dancing couples circled them in complete silence, shocked eyes stared up at Antonio.

Hair-trigger remark inspired by the moment, but it was out there, and there was no taking it back. Jesus, what was she doing to him? Springing something as monumental as the I-love-you without warning wasn't what he meant to do, and now she was standing there with the deer-in-headlights look.

Antonio felt the sheen of sweat pearling on his face. Jesus! Jesus, Jesus, could he have made things any worse? He knew better than to say those words unless he expected them in return. Not only did Isabella not echo the words, but her dumbfounded gaze was a majorly negative response.

How did you get out of a royal fuck-up like this one? Antonio couldn't take the words back, and as smooth a talker as he was, there was no smoothing this out.

But then, his mother would approve of Isabella. Antonio was sure she'd love her. After all, Isabella was her carbon copy: strong, smart, loving, independent, and determined. And he did love Isabella, so why profess what he felt?

Antonio kissed the palm of her hand, pressed it to his heart. "I love you, Isabella Farfalla. You're scored on my heart."

The words, the inflection, the emotion in his tone drenched in love, and Isabella raised a tender hand to his cheek. "You, too, are scored on my heart."

"I am?"

"Mmm-hmm. You have been since the first day you cooked for me."

"So, it's my cooking, you love."

"I can't boil water so, that doesn't hurt. But no," Isabella stroked his cheek with her fingertip, "I love you." She touched her lips to his. Eyes fluttering close, she pillowed her face against Antonio's chest.

When Etta belted out, she'd claimed her man, floating on celestial clouds, breathing in the scent familiar to her, Isabella floated with her man. In that instant, no one but the two of them existed in a perfect world.

On Etta's last note, Isabella skated fingers down his chest. "Let's get out of here."

"Great idea."

"Excuse me. Are you the Isabella Farfalla, Michaela's wedding dress designer?" The young twenty-something with the spill of fiery red hair asked. "She told us Isabella Farfalla designed her gown. Are you her?" When Isabella nodded, Fiery Red called out, "It's her," waving the group of excitable women over.

"Hi, I'm Ashley. This is Madison, Ainsley, Brooke, and Sharleen. We all have upcoming weddings and wanted to talk to you about designing our dresses," Ashley said, and the women's voices rose to an excitable squeak.

"I'm the first to get married. It's a spring wedding at Graydon Hall. I already ordered my dress, but Mommy won't think twice about cancelling it if you promise to design an original for me," Brooke said, fluttering her lashes at Antonio. "You're a tall, handsome one."

Antonio thought he saw a forked tongue slither out and decided to make his exit. "I'll meet you back at the table, Isabella. Excuse me, ladies." Turning to walk away, the comments that trailed made him wince, and Isabella smile.

Guiding the group of excited women away from the dance floor and toward the foyer, Isabella spent the next thirty minutes talking to them. Soon enough, the gathering grew to include mothers and mother-in-law's lobbying for their daughters. Giving assurances she'd accommodate everyone, Isabella gave them her card. The last bride-to-be on her way, Isabella went in search of a ladies' room.

Bypassing the CLOSED FOR RENOVATIONS sign, past the cordoned-off hallway away from the crowds where silence reigned, Isabella searched for a bathroom. Wending her way around the scaffolding wrapped in yellow CAUTION tape, past paint buckets, and other building material, Isabella spotted the LADIES sign.

Stepping to the bathroom mirror, she took a slow, contemplative look at herself in the mirror.

"Thanks to Michaela, you've become a wedding dress designer," she told her reflection.

Michaela's dress was a marketing dream. The mermaid gown garnered Isabella the brand recognition she'd hoped for. Five wedding dresses were sure to turn into a long list of customers willing to pay top dollar for her designs. Isabella would ensure they got the best she had to offer because those customers were her stepping stone to something bigger.

"Mama better start getting along with Sal because I sure as hell can't do this without him," she told her reflection before turning and heading into the first stall.

Stepping out of the stall, a wave of nausea swept through Isabella. Fear curled in her gut and took hold of every muscle in her body, paralyzing her. She hadn't heard the door swing open. She hadn't heard anything, but there he was.

"Hello, Isabella." The two simple words were slurred, unintelligible. His eyes were glossy, his hair tousled, and his tie was riding low and askew. "I haven't seen you all night." Joe waved the tumbler of whiskey, the liquid sloshing dangerously to the edge.

Female dread curled in Isabella's gut. Frozen on the spot, all she did was stare. The stink of alcohol assaulted her. Even from six-feet away, she smelled it radiating from him.

Joe tried to take a step and, in the process, lost his balance. Rocking back on his feet, he hit his head against the door. "Shit," he mumbled, clumsily reaching for the doorjamb for support. Stable on his feet now, he drank, wiped his mouth with the back of his hand. "Michaela told me how great you looked, but seeing you now makes my juices flow. That dress fits that tight body of yours like a glove." Eyes bright with the stimulation of alcohol scanned Isabella. His lingering gaze shot an alarming shiver up her spine.

Panic had Isabella's stomach turning, fear had her mind racing, but she forced herself calm. "Your wife, Michaela, is the one who looks beautiful," she said straight-faced.

"Michaela has nothing on you, Isabella. You're pure and whole. And the way your hair falls over those creamy, bare shoulders." He'd always imagined what it would feel like to run fingers through the dark tumble of hair. "Let me just say…" Joe's mind wandered, and he lost his balance again. This time he reached for the edge of the sink counter to prop himself up.

"I'd better be getting back to the table. Antonio will be looking for me." Isabella took a step forward to gauge his reaction. She held still when his expression hardened.

"Mr. Hot-Shit." Joe grudgingly barked the words. "You can do so much better than that pantywaist, Isabella. You need a real man. What you need is…" His mind shut down.

"I should be getting back to the table, Joe. Please let me pass." Isabella kept her tone levelled, hoping not to prompt his anger to surge.

His mind drifting, Joe's eyes glazed, and Isabella took the opportunity to reach for the door handle. Joe swung his arm with force to block her, almost knocking her off her feet. Isabella's lungs hitched, and running out of air, choked back the scream.

Instinctively she jumped back to put a safe distance from him. As drunk as Joe was, he was stronger and could overpower her.

"I'd dump Michaela in a heartbeat for you, Isabella, and she knows it. And oh, it pisses her off to no end." Joe blathered on incoherently as Isabella's mind raced, considering the angles.

"Michaela loves you, Joe." Isabella slowly reached into her purse for her keys. She remembered reading keys threaded between your fingers became a weapon.

"That'll be the day. Michaela only loves Michaela and money. And that goddamn meddling mother of hers believes the world revolves around her spiteful, envious, begrudging daughter. You know mother and daughter are exactly alike. It's enough to drive a man to fucking madness." The sheer bitterness in his tone struck Isabella.

She wondered where the anger came from or why he'd lie about Michaela and her mother. It had to be the alcohol talking, Isabella decided.

"Michaela's been crazy about you since high school." Hands at her back, Isabella threaded the keys through her fingers, fisted her hand. Her mind worked quickly. She needed to draw him away from the door and push her way past him.

"What about you, Isabella? Do you like me? I like you." Joe's eager eyes roamed over her as he took a step toward her.

"I like you, Joe." Isabella took a safe step back to draw him away from the door. "I like you a lot." She took a bigger step this time. She was pleased when he fell in step with her.

"Just not the way you like that pantywaist, Antonio." When she hesitated to answer, hot rage washed over his face. "Don't play me, Isabella. You don't want me anywhere near you. You never have, not in high school and not now." His hardened voice rose. The hot lick of anger edging his tone unnerved her, and Isabella took a calming breath to collect herself.

"I … I like you, Joe. I do. More so than Antonio." Isabella's words delivered in a sugary sweet tone mollified Joe. "Come closer to me, Joe."

Smiling, glassy eyes stared at her tenderly. "You like me, Isabella?" Joe took a shaky step forward when Isabella's lips curved into a sultry dare.

Isabella nodded. "I do, Joe. I didn't see it until now, but you're the man for me." Isabella lifted her chin, dared him to step forward.

A victorious smile played across Joe's face. "I knew sooner or later, you'd come to your senses." Draining the remaining whiskey, Joe took another step toward Isabella, closing the gap between them.

One step closer, and there would be enough distance between him and the door to make her escape. "I want you closer, Joe." At Isabella's invitation, Joe's mouth lifted at one corner, and he rushed to fall into her open arms.

The unexpected man's voice in the hallway distracted Joe and Isabella. Antonio's call gave Isabella the boost of strength she needed, and she shot forward, quick as a cheetah. With all her strength, Isabella pulled the door open. When Joe made to block her way, she threw her body's weight against him with force. Unstable on his feet, Joe stumbled. His hands reached out for support, but they latched onto air, and he fell to his knees. The sound of bone crunching against the floor tile was ghastly, but Joe was too drunk to feel pain.

Flat on the floor, Joe went still and silent. For a beat, Isabella thought to stop to check on him. However, instinct told her to get to safety and, she darted out of the bathroom like a bullet.

"Hey, I've been looking all over for you." In shock, the voice coming from the end of the hallway took her by surprise.

It took a few seconds to contain her rush of adrenalin. When she finally managed to compose herself, recognition set in. It was Antonio's voice. Isabella's mind worked fast.

Should she tell Antonio what just happened? She couldn't begin to speculate how the tale would spin in his head. What if he blamed her for provoking Joe's stalking? Maybe it was her fault.

Too many short skirts, too much red on her lips, the low cut blouses, and tight pants set him off. She did this to herself. She'd elicited his stalking.

She'd lose Antonio.

She wouldn't lose his support, of that she was sure, but Antonio would kill Joe, and she couldn't lose him. She loved him. He was the best thing in her life.

"I, ah, wanted to avoid the crowds, and I decided to take a detour."

"Docking your fans already? I never imagined you to do that." The eyes that slid over to Isabella quickly took on a look of concern when she walked into the light, and he noticed her pale face. "Are you okay? You're trembling." Antonio chained his arms around her.

"I'm... fine. I didn't expect anyone to be out here, and you startled me," Isabella said, looking past his shoulder toward the bathroom door. "Let's go home."

"Sure, whatever you want." Antonio pulled back to look Isabella in the eyes. "You'd tell me if there was something wrong."

"Of course. I'm fine, honest. I think I've just had a bit too much to drink. My head is spinning. Let's get Mama and Sal and get out of here."

"All right." Antonio draped an arm over her shoulder to soothe the palpable uneasiness in her.

FROM THE OPPOSITE END OF THE corridor, a pair of eyes lurked in the shadows. Watching Isabella sprint from the bathroom, reckless amusement filed *The Eyes*. Her sheet-white face and eyes wide with fear put a smile on *The Eyes'* face.

The fear, the panic that must have flooded Isabella at feeling trapped like an animal by a belligerent drunk, had satisfaction flowing in *The Eyes*.

How Isabella's mind must have raced formulating her escape plan.

It was an interesting turn of events for the woman who took, who stole what she wanted. Well, *The Eyes* was taking now. Isabella was getting her just desserts, and she needed to keep watchful eyes over her shoulder because this was only the beginning.

Chapter 24

IN THE PARKING lot of Michaela's magical castle venue, a round moon cast a soft glow over the city. Stars dotted a black-blue sky. Trees verging the grand building draped in the scarlet and gold colours of fall seemed ablaze against the dark sky. A handful of guests congregated in groups talked or smoked while others made their way to their cars.

"Antonio's car is this way, Mama," Isabella said when Maria turned in the opposite direction.

"Salvatore's offered to drive me home."

"What?" A bullet in the eye that burrowed straight into the brain was how Maria's comment felt to Isabella.

"The night's still young. You children go off and enjoy yourselves." Maria pecked Isabella and Antonio on both cheeks.

"You want Sal to drive you home?" Isabella didn't bother masking the shock in her voice.

"Don't worry, Isabella. I'll get your mother home safely." Salvatore's calm demeanour didn't reflect his galloping pulse or the thundering heart in his chest. The thought of being alone with Maria was something Salvatore had dreamed of for so long. Now that the opportunity was here, he doubted he could handle it.

Isabella cast confused eyes at her mother. "Are you sure, Mama?"

Maria nodded. "I'll be fine, honey," she said, leaving an open-mouthed Isabella watching her mother. The veneer of feigned cordiality erased from her face as she slid into the front seat of Salvatore's car. "It'll be fine." Maria mouthed to an open-mouthed Isabella as Salvatore drove past her.

"YOU WERE QUIET ON THE DRIVE home." Antonio helped Isabella out of her coat and draped it on the living room chair.

"Just tired." Isabella lied with a straight face as her mind raced with the night's events. The encounter with Joe, her decision to keep it from Antonio, and her mother's unexpected willingness to get into Salvatore's car circled her head in a continuous loop. Drained, she let her limp body tumble into the couch.

"How about a drink?"

"A strong one."

Antonio shrugged out of his jacket and headed into the kitchen, searching for the bottle of brandy and two glasses. "How about telling me what's bothering you?"

"It's this thing with Mama and Sal. It's thrown me for a loop," Isabella said, compartmentalizing everything else wrong in her life. "What do you think that was about?"

"It was about Sal driving your mother home?" Antonio handed her the tumbler of brandy, walked to the stereo to drop the needle on Chicago's greatest hits. Peter Cetera's breathy voice filled the room.

Just like a man not to see beyond the obvious, Isabella thought, sipping brandy. "Why, after months of tormenting him, would mama willingly get into his car and ride off into the sunset?"

Antonio furrowed brows in confusion. Would he ever understand how a woman's mind worked? "I thought you wanted to bring them together, and it's into the night."

"What?" Isabella propped her feet on his lap when he signalled her to do so.

"They rode off into the night. Technically it was night." Antonio slipped her shoes off.

"I'm serious. I wanted them to get along, but now I think maybe that wasn't such a good idea, or maybe it was. I don't know anymore."

The fear Joe instilled in her still fresh in her mind, and the thought of her mother with Salvatore, alone, had her in emotional turmoil. Maybe her muddled brain had her irrationally interpreting the look in Salvatore's eyes, but she thought she'd seen deep affection in them for her mother. She couldn't shake the feeling.

She wanted them to develop an amicable working relationship. Not something beyond that, and certainly not an intimate one, because the look she'd seen in Salvatore's eyes went beyond friendship.

Studying Isabella, as she paced the living room with frenetic energy, the thought rushed at Antonio. He snatched her in his arms. "No one, not Sal, not any man will replace your father," Antonio assured in the softest tone.

"I know that." Isabella sputtered with sharp anger, but all Antonio saw was worry in her eyes.

Isabella tipped back her head and closed her eyes for a moment before pinning them out the window. The night was silent, and she heard the cool wind sweep past the glass pane.

Antonio cupped her chin, raised her face to his. "Even if their friendship blossoms into something deeper, and that's a big if, Sal will not replace your father." Her tired mind and emotions collided in Isabella all at once, and she burst out crying. Antonio folded his arms around Isabella. "Please don't cry. Don't be sad."

"It feels like it's…"

"The conclusion of your father's life." Antonio finished.

"Yes." That was exactly it, Isabella marvelled. How did he always see through her with such clarity?

"It's not the conclusion. It's a new chapter. Your father is in your heart, thoughts, and memory. In you." He laid a hand on her heart, her head. "He'll never leave you. You're strong and intelligent, the determined woman you are today because of him. Never forget that."

She remembered her mother telling her that only once in your life did you come across your true soulmate, and Antonio was hers.

Chapter 25

MARIA'S GAZE NEVER left the road coming at them as Salvatore wound the car through the streets of downtown Toronto. Traffic was light. Except for a handful of people out on dog-walking duty, pedestrians were far and few. Homes were shrouded in darkness. The glow of light from storefronts closed for the day, and street lamps lit the night.

Whether because of the effect of her third glass of wine or the soft music flowing in the dance hall, or possibly the romantic atmosphere, to Salvatore's surprise, Maria asked if he'd like to go for a walk. The question knocked breath and speech out of Salvatore, and his response was in the form of a nod.

Maria saw the shocked look in Isabella's eyes when she turned toward Salvatore's car, but she couldn't explain her actions to her daughter because she couldn't explain it to herself. Why, after months of dismissing Salvatore, she wanted to be alone with him was as much a mystery to her as it was to Isabella?

Maybe seeing Isabella with Antonio, arms chained around one another on the dance floor, made Maria sentimental. Perhaps seeing the love in innocent eyes made Maria realize the time came to set aside her anger and hear Salvatore out. Whatever Maria's reason, the truth would come out tonight.

Guiding Salvatore toward Ashbridges Bay Park, he wound the car into the parking lot. A handful of cars, windows steamed, were parked a discreet distance from one another and away from blazing lampposts.

Salvatore pulled into the first spot he came to and turned to Maria. In shadows, her hair tumbling free around her face, she looked mysterious and beautiful. Maria had always underestimated her beauty, and tonight was no exception.

In the silver sequin, boatneck gown, she looked stunning. And he was glad Isabella had stuck to her guns even after Maria insisted a woman her age wouldn't be able to carry the deep V-back because she had, Salvatore thought.

"Is this okay?" He asked, and at her nod, he killed the engine.

For a long while, in silence, Salvatore waited for Maria to make the first move. When she reached for the door handle, he made a start for his door. Jumping out of the car, he rounded the hood to open Maria's door. His heart tumbled when Maria took hold of his offered hand as she elegantly maneuvered herself to her feet.

They walked past the grass-covered ground, beyond the children's playground, to the boardwalk hemming the stretch of white sand beach. The reflection of the luminous moon floating on the horizon rode over glass-smooth waters misted in a black haze. A soft, cool wind scented with lake and night danced its way through bare branches.

There was an exotic beauty to the night, and Salvatore's thoughts flashed back to the walks they'd made that memorable summer.

In companionable silence, Salvatore and Maria walked the planked boardwalk. It was some time before Maria pointed to a bench.

Nervously twisting the pearls at her throat, she said, "It's so peaceful and beautiful this time of night. Listen to the sound of the waves as they roll in and pull back out. I've always loved being near water."

"I remember." Salvatore reflected on the nights they'd spent making love on the beach under the moon's silver light with the Mediterranean Sea washing ashore. Afterward, with her head pillowed on his chest, they'd listen to the night, the calm, the sea whispering secrets. He wondered whether those memories were as vivid in her mind as they were in his.

"When Isabella was younger, we often came here." Maria fell silent when the elderly couple with the terrier puppy walked past them. "She loved playing in the sand, wading her feet in the water. We'd walk down to the end of the boardwalk, which leads to a craggy edge overlooking the lake. We'd sit on the boulders for hours watching the stars," Maria said reflectively.

"It sounds like a wonderful time in your life." He wished she had many.

"When did you receive the letter?" Her voice cracked at the question.

"Mid-January."

"That's about the time Angelo found out he had weeks left. He'd just been told his life is coming to an end, and his thoughts were on Isabella and me." Hot tears stung her eyes.

"He sounds like a good man, selfless and honourable."

"He is ... was." The tears streamed down Maria's cheeks, and Salvatore fished his handkerchief out from his pocket and handed it to her. "How did he find you?"

"Antonio told me Angelo steered him in my direction, but he did the legwork for him. He tracked my address down through the embassy and mailed the letter."

"So, Antonio knows its contents."

Salvatore shook his head. "The envelope Angelo turned over to Antonio was sealed. Antonio thinks one of the nurses wrote the letter for Angelo since he was too weak to put pen to paper. I believe the words are Angelo's." He felt his heart break at the sight of Maria's tear-stained cheeks.

"You came after you received the letter?"

"Yes. I immediately made the travel arrangements, but I didn't know the connection between Angelo and Antonio until I arrived in Toronto. Antonio told me Angelo was a long-time customer who laid out a dying wish for him to find me and get the letter to me the day he visited him at the hospital. Antonio vowed to do everything in his power to do so. The young man searched me out, sent the letter with instructions on where to contact him. Once I did, he set me up in one of his apartments. He helped me acclimatize to my new surroundings." He paused for a moment. "He led me to you."

She dabbed at her eyes. "So, Antonio knows nothing."

"No, I don't believe he does," Salvatore assured.

"He's an extraordinary young man. I can see why Isabella is drawn to him." Maria wiped her cheeks dry. "She hasn't told me as much, but I think she's in love with him."

"I suspect as much. And I believe he's in love with her."

They sat quietly for a time, only the lake moving beyond them. "If Angelo hadn't asked you to take care of us…?"

Anticipating the question, Salvatore jumped in. "Would I have come back for you?" He dug into his pants, pocked for a Nicorette, and popped it into his mouth to calm the nerves overtaking him. "I've always wanted to, Maria. I've known where to find you for some time." When her brows creased, he explained.

"It took me some time to find you, but I did—ten years ago. When I found you, I discovered you were happy, had a family, a husband who cherished you, and a beautiful daughter. I wasn't about to disrupt your life because I wanted to fill the void you left in me." Salvatore looked in her direction, and their eyes met. "I never meant to leave you, Maria. You have to believe me. And it certainly wasn't my intention to hurt you."

Maria gave him a direct look. "Then why did you disappear, Salvatore? Why did you leave without as much as a goodbye?"

"I didn't just disappear. I came back months later, but by then, it was too late. I was told you'd married Angelo and moved. That's all your mother told me. She wouldn't tell me where you were or how to get in touch with you."

"Did you expect me to pine away for you all those months after you left me?" Her tone was indignant, pained.

"I didn't know what to expect, but I had to come back to find you. I'd have come looking for you sooner, but family obligations didn't make it possible."

"Not one letter, not a call, nothing. I didn't know whether you were dead or alive. Eventually, I resigned to believing I was a summer conquest, a story to share with your friends over a beer."

Remorse reached up and grabbed him by the throat, but he plowed on with a desperate need to right wrongs. "I'm so sorry if that's what I led you to believe, but it's the furthest thing from the truth. Things got complicated." Salvatore broke off to compose himself. "The night I got the call from my family, I came to your house to let you know I had to go away for a short time to deal with a personal matter. Your mother answered the door. She wouldn't allow me to talk to you and asked me to leave you alone."

"You're lying. My mother wouldn't do such a thing."

He could hear the bitterness in her tone, but Salvatore brushed over her anger and pressed on. "She told me never to call on you again or contact you. I guess she knew who I really was."

"Who you really were?" The uneasiness creeping up her spine made her shoulders tense. "What does that mean? What are you saying, Salvatore?"

He grew quiet for a moment. "There isn't a good way to say this so, I'll just come out and say it. I was married when I met you."

The words came out at her so fast Maria wasn't sure she heard right. "You were married." She felt the bile rise in her throat. "So I was your mistress, a notch on your belt. I was a cheap romp between the sheets who fell for your words." There was temper in her voice, fire in her eyes.

He'd hurt more than her ego. He'd broken her heart. "Never think of yourself that way. I never did." Absently he reached into his jacket pocket for the cigarette he suddenly craved only to find it empty.

"I was such a fool to think, giving myself to you meant as much as it meant to me." Maria started to rise, but Salvatore grabbed her arm before she pushed to her feet. "Get your hands off of me."

"Please sit down. Please. You deserve an explanation." Salvatore's pleading eyes weakened her, and she took her seat, putting more distance between them. "It meant everything to me. You meant everything to me. And I meant it when I told you I loved you."

Maria let out a sarcastic laugh. "Right. So who was she? How long were you married? Did you have children? Why did you use me like that?" She lobbed the questions like projectiles, and when she realized the answers would only add to her pain, she said, "Actually, I don't want to know."

"Please, Maria, let me explain. I've waited so many years, travelled far to give you the explanation you deserve. You deserve that much. If it's not satisfactory to you, I'll leave tomorrow and never come back."

She stared at him as she considered. "Go ahead. Explain," she snapped when she decided she did deserve an explanation.

"My marriage was an arranged one, a business proposition between families. Her and my well-being were never considered. The first time we met, she told me she was in love with another man, but we both knew if she didn't marry me, her parents stood to lose a great deal, as did mine." Salvatore looked away from his kneaded hands over at Maria to make sure she was listening.

"My family has been in the winemaking business for almost a century. Although not wealthy, her family owned a large parcel of land, which my father had his eye on.

However, due to an age-old feud between the families, her grandfather refused to sell it to my father. My father wasn't the type of man to stand down. He vowed to get that land no matter what it took. I became the pawn. The marriage between us would make us family. It would sway her father to talk the old man into selling to my family."

Swamped by churning emotions, Salvatore paused to gather his thoughts, and Maria knew enough to stay silent.

"We were completely unsuitable. She was seventeen, and I was ten years her senior."

"I was one year older than her. Were we mismatched?" Maria spat.

"No, we weren't," he said softly. "She wasn't anything like you. She was immature, self-absorbed. Three months after we met, we were married. Whether we cared for one another or not was of no consequence to either family. It was a business transaction."

"You were a grown man, Salvatore," Maria hissed.

"Call it a family duty, cowardice, or a need to ingratiate myself to my disapproving father. I felt I had to do it." The unqualified understanding in her expression made him go on. "One year later, my family took possession of the property, lock stock, and barrel, and our marriage was already facing challenges. We were rarely intimate, and when we were, it was forced, detached, and cold. On one of our many arguments, she let it slip that her parents were pressuring her to have my child. By her family's reasoning, our child stood to fall in line to inherit my family's business and get their grasp into Mesi Winery."

Shock flew into Maria's eyes. "Mesi Winery? You own one of the largest wineries in Europe?" she squeaked, her tone incredulous. Yet another detail of his life he'd failed to disclose.

She hadn't made the connection, but how could she when she knew so little about Sal? The summer they spent together was focused on doing what young, carefree lovers do. Family history, drama, and details weren't what they wanted to talk about when they were together.

It would have never dawned on her to connect him to such a prestigious family, but then he'd never led her to believe otherwise. He'd told her he worked at a winery and left it at that. He'd never led her to believe he was but a simple farmhand.

"My father owns Mesi Winery, not me." Salvatore corrected. "The summer I met you, I'd decided to leave her."

Maria felt something catch in her throat. "Why didn't you tell me all this then? If you were planning to leave her, I would have understood. I would have waited for you." If only he had, things would have turned out so differently.

"My family is very complicated. I didn't want to raise your hopes. I wanted to make sure I could put the plan in motion to break ties with her before I involved you."

"What's her ... name?" Maria asked, not sure why she did.

"Her name is Luisa. The summer I met you, I'd decided to take a break. At that point, I had no interest in saving our marriage. I knew she was having an affair with the man she was in love with. We were miserable, and I'd never love her so, I figured why not let her live her life. I left for Sicily to work at one of my father's vineyards and left her at our house in Tuscany. For over one year, I lived in the town over from yours, working non-stop. I'd hear from Luisa when she needed money." Salvatore's eyes focused on some distant point.

"My life had become one-note, without direction, and then I met you, and everything changed." The eyes that gazed at her were full of love. "You gave me a reason to get up in the morning, smile, enjoy life, and fall in love with you. The best part was you made me feel loved. You meant everything to me, Maria. You were the air I breathed in every thought that filled my days. You filled my dreams at night. You made me smile. You were my everything."

Silent tears coursed down her face. "Then why did you leave?"

Salvatore watched Maria absently pull on the handkerchief with nervous hands. "The night I came to your house, I'd received a call from my mother. Luisa and her lover were in a car accident. They'd hit a truck head-on, or maybe it was the other way around. It was never determined. Anyway, both died on impact. I had to rush back to Tuscany that night. That was the reason I left so abruptly."

The knot at the base of her throat tightened, and all Maria could do was stare.

Salvatore went on. "Luisa had a two-month-old son."

"The child wasn't yours," Maria stated the obvious.

"No, he wasn't, and that wasn't the worst of it."

Her stomach clenched. "How could that not be?"

"During my absence, she'd moved her lover into our home. To conceal him, their affair, and everything that was going on, Luisa alienated her family and friends. The estrangement made it possible for her to have the baby without anyone knowing."

Seeing the effect of reliving the story on Salvatore, Maria said, "You don't need to go on, Salvatore. I'm sorry I've put you through this."

"I want to tell you everything. You deserve the truth." Taking a deep breath, he went on. "The baby only came to light after Luisa's death. Once the sequence of events was pieced together and the math done, everyone deduced he wasn't mine. My family and hers wanted nothing to do with the baby, a boy named Carlo."

Maria noted the muscles in Salvatore's jaw clench.

"The child tugged at me, and I felt a sense of duty to him. This poor innocent had done nothing wrong but to be born into unfortunate circumstances created by adults who should know better. When her parents abandoned him, I agreed to adopt him on the condition they sign away their rights to him. I didn't want them to blackmail Carlo, my family, or me later. They didn't hesitate to surrender all rights—at a price."

"You bought the child?" Maria regretted the statement when his eyes swam with anger and remorse.

"I had to for his well-being. Cheque in hand, the adoption was finalized. By then, seven months had passed when I came looking for you. That's when your mother told me you'd married Angelo and left Italy. I died when she told me."

Maria tilted her gaze up to Salvatore; saw the flash of pain run across his face. His eyes sparkled with tears, and absently she reached out to touch his arm.

"My whole world crumbled. I walked around aimlessly for days. When it finally dawned there was nothing left for me in Sicily, I returned to Tuscany. For weeks, questions rolled in my mind. I thought of looking for you, but I didn't even know where to begin. In the end, I decided I wouldn't. I wouldn't disrupt your new life."

Salvatore's story cut deep into her heart. The anger and resentment that consumed all these years flowed from her like a river running over its banks. "All this time, I've blamed you for deserting me and leaving me to deal with … things. And these past months, I've been so horrible to you."

"You haven't." Salvatore reached over to stroke her wet cheeks with his fingers. A hot punch of emotions swirled in both at the touch. "Never blame yourself, Maria. You were reacting to a situation I created. One I should have corrected long ago. I'm the one who let you down."

"I was hurt and angry, so hurt and so angry." She broke down and fell into his arms as naturally as she had years ago. "But that's not why I married Angelo or more why he married me, and why we left so abruptly."

Salvatore held her while she cried out her shock and guilt, surrendered emotions that had crippled her for so long. "You did what you had to do, Maria." He stroked her hair.

Maria pulled out of his embrace and looked into his eyes. "Angelo married me because I was pregnant."

Chapter 26

SALVATORE'S MET MARIA'S red-rimmed eyes. "I know Isabella is my daughter." There was no anger, no blame in his tone.

Maria's face went dead white. Maria was quiet for a moment as guilt, remorse, shame, and regret washed over her at once. "How long have you known?"

Glancing over at her, he reached for her hand. The warmth of it penetrated through to his bones, sending a wonderful shock to the system he hadn't felt for decades. "Not long."

"I'm sorry, Salvatore. I'm so very sorry for not telling you. Please forgive me."

The wall was down, he thought. It had crumbled right before his eyes. "I know you are, and you don't need to ask for forgiveness." Salvatore shrugged out of his jacket and draped it over Maria's shoulders when the cool midnight air made her shiver. When she started to speak, he cut her off. "I'll take you home now."

Maria remained silent for the entire ride home, and Salvatore fell into the silence she needed with her.

"Would you like to come in? I'll put on a pot of coffee," Maria said after Salvatore maneuvered the car into the spot in front of her apartment and killed the engine. Looking over at Maria, he saw the traces of tear washed mascara on her cheeks. "I doubt I'm going to be able to wind my mind down to get sleep." She looked up to Salvatore with fragile eyes. "Please, I'd like the company."

Maria's reserve broken, her heavy heart, the feeling of abandonment she'd carried with her all these years vanished. The man who'd left her, whom she'd resented, and hated all these years through his painful story, eroded the wall she'd erected and washed the pain she'd held for so long.

Their exchange made her realize he hadn't inflicted the anger and pain she'd harboured. Tonight she realized her hatred for Salvatore stemmed from her guilt of denying him the knowledge of his child. The secret out, the fear, anger, and hate afflicting her like a cancer faded away, and the love she once felt for him bloomed in her heart.

But they were different people now. So much had happened to them over the years. They'd led separate lives, had families of their own, endured experiences—good and bad—that changed them. They weren't the young, naïve couple they once were. She'd have to get to know him all over again, but this time, they would start from a beginning brimming with experience and wisdom.

Salvatore traced the curve of Maria's cheek with his finger. "I'd love the company."

Flipping the apartment lights on, Maria waved him to the kitchen while she made her way to the bathroom to wash her face. Salvatore was firing up the stove for the coffee to brew when she joined him. Watching him in her small kitchen with white painted walls, pressed-board cupboards, and the old canary-yellow appliances, he looked as if he belonged there.

She wondered if he sensed how much he'd stirred in her when he walked back into her life. Like a key turning in a long lost lock, he released memories and emotions she'd buried long ago. Guilt washed over her.

How could she be mourning a husband she'd buried months ago and had her heart feeling such strong pangs of love for the man who appeared into her life after a decades-long absence? What kind of woman betrayed the man who'd loved her and took care of another man's child?

Had Angelo known when she'd told him she loved him, her words weren't laced with the deep sentiment his were? Had he sensed it each time they made love? How could she hurt him that way? What kind of a woman was she? Angelo had his downfalls, but he'd been nothing but kind and loving.

Maria's scent flowed into Salvatore, and he turned to her. She'd washed all traces of makeup from her face, smoothed her hair into a ponytail, and changed into slacks and an aqua blouse. Salvatore couldn't take his eyes off her.

"I hope you don't mind. I set the coffee to brew."

"Of course not, but I'll take it from here."

"I have this under control." He returned the coffee tin to the cupboard and wiped the counter of stray grounds. "Take a seat and point me to the cups, spoons, and sugar."

Maria did and, in silence, watched Salvatore rummaged through the cupboards. He'd shed his tuxedo jacket and bow tie and had undone the first three buttons of his shirt. His once dark curls, a shock of silver now, were combed back into sophisticated smooth waves. Behind the silver-framed glasses, she could see the mink-brown eyes that sparkled in an olive face marked with lines tempered by the reality of life. So many years had passed, but he was as handsome as she remembered.

"Feeling better now?" Salvatore turned to shut the flame off on the sputtering coffee.

"Yes, thank you. I needed to throw water on my face. I looked quite the sight." She watched him pour steaming coffee into two thick-lipped espresso cups.

"I never noticed it." Salvatore's comment made Maria smile.

There was a stretch of silence before she said, "When did you figure out Isabella is your daughter?"

He set coffee cups on the table and slid into the chair next to her. "I sensed a familiarity, a connection with her the first time we met, but it wasn't until Antonio, and I were discussing Isabella's intention to purchase the buildings that I put it together. Antonio wanted my thoughts on the deal and showed me the paperwork she filled out for the bank, and I saw Isabella's birthdate."

A flash of guilt had Maria turning her eyes away from him to the dark liquid in her cup. Finding out about a daughter that existed for twenty-two years in such a random way was unacceptable. "I'm so very sorry, Salvatore. I should have told you about Isabella the moment you came to see me, but…"

Salvatore slid his fingers under her chin, tilting her face up to his. "We've gone over this already, Maria. I don't want you to blame yourself for anything. Circumstances led us both to make the decisions we made and take the actions we took. We didn't deliberately set out to hurt one another. Whether right or wrong, what's done is done. We need to focus on the now and the future."

"If I didn't let my anger and pride dictate my emotions, you wouldn't have found out you had a daughter in such a callous manner."

Salvatore gently wiped the tear that spilled down her face. "Please don't cry, Maria, and stop blaming yourself. I don't. It takes two to create a problem. Right now, all I want is for us to deal with this together. I promised you I'd be by your side every step of the way, and I will be. Thanks to Angelo, we're getting a second chance to right our wrongs, and we should embrace it," he said, reflecting on the day he received the letter.

The moment he read Angelo's letter, he sensed his life as about to be impacted in unimaginable ways. That he found a daughter, he knew nothing about all these years made the experience that much more poignant.

"Not a day has gone by I haven't thanked Angelo for writing the letter and bringing you and now Isabella into my life."

At the mention of Angelo's name, Maria's heart filled with overwhelming sadness. "I think of him often. I miss him so much." Maria pressed her lips together. "I'm sorry I shouldn't have said that."

Salvatore squeezed her hand. "He was your husband and in your life for a long time. You can never forget someone who's made such an impact in your life."

Her expression softened. "He gave so much to me, to Isabella, and never asked for anything in return. Angelo embraced Isabella as his own from the day we married. She was his princess."

"I can see that. She's very fond of him."

Shame and remorse were like two vicious, heavy blows on her chest. "I'm sorry we never told Isabella about you. We didn't want to confuse her." Instead, she piled lie after lie, setting the Jenga tower that was now crumbling. "And then time passed, and it became more difficult to tell her and… I need something stronger than coffee."

"I'll get it." Salvatore was half out of his chair when Maria gestured him back down.

Maria reached for the half-empty bottle of cognac in the pantry and walked it and two glasses to the table. "Isabella's birth was complicated. It left me unable to give Angelo children. Still, he sacrificed everything for her, for a child that wasn't his, a woman he knew never loved him as much as he loved her." She poured three fingers in each glass and took half of her drink in one gulp.

Maria remained silent for a moment.

"I don't want to make the same mistake twice. I need to make it up to Angelo. I want Isabella to see the letter. I want her to know everything Angelo's done for her. She needs to know how much he loved her and what a noble man he was," she said with determination. "And we need to tell her you're her father."

Salvatore reached for Maria's hand, enveloped it with his. "I want Isabella to know about me this very minute, but we shouldn't rush into this. We need to consider carefully. Angelo's death is still fresh on her mind, and she has a lot going with her business. This news may cause too much shock to her system. When the time is right, you and I will tell her, and we'll make sure she never forgets the sacrifices Angelo made for her, for all of us."

"Thank you. I was hoping you'd say that. I know it's a lot to ask, but…"

"I didn't know him, but based on his selfless letter, I could tell he was a good man, Maria, and he's the only father Isabella's known. Nothing will change that." As difficult as the words were to say, Salvatore felt indebted to Angelo.

Salvatore owed Angelo a mountain of gratitude for stepping in to look after Maria and Isabella when he didn't. He knew he would always feel that way because he understood firsthand that sometimes life takes you where it takes you, and you can only steer so much—sometimes not at all.

"We'll talk to Isabella together," Maria assured Salvatore, wondering what they would say, how Isabella was going to react.

"I'll leave it up to you to determine when you feel it the best time for us to sit down with Isabella."

"All right, but we shouldn't let it linger for too long. I'm afraid she may mistake our effort to protect her for deception and resent us. I can't hazard to guess how Isabella is going to react when we tell her. She may hate us all for lying and deceiving her. She may hate only me for not being forthcoming all those years ago. She may resent me for not telling her when you came into our lives. She may never see that Angelo agreeing to marry me was a gesture of love and that he and I married to protect her." A sharp jolt of panic hit Maria, and her nerves frayed.

"Stop speculating, or you'll drive yourself crazy with unnecessary worry. Isabella is smart, practical, and mature beyond her years. She'll be angry at first, but in time, when she's sorted through all the bits and pieces, weighed the pros and cons, she'll come around."

"I hope you're right." Maria deserved her daughter's hate, but Angelo didn't. Angelo deserved to remain in Isabella's heart and be thought of with pride and love.

Maria suspected Salvatore knew what she was thinking but said nothing. He held her hand, and the once familiar touch of this thumb tracing the contours of her hand made feelings buried for too long rush at her.

Her life was never going to be the same again.

Chapter 27

ISABELLA WALKED ANTONIO through the buildings, now silent from hammers, saws, and drills. Excitedly, she described her vision, and although she'd shown him the blueprint countless times, he intently listened as if hearing it for the first time.

Isabella explained the buildings, now one large unit, would house the six seamstresses—Hart Designs employees—enlisted by Gail. On the blueprint, she pointed out the drafting, cutting, fitting rooms, and retail floor.

The second floor boasted a T-shaped runway complete with a cocktail bar. Isabella explained her plan to host seasonal fashion shows featuring Kat. For the remainder of the year, the upper floor would be used as a salesroom for her wedding gowns. Since Michaela's wedding, gown orders had sharply increased.

Except for the two tall glass entry doors in the shape of her butterfly logo, which made a considerable dent in her budget, the main floor's interior decor was an extension of her original building. Rich, dark cocoa wood floors added a contrasting shock to the ivory covering the ceilings and walls. Brass, mirrored walls, and contemporary white veneer Italian display cases elevated the modern chic look.

"I'm planning on an April grand opening. I plan to hold my first fashion show with models strutting my original designs down the runway. Sal and I are already working on the two dozen dresses, Kat and four other models—of various sizes and shapes—will walk down the runway," Isabella told Antonio as he tried to keep up.

A dark, appreciative brow rose. "You have it planned down to the last detail. But didn't Kat start her training not long ago? Will she be ready for your show?"

"She'll be ready. Elsa and I are working closely with her. I'm expecting her any minute to discuss what I need from her."

Antonio's brow winged higher. "I don't doubt it. You could be very persuasive."

Isabella's lips bowed into a smile. "I have one more thing to show you." She took his hand and walked him to the back of the store, down the narrow hallway, past posts and beams, to be turned into storage, drafting, and sewing rooms. "And this is my office or my sane room. I had them prioritize its construction, so I'd have somewhere to work. "

A glass wall sheathed in bluish-gray blinds provided privacy to the spacious office. Polished mahogany cabinets covered one wall. There was an L shaped desk with a high-back leather chair behind it and two matching visitor's chair. A round glass table with four chairs served as a meeting area. Behind it hung the sketches of her first three designs.

With an approving look, Antonio followed Isabella's gaze. "Impressive. Does this mean I'm going to have to schedule appointments to see you?"

"Never." Isabella skated a finger over his chest, leaving a tingling sensation in its path. "You, Mr. Sabatini, are on my VIP list. You have twenty-four-seven access."

"I'm flattered."

"It's the least I can do for the man who encouraged me to follow my dream."

Antonio wrapped his hands around her waist, pulled her closer.

"You've done this all on your own. I'm very proud of you. I have no doubt you're on your way to becoming the next Coco Chanel."

"So, fame and money are why you're sticking it out with me, Mr. Sabatini?"

"That's one reason," Antonio teased, and Isabella plowed an elbow into his side. "And the other is because I'm crazy in love with you." He leaned in to glide his lips to hers.

"Much better."

Antonio twirled the loose curl around her face on his finger. "Will you be coming over tonight?"

Isabella nodded. "I'll be over as soon as I'm done with Kat. Say sevenish."

"All right, I'll have the chef cook us a nice meal," Antonio said, filling with anticipation.

"After dinner, we can decorate your Christmas tree while you tell me all about Tom Ritchie and his proposal to put The Café into his bookstores across the country." Knitting her fingers through Antonio's, they made their way to the front of the store.

"Or, we could come up with better things to do." Antonio looked at her with a twinkle in his eyes. "I'll pick you up."

"There's no need to make the trek back. I'll meet you at The Café."

"I don't want you making the trek alone. If your windows weren't covered up, you'd see the snow has been coming down hard." Antonio covered her mouth with his to silence the oncoming argument. "I'm picking you up."

"My knight in shining armour," she said, still spinning from the kiss.

KAT SHOWED UP AT QUARTER PAST six for her meeting with Isabella. Her hair and shoulders were peppered with snow, and her face had a rosy glow from the howling wind.

"I'm sorry I'm late, but it's a blizzard out there." Kat brushed snow off her hair and shoulders.

"I'm glad you made it. Drop your coat on the folding chair, and let's get to it. I need to get out of here by seven."

"Wow, this place is huge, Isabella." Kat took in the room, cluttered with building materials. The smell of sawed wood and paint hung in the air.

"It's a work in progress, but let me give you a tour."

Kat followed Isabella, intently listening as she went into more detail than necessary about her floor plans and the runway under construction. "It sounds so exciting." Kat's words tumbled out with interest as she followed Isabella into her office. "And look at this. Mrs. Johnstone will be so jealous when she sees this."

"Have a seat. Can I get you something to drink?"

"Water if you have it." Kat took the guest's chair and watched Isabella reach into the mini-refrigerator for two bottles of Perrier.

"How's your training coming along?"

"Elsa wasn't joking when she said it would be a lot of hard work, but I love every minute. My instructor says I'm at the top of the class." Kat fidgeted in her seat as she went on to tell Isabella what she'd learned, rising to walk the length of the office, catwalk style. "Do I look like a model?"

Isabella's smile spread. "You do. You have this in the bag, and you'll be more than ready for my first fashion show this spring."

Kat took the offered bottle of water, unscrewed the cap. "For you, Isabella, I'll make sure."

Isabella sank deep into the butter-soft leather of her chair. "I'm planning to invite seventy-five VIP guests. Sal is working on getting a couple of editors and photographers from major fashion magazines to attend. I don't know how he plans to do it, but he says he can get them. Do you know what that means, Kat?"

"Great exposure for your garments and your brand."

"Great exposure for you." Isabella reached behind her. "These are the two dozen designs I want you and the other models to walk down the runway. Elsa is working on booking the other models."

"Can I wear one of the wedding gowns, Isabella? They're sexy and dreamy," Kat said, flipping to the last board.

"I designed those two with you in mind. You have the height and the body type to carry the strapless, mermaid lace and the ballgown. They're going to fit you like a glove."

Kat took a closer look at the sketch. "That plunging neckline on the mermaid dress is pretty daring. I love the Mantilla veil on the ballgown, and the cathedral-length one for the mermaid is angelic. Are those Swarovski crystals on the bodice black?"

Isabella gave Kat an arched look. "You're becoming well versed."

"I thought it important to learn to appreciate the designer's artistic vision. You know, like appreciating an artist's painting," Kat said, so sincerely Isabella could only smile.

"I made the plunging neckline purposely low, and those are black Swarovski crystals. They give the shock-factor I want." Isabella took the sketch from Kat to look over what she thought was her best design yet.

"I'll work doubly hard, Isabella. I'll make sure I'm ready for your show." Kat took the last of her Perrier.

"Good. I'll need you in for a few fittings. I'll let you know when."

"This is so exciting." Kat giggled, sounding remarkably girlish. Kat raised her Perrier bottle, tapped it against Isabella's in a toast. "My first runway show, my mom is going to be over the moon when I tell her."

The sound of approaching footsteps drew the women's eyes toward the door. His tousled hair dripped wet with snow, his unshaven face had days-old stubble, and his shirt was untucked, unevenly buttoned. Isabella picked up the smell of bourbon, and he was barely able to stand up on his own two feet.

It was the worst she'd seen Joe. Although Isabella recognized Joe's deep state of confusion, it didn't diminish her sense of impending danger.

"Kat, why don't you get going now?" Isabella said quietly.

"I'm staying with you," Kat said, sensing Isabella's uneasiness as hers sent her heart racing.

Joe's glassy eyes filled with confusion when he saw two women, and he strained to make out the blurred figures. Joe looked from Isabella to Kat and back. It took some time for his muddled brain to put it together.

"Who the fuck are you?" The slurred words aimed at Kat.

"She's no one in particular, and she's leaving," Isabella answered before Kat could. "Anyway, it's me you want."

The corner of Joe's mouth lifted into a smirk at the sound of Isabella's voice. "Yeah, it's you I want, Isabella."

"Kat's leaving now, Joe. Let her by." Isabella's tone was firm.

"Are you sure, Isabella?" Kat mimicked Isabella's tight grip around the water bottle's neck.

Joe's attention temporarily distracted as he rummaged through his pockets, Isabella seized the moment. "There's a telephone by the entrance. Call Antonio at The Café." Isabella whispered the number. "Tell him I need him. Then I want you to get out of here. No buts, Kat, do as I say." Isabella took the bottle from Kat into her empty hand. She planned to use it as a weapon.

Kat nodded and waited for Isabella to cue her exit. When Isabella did, like a seasoned runner, Kat sprinted past Joe and down the hall. Joe's mind floating on bourbon, he tried to piece together what just happened.

In the eerie silence, Isabella's eyes fixed on Joe. She watched him lean on the doorframe for support as he struggled to pluck a cigarette from the pack. Isabella's eyes followed his unsteady hand as he tried to plug the cigarette into his mouth before attempting to connect flame to tip. When he finally managed it, Joe inhaled deeply then flicked lustful eyes to Isabella.

"You look damn good tonight, Isabella. How about a kiss?" Plucking the cigarette from his mouth, he puckered his lips into a distended pout.

White knuckles wrapped tighter around the neck of the Perrier bottles. "You're drunk, Joe. You need to go home to your wife, Michaela. You're married now, remember?" Isabella's tone remained steady, although the fear gripping her went bone-deep.

"I know exactly what the fuck I'm saying," Joe growled. "It won't bother Michaela if you become my sideline booty call. I have her…" Joe went silent when his train of thought derailed. His mind un-fogged again, he finished his thought. "Approval."

Thinking it best not to address the ludicrous comment, Isabella said nothing. Instead, she planned her escape in her mind. She needed to get him away from the door he blocked.

"You don't believe me, do you? I can see the doubt in your face. At least I think it's doubt." Joe waved the cigarette erratically in the air. "Call her and ask her. She's completely good with me rolling in the sheets with you. And there's nothing more that I'd love than to spend a night in bed with you, Isabella. I'd show you what a real man is." He took a lurching step forward.

"Stay back, Joe," Isabella told him, keeping her tone as steady as possible.

"I want to touch you, Isabella." Joe took a step closer, and Isabella felt the panic bubbling in her throat, but she wouldn't show it.

"Don't come any closer, Joe. I'm warning you." Waving glass bottles at him in a lancing motion, Isabella moved behind the chair to use as a buffer.

Joe flicked the cigarette onto the floor. "You get me hard when you're this feisty, Isabella." Salacious eyes that looked almost transparent ogled Isabella as he closed the distance.

Close enough, he slammed his bulk against the chair with force to pin her against the wall. Trapped, Isabella did the only thing she could she lunged the bottles at Joe. The first one flew past his right shoulder. The second one hit him on the forehead forcefully enough to draw blood.

"What the fuck, Isabella." Joe shrieked, raising his hand to the gash dripping blood over his eyes and down his cheek.

The rage burned hot in Joe now, and he swung his right hand to latch onto Isabella's wrist. She flailed her arms to avoid his grasp, but he managed to take hold of her. His touch made her skin crawl.

"Let go of me, Joe," Isabella gasped in panic. Frantically, she tried to pull away, but even in his drunken state, Joe overpowered her. He was built like a bull and just as strong.

"You're a feisty one," Joe said, with a brash smile.

Arching back with the weight of her body, Isabella tried to pull away. Joe's response was a growl, wild, and primal. It made her heart speed up at twice the rate, and she went still.

"I'm sorry, Joe. I'm… I'm sorry," she stammered. "I won't fight you anymore."

"You promise." Joe's grasp on her wrist was hurting her.

"I promise." Isabella's sugary voice swayed Joe into releasing his hold. That's when she lunged a right punch at his face.

The ring on her finger connected with Joe's lip, cut it open. Blood flew in a grisly spray when she jabbed a second punch at his mouth. Joe could taste blood; she could smell it.

Joe wiped his mouth with the back of his hand. "You fucking bitch, Michaela. Look what you've done."

Flickering angry eyes at Isabella, Joe slapped her hard enough to brand and cut her cheek open deep enough to spill blood. Her wind gone, Isabella wheezed for air to fill her lungs. She could never match Joe's strength, but her survival instinct wouldn't allow her to succumb to him, and she frantically struggled to pry herself from his hold.

Fear replaced with her instinct to survive, Isabella shouted, "Let go of me, you sonofabitch," throwing blind punches.

Isabella threw enough punches for her fists to connect with Joe's ear, jaw, and his left eye when he turned to dodge them. The impact made Joe's head spin and he wanted her to stop.

His hand blindly reached for Isabella's throat but instead caught the front of her shirt. The contact of hand against skin excited him. He imagined she felt the same thrill coursing through her. He'd show her what it was like to have a real man, his foggy brain mused.

Joe tugged at silk until the pearl buttons from her shirt popped. One by one, they fell, tapping on wood as they bounced and scattered. His glassy eyes lit up when he caught sight of the ripe swell of her breasts spilling over black lace. Frozen with fear, Isabella stood there as Joe's breath came fast and shallow as he eyed her like a rabid animal does its prey.

"Those look better than I imagined." Fine spit sprayed Isabella's face. The sound of his breath coming in excited gasps made the hair on her neck stand on end.

Shaking herself out of her paralyzing fear, Isabella crossed her arms to cover herself. The gesture infuriated

Joe, and he reached to pull her arms away. As he did, Antonio's hand whipped up to snag Joe's arm.

The sight of Isabella's torn shirt, the gash on her cheek, the terror on her paled face unleashed a fit of ferocious anger in Antonio that aimed to maim. Antonio spun Joe around until they were face to face.

Eye to eye now, Antonio met Joe with a murderous look. "You fucking sonofabitch." Antonio barked, his eyes dark with the furious wave of rage that washed over him.

Trying to establish face recognition, Joe's drunk gaze studied Antonio.

"Don't you ever lay your hands on Isabella again? You hear me, you drunken sonofabitch?" Antonio's hands gripping Joe's shoulders with vice strength, he propelled him against the wall making his head bounce hard. Clamping his left arm against Joe's neck, Antonio pressed down until Joe gasped for air. Antonio pressed harder. "You want to threaten anyone you threaten me, you motherfucking coward. Don't ever come near Isabella again. You hear me, Joe?"

Isabella recognized the look of murder in Antonio's eyes. As much as the thought of Antonio punching Joe to unconsciousness pleased her, Isabella couldn't bear the idea of him ending up in jail. "Don't, Antonio. Please don't." Isabella cried out when she saw Antonio's right hand form into a tight fist.

Intent on bashing Joe's face, Antonio ignored Isabella's pleas. "Let go of me, Isabella. I need to punch the fucking drunk out of him. I need to hurt him." Antonio tugged his punching arm lose from Isabella's grip.

"I don't want you to go to jail. They'll end up charging you for throwing the first punch, and he's not worth it. Please, Antonio, for me, don't do this. I don't want to lose you." Isabella's pleading words penetrated Antonio's ears this time, and he lowered the fisted hand. "Let him go, Antonio."

Reluctantly, Antonio loosened his chokehold. "You're lucky she stopped me. I'd have beaten the shit out of you if it wasn't for her," he said, watching Joe struggle for air. "Get your bourbon-soaked ass out of my sight before I change my mind and beat the shit out of you. Next time you think of breathing the same air as Isabella, you better think twice. Because I promise you, Joe, I'll kill you. Do you hear me? I'll kill you with my bare hands and enjoy it."

Whether from an alcohol-induced fearlessness or out of sheer stupidity, Joe creased his mouth into a contemptuous grin and looking into Antonio's eyes, he said, "Pfft. You're a fucking pussy. You don't have the balls."

The muscles in his jaw clenched, Antonio closed in on Joe. The red-hot rage in his eyes made Isabella fear for Joe's life.

"Get out, Joe, before..." Isabella didn't get a chance to finish when Antonio's knuckles connected with Joe's face. The sound of knuckles against jaw was sickening.

Antonio landed a few more blows to Joe's face. Each felt more satisfying than the first. Joe's wind gone, he struggled for air. Wheezing, Joe stumbled to his knees, then fell on all fours. In a matter of seconds, Joe was face down on the floor.

Gagging for air, Joe took in big greedy gulps as a pool of blood spread on wood. Isabella wasn't sure where the blood came from, but she could taste it, smell it thick in the air.

"Please don't, Antonio." Isabella cried out when she saw Antonio raise his right foot to deliver a blow to Joe's side. Her whimpering cries permeated into Antonio's rage, and his foot froze mid-air.

"Next time you accost Isabella or come anywhere near her, I won't be as forgiving," Antonio barked the fury laced words to a passed out Joe before turning to Isabella. "Are you all right?"

"I'm fine." Isabella fell into Antonio's arms.

Heated temper waned into concern, Antonio pulled back to scan her. "Did he lay a hand on you?"

"No, no, he didn't," Isabella assured him.

Antonio draped his coat over Isabella and chained protective arms around her. For a long time, he held her trembling body. "Has he done this before?"

The fear of his threat to kill Joe looming in her mind, she said, "No."

Her response came too quickly to sound believable, and the sour waves of nausea rose in Antonio's stomach. "This isn't the first time he's accosted you, is it? Answer me, Isabella."

Isabella returned a subtle shake of her head.

"Joe's done this to you before? Hasn't he, Isabella. Answer me." Unable to suppress the guilt in his voice at failing to protect her, his words came out harsher than he intended.

Angered by the unwarranted raised tone, Isabella pulled away. "I said no," she snapped.

He wasn't getting the full story. He sensed it. Still, Antonio turned to face Isabella with an expression akin to an apology. "I'm sorry. I'm worried about you." His voice dipped to an apologetic register

"I know."

Antonio pulled Isabella back in and chained arms around her. "I'm having the police pick him up. A couple of days behind bars will make him think twice about approaching you again. And we're telling your mother about this so she can keep an eye on you."

When she opened her mouth to agree, he mistook it for dismissal and pressed on without allowing her to get a word in. "I don't want a repeat incident. If he so much as breathes in your direction, I want you to let me know. He's fine when he's sober, but if today is any indication of what he's like when he's drunk, he's dangerous, Isabella. If he so much as touches a hair on you, I'll kill him." Although the words were said in a calm tone, the violence in his eyes told her he meant every word.

"Please don't say things like that." Her stomach did one hard shudder. "He's not worth it. Promise me you won't do anything crazy."

Despairing eyes looked down at her. "I don't know what I'd do without you. I don't know what I'd do if anything happened to you." Eyes overflowing with the fear and pain brought on by the thought of losing her clung to Isabella.

"I'm sorry I put you through this."

Brushing the hair from her face, Antonio looked deep into Isabella's eyes. "Don't apologize. I don't ever want you to apologize for turning to me when you need me. I'd do anything to protect you. I need you in my life. Do you understand that?" Antonio held her tighter, and she let her face fall into his chest. His lips brushed over her hair, and he took in her sweet scent to soothe his fears. "I couldn't live without you. I wouldn't know how to. Do you have any idea how much I need you in my life?"

She didn't know until then. "I need you too, and it's why you need to vow you won't do anything rash and stupid. Please, promise me, Antonio."

"I promise." Cupping her chin, Antonio brought her face up to meet her lips. "I'll walk you to your apartment. Then I'll come back to deal with this." Antonio said, looking down at the passed out Joe.

ISABELLA DIDN'T LEAVE ANTONIO'S SIDE. EMOTIONS were still too raw in him, and she feared what he might do to an unconscious Joe. Besides, she needed the satisfaction of seeing Joe hauled away by the police.

Chapter 28

ANTONIO CALLED MARIA to the store. Within minutes, she was there—Salvatore by her side. Wide-eyed, Maria and Salvatore's eyes darted from Isabella to a passed out Joe, then to Antonio as they listened to the horrific account.

"Why didn't you mention any of this before today, Isabella?" Maria's face, a mask of distress, didn't prevent Isabella from noticing Salvatore's soothing arm around her mother's shoulder.

"I didn't think it would escalate to this. I didn't want to worry or upset you unnecessarily." Isabella wrapped Antonio's coat tighter around her to conceal the ripped blouse.

Maria studied Isabella with a motherly eye. Isabella was a grown woman, but to her, she was her little girl, and she'd protect her to the ends of the earth. "This has to do with a dangerous drunk, who aims to cause you harm, and if my gut tells me, this isn't the first time he's accosted you." All eyes turned to Isabella.

When the silence lingered, with the concerned tone of a father, Salvatore said, "You will have to be more vigilant here on, Isabella. We'll all have to be more vigilant and protective of you. I'm afraid for your safety, of what he may end up doing to you."

"I'm with Sal on this, Isabella." Antonio cut in before Isabella countered Salvatore's comment, whom she was still working out in her mind why he'd walked in with her mother.

Was he at the apartment with Maria this whole time? Why, why would he be there, and how long had this been going on? The questions cycling through her mind, Isabella pressed fingers to her temples where the headache built up.

"Please stop. All of you stop. I agree something needs to be done, but what? The cops won't do anything until Joe's caused physical harm. I can apply for a restraining order, but what good is that going to do except weigh me down and affect my life, my business."

Antonio ran fingers through his hair. "I don't care what it does to your business. It's you I'm worried about."

Salvatore and Maria simultaneously added, "I agree with Antonio."

"I'm not about to throw away months of blood, sweat, and tears because of a drunken bully. I refused to be bullied." The pain was now throbbing at Isabella's temple, beneath the eyes.

"He's not just a drunk, Isabella. He's a dangerous man who, for reasons unknown, is after you. Kat picked up on that tonight. Why can't you?" Antonio set his teeth against temper.

"You can't make unilateral decisions on my behalf. I have a business to run." Isabella charged back. As much as her eyes flashed anger, deep down, she knew they were right.

Setting aside the turmoil of emotions swirling inside her, Maria stepped in as the voice of reason. She knew her daughter. She knew what Isabella needed to hear. Maria understood it was difficult for Isabella to let go of her independence. Unlike Salvatore and Antonio, who felt

Isabella was reacting defensively, Maria recognized her daughter's pushback was due to fear.

"Joe has shown to have dangerous tendencies, and you can't take this lightly. We'll file a restraining order." Maria raised a hand to silence Isabella when she started to speak. "The restraining order is a means of ensuring the police take you seriously if charges need to be pressed. We'll get our lawyer to process the paperwork and submit it on your behalf. It keeps you out for most of the process and ensures confidentiality for as long as possible. In the meantime, swear to me that a staff member, Salvatore, Antonio, or me, will accompany you at all times. There's strength in numbers."

"That's unrealistic. I have meetings to attend. I'm not taking a chaperone with me everywhere I go." Isabella rolled her eyes, prompting Salvatore and Antonio to voice their annoyance at her lackadaisical attitude.

When they began to speak, Maria shot both men a withering look, and mouths closed tight. "Try to schedule them in-house, and if you must go out, take Gail with you to every meeting possible. She'd be happy to shadow you." Maria articulated a female perspective with a viable solution.

Isabella's face twisted into a sour expression but relented. "Fine, you win, Mama. I'll call David Strubb Monday morning about filing the restraining order. I'll talk to Gail, and I'll make sure someone's with me at all times."

Isabella noted the relieved look on Antonio and Salvatore's face. "Question is, how long am I going to do this for?"

Maria wrapped a protective arm around her daughter. "Let's take it one day at a time for now. We'll work through this together. Now, let me put a call to Becca. She's the police chief's wife." Maria explained when brows furrowed. "She's a uniform customer whom I've befriended over the past few months. I'm sure she'll be happy to get her husband to help us out."

"Their friends with Joe's parents," Isabella pointed out.

Maria gazed over at a passed out Joe. "Maybe, but Becca is a woman and the mother of teenage daughters."

AFTER MARIA RECOUNTED HER STORY, TO Becca she put her husband on the line.

Maria pled with Chief McNeill to keep Isabella's name off the record. The school board wasn't bound to overlook the imposing dangers of a drunk stalking Isabella. With a defiant tone, Maria told Chief McNeill she wanted Joe arrested and incarcerated for as long as the law allowed.

"I need you to protect my daughter. I need you to keep him away from her." Maria pled.

The conversation from there on became one-sided as Maria listened to Chief McNeill, nodding as she made a mental note. The conversation broke with Maria giving Salvatore's license plate number.

"It's all set. Chief McNeill is sending a couple of police officers to arrest Joe on suspicion of car theft and attempting to operate a vehicle while intoxicated," Maria told them when she hung up the telephone. "Antonio, Salvatore, you'll need to haul Joe's body out to Salvatore's car. Make it look as if he tried to break into the car and prop him up to look as if he's turning the engine over. Once that's done, Antonio, you take Isabella to your place. We need to distance her from this mess. All right, chop, chop boys, we have work to do." Maria clapped her hands to mobilize the speechless trio.

THE SNOW STOPPED FALLING, BUT THE wind picked up, making the night air unbearably cold. The heat blowing from the car vent fogged the windows and made it difficult for *The Eyes* to watch the scene across the street play out.

As cold as it was, *The Eyes* rolled the car window down to get a better view of the two undercover officers hauling Joe's drunken ass out of the Pontiac and fling him into the back seat of the unmarked Dodge. Bringing the police into the picture wasn't an eventuality *The Eyes* accounted for, but Joe was such a useless fuck.

Joe's stupidity was going to delay the final steps of the plan's execution by days.

Fuck! Fuck, fuck, *The Eyes* rammed hands against the steering wheel as the Dodge drove off.

The only consolation was that Isabella was running scared. Looking over her shoulder at every turn was what the bitch deserved for taking what wasn't hers.

Chapter 29

ISABELLA'S HEAD PILLOWED on Antonio's chest, he held her. The chilling events fresh in his mind, the fear of loss reeling in his mind, Antonio stroked her hair until the sleeping pill took effect, and she slipped into sleep.

Tonight Antonio wouldn't sleep. Tonight he'd watch over Isabella.

Clearing sleep from his eyes, Antonio watched Isabella in sleep. Listening to the gentle rhythm of her breaths, he hoped her dreams were pleasant ones, devoid of the darkness that touched her tonight.

At the thought of the harm she may have come to at Joe's hands, anger burned in Antonio. Isabella had come to mean too much to him. He didn't know he could love anyone as much as he loved her. The love he felt for Isabella motivated him to extraordinary lengths to protect her, but he couldn't be there for her around the clock.

Isabella agreed to Maria's suggestions, but with a business to run, restraints like those she'd agreed to were difficult to maneuver when life pulled you in every direction. No one understood that better than he did. He couldn't watch over Isabella twenty-four-seven, and the thought of what Joe might do if she so much as got distracted for a moment left him feeling angry, helpless, and fearful for her life.

His need to protect Isabella was too strong in him to cast aside.

Antonio spent the rest of the night deep in thought. No matter how he played the scenarios in his head, he circled back to the only solution.

Pulling Isabella closer, he set anxious eyes out the window to wait for the morning sun to introduce a new day and set the gears in motion.

ISABELLA SHIFTED RESTLESSLY IN SLEEP. DREAMS of flowing blood so real she thought she could taste cycled in her mind. There was a vision of a confrontation, an attack on her. The images now sharper, she saw Joe coming at her, watched Antonio block him with the punches he delivered, the blows that knocked him off his feet. She heard Joe taking big thirsty gulps of air to fill his deprived lungs as the bright, red blood pooled around Joe's head.

Isabella heard Antonio's threatening words telling Joe he'd kill him with his bare hands.

She saw Joe's beaten lifeless body.

Panic crushed her chest, shut off her air, and she bolted up in bed. Isabella reached for Antonio. He wasn't there. A stronger surge of dread overtook her. Her eyes widening, Isabella looked around the room. When she didn't see Antonio, her breaths came fast. She shut her eyes to remember.

The memory was coming back. She'd gone home with Antonio. He'd tucked her in his bed, held her until her exhausted mind succumbed to sleep.

She remembered nothing happened to her or Antonio.

Brushing sleep out of her eyes, she scanned the room again. There was no sign of Antonio.

"Antonio," she called out.

"Good morning." In a white T-shirt and jeans, dark, wet hair clinging to his neck, Antonio popped out from behind the partition and rounded the kitchen island. "I hope I didn't wake you," he said, aiming a look up to the bedroom.

She watched him make his way to the window. "What time is it?"

"It's almost noon." Antonio rolled the blind up to let shafts of bright sun fill the room.

Isabella wrapped her arms around folded legs as he crossed to her with the tray of food. "I slept through all this?" she said when the sound of flowing traffic and street noise and the din of conversation from the cafe below fully awakened her senses.

"You did. You were tired. You slept all night soundly. Brunch will be served in bed in a minute." Antonio set the tray on the bed.

"Those sleeping pills work well."

"They do. As I said, you slept well all night."

"Did you sleep?"

He picked up the steaming cup of coffee and handed it to her. "I wanted to … watch you in sleep."

She stopped her drinking mid-sip. "All night?"

"Mmm-hmm."

Love spurt right through the heart. "My dad did that when I couldn't sleep."

He leaned in to glide his lips to hers. "How are you feeling?"

"Better. I guess."

"You'd tell me if you weren't." Isabella nodded, and Antonio left it at that. Nagging wouldn't result in a good outcome. "I spoke to your mother this morning. She told me Joe's in custody he'll be spending two to three months in jail. Chief McNeill will see to it. Joe blew beyond the allowable limit. His body's alcohol content was to the level of alcohol poisoning. They're shocked he's alive."

"That's terrible." Isabella watched him pick up the second cup of coffee off the tray.

"Don't tell me you're feeling sorry for him." He watched her fuel herself with coffee.

Setting her cup down, she reached for the scrunchie on the night table and bundled her tangled hair into a ponytail. "To be honest, I'm not sure what I'm feeling."

Antonio slid onto the bed next to her. "Eat something. You hardly touched your dinner last night."

Isabella picked up a slice of buttered toast, topped it with scrambled egg. "If you don't mind, I'd rather not talk about Joe."

Stretching his legs out, he crossed bare feet at the ankle. "All right," he said, sipping coffee.

"I'm fine. Really, I am," Isabella said when Antonio eyed her over the rim of his cup.

"You were attacked, Isabella." Anger tightened his belly at the memory.

"Almost attacked." Isabella pointed out.

"Don't dismiss it as something trivial." Antonio struggled to keep his temper from flaring.

"I was rattled last night, but I'm fine now. Especially knowing Joe's behind bars and the less we talk about him, the faster I can move on. Besides, I don't want this darkness touching our lives any longer."

"Okay, no more talk about Joe for now, but I'll be here for you when you want to talk."

Knowing Isabella as well as he did, persuading her to entertain a conversation she didn't want to enter into would end up in her shutting down. The woman was obstinate and unyielding when she set her mind to it.

"I know you will be. You look tired."

"I'm fine." Antonio took a bite of toast, chased it with coffee.

"I'm sorry, that's my fault, isn't it?"

"It's not your fault. It's Joe's fault." Feeling the weight of his fear, he closed his eyes for a moment. Calm restored, Antonio reached over for the loose strand of hair on her face, curled it on his finger. "I need you in my life, Isabella. I'd do anything to protect you, to make sure you remain a part of it."

"I, too, need you in my life." Isabella's mind flashed back to his threatening words to Joe. Knowing he wouldn't hesitate to act on them if the situation arose, she said, "You promised me you would never do anything to take you from me."

"I'm sorry if I scared you."

"Me too." Isabella watched Antonio stare down at his coffee, seemingly lost in the dark liquid. "A penny for them."

"You and I have come together for a reason, and I want to continue to explore those reasons. Not just today or tomorrow, but for the rest of our lives." Isabella studied Antonio, trying to understand what he was going on about. "I want you by my side on this journey through life." There was a short hesitation. "What would you say to us getting married next weekend?"

The emotional upheaval and stress pushing its way into his voice, she rested a hand on his cheek. "I love you, and I'd love to ride this journey with you, but only when the time is right. I think right now, the angst lingering from last night is making you say this."

"Maybe, probably, but the one thing I am sure of is that I want you always with me. I'm never happier than when we're together."

Isabella reached for Antonio's hand, liked the feel of it casing hers. "Me too, but making a rash decision, one that will affect us for the rest of our lives, based on what happened last night is not the right way to go."

"If you don't want to marry, just say so," he spat.

She looked at him beyond the anger, which she understood stemmed from fear, out of his need to protect her. This was love, she thought. "I know you don't mean that. I know you know I love you and I want to marry you. I want to make sure this is what you want."

Antonio touched a hand to her cheek. "Maybe I'm making a rash decision, but how I feel about you is real. I've felt this way since the first time we kissed. You fill my dreams at night and my thoughts always. I love you, Isabella, and I want you by my side … always."

"I, too, want you always by my side." She eased closer to him, her eyes on him. "You're sure about this, Antonio?"

"I am. Marry me, Isabella."

"I have horrible habits you know nothing about."

"Who doesn't?"

"You've only seen the dating Isabella. You haven't seen the cranky-morning Isabella."

"You haven't seen how cranky I can get when things don't go my way." He countered.

"I need to devote a lot of time to my business. You know it's just getting off the ground, and there's so much more I need to do. That's non-negotiable."

"The franchising deal with Tom Ritchie is bound to become time-consuming."

"I want only one marriage in my life. Meaning we're both still fairly young, and this can't be a trial run."

Antonio lifted her hand to his lips. "I can't guarantee what the future will bring. Life throws challenging hurdles at you every day, but I can tell you with certainty that I love you as I've never loved anyone before. Aside from that, what else matters?"

Take risks and chances, Isabella. Live for today, not for tomorrow or the day after because today is here now, and the now is the foundation for your tomorrow.

Her father's words bouncing in her head, she said, "All right, let's get married."

"You mean it?"

She leaned in, touched her lips to his. "I do. Can we have a Valentine's wedding?"

His smile spread. "That only gives you eight weeks to plan the wedding."

"It's enough time. I don't want a big do. I'd like to have a small reception. Invite Gail and the staff, Mrs. Cropper, Mrs. Johnstone, and Kat. I want to make myself a simple wedding dress." Isabella explained, and in the excitement of the moment, she was happy Antonio didn't notice her omission of Salvatore's name. If Salvatore was spending time with her mother, she wanted him gone.

"I'm good with that." Antonio slid the night table drawer open and reached for the ring.

On bended knee, he held up the heart-shaped ruby surrounded by tiny diamonds. "It was my mother's ring, handed down from the generations of Sabatini's."

A sunburst of love that left her speechless descended on her.

When the deafening silence reigned, Antonio said, "I know it's a simple ring. If you don't like it, I can get you another one."

"It's perfect. I love it," Isabella said when she found her voice.

Antonio looked deep into her eyes. "All right then, Isabella Farfalla, will you make me the happiest man alive. Will you join me on this journey through life as my soul mate, my best friend? Will you marry me?"

Isabella kept her eyes on Antonio. "I can only answer after you promise me that you will also have the same impact on my life?"

Crystal blue eyes swam with love. "I promise."

"I'll marry you. I will. I will. I will." The words tumbled out with giddy excitement.

Antonio slid the ring on her finger. "Thank you for agreeing to be a part of my life. There's no one else I would rather have beside me on this journey than you."

Part III

Truth

The truth is rarely pure and never simple.

—Oscar Wilde

Chapter 30

MARIA CAUGHT SIGHT of the ring on her daughter's finger when she and Antonio walked into the apartment. Joy spilled from her eyes as she hugged her daughter. "I'm so happy for you, honey," she said, locking away thoughts of Joe. Tonight he wouldn't blacken their lives.

"You knew Antonio was going to propose?" Isabella asked, seeing the telltale signs on Maria's face.

"I did. This young man called me this morning to chat about asking for your hand in marriage. I'm thrilled to welcome a wonderful son into our family." Maria pecked Antonio on the cheek. "I couldn't have asked for a better man for my little girl."

"I'll take good care of her," Antonio assured Maria.

"I know you will. This calls for champagne. I picked one up this morning. It's in the fridge," Maria told Antonio as she and Isabella settled into the living room couch.

While Antonio busied himself in the kitchen, opening the bottle and rummaging through the cupboards for glasses, Isabella told Maria about their plan to wed in a few short weeks.

Maria's eyebrows rose. "That doesn't give us much time."

"We don't want anything extravagant, a simple church wedding, and an intimate reception afterward." Isabella went down the list of people she wanted to invite.

"That's by her choice. I told her she could have as big a wedding as she wants." Antonio walked into the living room with the champagne bottle and glasses.

"He did, but I, we, want a simple affair."

Pomp and pageantry weren't who Isabella was, but Maria suspected her daughter's reason for the toned-down affair had more to do with Angelo's absence from her special day.

"It's your day. Whatever you say goes," Maria said automatically. "One thing I insist on is you wear a wedding gown and that you allow me and Salvatore to make it for you."

"I don't know if a wedding gown is possible, Mama. It's only weeks away. I was thinking more of a floor-length peach dress."

Maria drank champagne to drown the words. In her days, white was what brides wore, but her daughter wasn't an average bride. "Peach it is, and Salvatore and I will make it possible," Maria said, and Isabella knew better than to argue.

The three toasted to new beginnings, and an excited Isabella went on to tell her mother of her wedding must-haves. Knowing better than to come between two women making wedding plans, Antonio sipped on champagne and silently watched on as mother and daughter exchanged ideas.

A half-hour into the planning, Salvatore opened the door to Maria's apartment. He didn't have to listen to the conversation for long to determine Isabella accepted Antonio's proposal.

When Maria hung up with Antonio, believing Salvatore should share in his daughter's moment, she called him and asked for him to join them at the apartment. Salvatore turned the invitation down, suspecting Isabella wouldn't welcome the intrusion but relented when Maria insisted the time to tell their daughter everything had come.

Salvatore's heart drummed in his chest at the idea of sharing in his daughter's special day. He'd missed so many of them. Still, he questioned Maria's decision. Maria, however, contended they shouldn't postpone any longer. Isabella was entering a new phase of her life, and he needed to be a part of it. He needed to walk his daughter down the aisle because if the thought had crossed her mind, it had crossed his.

Nerves bouncing, bracing himself for what was to come, Salvatore cleared his throat to announce his presence. Maria waved him in. Walking into the living room, Isabella's frown of confusion didn't escape Salvatore.

"So, she said yes."

"She did." Antonio took Salvatore's outstretched hand for the congratulatory handshake.

"You knew?" Isabella's voice rose noticeably.

Salvatore nodded but didn't elaborate as Isabella's eyes demanded. "I wish you both a lifetime of happiness."

Unable to wrap her head around Salvatore's intrusion into the family moment, Isabella remained stoic when he leaned in to peck her on the cheek. This new development took priority over everything else, and her gaze swivelled to her mother in search of answers.

"I don't understand. Why is Salvatore here, Mama?" Isabella watched her mother eye him as if exchanging coded messages. "As long as I'm on the topic, how did Salvatore come to be with you last night when you came down to the store? Was he here at the apartment with you all night?"

"Isabella, that's very disrespectful, and none of your…" Maria stopped short when Salvatore shot her a cautionary look.

"Really, Mama, I'm disrespectful. Daddy hasn't been gone a year yet, and you're already…"

"Honey, Salvatore, and I need to speak to you." Maria cut Isabella off before she said something she'd regret.

"Go ahead." Isabella's temper flared.

Noticing Maria's agitation, he jumped in. "Please have a seat, Isabella. Please," Salvatore repeated when Isabella turned defiant.

Antonio nudged Isabella onto the couch. "Would you like me to leave?" Antonio directed the question at Salvatore, but Maria answered him.

"No, honey, I'd like you to stay. You're a part of the family now."

Isabella said, "I'd also like you to stay. I'm not sure what this is all about, but you're my family now, and whatever involves me involves you."

Isabella watched her mother take a deep breath, and in the moment of silence that followed, everyone in the room became conscious of Maria's uneasiness. "Angelo loved you very much. He was so proud of you, honey. He'd never do anything to hurt you. And I know he'd be so happy to know you're marrying Isabella." Maria flicked her eyes to Antonio before turning her gaze back to her daughter. "There's nothing he wouldn't do to ensure your happiness."

"I know that, Mama." Guardedly, Isabella watched her mother a blend of nerves and tension, nervously spin her wedding band. "Say what you have to say, Mama."

"I think it's best if you read this before we go on." Maria Reached into her shirt pocket for the envelope and handed it to Isabella.

Isabella inspected the face of it before taking out the letter, wrinkled and brittle from handling. With Antonio looking on, Isabella read. As she got further down the page, her colour vanished. The tears stinging Isabella's eyes, she covered her mouth with her hand to stifle the sob as she looked to her mother for an explanation.

"Angelo wrote the letter during the last few weeks of his life." Maria's voice broke with emotion.

Isabella's heart sank deeper in her chest when she reread, this time more slowly, taking in every word. When she was finished, she looked over to her mother with a pained look. "I don't understand any of this. This letter is not from Daddy. It's not his handwriting. I'd recognize it."

"He was too weak during that time. He likely got someone in the hospital to write it for him." Maria's tears spilled down her cheeks.

Mopping tears from her eyes, Isabella looked over to Salvatore. "If he was too weak to write the letter, how did he manage to get it sent off? How did he even get your address? Did he have it all along?" Her voice choking, Isabella lobbed the questions out like a tennis ball as they rolled in her head.

"I mailed it." Antonio jumped in with the unexpected admission.

"You, what do you have to do with this?" Isabella wasn't entirely sure what she was experiencing.

"I went to see your dad at Christmas time. During my visit, he asked me to help him locate Sal. I did and gave your father the information. Next thing he hands me the envelope, asked me to mail it. He told me if Sal didn't answer back, I should do anything I could to talk him into coming to Toronto to meet you and your mother. I didn't ask any questions."

Isabella pressed a hand to her stomach. Antonio brought Salvatore, a man her mother loved more than her father, a man who looked to replace him, into their midst. Although she didn't understand how Salvatore fit into the picture, Isabella perceived Antonio's actions as an act of betrayal.

Isabella's eyes went dark and turbulent at the thought her father, who'd sacrificed his life to provide, loved them as much as he had, who to his dying day gave and gave, left this earth feeling unloved. Fresh tears sprang to Isabella's eyes, and the pressure in her chest was heavy and tight.

The hurt in Isabella's eyes made Antonio's stomach twist into tight knots. "It was a dying man's wish, Isabella. How could I not do as he asked me? I didn't know what it was all about. When I found out Sal was a skilled tailor, I assumed your father asked for his help to keep the business going. He told me he was leaving you and your mother in debt, and he didn't want you to deal with it alone."

Isabella's mind raced as she tried to process everything. "I don't even know what to think anymore. You could have told me about sending the letter," The cold, steely glint she aimed at Antonio matched the steel in her tone.

"I'm sorry I didn't, but your father asked me not to say anything, and I didn't think it was my story to tell. I didn't know the contents of the letter. I assumed your mother did. I'm sorry." Antonio lifted his shoulders and let them fall. "All I did was to fill a dying man's wish. It was what your father wanted, Isabella."

"Antonio's right, honey. He has nothing to do with any of this. It has to do with Angelo, Salvatore, you, and me," Maria said, on seeing the look of betrayal sweep over Isabella's face.

The pressure at the base of her throat made Isabella's chest compress. Needing time to think, the fear from last night lingering in her, absorbing the unexpected deluge of information coming at her now, Isabella waved a hand to silence everyone. For a long while, the air hummed while Isabella reread Angelo's letter.

"To his dying day, daddy was such a loving man. On his dying bed, he's thinking of us." Her father had been her hero in life. In death, her love grew tenfold for him, as did the anger for her mother. "You hurt him. You broke his heart." The look Isabella aimed at her mother was sharp enough to cut diamonds. "And even after this letter, you can say he's not the love of your life." The bitterness rang clear in her voice.

Maria's eyes swam in tears when she lifted them to Isabella. "I love Angelo very much, honey. He was good to me, to you."

"But he wasn't the love of your life." Isabella injected with a caustic tone. "Don't say anything else, Mama. I don't want to hear what you have to say." Isabella broke into a flood of tears.

"I never gave him a reason to think so. I don't know why he'd say that."

"But you didn't love him, did you, Mama?" Maria's silence spoke volumes. "You don't have to voice your feelings for people to understand how you feel. If you didn't love him, he would have sensed it, felt it in his bones. Daddy would have known." She felt an unimaginable ache at the thought of the depth of her father's heartache all these years, knowing he was never loved as he loved.

Emotions swimming, Isabella twisted her ring round and round, wondering how she'd feel if Antonio didn't love her as she loved him. The mere thought of it was unbearable. How could her mother put her father through that? Then why would he marry a woman he knew didn't love him? Why would she marry a man she didn't love? The questions circling in her head, she turned to Salvatore.

"And you moved in the moment you got a chance. This is our home. You're intruding in our family moment." Heat flashed in Isabella's eyes.

Maria opened her mouth to rebuke her daughter, but understanding it was Isabella's anger talking, Salvatore shook his head.

"If that's who you loved," Isabella tilted her chin to Salvatore, "Then why did you marry Daddy? Why marry a man you didn't love? Is everything you've told me about your life a lie?"

Maria shook her head. "Angelo and I did meet as children. We grew up together, were best friends. We loved each other as friends. But as we got older, his emotions for me developed into romantic love, which I, unfortunately, couldn't return, and I told him so. He understood, and we remained best of friends."

"You haven't answered my question, Mama. Why did you marry a man you didn't love?" Isabella pushed Antonio's hand away when he rested it on hers.

There was no getting away from it now. Quick, like tearing off a Band-Aid from a raw wound, Maria thought.

"I was one month pregnant when Angelo insisted on marrying me to save my honour. We got married right away, and when I started showing, we left Sicily." Maria explained.

When the swift realization she wasn't Angelo's daughter hit her, it felt like a bare-fisted punch to the gut. Faces, voices, and sounds became a blur. She was in a nightmare. That was it, a terrible nightmare. She hadn't heard what she'd heard. She was in a deep sleep, and she could stop the dream by shaking herself awake. Isabella did that, but when she opened her eyes, nothing changed.

She was awake. The moment was real.

Her whole life had been a lie.

Isabella looked at her mother. "If Daddy isn't my father, who is, Mama?"

There was a stretch of silence as the pieces of the puzzle came together in Isabella's head. When the last part fell in place, the answer came, and Isabella felt her lungs choke. Paling white, her eyes fixed wide in shock.

"Oh, my God." Emotions raging, Isabella looked over at Salvatore. "You're my father."

Maria's eyes welled with fresh tears flickered up to Isabella. "Yes, Salvatore is your biological father." The weight of guilt burdening her for decades rolled off her shoulders like an avalanche. There was a long road of healing ahead but saying the words felt so liberating.

At Maria's admission, Antonio's reaction was one of pure shock. Salvatore remained silent, but Maria's focus was solely on Isabella as her daughter fought to get her thoughts into a rational order.

"Jesus, I don't know what to do with this information. Daddy knew all along. That's why he wrote to you from his death bed?" Isabella gave Salvatore a long, hard stare.

Maria interjected before Salvatore could answer. "Angelo knew everything, Isabella. It was his idea to marry, to leave Sicily. You know what small-town mentality is like. He wanted you to have a life away from prying eyes, away from the hurtful gossip." Maria dabbed at her eyes with the handkerchief Salvatore handed her.

Flushed with anger, with a killing glare on her face Isabella turned to Salvatore. "If you're my father, where have you been all this time? Why weren't you here? Why did you abandon us? Wait, do I even want to hear your sorry ass excuse?" Isabella bolted to her feet and crossed the room to put distance from everyone.

"Isabella, this is difficult for all of us," Maria said in the calmest voice she could muster. "I met Salvatore the summer of fifty-nine. He was working at one of his family's wineries. He decided to take in my town's festival that Saturday. I was tending your grandfather's peanut cart when Salvatore walked up to buy a bag." Maria hesitated for a moment when the memory of that night came to her.

"We got to talk, small talk, the weather, the week-long summer festival, and before I knew it, we were spending every waking minute of that summer together. In the process, we fell in love. Toward the end of the summer, Salvatore disappeared."

"Leaving you knocked up." Isabella lobbed the words meant to slap Salvatore from across the room.

Salvatore rested a hand on Maria's arm. "Let me."

With a swell of emotions, Salvatore recounted his story. He told Isabella about the land his father was desperate enough to bargain for with an arranged marriage. Everyone went still when Salvatore told them about his discovery of Carlo.

Isabella's anger turned into shock. "Jesus! Your son is Carlo Mesi, and you're the Salvatore Mesi."

Salvatore gave her a subtle nod, and Maria went on to explain when Antonio's brows knit in confusion. "Salvatore and Carlo own one of the more successful couture houses in Milan. The Mesi brand is known worldwide and highly sought."

"I suspected all along you were more than a small-town tailor. You were far too good, but I dismissed the idea since Carlo is the face of the company," Isabella pointed out.

"I named it after Carlo because I wanted him to have a sense of self-worth when he grew up. I didn't want him to feel disenfranchised when he came to know of his past. I felt I owed it to him to give him a name, a sense of direction, the self-esteem he deserved. I was a tailor. By trade, I still am. It's what I trained for and what I love to do. Once I adopted Carlo, I broke ties with my family and built the company on my own. And now Carlo, who's one year older than you, has taken the company over with the help of the only sister I've kept in touch with."

"Salvatore has been your financial backer, not Antonio, as I'd suspected." Maria rested a hand on Antonio's arm.

"I don't want to minimize Antonio's contribution. He helped you from the onset. He guaranteed the initial loan Mrs. Johnstone gave you, which got you started, but I took over when I arrived in Toronto. I took care of you, and your mother as Angelo asked of me. All I did was give assurances to Mrs. Johnstone."

"Sal and I were simply safety nets, nothing more." Antonio rushed to assure when he sensed Isabella tensing up.

"What you've accomplished has been your own doing. It's through your drive, determination, and entrepreneurial acumen that you are where you are today. It took guts, vision, and hard work. You, Isabella, single-handedly got to where you are today." Salvatore pointed out.

She would have rebuked everyone in the room for interfering in her life, in her business, but at that moment, nothing mattered. Her world was turned upside down, and nothing felt real.

Isabella rubbed at her temple to relieve the increasing thumping pressure. She needed time to work through emotions, the aching sadness for the only father she'd known, for the father whose life lacked the loved he deserved.

The pained expression on Isabella's face was replaced with anger. Her face went hard, her eyes sombre when she turned to her mother. "Is there a reason why you only had me? Did you hate Daddy that much?"

"I didn't hate Angelo. I loved—love—him. Not in the way he loved me, but I love that dear man. I wanted to give him children, and he wanted you to have siblings, but I couldn't bear children after you. I wasn't lying when I told you I almost lost my life giving birth to you. The medical technology that exists today wasn't available two decades ago." Maria dabbed her eyes dry.

"Regardless of everything that's happened, Isabella, I want you to know Angelo, and I love you with all our hearts. You are the best part of our lives. You've always been very much loved, Isabella. Never doubt that."

Isabella's emotions bouncing like a yo-yo, her tone was calm when she asked Salvatore, "And why didn't you have any more children?"

"I never married. After losing your mother, no woman measured up to her." Salvatore's eyes flowing with emotion looked over at Maria. When their eyes met, Isabella saw the deep mutual love they had for one another. Her heart constricted, and she felt an aching sadness for her father.

The warmth of Antonio's hand struck Isabella, and she related her mother's circumstances to herself. She couldn't imagine what it would be like if she lost Antonio. He was her first love, the man who'd come into her life when she needed a friend. Antonio had brought meaning when she thought life had none. He was her crutch, her sounding board, her steadfast supporter, her friend, her lover, and no matter where life took her, he'd forever be in her heart. She'd never love another man as she loved him.

Isabella made her way to the window. Tree branches hung low under the weight of the snow that had sheathed the city under a sheet of white. Above, the moon was sliced in half, its glow sharp in the dark sky.

Isabella's gaze fixed beyond the window, she said, "Sal, you're a good man. Daddy believed so, and therefore I do too. You've been good to Mama and me, but I don't know what to feel, feel, and think. I need time to sort all this out in my head. I need time to mourn, to grieve for the only father I've known until today. As Daddy said, 'I believe that in the overall scheme of things the sum of one's life is no more than a series of overlapping stories, which defines us, make us who we are, who we become.'" Isabella paused a moment, and everyone sensed the struggle going on inside her.

"Your stories were set in motion long ago, where mine feels as if it's beginning all over again, and I need time to determine how I will write my next chapter. I'm sorry, I hope you understand." Salvatore's eyes met Isabella with understanding. "If you don't mind, I need to be alone right now. I need to be alone for a while."

Antonio walked over to Isabella. "Do you want to come back to mine?" When she shook her head, he said, "All right. You call me any time of day or night if you need to talk."

Head bowed, shoulders sagging, Isabella headed to her bedroom, where she remained for the rest of the night— crying.

Chapter 31

THE DAYS THAT followed were filled with sleepless nights as Isabella's mind splintered in different directions as it cycled between the emotions and thoughts assailing her. Focusing was a challenge when her mind floated on thoughts of a biological father she didn't know existed until a few days ago and a mother who'd deceived her her entire life. With so much stirring in her head, Joe's assault was cast to the back of her mind.

Then there was the man who'd been by her side all her life, whom she desperately missed. How could Isabella give in to the idea he wasn't her biological father? How was she to deal with this overload of lies and deception? How could she decompress with the cloud of misery hovering over her?

Leaning back in her chair, she raised fingers to her temple to soothe the pounding headache. She forced herself to clear her head, to find the needed calm. Reaching into her desk drawer for the bottle of Tylenol, her thoughts drifted to Antonio.

Isabella hadn't seen Antonio since the day he slid the ring on her finger. He gave her the space she needed. He called to check up on her often, but their conversations were short and succinct. Most nights, mentally drained to do anything, she'd head straight to bed.

Salvatore and Maria were prudent enough to keep out of Isabella's way. They gave Isabella the space she needed to sort through her emotions and disengage from anger, hate, and resentment. Isabella was glad they kept their distance because she wasn't ready to talk.

A few days ago, the man who'd wandered into her life was her employee. Now, he was her biological father. Isabella still didn't know what to do with that information, what to think, how to think. Then there was the man she'd just buried. Was she supposed to replace him with a man who'd never been there for her, a man she didn't know?

Isabella understood life brought unexpected twists you had no control over. Still, she couldn't help but harbour resentment for her mother for letting her live a lie. Her mother had done what was best under the circumstances. She could deal with that part of the equation, but she couldn't come to terms with the anger stemming from her mother's treatment of her father.

In Isabella's mind, making a man who'd given so much of himself to feel unloved all these years was reprehensible. No one should die feeling unloved. That was worse than the months of suffering he'd endured from the disease that consumed him.

There were days Isabella felt as if her head swam in a sea of emotions as she struggled to make sense of her tainted life—of everything. Why was it taking so long for her to sort through it all? She was a practical, logical woman used to dealing with complications. Antonio was right when he told her logic didn't apply to the emotions of the heart.

Isabella popped two extra Tylenol and buzzed Gail on the intercom. "No, Gail, there's no need for you to accompany me. I need to get away for a bit by myself... Yes, I'm going to Antonio's. ... Yes, no detours, straight there." Isabella reached for her coat and, cradling the phone on her shoulder, shrugged into it.

"Yes, I promise I'll call you as soon as I get to The Café... I know Mama will kill you if you let me wander off by myself, but I need to wander right now. Besides, Joe's still in jail, so I won't be in any danger. ... Yes, I promise I'll call you the moment I set foot in the door." Isabella gave a silent sigh. Reporting her every move wasn't getting easier.

"No, I am not heading out there for a booty call... It will relieve my tension, will it? ... No, I am not doing that. ... Jesus, Gail, filter. Filter. ... Jesus, is that even physically possible? Never mind, I'm hanging up now." Isabella held back a snort of laughter. Gail always managed to put a smile on her face, Isabella thought, slinging her purse on her shoulder.

THE JANUARY WIND CARRIED THE SHARP taste of winter, and even with the spill of bright sunshine, it was bitterly cold. Yet, hoping to clear her head, Isabella took the four-block stretch to The Café at a leisurely pace.

Crossing the light on green, Isabella reflected on the first time she made the walk in the same confused state. So much had happened since then. Her life had taken one hundred and eighty-degree turn. Isabella thought of Angelo and felt the emptiness in her heart. He was always there when she'd needed him. He'd always known what to say to ease her mind.

Isabella didn't doubt Salvatore was a good father. He'd been a great friend—she guessed that was the right term—looking after her and her mother as he had. But she didn't know the man. Not that she blamed Salvatore for not being in her life. After hearing his story, she understood. She did. Sometimes life had a way of working against you. She'd learned that dealing with her father's illness and his death.

But how was she to embrace a man she'd known a few months? How could she allow him to replace the man she'd call father all her life?

There were so many questions and no answers.

Her mind drifting, before Isabella knew it, she was walking through the doors of The Café. The hard leaps her heart made the moment she saw Antonio made her realize how much she'd missed him. For a long while, she watched him. The thick, dark locks she enjoyed running her fingers through fringed his handsome face, and there was a confident aura in the blue eyes drifting from the paperwork in his hands to the man sitting across from him.

Antonio wore his customary attire of jeans and a white cotton shirt; sleeves rolled up to the elbow. She'd have another talk with him about that. Now that he was about to become a household name, he needed to update his tired wardrobe. Not an easy task since Antonio always opted for comfort over style.

Sensing she was intruding on something more than coffee between friends, Isabella took a seat at the bar. As she was about to do so, Antonio caught sight of her and waved her over to the table.

"Hi." His eyes took on a tender look as he leaned in to brush his lips on her cheek. The subtlest hint of her perfume slid into him, stirring his insides and reminding him how much he'd missed her these past few days. "I'd like you to meet Tom Ritchie. Tom, this is Isabella Farfalla, the lady I was telling you about."

Tom rose to his six-two frame and drowned her delicate hand in his large, strong one. His dark eyes stared at her with a twinkle as Isabella sized him up. He was ruggedly handsome, with skin tanned the colour of honey, and a ring-less finger.

Antonio told Isabella Tom Ritchie was in his late sixties, but aside from the crown of silver waves, his striking face showed few signs of his age. He had a pleasant smile, which came with an equally affable demeanour. Under the brown tweed jacket, he wore jeans and a plaid shirt. She expected to see a cowboy hat and a horse nearby, but the British accent, which added a note of sophistication, told her he was anything but a cowhand.

"It's a pleasure to meet you, Mr. Ritchie." Isabella locked eyes with him.

"Call me Tom, luv." He signalled the seat he cleared for her. "Antonio tells me you designed the interior of The Café, his uniforms, and logo," he said in the distinctly British that rolled off his tongue like a fine melody.

"I did. Thoughts?"

"You did a fine job. It's unique and eye-catching. I've been mulling a re-design for my bookstores for some time. Now that Antonio and I are entering into this deal, they'll surely need the update. We'll be the first retailer to offer customers the combined cafe-bookstore concept," Tom said, with a satisfied smile.

"It's a great cross-merchandising concept. Your slogan should be…" Isabella fell into thought. "A great book and a good cup of coffee are life's great pleasures."

Tom's eyebrows winged up. "I love it. You and I are definitely going to sit down for a chat in the coming weeks."

"I'd like that, but you know that I'm a clothing designer."

"You can make an exception for me."

Isabella tapped her chin with her finger. "Well, seeing as my future husband stands to benefit, I'll put some ideas on paper for you to review."

"I knew it. She's marrying me for my money."

Isabella poked Antonio in the ribs. "I have my own. Thank you. I'm doing it purely for altruistic reasons."

Tom's eyes lit with a smile. "Well, whatever the reason, it sounds good to me, and I'm sure I'll like what you come up with. Call my office when you're ready." He turned over his business card to Isabella.

"Well, my lad, I'm not going to take up any more of your time. I'll leave you to look after this young lady. I'll have my secretary coordinate a time to meet with our lawyers to sign off on the paperwork ASAP. We need to finalize everything this week. I leave for London Sunday, and I'd like to conclude everything before I leave so we can get straight to work on the project on my return."

"We'll get it done, Tom," Antonio assured.

"That's a lovely accent. Where in the U.K. are you from?" Isabella asked.

"London." Tom gathered papers, dropped them into his briefcase.

"London's on my bucket list. It's the fashion capital of the world, and I've heard the shopping is to die for. Your wife must go crazy when she's there." Isabella watched Tom take the last of his coffee.

"If she's spending money, she'd better be using her husband's credit card. She and I have been divorced for years now." Tom picked up his briefcase.

Perfect, Isabella breathed under her breath. "I'm sorry I shouldn't have said anything."

"No need to be sorry, luv. I sure as hell am not. The woman was a heap load of trouble." Lips, firm and full, curved. "It was nice meeting you, Isabella, and it's a pleasure doing business with you, Antonio," Tom said, pumping his hand.

"That's a lovely accent. Your wife must go crazy when she's there." Antonio mimicked Isabella when Tom left.

"I just wanted..."

"I know what you wanted. You think he's perfect for Mrs. Cropper."

"Well, he is. He's tall, dark, handsome, and single." Isabella ticked the points off on her fingers. "And he seems like a genuinely nice man."

"I already thought of that, but can we please not get into matchmaking until I sign off on the deal. I don't want this deal to go south on me. If everything works out, he's going to be putting a compact version of The Café into every one of his larger bookstores across Canada. That's over sixty-five locations with an additional fifty in the coming five years. Ritchie's Bookland and The Café is a perfect marriage." Antonio gathered his paperwork and dropped it into a file folder.

"And it's a stepping stone from there for me to franchise out and..." He set off excitedly droning on about every minute detail of his plan to conquer the cafe world. "What?" he asked when he caught her staring at him.

"You sound like me when I'm excited." Her mouth twisted into a smile.

"Never mind that." Antonio brushed his lips to hers and settled back into his seat. "Am I forgiven?"

"You are."

"Thank you." He ran hands along her arms. "How are you?"

"Going crazy. I needed to get out of my office. I haven't been able to concentrate on anything since the talk," she said, taking the last of Antonio's coffee.

"Let's go upstairs where we can have more privacy, and you can tell me all about it." Antonio waved to Marco and signalled up to his apartment.

Upstairs, Antonio dropped the file folder on the coffee table and hung Isabella's coat on the rack.

"I've missed you." He brushed away the errant strands spilling over her face.

"I'm sorry, but this whole thing with Sal and Mama, and the renovations, and…"

Antonio brushed his lips to hers to stop her talking. The tenderness of his kiss had her belly doing somersaults and leaving her breathless. "That's better. I'll get some wine. It'll help you relax. Then you can tell me what's been going through that mind of yours."

Her hand whipped up to snag him back when he started to step away. "I've missed you too," she said, playing her mouth over his to get a deeper taste of him. "I needed time to think things through."

"I know. Take a seat on the couch while I get that wine. Are you hungry? I can get the chef to whip something up," Antonio called out from the kitchen.

"Maybe later. Right now, I need to call Gail to report in like a two-year-old," Isabella said with an irritated tone, and Antonio let slide. Now wasn't the time for a lecture.

Although Joe was behind bars, Maria thought it best Isabella get into the routine of Gail shadowing her or reporting in to her when she ventured out on her own.

When Isabella hung up, she fell back onto the couch and watched Antonio walk the bottle of Zinfandel and glasses to the living room. "Tom seems nice."

Antonio poured two glasses, handed Isabella one. "He is. I've enjoyed doing business with him. By the way, you know that once the project gets off the ground, I'm going to have to travel."

Knowing where the conversation was heading, Isabella jumped in. "You don't have to worry about me. I've put all the recommendations you and Mama suggested into practice. Gail goes with me everywhere, and we all know she'll watch out for me. When she's not with me, there are workmen and staff and…"

"You've made your point. I want to make sure you don't give that animal another opportunity to lay a hand on you. While Joe's locked up, we can all breathe easily, but unfortunately, they can't keep him in forever."

Isabella rested her feet on his lap. "I know. Doesn't seem right, does it? He terrorizes me, and I now I have to watch my every move."

"Chief McNeill has done the impossible by keeping him locked up for this long. He's already told your mom he won't be able to keep him in much longer."

"I know. I promise I'll take every precaution," Isabella said when concern flashed over Antonio's face. "Can we please not talk about Joe?"

"Okay. What would you like to talk about?" Antonio set his glass down and took to running his thumb up and down the soles of her feet.

"That feels great. Let's talk about the wedding. Gail's been a Godsend. She's helped with a lot of the planning."

Antonio's brows knitted together. "Your mother hasn't been involved in the planning?" Antonio watched Isabella's eyes focus on the wine in her glass. "Your mother will forgive you for not involving her, but if I know you, you're going to end up regretting it tenfold."

"I'm still so angry with her I can't even… Ugh, I can't talk to her right now." Isabella rose to pace the room.

"May I put in my two cents?" Antonio said, volleying eyes to keep up with her stride. "I don't think you have so much of an issue with the revelations made by your mother and Sal. You're a practical person who understands that circumstances sometimes dictate the direction our lives take. I know you understand although we have options, sometimes they're limited, and the best we can do is to choose the most suitable for the circumstances." Antonio patted the seat next to him.

"You know there's no right or wrong answer here. It's not as if your mother deceived your father. Angelo made his decision to marry your mother, knowing what he was getting into. Sal's circumstances, unfortunately, took his life in another direction. Angelo loved your mother very much, and I think she gave him a certain amount of fulfillment throughout his life. He says so in his letter." Antonio could see the tears brimming in Isabella's eyes, but he forged on.

"The fact your mother's heart belonged to Sal is something she couldn't help. Human beings are emotionally inept because, most often than not, we're governed by our feelings. I think what's bothering you is that you think that by accepting Sal as your father, you're betraying the man who raised you and devoted his life to you. The man you love and see as your father." Antonio wiped the tears that began to stream down her cheeks with his thumbs.

"You're doing no such thing by accepting Sal as your biological father. Angelo will always be a huge part of your life. He was there during your formative years, the more important years of your life, by choice. You are the woman you are today because of him."

Isabella listened in silence, and seeing the logic in his words, her expression softened.

"Your father, mother, Sal, you, even Carlo now, have an undeniable connection that intertwines your lives together. Like threads that tightly weave into a colourful tapestry. Although your father was the starting thread, you're the heart of it, and he wants you to weave all the threads of this tapestry together. It's why Angelo brought Sal into your life."

Antonio framed her face with his hands, kept his eyes direct on her. "The most important thing you need to know is that you are loved, Isabella, by Angelo, Maria, Sal, and me. Never doubt that." Antonio reached to wipe the tears streaming down eyes filled with gratitude. The thoughts he'd so clearly articulated was precisely the answer she'd been searching for days.

"Angelo was a great man. I only wish I could be half the man he was for you." His last words released a flood of fresh tears in Isabella, and she fell into Antonio.

Solid arms wrapped around her, she let her tears wash away the anger, confusion, and hate bottled inside her.

Chapter 32

THE METRO DETENTION Centre, a minimum-security facility, had a classic prison feel. Tall concrete walls, heavy iron doors, and the redolent smell of stale cigarette smoke and despair hung thick in the air. The doors opened at nine, and most visitors there that morning appeared to know the drill and automatically lined up single file to pass through the security check.

Michaela, however, couldn't have been more conspicuous amongst the visiting crowd. In Ferragamo boots, a tan cashmere coat, and flowing blond hair, she stood out like a sore thumb. She refused to comply with the guard's request to strip her coat, gloves, and jewelry but conceded when she was denied entry. Joe wouldn't be pleased if she didn't show up today. She'd postponed the gruesome experience for three weeks, but who could blame her? He brought on the state of affairs he found himself in, and she sure as hell didn't deserve to be there.

She still wasn't clear on why he was there for so long. On his two calls home, Joe spent most of the time cursing her or unintelligibly blathering. She didn't deserve any of it.

Reluctantly, Michaela took off her diamond ring and matching earrings, set them on the tray before being scanned. If that wasn't debasing enough, she had to submit to the degrading pat-down, which she believed, the guard enjoyed too much.

It was more than a person should endure.

Scanned and cleared, a guard motioned all visitors into the drab room with concrete walls washed in gray and barred windows. Everything in the place bore the stains of years of cigarette smoke and indifference. Michaela's nose wrinkled in disgust when stale air and rancid body odour slid into her. God knew what nasty germs had settled into her lungs by breathing that revolting air. The entire experience was objectionable, and Michaela couldn't believe she was in the midst of it. How could Joe put her through this?

Michaela eased herself down on the frayed seat mended with black tape in front of her. The last thing she wanted was to delve further into the depths of the room and expose herself to the vile people in it. God, she hated this place like off-the-rack. Why would anyone want to end up there?

There had been so many rules: don't wear this, don't carry that, show up on time. Michaela was searched, prodded, and asked insolent questions. Did she have any illegal substances on her person? Michaela didn't know what on her person meant, but did she look like the type that would? Couldn't they see she was above anyone in the room? It was the most demeaning experience.

Add insult to injury, she was thrust amongst the tawdriest people whom Michaela was certain had crawled out from the depths of the earth. The woman to her right had squeezed her shapeless body into leopard-print spandex pants and topped it with a blinding purple shirt. The side knot, for that touch of sex appeal, wasn't. Her rotund face looked as if she'd buried it into her makeup bag until she was doused with every one of its contents. Her clown-like makeup emphasized the dry, red mop of hair soaked in hairspray. The woman risked her life every time she lit a cigarette. She looked like a troll doll, and Michaela wondered how anyone allowed themselves to be seen in public looking like that.

To Michaela's left, the gaunt sliver of a woman with two missing front teeth, thin lips, hollowed brown eyes, and long, oily hair depicted the essence of the quintessential degenerate junkie-slash-prostitute. Not that she knew firsthand what they looked like. Her knowledge came from television cop shows. From her nervous twitching, Michaela concluded she was high at that moment.

Michaela's skin crawled. She hoped Joe appreciated what she was enduring for him. This wasn't what she'd signed up for when she married him. For better or worse, didn't mean visiting your husband in a disgusting jail.

"Pick up the goddamn phone." Joe mouthed from behind the Plexiglas in desperate need of a wipe down.

Joe's eyes were lucid and sharp. He had weeks' worth of facial hair, and his dark hair hung in a tangled mess around a gaunt face. He wore orange prison garb, which did nothing for his complexion or appearance, Michaela thought.

Hesitantly, and with disgust in her eyes, Michaela reached for the handset, wiped it clean before pressing it to her ear. "How are you, baby?"

"I'm in jail. How the fuck do you think I am? Where the fuck have you been? I've been in here for three weeks, and you're only showing up now." Fury edged Joe's eyes and tone.

"I've been busy." Michaela shot back with anger.

He wasn't the least bit appreciative of the unsettling experience she was enduring by being there. Not that she dare voice the thought. The last thing Michaela wanted was to set Joe's temper off. And she sure as hell wouldn't dare tell him that if the degenerates she saw today was an indication of what she'd have to face on future visits, he wasn't going to see her again until he was released. Glass between them or not, Joe was a scary man when his temper flared.

"For three weeks? What exactly has been keeping you so fucking busy that you couldn't take the time to see me or take my calls?" Joe's fisted hand banged against the table with the irresistible urge he had to throttle Michaela.

Michaela didn't see the reprimanding headshake the security guard gave Joe when she became distracted by Troll-Woman's soft moans. Grimacing, Michaela shifted further away when she deduced Troll-Woman was having telephone sex with her toothless boyfriend.

"Michaela, focus."

"Yeah, yeah. For one, your family has been nothing but a royal pain in my ass about this whole thing. They haven't lifted one finger to help. Your father refused to call Chief McNeill, and all your mother does is shed crocodile tears." Michaela considered, then shedding her tears. That always weakened Joe's temper, and right now, she needed to get him into a calm space.

"Your father wouldn't let your mother or me come to see you. He said the best thing that happened to you was to end up here. That maybe now you'd learn your lesson and that if it was up to him, he'd leave you locked up for as long as possible. He doesn't know I'm here. I just had to sneak out of the house to see you. I miss you, baby." Michaela's pouting mouth only managed to get a grunt from Joe. "Two, your new lawyer has kept me occupied with mounds of paperwork."

"New lawyer?"

"Your father said you'd become a liability to his construction business, and he no longer wants you involved with it. He's threatened to take you off the payroll and cut you off from your trust fund unless you stop—what is it that he called them?—shenanigans, and you know I don't make enough money at the bank to support our lifestyle. What are we going to do, baby?"

"Never mind all that." The whirr of the ceiling fans drew Michaela's attention. "Focus, Michaela. What's that about a new lawyer?"

"Your father pulled his lawyer off your case. He said he had more important business to focus on than you. So I got you another lawyer, but you know he's never going to be as good as Martin."

"Fine, fine, so when is he getting me out of this shithole." Joe's movements were becoming agitated.

"Stanley, that's your new lawyer, claims it'll be a few more days before he can get you out." When Michaela saw the oncoming outburst, she rushed to quell it. "I'm working on getting you out, baby. I need you home. You know. A girl can't go on taking care of herself." Michaela's lusty gaze from under over mascaraed lashes distracted Joe.

"How have you been taking care of yourself?"

"The way you like me to when you watch, and I'm thinking of you the entire time," she whispered, skimming fingers over her breasts and drawing his eyes.

They weren't brazenly exposed as they usually were, but Joe could see the mound of taut flesh and pebble-hard tips pressing against red silk. It sent his mind racing. The thought of defiling her there and then made his anger fade, and he licked his lips. At the desirous expression on his face, Michaela traced the full ruby-red painted lips with her tongue. Joe absently leaned into the Plexiglas and hit his head in the process.

The familiar look of sexual yearning in Joe's eyes strong, Michaela cupped the receiver with one hand and whispered, "Picture me bent over in front of you with nothing but my garter belt and the black lace thigh high stockings you love. You doing to me what you like best. Can you hear the slapping sound of hot flesh on hot flesh as you wildly thrust in and out of me?" Michaela caught her bottom lip between her teeth.

Joe's breath hitched, and his blood swam hot as the image flashed in his head. He could hear Michaela's greedy moans, her desperate pleas for him to move faster, harder, and he felt himself go steel hard. Now he'd have to go back to his cell and work the tension off on his own. He'd do so with images of her in the positions she was more than willing to contort herself to heighten his pleasure scrolling in his head.

Joe's mood softened, and Michaela clamped on that to keep him calm. "I want you to keep that image in your mind until the day you come home to me. We have to make up for lost time, baby." Michaela's voice thickened as he liked.

"All right," Joe murmured, with a rabid look in his eyes.

When Michaela started to drone on about some nonsense or other, Joe's eyes focused on the mouth with the suction capability of a Hoover. Michaela could suck the nails off a cement wall, and he envisioned her on her knees, hoovering him with the express aim of making him explode in her mouth. Lust bulleted straight to his loins.

"And Isabella is getting married in a few weeks, on Valentine's Day. Of course, I'm not going to the wedding, not with you being here. And…"

Michaela's words slapped Joe back to the moment. "What did you just say?"

"That I love the new song, Say Say Say, by Paul McCartney and Michael Jackson."

She was such a dolt, Joe thought. "Before that," he growled.

"Oh, Isabella and Antonio are getting married on Valentine's Day." Michaela watched his mood darken, and she could have kicked herself for mentioning it.

"When did this come about? I didn't know she was engaged."

"They just got engaged. It's a shotgun wedding." The disappointment on Joe's face cut deep into Michaela. On the sharp pain of betrayal, she angrily shot back, "Why do you care so much about Isabella getting married, Joe?"

Seeing the agitation in Michaela's eyes, Joe answered her in a carefully modulated voice. "I don't. I wondered if she went and got herself knocked up to get at his money," he said, playing the gossip angle Michaela enjoyed.

"Hmmm, I wondered about that, but it's not like Isabella to do something so reckless. She's too calculating. She has been since she was a kid. Maybe Isabella's so in love with Antonio she couldn't wait to be married to him." Michaela unbuttoned another button on her shirt to let her ripe breasts spill over for him to enjoy. "Better, baby?" Joe nodded with approval. "They've missed you. Can you taste them from there?"

"I've missed biting on your nipples, letting my tongue wander between your thighs."

"You just got me all wet." The unexpected shrill of a ringing bell startled Michaela. "What's that?"

"Visiting hour is over," Joe said, in a seemingly relaxed tone.

"Oh, okay. I'll see you in a few days, baby. By the way, I'm not wearing any underwear," Michaela commented with a wink, and for his viewing pleasure, she sashayed out with an overstated sway of her hips.

Chapter 33

THE FEBRUARY MORNING brought with it a textured sky. The sun danced between layers of blue and dark clouds, unable to make its mind up whether to come out or hide. A cold northern wind nipped the air, and in a few hours, snow threatened to blanket the city. Still, today nothing and no one was going to hamper Isabella's mood. She was getting married, and that was all that mattered to her.

Isabella dabbed a layer of red lipstick, wiped the excess with a tissue. She fussed with her hair and straightened the tiara that held the cathedral lace veil in place. The veil, a Salvatore Mesi design, was handmade with red Swarovski crystals to match the flowing floor-length gown's bodice.

Everything in place, Isabella took a slow, contemplative look at herself in the mirror, smoothed the front of the peach Mikado silk dress. Looking herself over in the floor-length mirror, Isabella couldn't imagine wearing anything else. She was glad Salvatore and her mother hadn't listened to her angry outburst when she'd turned down the offer to make the dress.

Temper flaring, she'd told her mother she wanted nothing from her or Salvatore. But as the days passed, her anger settled to a mild simmer, and the answers to the endless questions roiling in her head became apparent, and her pain faded. Now, looking at herself over in the floor-length mirror, Isabella couldn't imagine wearing anything else.

There was still a cauldron of emotions to sort through. Everything was too raw in her to embrace this new reality overnight, but opening the lines of communication with Salvatore and her mother, as Antonio persuaded, made the pain fade into a dull ache. Like it or not, Maria was her mother, and Salvatore, her biological father.

Isabella ran fingers over the waterfall of diamonds that dangled from her ears—Antonio's wedding gift. As she eyed herself in the mirror one last time, the answers to the question she'd mulled over in her head came quickly.

"Are you ready, honey?" Maria peeked her head in the room.

Maria's eyes drifting to her daughter, they welled up. The girl who'd run to her when she'd scraped her knees, whose bedside she'd sat by when she had the chickenpox, and the measles, looked like an angel. The helpless child whose many colds she'd nursed, whose scraped knees she'd mended, was no longer a helpless little girl, but a beautiful, strong, confident woman, and she was getting married today.

Pride flooded Maria like a river overflowing its banks.

Isabella had been a perfect daughter to her and Angelo, and in time, she would be to Salvatore. Maria didn't doubt when the emotional storm settled in Isabella, she'd embrace Salvatore as her father. Not because his blood flowed through her or because Isabella felt a sense of obligation to Salvatore, but because of the loving person she was.

She would miss her daughter, but Isabella couldn't be in better hands. Antonio loved her. He'd keep her safe and make her happy. That, in Maria's opinion, was the measure of a good man.

"How do I look?" Isabella turned to face her mother.

"Beautiful, that dress is the essence of you."

"It is. It's as if Sal read my mind."

Maria thought the same when Salvatore first showed her his vision sketched on paper. "He did have some help, you know," Maria said with a soft smile.

"He did. Thank you, Mama." Isabella wrapped loving arms around her mother. "What do you think Daddy would say?"

Maria snatched a tissue from the box when the tears sprang from her eyes. "He'd be beaming with pride at his beautiful daughter."

"I hope so."

Maria watched Isabella gnaw on her bottom lip, a gesture that told her her daughter was considering her next words. "What is it, honey?"

"What do you think Daddy would say to I asked Sal to walk me down the aisle?"

Maria felt something catch in her throat. This was a step to embracing Salvatore into her life. "Is that what you'd like to do?"

"It feels like the right thing to do."

Cupping her daughter's chin, Maria raised her face until their eyes met. "Then, Angelo understands your decision. All he wanted was for you to be happy."

Despite the ache, Isabella felt at Angelo's absence from her special day, her lips curved into a smile. "I know. I miss Daddy, Mama," she said, falling into the cradle of her mother's arms.

"So do I." Maria shushed and rocked her daughter, hoping this wasn't the last time. "Now, we can't have you crying." Maria dabbed at the tears on Isabella's cheeks. "You'll end up smudging your makeup, and we don't want anything happening to this perfect face."

Isabella looked into her mother's eyes. "You love Sal."

The comment surprised Maria. "I…"

"He loves you. I can see it in his eyes when he looks at you. His face lights up when you walk into the room." The words triggered a swell of guilt in Maria. Although Salvatore and her coming together was what Angelo wanted, Maria couldn't help feeling she was betraying him. "Don't feel guilty about your feelings for Sal, Mama. Daddy wanted you to be happy. He wouldn't have brought Sal into your life if he didn't. Love and understanding filled Isabella's eyes. "I, too, want you to be happy. I don't want you to be alone, especially now that I'm moving to Antonio's apartment."

"Thank you for saying so, but as much as I…"

"Love him." Isabella finished when Maria fell silent. "You can say it."

Maria lifted her hands to cover the one on her shoulders. "Salvatore and I need time to get to know each other all over again. A lot has happened to both of us over the years. We're different people now."

"I know. I just wanted you to know whatever you decide. I'm okay with it."

"Well, enough, blubbering." Maria took a seat at the dresser, and eyeing herself in the mirror, said, "Fix my makeup, and let's get you married."

THE MOMENT SALVATORE SAW ISABELLA HE stopped in his tracks. A complete hush fell in the room as a speechless Salvatore stared at Isabella—at his daughter.

She'd just come into his life, but his love for her flowed like a raging brook after a rainfall. Salvatore wanted to tell her as much. He wanted to tell her how proud he was of her, how honoured he felt to be her father, but her eyes told him she wasn't ready yet to embrace him. He feared losing her all over again.

The daughter he'd just found, whom he was getting to know, was embarking on one of her most significant life-changing moments. He'd missed so much of Isabella's life, and after today, her life with her husband took her in a new direction—away from him.

Tucking his fear aside, masking the emotional turmoil pulling him in all directions, Salvatore flashed Isabella a smile. "You're the most beautiful bride I've ever seen," he said, staring at her.

"It's all due to the brilliant dress designer." She walked over to lift the bottle from the bucket and poured two glasses. "Please have a seat." She handed Salvatore a glass.

"Is everything all right?" Salvatore watched Isabella take the seat next to him and drink deep.

"I wanted to apologize. I've been cold and distant these past few weeks. But…"

Salvatore cut her off. "You don't need to apologize. It's a lot to take in. We've sprung so much on you, years of history, secrets, and a past you knew nothing about. It's a shock to the system. I myself am wrapping my head around this whole thing."

"It is. You and I have a lot of talking to do. If you like, we can do that in the months to come. I want to get to know you."

The unexpected words made Salvatore choke with emotion. "I'd like that very much."

"You know it's going to take me some time. So I need you to be patient with me."

Salvatore nodded. "Take all the time you need."

Isabella smiled at him. "I had a chat with Mama. I want her to be happy, and you do that for her. Make her happy."

Angelo's heart warmed. Her approval and acceptance of his evolving relationship with her mother was a stepping-stone to their evolving relationship. "I will," he said, after a moment.

"I'm counting on it." Isabella paused for a moment to stall. Asking Salvatore the question was harder than she thought it would be. She sipped on wine for courage with Salvatore watching on. "I wondered how you'd feel about walking me down the aisle." Isabella felt an odd pleasure at saying the words.

Salvatore's breath was knocked out of him, and there was nothing but silence in answer. From the moment she and Antonio announced their engagement, he'd imagined their arms linked as he proudly walked her down the aisle to begin her new life. Never did he expect that dream to become a reality.

Through the blur of tears and choked emotion, his smile spread from ear to ear. "I'd be honoured to walk you down the aisle, Isabella," he said, with a watery laugh.

THE EYES WATCHED THE PERFECT LOOKING couple, hands linked and all smiles emerge onto St. Catherine's Church's steps. *The Eyes* could see Isabella's eyes glow with happiness as she looked over at Antonio. The final piece of her fairy tale had fallen in place.

Now, the final piece of *The Eyes'* long nursed hatred would also fall in place.

Chapter 34

BUSY SCHEDULES DIDN'T allow for an extended honeymoon, and Isabella and Antonio settled for the next best thing, a luxurious weekend getaway at the Windsor Hotel—compliments of Salvatore.

Exiting the elevator on the penthouse floor, without warning, Antonio swept his bride into his arms and carried her down the brightly lit hallway.

"Am I to expect to you taking such liberties now that I'm your wife?"

"Only when I mean to spoil you. Complaints?"

Lips bowed, Isabella's mouth came down to meet his. "Not from me."

"You taste so much better now that you're Mrs. Sabatini."

"I do, do I? I'll need another taste, to decide whether you taste better as my husband," Before he got a word out, Isabella poured herself into the long, passionate kiss. "Still undecided. I need to do that again."

His eyes lit with laughter. "Luckily, you'll get plenty of that tonight," he said, with a wicked wiggle of eyebrows.

Isabella's euphoric laughter had the elderly couple at the end of the hallway swirling in their direction, he with a look of envy and she with one of understanding.

"Here we are, Mrs. Sabatini. Reach for the key in my jacket pocket."

The moment Antonio threw the door open to the honeymoon suite, the scent of roses from the bouquets spearing from vases around the room met them. Unchained Melody drifted from the living room radio. Together with the flicker from dozens of candles, their flames swaying in a sensual dance turned the room into a romantic nirvana.

Antonio followed the trail of rose petals, past the living room to the bedroom where hundreds of petals in the shape of an enormous heart spread over the ivory comforter.

"Very romantic, Mr. Sabatini. I think I'm falling in love with you all over again." Isabella's gaze, slow and lazy, stayed on him when he set her on her feet.

"I wish I could take credit for all this, but I'm guessing Sal, or more so your mother did this, down to the bottle of Cristal nestled on ice." When Antonio mistook her deep sigh for disappointment, remorseful blue eyes flashed to her. "You know I would have done all this for you if I had the time. It's just that with working on Tom's project, and…"

Isabella pressed a finger to his lips. "My sigh was one of happiness, not rebuke. That they thought to do this for us makes my heart swell."

Breathing a sigh of relief, he said, "So, I'm still getting lucky tonight."

Her elbow plowed into his side. "I knew it. Now that we're married, the romance is dead."

"Never." He touched his lips to hers. Her lips were still tingling when he pulled back to say, "By the way, I didn't know your mother was such a great dancer."

Isabella watched Antonio shrug out of his suit jacket and toss it at the foot of the bed. Loosening his tie and the first few buttons on his shirt, he crossed to the bar. He was gorgeous, and all hers. The deep, penetrating warmth made her pulse gallop, and he was definitely getting lucky tonight.

"I didn't either. My father wasn't a dancer." Isabella tossed her shoes off, shed out of her dress to change into a loose, thigh-high T-shirt while Antonio poured champagne into two flutes. "Mama and Sal looked happy together, didn't they?" Her voice held a mixture of delight and sadness.

To divert her thoughts, Antonio said, "Mrs. Cropper and Tom hit it off. They were inseparable all night."

She slid into the seat next to Antonio at the couch facing the picture window. "I knew they would. It's why I went out of my way to seat them at the same table. From the moment I introduced them, it seemed like they'd known each other all their lives. I truly hope the romance carries beyond tonight. I'd like to see Mrs. Cropper have someone in her life. She's wealthy beyond her needs, and what she needs now is to enjoy the fruit of her hard work with someone special." Sipping on Cristal, Isabella's eyes flickered out the window.

A curtain of white flakes fell from the night sky and drowned the sparkling lights of a sleeping city. On the radio, Styx sailed away as Kenny's twangy voice glided in.

"Well, from what I saw, Mrs. Cropper had her hooks deep into Tom, and I sense she's not the type to surrender her prey easily." Antonio followed the comment with a cheerful laugh. "I didn't see your aunt and uncle."

"In the end, they decided not to attend, but I wouldn't have either. Although Joe was released last week, they'd be questioned, and how could you justify their son-in-law's incarceration."

"I have to confess I'm glad they didn't come. I never wanted them there." Antonio had a lot more to say on the topic of Joe's release and her family's association with a stalker, but Isabella purposely cut him off.

"From the Surprising-File, I thought your best man Marco was more Kat's type. You know they both have that shy thing going, but in the end, he and Gail ended up on the dancefloor all night."

"I caught that too, and knowing Gail, Marco will be showing up to work on Monday with a smile on his face that will last for days."

"Why do you say that?"

"Marco asked if he could use my apartment for the weekend. He didn't want to take Gail back to his. He has a roommate, and he was sure Gail was the type of woman to need thicker walls than those at his place."

Isabella burst out laughing. "I don't doubt he's right about that. The woman has no filter and no shame."

"That's what I figured. I hope they don't break anything."

When their laughter died, Isabella rested her head on her updrawn knees. "I'm glad I asked Sal to walk me down the aisle."

"It was a nice gesture. The pride and love in his eyes as he walked you down were priceless. I suspect that's a memory he will take to his grave."

"I know." Isabella thought back at the bittersweet moment as the back of her eyes stung for the father she'd lost and the father she now found.

"Let's make our memories, Mrs. Sabatini," he said, scooping her into his arms.

Chapter 35

MONDAY MORNING CAME too soon, and loading the overnight bags into the limousine for the drive home, Isabella and Antonio slipped back to the regular rhythm of their lives.

"Don't forget I'm picking you up tonight," Antonio said, sliding beside Isabella.

"I don't know when I'll be done. It'll probably be late. I have two days of catching up." Isabella reached to turn the radio on and stopped tuning when she heard Christopher Cross happily sailing away to tranquillity. "I love this song."

"Don't change the subject, and it's precisely why you should call me. I don't want you making the walk alone, late at night." Antonio gave each word separate weight.

"Don't worry about me."

"I do worry. I know how difficult it is to relinquish your independence, but promise me you'll call me. Please, Isabella." Antonio's voice sounded too tender for her to roll her eyes in frustration. "Joe's not behind bars anymore, and I'm not letting you make the walk back to our apartment alone."

At the sound of the word *our*, Isabella was reminded they were now a *we*, an *us*. Her obligation to Antonio crystalized into something more profound than she'd felt before and capitulated. "I promise I'll call you."

"I want you to be safe." Antonio brought their linked hands to his lips. "And don't forget to remind your mother I'm out of town Friday and Saturday." Antonio smothered the quick pang of guilt at leaving her alone, but he fought to grind it down.

His business venture with Tom Ritchie underway, he'd be away from time to time. Until The Café, installations were up and running, travelling was going to become routine. There was construction to supervise, personnel to hire, equipment to source, and training to complete. As much as he relied on Marco, his new regional manager, the position was too new to let him fly solo.

He managed to get Isabella to promise to stay at her mother's apartment on the days Antonio was away. He only hoped she followed through. The woman was as stubborn and unreasonable as they came.

What part of they were now husband and wife, a couple, didn't she understand? What part of whatever she did now affected him as well, didn't she get? What part of he couldn't survive without her did he need to prove over and over? Before her, his universe was a random chaotic sequence of meaningless events. She'd brought reason and purpose to all things in his life.

"Please, Isabella. Tell your mom, Sal, and Gail I'm going to be out of town. Promise me you will."

How could she turn the pleading blue eyes down? "I promise," she said, leaning to him and brushing her lips to his.

"You're not just saying that," Antonio said when Isabella's eyes went thoughtful.

She shook her head. "I was thinking of inviting Sal to dinner during my stay at my mother's."

Understanding the comment was made with a heavy heart, Antonio offered his thoughts. "I think you should do it. It's dinner, Isabella, a nice gesture. I'm…"

"We're an us now, and I want your input," she said when he hesitated.

"Are you emotionally ready for where dinner will lead?"

The limousine came to a quick stop at the red light, and Isabella and Antonio slid forward on polished leather. "No, but I need to get to know him."

Seeds of curiosity were sprouting, pushing through the hurt and anger, and Antonio reached for her hand. It was small and delicate, but as strong as she was.

"Whatever decision you make, I'll support you. I just want you to understand once you cross that line, there's no going back."

"I know, but I feel I need to bring us together to talk, don't you think?"

"That sounds like a step in the right direction."

"I know you'll always be supportive of whatever I do, so I think I should come clean."

Antonio swivelled fretful eyes in her direction. "Do I need to be worried?"

"Relax, it's nothing crazy. I've been digging through magazines looking for articles on Sal."

That she had done so spoke volumes, Antonio thought. "It's only natural you want to know about his life." Antonio raised a finger to silence her when she jumped to interrupt him. "Don't feel guilty. Angelo introduced him into your life. He wanted you to know him. He wanted Sal to play the fatherly role in your life."

Isabella's eyes absently followed the flight of passing traffic out her window as the limousine wound its way through morning rush traffic. "It still feels awkward, you know."

"So, what did you find out?"

"Not much. There were tons of articles, but all were about Carlo, who I guess technically is now my brother." She had to absorb that. "Anyway, there wasn't much on Sal. I may have to dig further back into the archives. Carlo has been the face of the company since he was a teenager. I'm not sure if it's because Sal wanted Carlo to shine or because he's a private man. The few articles I found on Sal say that although he comes from money, he built his business from the ground up with no financial backing from his wealthy family."

Like her, Isabella thought, his driving ambition to succeed was due to an overriding desire for financial security. Along the way, he thrived and proved to his family he could stand on his own two feet.

"Based on the articles I've read on Carlo, Sal's pride and love for him, a boy who may have ended up under far different circumstances if it weren't for his generosity, is heartfelt. It's that of a father. I've also found out there's an estranged family. I have grandparents I know nothing about and whom I think I want to meet. They're in their seventies, and time is of the essence. I know Sal has one sister, my aunt. She's the one helping Carlo run the company. I want to meet her and find out if there are other aunts, uncles, and cousins."

Antonio lifted a hand, ran it over her hair. "It's reasonable and normal to want a family."

"You, Mama, Michaela, and her parents are my family."

He saw her eyes glancing sideways, then away in guilt. "Look at me." She turned to meet his eyes. "We are your family, but you want to be part of something bigger. We'll start our own family soon, and you want our children to have a safety net, people they can turn to and be able to rely on."

This was why she loved this man. He knew her so well and knew the right thing to say—always.

"You have a brother and a family to get to know. Don't you think it's time you stopped speculating and digging through the archives at the library? You have the best source readily available—Sal. He's at your disposal, and I bet more than willing to answers your questions." He uncapped a bottle of water, turned it over to Isabella.

"My only suggestion is that you make sure you're ready for the answers. Sal is your biological father. That connection runs deep in your veins. Emotionally, this is a big step, but it's one Angelo would want you to make." He looked at her face, looked into her eyes. "You don't love Angelo any less if you open your heart to Sal."

Isabella pressed against him, burrowed into him. "I love you."

Chapter 36

ANTONIO SET THE tray topped with pastries, a cup of steaming coffee, and fruit salad in front of Isabella.

"Three months into our marriage, and I'm still getting breakfast in bed. If you keep this up, I'm going to end up expecting it every morning for the rest of our lives." Isabella mulled her options over before choosing a croissant and slathered it with jam.

"I, my beautiful wife, will be more than happy to serve you breakfast in bed as long as you're willing to do what you did for me last night." Antonio threw her a wicked grin and touched his lips to hers. "Mmm, strawberry. Enjoy your breakfast while I take a quick shower," he said, as she brought the mug to her lips for a jolt of caffeine.

Isabella's cup stopped midair when ten minutes later, she watched Antonio step out of the bathroom. His body and hair glistened from the shower's dampness, and he had a white towel wrapped low around his hips. He was beautiful, she thought, with a quiet sigh of appreciation as the slow, liquid warmth spread from her belly to her thighs.

Becoming self-conscious of her rumpled appearance, she tamed her hair and clamped it back with a blue scrunchie. "I must look a mess."

"You could never look anything but beautiful to me," Antonio said, massaging the wet ropes of hair dry.

"I hear the fearful married-man tone in that compliment." A smile came to Isabella's eyes as she stuffed her mouth with croissant and chased it with coffee.

"There's nothing to be fearful about when you tell the truth."

"Hmm, smooth save as always." Isabella licked strawberry jam from her lips.

"By the way, my hotel info is all there." Antonio pointed to the pad on the bedside table. "I'm sorry, but my four-day trip may extend into one week. Tom passed your sketches to Peter, his architect and eldest son. Both believe your ideas are fresh and innovative. They want to implement the changes at every location in conjunction with the installation of The Café."

"Men of good taste." Isabella set the tray aside.

"Anyway, Peter wants my input and has asked me to go along with him to survey the stores."

"This is new information. When did all this come about?"

Bare-chested, jeans still carelessly unfastened, he did a quick whirl. "This morning, we've been on the phone for a couple of hours discussing it. I know it's very last minute, but I promise I won't extend the trip for longer than I have to. One week tops."

"Don't apologize for looking after your business."

"Our business," he reminded.

"Yes, our business, which makes it that much more vital that you do what's necessary," she said staunchly.

Antonio's eyebrows drew together. "Hmm, it does, does it?"

"It does so, take all the time you need for your trip."

"I will, but until then, promise me you'll take care of yourself." Hearing her impatient hiss, Antonio said, "Promise me, Isabella."

The look he aimed at her that could have moved mountains. Having no choice but to relent to his piercing gaze, she sang out, "I promise, I promise."

"That's better. I know this is an invasion of your life…"

"You think. I don't go anywhere alone anymore. There's always an entourage with me." Her tone said how tired she was to have every minute of every day choreographed.

"Gail doesn't an entourage make, and it's only temporary. Look, I get it, I do, but Joe is out there, and although we haven't seen or heard from him in months, I don't want you to become lackadaisical and let your guard down."

Setting her impatience aside, Isabella moved to assuage her husband's concern. "I'll be careful. I'll make sure I'm always with someone, and everyone at the store has been instructed to lock the doors if they're the last ones out, and believe me, Mama and Sal won't be leaving me alone for one minute while you're gone." When Antonio's eyes registered relief, Isabella stopped offering assurances. "Tom's counting on you to make the marriage between his bookstore and your cafe a success. That's what you need to focus on."

"I don't even think Tom's giving this project a second thought anymore. Now that he and Mrs. Cropper has become an item, he's left everything in Peter's hands. Have you seen those two? They're like teenagers in love." Antonio rummaged through drawers for socks.

"They're in love, and I'm so happy for Mrs. Cropper? She deserves this."

"She does, but really to be so…" He searched for the appropriate word, "demonstrative in public and at their age."

"At their age, they don't want to delay gratification." The comment got her a cocked brow. "Her words, not mine. Take what you will from that. Either way, I think they're adorable. They're good for each other. Not to mention that Tom's so hunky and they make such a cute couple."

Antonio rolled his eyes. "Tom, hunky? Really?"

"Really." Stretching legs out, Isabella crossed them at the ankles. "Tom's a looker. That thick shock of silver hair, that dreamy accent, and for a man his age, he's fit. Or so, Mrs. Cropper tells me." Isabella gave Antonio a wink.

Antonio threw his hands, palm out, in the air. "Please stop. We've now crossed into the too-much-information territory."

Isabella snorted a laugh. "My only concern is that Mrs. Cropper now wants me to help her manage Textile Depot, and I'm not sure I can meet her expectations. You know as well as I do, no business owner thinks anyone can run their business as well as they can."

"This is new information. When did she mention this?" Antonio reached into the closet for a white shirt, shrugged into it.

"Yesterday, when she called me to let me know she and Tom were heading off to Hawaii for a few weeks, and if I wouldn't mind keeping an eye on the place."

Antonio rolled his sleeves to the elbow. "Isn't Toya her right-hand person?"

"She is, and she's very competent, but in my opinion, too inexperienced to be left in charge of everything. I'll have to get Gail over there for a few days, and I'm going to have to come up with a solution for Mrs. Cropper soon because she and Tom are scouting the island for a love palace to live in sinful pleasure. Again, her words. She giggled like a schoolgirl when she said that." Isabella snickered at the memory of Mrs. Cropper's girlish giggles. "Anyway, she alluded to the fact I should consider buying her out."

Antonio cocked his head from the closet. "That's excellent news, isn't it?"

"Merging Textile Depot with my company is a perfect marriage. My only problem is financing."

Antonio hauled out his carry-on and garment bag, set it on the bed. "If you feel the purchase is beneficial to your business, we'll work it out. Worse comes to worst, you can ask…"

"Let me stop you right there. I'm not asking Sal for money."

Antonio scrutinized his prideful wife relentlessly, twisting her wedding ring. "He'd be more than happy to help you out, especially if it's a sustainable investment."

"I know, but well, we've just started to bond, and it's working out well. The last thing I want is to bring money into the equation. I don't want to give Sal the impression I'm interested in him for his money."

"He'd never think that, Isabella. He's your father. He would do anything for you." Antonio took her silence as a sign they'd exhausted the topic. "Have you heard from Kat?" He dropped the armful of underwear and undershirts into the carry-on with no finesse for order. As she lunged into folding and organizing, Antonio wrapped a protective arm around his carry-on. "It's underwear. I got this," he said short of a growl.

Holding back the snort of laughter at the male response, Isabella sat down on the edge of the bed. This, she thought, was one of those quirks he'd warned she'd have to adapt to.

"Elsa, my friend from the modelling agency, has Kat focused on one-on-one coaching for the next few weeks. So I haven't seen or heard from her since the store opening when she rocked my runway show." Isabella watched Antonio crouch on all fours to fish for shoes under the bed.

"She's a natural. The girl is destined for a successful modelling career, and she did a great job." Antonio sat at the edge of the bed to slip his feet into tan loafers.

"She is, and she deserves it. She's worked very hard. You know, for days before the show, she'd jump from her bank job to her modelling training. Then, she'd head to the store and spend an hour practicing her walk down my runway. At one point, she was coming past closing hours and asked for a key to the store. In the end, it paid off. She won't take the credit, but because of her, I got the write-up in Vogue and Wedding Bells and why they've both offered me a five-page spread feature in next spring's issues," Isabella said, reflecting on Kat's spectacular performance.

"Don't underestimate your talent. It was your garments that caught their attention." Antonio tapped a finger to her nose as he bounced to his feet. "You, my beautiful wife, are a shrewd, talented, risk-taker just as I like my women. The way you managed to handle Fizz when she crashed the modelling show is a perfect example." Antonio swivelled his gaze toward Isabella as he threaded his arms into his leather jacket.

Conjuring up the memory, Isabella couldn't help but snicker. "You mean Gail managed to handle her perfectly. She's the one who spotted her in the crowd and was the one who had me say," she dipped into her memory. "I'd like to welcome my former employer and now a competitor to the show tonight. Her respect and admiration for my career and my artistry run so deep that she's gone as far as crashing tonight's event. Thank you for your support. Fizz Hart, everyone. Please, Fizz, stand up, and take a bow."

"She turned so red I thought she was going to self-combust." Antonio let out a booming laugh, and Isabella joined in.

"I wonder what shade she'll turn next summer when she sees three of my dresses replacing part of her line on store shelves, which in essence is my old line. I know it's only a test run in five Toronto stores, but that is a manufacturer's worst fear. At this rate, I'm right on track to take over Hart Designs in five years. I've already taken on all their best seamstresses, and Gail and I are in talks with their top salespeople. They should be on my payroll by late summer."

Antonio watched her eyes take a satisfied look. "Mrs. Cropper is right. I'd better make sure never to piss you off. I may find myself short of appendages I dearly treasure."

Isabella snorted at that. "I would never think of savaging that beautiful body, not unless you asked me to. For example, if you asked me to do so now before you leave on your week-long trip, I'd be more than happy to do so." Her smile was sly as she slid the bedsheet back.

Riding on the thrill of a pre-business trip booty call, in a matter of seconds, Antonio toed shoes off and left a tornado of clothes in his path.

Chapter 37

UNDER THE HUM of spring rain, Maria and Salvatore huddled close under the umbrella as they made the short walk from Mama's Pizza to her apartment. Over a pepperoni pizza and a cheap bottle of Chianti, they'd spent the past couple of hours talking and reminiscing.

The entertainment, an ageing accordion player, was tone-deaf. The red and white checked linoleum-topped table wobbled, but in Salvatore's mind, it had been a perfect romantic dinner. Another memorable night to add to the many they'd shared in the past few months.

After decades of separation and the life-changing events they'd endure, the idea of reviving what they once had was inconceivable. When it happened, it staggered Salvatore, and he had Isabella to thank. Without Isabella's encouragement and approval, Maria would not have allowed him back into her life so easily.

When they came together, the love they'd shared years ago bloomed in their hearts. It was as if time hadn't passed, and they were reliving the memorable summer of 'fifty-nine when two young, impulsive people fell in love.

There had been many women in his life willing and eager to be at his beckon. It was a perk of wealth, but they were shallow, plastic, needy. He'd admired those who were unashamedly frank about being interested in his bank account and did everything necessary to retain his interest, but he quickly became bored with them. They weren't Maria, and none had stirred the emotions in him she had. None had filled the void or left him feeling as complete as Maria did. They hadn't kept him even a little off-balance, as Maria did.

It never ceased to amaze Salvatore how even today, a simple vision or a thought of Maria filled him with a formidable need to be with her. The heart is fickle, it knows what it wants, and Salvatore's heart wanted Maria.

Maria would never be the type of woman who strolled into his life and left satisfied with diamonds or rubies. Not Maria. She made him work for her attention all those years ago, and this time around, she made it clear from the onset his fame and money didn't interest her. Angelo, she told him, despite her shortcomings, always fulfilled her needs. He'd made her feel special and as loved as a woman could feel.

A tall order, but if that was what it took to get Maria back, it was what Salvatore would do because his love for her was stronger now than it had been in his twenties. He was wiser now. He'd endured the tests of life, which made him realize Maria was the only woman for him, and he loved her more than he imagined a human being could love another.

The same pressing need to be with Maria he'd felt then rushed at Salvatore when they reconnected, but he knew better than to press her. Maria was a strong-minded woman who demanded more from a man than frivolous attention, compliments, or platitudes.

The man Maria committed to had to prove to her their relationship was based on love, respect, and devotion. The man who stood by Maria's side had to be there for a lifetime. That resolve pulled Salvatore to her as the moon pulls at the earth.

Now that Maria was in his life again, Salvatore was never going to let her go. Their bond was no longer tenuous. They had a daughter. They were a family, but their relationship was new, and he still had to tread carefully. Maria was as delicate as she was tenacious.

This time around, he believed they'd spend the rest of their life together. He sensed Maria, too, thought that to be the case when he took her hand to lead her to his bedroom. There was hesitation at first, but in the end, it waned, and she willingly followed him.

It was their first time together in over two decades, but the love he'd seen in her eyes twenty-three years ago was there when he'd looked into them as he made love with her now.

Salvatore's heart swelled at the memory of that night and the nights that followed since. Not only because of the love they'd shared when they came together, but at the thought, their nights together ushered new beginnings, a life together—the life he'd craved all these years.

Salvatore wished he and Maria could be together tonight. He had a strong urge to chain his arms around her to taste those petal-soft lips, but he'd have to put the thought aside. Isabella was staying at the apartment.

With Maria dry in her apartment, Salvatore started on the short walk to Isabella's store. He'd invited her to join them for dinner, but Isabella passed, claiming she had paperwork.

It was eleven, and the night was silent. Rain-soaked roads and sidewalks glistened under the reflected lights from street lamps. The night, the stars, the moon, and the rain were perfect, Salvatore thought.

Life was perfect.

Salvatore's smile over thoughts of his future with Maria and his newfound daughter faded when he found the front door to Isabella's store ajar. An eerie chill shot through him. Had he left the door unlocked? As the last one out, hadn't he locked the door behind him? Of course, he had. He wouldn't be so careless. Salvatore searched through his memory. He distinctly remembered closing the door behind him and locking it. He was certain. He'd never put Isabella in harm's way.

Or had he?

Jesus, hadn't he locked the door?

The hairs on the back of Salvatore's neck stood on end when he threw the door wide open and saw the wet imprint of a man's boot leading to Isabella's office. Panic crushed his chest, shut off his air. Salvatore's heart thundered in his as the horrifying thoughts rushed at him.

Jesus! Jesus, Jesus, he screamed in his head. The thought his carelessness might have caused Isabella harm, without regard for his life, Salvatore charged toward his daughter's office.

Ears roaring, blood pounding in his head like a warrior, Salvatore threw the door to Isabella's office wide open. Everything in the room appeared undisturbed. Files were neatly stacked, every pen in its holder, every paper clip in its place just as Isabella kept it. Still, his gut told him something wasn't right.

He sprinted toward the storeroom and office and saw no one. His panicked voice called for Isabella. There was no answer. Fear caught in his throat, and he raced down the hall. Alarm trembling in his voice, he called out for Isabella. There was no answer to his anxious cries.

Throwing doors opened, flipping lights on, he frantically ran from room to room. The showroom, the sewing, fitting, and the cutting room were empty. There was no sign of Isabella.

Salvatore ran back to Isabella's office. This time he walked around her desk. His breath hitched at the vision of his daughter on the floor, out cold. She was pale as milk.

Salvatore rushed to Isabella's side. Calling her name, he knelt beside her and checked her breathing, her pulse. Finding it normal, he said a silent prayer.

Fury replaced relief at the sight of her raised skirt. Her panties lay inches from her body. Her shirt was torn, its buttons scattered on the wood floor. The gash on her right cheek was stained red. Her hair was a tangled mess, and Salvatore could see the broken fingernails used to claw at her attacker.

Everything seemed to wash over him at once: anger, guilt, fright, remorse, and shock. The bile rose to his throat and choked him. This was his little girl.

Salvatore's eyes darkened with a murderous rage. Shaking with a fury he could almost taste, all Salvatore could think of was retribution. The need to kill, maim the person who committed this crime against his beautiful daughter seeped into his bones with the intensity of a tidal wave.

As quickly as the fury came, it died from his eyes when the screams inside his head told him to focus on taking care of his daughter.

Armed with a sudden surge of adrenaline, Salvatore bent down, scooped Isabella off the floor like a rag doll, and carried her limp body to the couch. Shrugging out of his coat, he covered Isabella before he rushed to the telephone.

He called the first person he thought of. When Maria answered, in succinct sentences, Salvatore recounted his story. Mid conversation, Maria dropped the telephone and rushed out of the apartment.

Turning anxious eyes to Isabella, he tapped her left cheek, begging her to come to. When she didn't, Salvatore fretted over the arrival of the ambulance. It was then he realized he hadn't called them.

"Jesus, Salvatore, focus, focus," he chastised himself as a new wave of guilt came stronger and harder.

Scramming to his feet, Salvatore rushed to the telephone. As he started dialling 9-1-1, he heard Isabella moaning and dropped the handset.

"I'm here, honey. Do you know who I am? Do you know where you are?" Salvatore asked, frantic, assessing her state of mind, but Isabella continued to moan Antonio's name. "Honey, I need to step away for just a moment. I need to call for an ambulance."

Her eyes rounded wide with fear. "No ambulance." Isabella struggled to get the words out.

"You're hurt, Isabella, and you've been... We have to get you to the hospital."

"No ambulance," Isabella repeated, her tone defiant.

"Honey—" The front door's musical chime distracted Salvatore. Looking up, he saw a flushed Maria arched at the office door.

Maria's heart shot up to her throat when she saw Isabella's limp body on the couch. A flash of shock overlaid the flush of anger that washed over Maria.

"Oh, my God!" Rushing to her daughter's side, Maria fell to her knees. "Isabella, can you hear me? Isabella, talk to me."

Maria's eyes flashed with anger when Isabella turned toward her and saw the gash on her cheek but bit back the emotions inside her. Instead, she gave her daughter a comforting smile when Isabella's dazed eyes opened wide enough to meet her mother's gaze.

"I'm here, honey," Maria said, running a hand over Isabella's hair. "Are you okay? Are you hurt?"

Isabella looked up at her mother through mascara-stained eyes with a mollifying expression.

Maria's heart was beating so fast she felt it would jump out of her chest, but she fixed a calming expression on Isabella's face. "It's going to be okay, baby. Let me get you some water."

"I'll get it. You sit with her." Salvatore set Isabella's head down on Maria's lap when she took his seat.

"You're hurt," Maria said, eyeing the gash stained with blood.

"I'm fine, Mama," Isabella murmured.

"Who did this to you? Was it that bastard, Joe? Because if it was, so help me God, I'll kill him," Maria said, with a maternal fierceness that surprised even her. "When the hell are the ambulance and police going to be here?" Maria demanded when Salvatore walked back into the room.

"No ambulance. No police." Isabella looked up to her mother with an unwavering gaze

"But, honey, you need to go to the hospital. We need to report this to the police." Maria raised the glass of water to Isabella's lips, but she waved it away.

"No. We don't." Isabella's voice was firm.

"I can call the chief of police right now. I'll ask him to keep this quiet," Maria said, understanding Isabella's need for privacy.

"No chief of police, no ambulance. Promise me you will call no one. Promise me, Mama."

Maria didn't answer right away, but when Isabella's piercing eyes demanded assurance, she relented. "All right, I promise," she vowed, not wanting to upset Isabella any further as her mind circled the thought she wouldn't allow whoever did this to her daughter to get away with it.

"Take me home, Mama." Isabella's pleading eyes arrowed straight into Maria's heart, and she bit back the tears.

"Of course, honey. Salvatore and I will help you back to our apartment, and we're not letting you out of our sight. Not until Antonio gets back."

At the mention of Antonio's name, Isabella's heart began to thud in her throat. With tears spilling down her blood-smeared cheek, she said, "Antonio must never know. You and Salvatore must promise me Antonio will never be told about this."

"But, honey."

"Antonio must never know, Mama. You and Salvatore must promise never to tell him or anyone about this."

Only when Maria and Salvatore nodded did the panic ease out of Isabella's eyes.

FULL OF ARROGANT ENJOYMENT, THE EYES watched the scene unfolding across the street. Arms wrapped over Salvatore and her mother's shoulder, *The Eyes* watched Isabella struggle to walk to the apartment. *The Eyes'* mouth twitched.

Today, *The Eyes* thought was sure to come between Isabella and Antonio. It would put an end to the torment

The Eyes had endured all these months by watching over the utopian life Isabella stole.

Chapter 38

FORCING HERSELF TO look into Isabella's haunted eyes, Maria tended to the cut on her cheek. Fortunately, it was superficial and didn't require stitches because Isabella remained insistent on not seeking medical help or involving the police in the equation.

Maria wiped, sterilized, and taped. Isabella said nothing, and Maria fell into silence with her. Now wasn't the time for questions or rebuking. Isabella was in shock and needed time to process. What Isabella needed was rest to calm her nerves and mind. And she'd get that calm in the familiar and comforting surroundings of pink splashed walls and the collection of stuffed animals from her childhood.

After talking her daughter into taking a sedative to help her sleep, with Maria by her side, Isabella slipped into sleep.

For a long while, sitting at the edge of Isabella's bed, Maria held her daughter's hand, watched her, and listened to the rhythmic rise and fall of her breaths as she slipped into sleep. Colour had flooded back into Isabella's face, and aside from the gash running along her right cheek, there were no visible scars. Knowing her daughter as she did, Isabella wouldn't admit to others, and without medical or police involvement, there would be no proof.

The visions of Isabella's attack came at Maria like bullets. As the images roiled in her head, it fueled hate and anger and brought tears. Isabella hadn't pointed the finger at Joe, but Maria sensed in her bones that he was responsible. The drunken, soulless sonofabitch was responsible for soiling her daughter and stealing her innocence.

The strangling feeling at Maria's throat made it almost impossible to breathe.

The physical scars would heal in time. The emotional ones would seep deep into Isabella's soul, immerse themselves in her mind and stay with her tormenting her for all her life.

A hot fury spread through Maria—at herself. She allowed this to happen. She didn't protect her child, as a parent should, because she was too distracted with her own life. She shouldn't have left Isabella alone at the store even after she insisted she and Salvatore keep their dinner date.

She should have stayed with her daughter when she'd told her she had mounds of paperwork to go through. There were so many should-haves, could-haves coming at Maria she hadn't seen—or bothered to notice.

It was too late for all that now. Her daughter was scarred and broken, and all Maria could do was apologize.

WATCHING MARIA STROKING ISABELLA'S CHEEK AS the tears streamed from her eyes made Salvatore's heart squeeze tight. The sight made his guilt come in unrelenting waves, and his mood blackened darker than it already was.

Salvatore understood Maria's tears were not shed solely out of sadness for the daughter she watched in sleep but out of remorse.

The thought of the two most important women afflicted with an undeserved pain and an emotionally harrowing memory that scarred both for life made his stomach clench. He wanted to punch his fist into the wall, into something hard that would damage and bloody it.

The strangling feeling this may have been his fault choked Salvatore. He'd been wracking his brain all night, going over the angles. Did he lock the front door when he left to pick Maria up? No matter how he spun it in his head, it came back to yes he had, but there was no sign of tampering with the lock or damage to the door.

The cold prickle of fear stabbed at Salvatore like sharp needles. There was no one else to blame for the consequences of his carelessness but him.

Salvatore closed his eyes, gave it a minute for the storm of emotions to settle. With a clearer head, he cleared his throat to get Maria's attention. "I'll keep watch over Isabella. You should get some rest," he said, from the bedroom door when Maria's eyes rose to him.

Maria shook her head. "I want to stay with her. I need to be by her side when she wakes."

"She won't be waking up for some time. The sleeping pill knocked her out. You grab a few hours of sleep. You'll need to be rested if you're going to look after her when she wakes."

Maria lifted her hand to cover the one on her shoulder. "All right, if you promise to come to get me the moment she wakes."

"I will, the moment she opens her eyes." Salvatore helped Maria up and, aware of her need to be comforted, wrapped his arms around her.

"Why, why would anyone do this to our perfect daughter? She doesn't deserve this." Maria pressed her face into Salvatore's chest and let herself cry.

"Shhh, we'll talk later. What you need right now is some rest." Salvatore steered her to the bedroom.

Emotionally and physically drained, Maria fell asleep within minutes of her head hitting the pillow. Salvatore covered her, and with a kiss to her forehead, closed the door to the bedroom.

After checking on Isabella, he made his way to the kitchen and dug out the Chivas Regal bottle. Pouring himself two fingers, Salvatore took the drink in too quickly for pleasure, winced when the alcohol hit him. The drink gave him just the right amount of kick he needed. Pouring liberally this time, he refilled his glass and crossed to the living room sofa where he sunk his weary body.

Eyes fixed out the window. The storm that had threatened to come all evening struck minutes earlier. A thick curtain of rain fell out of a darkened sky, beating hard against the window. Startling rumbles of thunder rang loud as lightning cut through the darkened sky.

Tapping his finger on his glass, Salvatore contemplated calling Antonio. He soon enough pushed the thought aside. He'd speak to Isabella first about telling Antonio everything. Hopefully, when her mind was clear, she'd be able to think straight and decide to bring Antonio into the fold and press charges against that animal.

Salvatore wondered why Isabella insisted on keeping the incident quiet. He didn't believe it was for fear of losing Antonio. There was no doubt in Salvatore's mind Antonio would never turn his back on Isabella, even after such a personal violation.

A personal violation on his little girl, Salvatore thought, tightening his grip on the glass. The feeling of needing to strike something, to break something to pieces, was back, but he cast it from his mind.

His thoughts back on Antonio, Salvatore concluded Antonio loved Isabella, and nothing could ever come between them. Knowing Antonio as well as he did, Isabella's experience would only bring him closer to her.

With that calming thought, Salvatore closed his eyes to rest them.

IT WAS FIVE A.M. WHEN SALVATORE heard Isabella stirring in her bed. He shot up from the sofa and rushed to her side. Hazel eyes looked down at Isabella from rimless glasses. At the sight of the eyes shadowed with fear and the tears that streamed down from them, his heart ached.

Taking his daughter into his arms, Salvatore pulled her closer, soothed with a fatherly touch. "Shhh, it's all right, honey. You're safe now," Salvatore whispered.

Wrapped in the comfort of her father's arms, Isabella let herself cry. When she had no more tears to shed, she said, "Mama?"

"She's asleep. How are you?"

"I want to talk to you."

"Okay, let me get your mother?"

Before Salvatore could get to his feet, Isabella nudged him down. "No, I want to talk to you alone. Mama won't listen to me as I know you will." Isabella closed her eyes briefly. "Antonio must never find out about this," she said with a direct gaze.

"Honey, Antonio needs to be told. If you're scared of him not understanding, you know he would never turn away." Salvatore assured.

Isabella let a beat of silence hang. "I'm afraid of what he'll do to Joe," she said, for the first time admitting Joe was her attacker. "I'm afraid he'll kill him."

A stunned look came with shock. "Why would you think that?"

"He's said as much. I saw the hatred and contempt for Joe in his eyes the first time he beat him up." Goosebumps rippled on her skin at the memory.

"Honey, they're words people say in anger. I don't think he meant…"

"He'll kill him if he finds out what he did to me, and I can't stand to lose him. I don't know how I'll survive this without him in my life. I need Antonio now more than ever."

Her emotions fear, pain, and angst, a sense of loss became his then, and all Salvatore wanted to do was take it all away. "That's why you didn't want me to call the ambulance or the police?"

Eyes downcast, she pursed her lips. "I don't want anyone involved. I don't want anyone knowing about this."

All Salvatore wanted to do was comfort her then, do as she asked, but he was her father and responsible for her well-being. "Honey, we need to report this to the police. You have a restraining order against Joe, and the repercussions will be great for him."

"I won't be pressing charges. I need you to promise me this will remain between you, Mama, and me." Isabella's face was cool, her gaze unyielding. "Promise me you won't say anything. Promise me you'll talk Mama into keeping this quiet."

A thundering silence fell, and the only sound in the room was the battering rain against the window. As much as Salvatore questioned Isabella's decision, he understood her fear of losing someone she loved. Salvatore understood that Antonio's absence from her life when she most needed his emotional support was tantamount to abandonment and rejection, affecting her healing process.

The sheen of tears on Isabella's eyes, against his better judgment, swayed him to agree. "I promise, and I'll speak to your mother. However, you need to promise that whenever you need to talk about this or need a shoulder to cry on, you'll turn to your mother and me, if necessary, a professional. I don't want you keeping this bottled up. We'll be here whenever you need us." Salvatore searched Isabella's face for an answer.

"I promise."

Chapter 39

MARIA'S EYES FIXED wide in shock, she closed her bedroom door behind her. "Why would you agree?" she said, in response to Salvatore's promise.

The quivering waves of sadness and pain that filled Isabella's teary eyes flashed at him. "She begged me, Maria."

"She's young and scared."

"Whether she's scared or not, I promised Isabella, and I can't go back on my word. I've just started to build a relationship with her, and I can't compromise her trust in me at this point." Salvatore paced the room to burn nervous energy.

Maria laughed bitterly at that. "Well, I can. I'm her mother, and I know what's best for her."

"And I'm her father." Salvatore was quick to remind.

"It's not a minor crime, Salvatore. She's been…" Maria couldn't bear to say the word, let alone think it had happened to her flesh and blood.

At Maria's hesitation, Salvatore felt the punch to his stomach, and the anger sprang hot to his throat. His little girl was assaulted. He'd drive his fist right through the wall if Maria weren't there.

A fit of smouldering anger rose in Salvatore to a point he never thought imaginable. He was a religious man, but at that instant, the rage coursing through Salvatore, he wished Joe a violent, painful death. Worse, he wanted to be the man to cause it. Unfortunately, that wasn't an option in a so-called civilized world where a predator was allowed to roam free until he committed the vile act of assault on an innocent woman, and her only recourse was to disrupt her life.

"Don't you think I know that?" The sting of guilt in Salvatore's voice carried across the room.

"Then why would you entertain her ludicrous request?" Angry eyes demanded an explanation.

Salvatore pinched the bridge of his nose as the pounding headache began to throb behind his eyes. "Because…"

"Because why, Salvatore?"

"I gave her my word, Maria."

"You can't always give in to a child. We're the adults, the parents who are supposed to be wiser, know better. That's not what a father does, Salvatore." Maria's comment left him feeling slighted, and he turned injured eyes out the window.

Trees, like his pride, were weighed down with the rain hammering at them all night, and the air carried with it the pungent smell of wet earth.

"I lost my daughter once. I'm not losing her again. This is what she's asked me to do for her, and damn it, Maria, I'm doing it." The words came out harsher than he'd intended.

She'd hurt him; hurt his pride and heart. "I'm sorry for lashing out. It's just this whole thing has me rattled."

"I know." Salvatore took her hand in his. "I'm sorry too for lashing out. It's just that…"

"What is it, Salvatore?"

He lifted a frustrated hand, ran it over the thick mop of silver hair. "I think this is my fault."

Maria whirled on him. "Why would you think that?"

"I think I left the door unlocked," Salvatore blurted out.

Maria stiffened. "What are you saying?"

"I've racked my brain over this, turned it over in my head repeatedly, and the only conclusion I come to is that I left the door unlocked. There was no sign of break and enter. How else would Joe have gotten in? It's my fault. I let this happen." Tears blurred his vision. "What kind of a father am I that I didn't protect my daughter from something like this?"

Anger clawing at Maria all over again, she wanted to strike out and would have if his voice hadn't sounded sapped, and his cheeks weren't stained with tears.

Maria felt exhaustion claim her. "It's not your fault, Salvatore. I don't believe for a moment you would have been so careless to put your daughter in danger."

"Did you hear what I said, Maria? There was no damage to the door. Joe just walked in."

"There's another explanation for this. There has to be. Isabella made it a point to walk through the store every night after everyone left to check all doors were locked. I'm certain she did it tonight."

"You think so?" Salvatore said with the prospect of hope in his voice.

"It's one of the procedures I put in place and enforced. This is not on you."

Grateful eyes tilted to Maria, and he laid a hand on her cheek. "Thank you for saying so."

Eyes tender in apology gazed at him. "I didn't mean to say you're not a good father."

"I know."

"We need to find another solution to this problem while keeping our word to our daughter. We need to make Joe disappear from her life."

"I already have," Salvatore said, without a second's hesitation.

Chapter 40

THE STAFF GONE for the day, Maria and Salvatore sat across from Michaela in Isabella's office. Looking stunning in a white silk suit, Michaela studied Salvatore and her aunt from long-lashed blue eyes.

"It's nice to see you, Auntie Maria. It's been a long time since we last spoke." Michaela let her eyes rove the office.

Eyes cocked in appreciation at the stylish décor. Straight lines, polished wood, leather, and framed pencil sketches on the wall came together nicely, she thought. Michaela had to admit Isabella had a tasteful eye. If it were her office, the only adjustment she'd make was to make it larger. If she had the money Isabella had, she'd flaunt it at every turn. After all, wasn't that what money was for?

"This isn't a social call, Michaela," Maria's tone was audibly ungracious.

"Oh." Michaela's smile waned into confusion. "What can I do for you?"

Salvatore stepped in. "We want you and Joe to leave the country by the end of the week," he said plainly.

Michaela turned blue eyes in Salvatore's direction. "Excuse me. Why, why would I do that?"

"Joe, your husband, assaulted Isabella a couple of days ago." At Maria's snapped words, Michaela made a noncommittal sound.

"And unless you and Joe leave the country by the end of the week, we'll be turning him over to the police." There was a furious edge to Salvatore's spat words.

Michaela's face flushed the colour of her ruby-red lips. "How dare you insinuate such a thing of my husband?" She sprang to her feet in one fluid motion. "If you truly believed Joe assaulted Isabella, you would have already turned him in."

With a rage that dug deep, Maria started to tell Michaela of Isabella's bedridden state since the attack but opted not to. Only a mother could understand the feeling of utter helplessness that swamped you when watching your daughter cry herself to sleep at night or seeing how fearful she was of everything, how much she hurt.

"Sit back down, Michaela." Maria didn't raise her voice, but the hardened look on her face made it plain to Michaela she better do as told. She sat. "We haven't turned him in as a favour to Isabella," Maria said, struggling to contain herself as the image of Isabella's limp body flashed in her mind.

"Why would Isabella not press charges or turn Joe in if he assaulted her? Well, tell me?"

"We don't have to explain ourselves. You're married to a belligerent, dangerous alcoholic, who's hurt Isabella, and whether you like it or not, I'm telling you that you and Joe are leaving the country by the end of the week. You can both move to hell for all I care, but you're leaving and taking that useless excuse of a man with you." Maria's gaze was unyielding, and Michaela knew she meant every word.

"This should cover your travel expenses and the transition to your new home." Salvatore handed Michaela a bank draft.

Michaela's eyes darted to the dollar amount. "If you think this pittance is enough to entice me to admit my husband's involvement in your ludicrous allegation and pack up and start fresh elsewhere, you're sadly mistaken." She let pieces from the torn bank draft fall on the hardwood like confetti.

Maria's eyes bore into Michaela. The woman before her wasn't the person she knew, the girl she'd babysat as a child, the niece she'd loved like a daughter. In Michaela's blue eyes, Maria saw a ruthless, greedy, unfeeling woman. It was a dark, ugly side she hadn't seen before.

Salvatore's jaw clenching, he asked, "What do you want?"

"Well," Michaela let the sentence hang to keep him just a little off balance. She wasn't about to settle for a measly seventy-five thousand dollar one-time deal. "You're asking me for a lot, and the way I see it, one hundred thousand dollars, yearly, indefinitely, sounds about right," Michaela said, her tone overflowed with confidence.

Having seen the Mesi name on wine labels and fashion apparel through Italy during her honeymoon, Michaela did her homework. The old man was loaded. Joe's family wealth was chicken feed compared to the old man's.

Whether Joe did what they said or not was of no consequence to Michaela. This was the answer to her dried-up bank account. Besides, a few million dollars wasn't going to break the old man.

"Fine," Salvatore said, without a second thought. The shock to his swift agreement didn't register on Michaela's face, but she immediately regretted not asking for more.

"Before I hand the cheque over, you and Joe will sign this legal, binding agreement stating you will never set foot in Canada again. If you or Joe even thinks of breathing the same air as Isabella, the agreement becomes null and void, as do the payments. There are other clauses, including that if word of the ... incident gets out, the agreement terminates, and all money paid out must be repaid with interest. Understood?" Salvatore's piercing eyes remained on Michaela.

Michaela bit her bottom lip to control the shudder of triumph bubbling inside her. "I'll sign it. Joe will too. He does what I tell him," she said, with a smugness Maria wanted to slap off her face.

Rising to her feet, Michaela picked up the contract off the desk and tucked it into her Hermès tote. "I'll have it back to you first thing in the morning. Have my cheque ready." Crossing the room, Michaela stopped at the doorway. Her eyes fixed on Maria and Salvatore. "This is in no way admitting Joe did what you say, but you have my word he and I will be gone by the end of the week," she assured before walking out the door.

Stunned, Maria shook her head in disbelief. "I don't recognize that girl."

"I'm just glad this is over and done with. Joe will be out of Isabella's life, and she will at least be able to live her life without fear."

Maria curled her fingers around his wrists to hold him when he began to stand. "This could end up costing you millions."

Salvatore looked at Maria. "It's only money. Isabella's ... our daughter's well-being is priceless to me."

Something inside her burst like sunlight, and leaning in, she lay warm lips on his. "You're an excellent father."

The words filled Salvatore with profound happiness.

Chapter 41

February 2007

TWENTY-FIVE YEARS later, sipping cappuccino on the patio of the out of the way Milanese cafe, Isabella reflected on her life.

The years that followed that horrible day were difficult ones. Putting the assault behind was as big a challenge as carrying the lie with her all these years. In due course, with Maria and Salvatore—whom in time became Dad—by her side, Isabella was able to move past it and get on with her life.

After Antonio's return from the Vancouver trip, he saw the physical bruises on Isabella's body and detected emotional changes in her. He chalked it up to the terrible shock she endured when she lost her footing and fell down the stairs at Maria's apartment. A brush with death tends to have that effect on a person, he reasoned.

Many times Isabella came close to tell Antonio about that horrible night. On several occasions, she almost told him everything, but fate intervened every time—or so she believed. In Isabella's mind, not telling Antonio proved to be the right course of action when she saw the love in his eyes for the beautiful baby girl she gave birth to nine months later.

When Isabella watched the joy in Antonio's eyes the first time he held Bianca and his excitement at becoming a father, she couldn't sever the bond with a questionable reality. To cast doubt and bring such ugliness into Antonio's and her daughter's life wasn't an option. On the day she gave birth, Isabella decided she'd take the secret of the worst night of her life to the grave.

Isabella had misgivings about Bianca's origins, but as her beautiful daughter grew older, she saw Antonio in her eyes, her smile, and there was no doubt in Isabella's mind Bianca was his child. That made it easier for Isabella to get on with her life and put the past behind her.

Still, the anger, pain, and fear of her violation stayed with her. No matter how she tried to compartmentalize that ugly time of her life, it wasn't something she could altogether forget. Regardless, Isabella believed she'd made the right decision. Keeping that vile time of her life from permeating her life, her marriage, her family was the right thing to do.

"Would you like another cappuccino, *Signora* Farfalla? I make you a nice hot cup to keep you warm," Giorgio offered, wondering why she insisted on sitting out on the patio in February.

Isabella folded the morning's newspaper and tilted her gaze to the man who'd served her countless cappuccinos over the years. "No *grazie*, Giorgio."

"My wife, she say molto grazie for the Farfalla leather—*come si chiama*?—I think she call it a tote." Giorgio draped the dishcloth over his shoulder after wiping her table. "She go crazy when she see it. Crazier than when I ask, she marry me."

"I'm sorry." Isabella bit back a smile.

"No, you no be sorry. She get very happy after." The lines on his face creased with a wide smile, and he winked at Isabella.

At that, Isabella let out a soft rolling laugh. "Well then, I'm glad she liked it."

"Are you sure you no come inside where it's warmer?" Giorgio raised his chin to gesture to the empty tables around her to make his point.

"I'm fine out here, Giorgio. It's going to get warm soon." Slipping her gloves off, Isabella looked up to the morning February sun beginning to pour hot and bright through the bad-tempered clouds drifting away.

Giorgio shrugged his shoulders. "*Va bene*. You wave to me if you need anything. I keep an eye on you."

Alone again, Isabella relished in her solitude. Savouring her cappuccino and enjoying her morning me-time Isabella thought about her life, focusing on how complete it was.

Her thoughts drifted to the man whose selfless act set her life in the course it took. Isabella often wondered, as she often did, that if Angelo had not written the letter to Salvatore, how her life would have turned out.

There was a tear in her eye as the words etched in her memory fisted around her heart. Not a day went by when thoughts of Angelo didn't fill her mind. Angelo was gone for almost half of her life, yet the impact he made during his short life was meaningful. Isabella would carry his memory in her heart forever.

Isabella hoped Angelo was proud of what she'd accomplished. She had a beautiful family, a loving husband in Antonio and a wonderful daughter and son in Bianca and Christian. She had a thriving business, and her brand was globally recognized. All she'd done and everything she'd achieved was partly because of him.

Isabella crossed one slender leg over another and, taking a long sip of her cappuccino, eyed her surroundings. Centuries-old cobblestone roads, the sight of spectacular palazzos, and the fantastic food people from all over the world travelled to Milan for, in Isabella's mind, made the city as perfect as it was.

Isabella fell in love with Milan the moment she set foot in the ancient city years ago. Not because of its international recognition as one of the world's fashion centers or because it was where she drew her inspirations for the Isabella Farfalla collection found at her stores across the globe. Isabella loved Milan because it was where she'd met her newfound family, who'd warmly welcomed her.

Isabella, Antonio, and the children made the trip to Milan twice yearly for fashion week. Antonio came for the culture and ambiance, which Milan had plenty to offer. Although much of his time was spent looking for the next new concept to provide The Café franchisees, now numbered five hundred across North America. Bianca came because she was as passionate about Milan as her mother was. Unlike her mother, though, Bianca set aside time to indulge in her favourite pastime, eye-shopping—as she called it—for Italian men. Her twenty-two-year-old son, Christian, tagged along for one reason, the Italian women he claimed he couldn't live without.

In the end, though, they travelled to Milan for the sole purpose of supporting Carlo when his collection walked down the runway at Milan Fashion Week. Isabella, Antonio, Bianca, and Christian were always front row center as Carlo's collection, catwalked by supermodel—and wife of fifteen years—Kat LeBlanc, made its way down the runway during the weeklong fashion extravaganza.

After the show, tradition dictated, the generations of Sabatini's and Mesi's, along with Tom and Rita Ritchie, Gail and Marco, their five rambunctious children, Kat and Carlo, and their twins congregated at Salvatore's and Maria's Villa on *Via Giancinto Collegno*. The home Salvatore gifted Maria on their wedding day twenty years ago served as their winter home and was the bi-yearly family gathering venue.

Everyone came together at the villa as a celebration of family and, in honour of Carlo, who, as an accepted Mesi, never failed to bring pride. Even Granddad Mesi, in time, grew to respect and appreciate Carlo's talent for his artistic designs and worldwide recognition.

There would be tons of food, which Maria and the Mesi women spent days preparing. There would be loud arguments, criticisms for anything and anybody, and gossiping, so much gossiping. But at the end of the night, everyone made sure to log the date of the next family event into their calendars. Everyone's life revolved around it.

When Isabella's cell phone rang, her immediate reaction was to scowl at the intrusion. She'd forgotten to turn it off, and the constant ringing was imposing on her quiet morning me-time. Isabella reached into her purse to shut it off. It was then she heard the man's voice.

"Isabella?" The subtle scent of her perfume hit him, nagged at his senses, and emotions long buried stirred and rushed at him with tidal wave force.

Isabella turned, and he caught sight of her face. She was as beautiful now as the last time he'd laid eyes on her. Hazel eyes aged as fine whiskey mesmerized him as they always had. Her face was as delicate and beautiful as he remembered with few traces of years gone by. He was pleased. It meant she'd had a happy life, full of love—what he'd wished for her.

Squinting against the blinding sunlight, Isabella tried to bring the man into focus. Never taking his eyes off her, he watched her fish through her purse for her sunglasses.

"May I join you?" The man's voice was gentle, his tone soft and familiar, but as deep as she searched in the recesses of her mind, Isabella couldn't place it.

"I'm sorry, do I know you?" Isabella flashed a quick smile that left him staring at her. It was as he remembered it.

"Yes," was the response. Just then, a gust of wind rushed the chestnut waves, making it swirl into the air like wings. He thought she looked like an angel.

"I'm sorry, this sun is strong, and I can't see a thing," she said, perching gold-rimmed Mesi's on her nose.

Shaded eyes now met the man's face, and although decades had passed since she'd last seen him, Isabella immediately recognized the face. The distinct jolt of panic sent her heartbeat racing and made her chest constrict.

The man before her was Joe Smith.

Although they couldn't have been more different for each, memories with painful intensity flashed to both of them.

Joe had no resemblance to the drunken, terrifying man she came to fear. His coal-black eyes were vibrant and serene. The anger she so vividly remembered was replaced by a harmonious expression. The dark wavy hair had wisps of gray woven through at the temple, and he sported a fashionable stubble. He looked stylish in the black suit she recognized as a Carlo Mesi.

It had been a long time since she'd laid eyes on him, but there was no doubt the brilliant eyes staring down at her were those of a changed Joe Smith.

Appearances, however, offered no assurances, and Isabella nervously looked around her for some form of protection.

Although Joe couldn't blame Isabella for her reaction, it stung deep, and he almost reached out for her hand to calm and soothe. The repulsed expression that filled her face drove him to thrust his hands deep into his pants pockets.

"I'm not here to hurt you, Isabella. I just want to talk." Joe assured, smiling a little, hoping to placate her visible anxiety.

A lifetime of buried anger bloomed into hate, resentment, and fear, and she snapped, "Don't come any closer, or I'll scream for the police."

Joe detested himself for being the reason for her angst. He imagined the darkness that had filled her heart and soul all these years. He sensed the anger and hate she harboured for him were in her blood. He presumed it went bone-deep.

"Please, Isabella, I just want to talk," Joe repeated, watching her nervously shift in her seat.

"There isn't anything you can say that I want to hear." Isabella's voice was hard as steel, cold as a polar vortex.

All those years ago, Joe stole her dignity, set her life in turmoil. He snaked his way into her mind, stole her trust and faith in humanity, and everything she believed in. For a short time, the aftermath of his attack drained her of her creativity, which affected her business. Worse, Joe nearly destroyed her relationship with Antonio—the one perfect constant in her life. That was when Isabella decided to reclaim her life by doing the unthinkable.

She forgave Joe.

She forgave him, even knowing deep down he took a part of her she'd never get back. Forgiving Joe for the ugliness he'd brought into her life and tearing the fabric of the life she'd built saved her. It took a lot of soul searching and a strength she didn't know she had, but she did it.

Forgiveness was the only way Isabella saw to find peace within herself, to hang on to everything dear to her. It had been the most difficult thing she'd done, but once she navigated through that hurdle, Isabella was able to get on with her life.

That Joe had inexplicably disappeared from her life after the incident contributed to her healing. She often wondered if Salvatore and Maria had anything to do with Joe's sudden departure since both assured her, with definitive certainty, she never had to worry about him again. A few times, Isabella thought to question Salvatore and her mother, but fearing what the response might be, she thought it best to let sleeping dogs lie.

Joe watched Isabella bolt to her feet. "We have nothing to talk about." Her need to get away, to put distance between them, was palpable.

Shame washed over him, and he rushed to say, "I want to apologize for … everything, Isabella. I want to tell you I never meant to hurt you. I'd never do anything to hurt you, Isabella. I…" There was a moment's hesitation. "I loved you, Isabella."

The words, the tone in which they were delivered, sent a flush of shock in Isabella, and she stopped, rooted to the spot.

"I loved you, Isabella." This time the words floated from Joe like a melody behind her stiffened back. "I would never have caused you harm. You have to believe me. I haven't stopped blaming myself for what I did to you. I'm so very sorry I hurt you and caused you so much pain, Isabella," Joe said with a gleam of moisture in his eyes. "I … want to apologize. I know it's not much, but I want to tell you how sorry I am. All I want to do is talk, to explain, Isabella." The words were said with remorse, and she heard the sincerity in Joe's tone.

Joe's words spinning in her head, he watched her raise eyes to the sky and let the warmth of the sun fall on her face as she contemplated. After a long while, Isabella turned. The expression she saw on his face was one of regret, pain, and remorse. In Joe's eyes, she saw a genuine plea for forgiveness.

Pouring over the idea, some more Isabella debated what to do. Giorgio's smile coming at her from behind the cafe window swayed Isabella to take the chair Joe pulled out for her.

"May I get you a coffee?" He slid into the chair across from her.

The silence stretching seconds longer, Joe went ahead and waved Giorgio over, and sang out an order in melodic Italian for two espressos. "It's taken me a long time to muster the courage to face you, Isabella," Joe confessed when they were alone again.

The silence hovered between them before Isabella gathered the courage to ask the questions she'd wanted to pose all these years. "Why did you do it, Joe? Why did you need to cause me so much pain? Why did you need to steal a part of my life?" Her nerves coiled tight as the memory of that day surfaced from deep within to flash into her mind. "I didn't deserve what you did to me."

Seeing the pain that filled Isabella's eyes, the guilt weighing him down all these years came in waves. "No, you didn't deserve any of it, and I'm so very sorry I caused you so much pain and filled your life with such ugliness, Isabella. I've lived with the guilt all these years."

Isabella stared hard into Joe's eyes. "I wish all I had to deal with was guilt. You stole my innocence, my confidence, my courage, my sanity. You broke me. I was broken for a long time."

She seemed so fragile, so small, Joe thought, and the guilt rolled into him like a thick fog. "It's why I need you to allow me to tell you my story. The entire story."

Angry, piercing eyes fixed on Joe. "There's no story you can tell me that can justify what you did to me."

Joe went silent as Giorgio approached the table with their coffees. When they were alone again, he waded into what he'd waited to tell Isabella for so many years.

"After I was taken to jail, my father put his foot down. He'd had enough of my shenanigans. He told me I was an embarrassment to the family and negatively affecting his construction business. He took me off the payroll and cut me off from my trust fund, saying he would no longer finance my alcoholism. When Michaela found out, she panicked. There'd be no money to support the lifestyle she and her mother had become accustomed to, and that's when both set off to hatch the plan for me to break into your store and…"

Isabella cut him off there. "You're lying. You're making all this up. I don't believe it. They're family, and to accuse Michaela and Auntie Nina of scheming against me is …"

"The truth, Isabella."

"They wouldn't hatch such a vile scheme against me. You're looking to pin the blame on Michaela for something you did." Anger ripped through her words.

"I'm not, Isabella. Michaela was jealous of you for many reasons. She and her mother detested your success and how, in Michaela's words, 'everything came so easily to you because you stole everything.' It took me some time to figure out, but I believe the only reason she pursued me in high school was because of how I felt for you. She couldn't allow you to benefit from my wealth. She couldn't let you get a leg up on her. She married me as a last resort."

He watched the frown of confusion crease her brows.

"When she found out of your relationship with Antonio, she lost it. You see, she claimed to be in love with him. Michaela was, is, a bagful of crazy," Joe said when the awkward silence hummed between them.

"Michaela didn't know Antonio as anything other than through social contact. She was a customer," Isabella said, and Joe couldn't escape the feeling she felt as if he was concocting the whole story to absolve himself.

"I didn't know you either, Isabella, not really. You didn't even consider me an acquaintance, and yet…" Joe stopped and lowered his gaze to the dark liquid in his cup, becoming seemingly lost in it. "When Michaela and that mother of hers, you know she was the instigator of everything." Joe's expression hardened, and Isabella heard him deeply breathe in and out while counting back from ten until it softened again.

"I'm sorry. It's a calming technique. Anyway, Nina was one envious, vindictive bit … woman who fueled her daughter's greed and spitefulness. When mother and daughter found out, Antonio was sidling himself to you, and worse that he was financially supporting you, well guaranteeing your loan jealousy gnawed at their insides."

Joe explained when Isabella's brows knitted in surprise at the knowledge that Michaela's only reason for working at the bank was to have access to everyone's information. Working at the bank allowed her to keep her mother and herself abreast of everyone's finances.

Joe breathed deeply again, counted back from ten. "Anyway, when Michaela found out Antonio was helping you, the anger that seethed in her became scary. I'd never seen her like that. That's when she set out to hurt you and turned me into her conduit for the pain she wanted to inflict."

Isabella stared at Joe with a steadfast gaze of disbelief.

"From what I've pieced together, in the beginning, all she wanted to do was have me get a bit physical to intimidate and make you emotionally unstable."

The words struck Isabella with their full shock value, and as she processed the information, her throat squeezed so tight, it obstructed her breathing.

"It gets worse, Isabella."

Her eyes fixed wider. "How could it possibly get worse?"

"Things took a turn when your mother and Sal came to our wedding as a couple." Joe gave each of the last three words separate weight to stress the point.

The fact Salvatore was her father remained between Maria, Antonio, and Salvatore for the longest time only because Salvatore understood Isabella's need to make her mark in the world on her own.

"What do Mama and Sal have to do with anything?"

"If you recall, Michaela and I honeymooned in Italy. As we toured the country, she saw the Mesi name everywhere: wine bottles, clothing, sunglasses, shoes, even perfumes. It piqued her interest, and she dug deeper. Not only did she find out he owned the Carlo Mesi Couture Company, but that he was the son of the Mesi Winery magnate." He picked up his coffee, drank to wet a dry mouth.

"All that sent Michaela over the edge. She couldn't understand why, as Michaela put it, 'you and your mother had all the luck in the world.' The anger that bubbled in Michaela when it became clear of your newfound wealth burned in her hotter than the fires of hell. My family's money became chump change to her. No amount of money was ever enough to satisfy Michaela's penchant for expensive clothes and the lifestyle she thrived on. That's when she concocted the plan to…" Joe fell silent, his mouth set like stone.

"If this is true if it was all Michaela's doing, why would you go along with it?" The bile rose hot in Isabella's throat.

"I would never have been a willing participant, but you have to understand I wasn't mentally equipped to figure out she was manipulating me. I didn't piece any of this until years later, when I sobered up and got into therapy. Before then, Michaela's hold on me was one that I couldn't break from. She knew how to push my buttons. She provoked me, fueled my addiction, which made me mentally unstable, and I became even more dependent on her. I tried for months to break away without luck. I tried,

I did, Isabella." Joe set off on his backward count again and continued when he calmed down.

"I tried to get help for my alcohol addiction, which by the way, started when I got together with Michaela. But it's difficult to succeed at anything when the person closest to you, the person you trust and depend on, jeopardizes your progress at every turn. Every time I got a step ahead of my addiction, she'd tempt me with alcohol and set me back ten. She did it so often I decided to succumb to the fact I'd always be a drunk, and I gave up trying to overcome it." Joe was pleased he finally had Isabella's attention and that she was accepting his word as truth.

"Why didn't you leave?" Isabella's face now reflected genuine concern.

"I had nowhere to go. My family had disowned me. After I married Michaela, my friends all disappeared. They hated her and the person I'd become. As for her parents, well, I think that's self-explanatory."

Isabella couldn't fathom not having her loving family, who had been by her side every step of the way. She imagined the desperation Joe felt at having no one to turn to, no safety net to fall back on during the darkest hours of his life. For a brief moment, her eyes had an apology forming, but his words broke into the thought.

"What I know about that night came from Michaela because I don't remember most of it. I've spent two decades going over the events of that night in my head. One thing that stumps me, no matter how I piece it together, is how I got into your store. It was late, and your front door had to be locked."

Isabella nodded. "It was. I've often wondered how you managed to get the door open. I'd done a walk-through of the store to ensure all the doors were locked."

"In the drunken state I was in, I could barely walk, let alone maneuver something as small as a key into such a tight space as a lock. I'm almost certain Michaela unlocked it. I faintly remember someone there with me, but I can't put my finger on who it was. I was so drunk. I just know there was no way I was capable of unlocking the door on my own. Someone had to have opened it for me."

"Let's say she did open it. Where would she have gotten a key? The only people entrusted with a key were me, Antonio, Sal, Mama, Gail, and Kat, and there's no way any one of them would have surrendered a copy to anyone outside of the group."

"Wait, you had someone on staff named Kat?" The name triggered his memory. "Did she go also go by Kathleen?"

Isabella felt her stomach clench. "Yes."

Joe reached deep into his brain for an image of the woman he'd seen at his house once. "Was she a young, tall, blonde girl with large blue eyes?"

Isabella felt the sucker punch to the stomach, robbing her of breath. "Yes, but Kat would never have done anything to hurt me. She will never have given anyone a copy of the key if that's what you're insinuating. I'm the one who helped launch her modelling career. If it weren't for me, she would still be working as a receptionist at the bank."

"She worked at the bank?" With a flashback, the memories were emerging, bringing it all back. He remembered the late-night calls from Michaela to

Kathleen, the threats, the demands. "Michaela was blackmailing a Kathleen. I don't know her last name. I just know she worked at the bank alongside Michaela. She'd caught her siphoning funds from petty cash. It was a negligible amount, and she eventually replaced it. Still, by then, Michaela had gotten a hold of the information, and she was threatening to report it to the bank manager and police." The visit by Kathleen to the house was now stronger in Joe's mind. "I can tell you she came to the house to drop off an envelope for Michaela days before that night."

The mussels in her stomach tightened. "That could have been anything."

Joe cocked a brow. "It could, but Michaela could be very persuasive. I wouldn't doubt it if it was a copy of the key to your store Kathleen or Kat dropped off. There are no coincidences where Michaela's involved."

The utter shock in Isabella's eyes made him want to stop, but he came needing to tell her everything, and that's what he did.

"It took me a long time, but eventually, I learned not to underestimate Michaela. She's a venomous viper with an unrelenting bite, especially so where you're concerned. She's consumed with abnormal envy and jealousy when it comes to you. You had it all, and her life's goal was to take it away, to destroy you."

"At first, she thought she could compete with you, and she set out to match your every move, your every success. She doesn't have your intelligence, your drive. Her failure to keep up with you fed her hate and anger. When she realized she couldn't compete with you, she became crazed, batshit crazed. She made so many demands of me. Demands I couldn't meet and in time sapped my energy, my passion for life. I lost my will to live." Hate roiled inside Joe at the thought of her denigration for his inability to meet her relentless demands. Count back, Joe, he told himself.

"Anyway, I've wracked my brain thinking about that night, and no matter how I spin it, I don't think I was able to do what she told me I did to you. All I remember was passing out and taking you down to the floor with me. I remember, in somewhat of a blur, your head bouncing off the hardwood." Shoulders hampered with guilt and regret hunched.

"I blacked out, so I don't know what happened, but I can tell you I was too drunk to be … physical. I mean, when you're that drunk, a man can't…" He let the sentence trail, but she was clear on his meaning. "Every indication leads me to believe I did nothing but pass out on your office floor."

"But I was…" Isabella hesitated, searched for the suitable word, "undressed."

Joe's brows furrowed in confusion even as he fought off the shiver of disgust that crept up his spine. "Jesus. I wasn't aware you were. I don't know how. I don't recall doing that. I can tell you that I'm as certain as one can be that I didn't follow through. That nothing happened. I was just too drunk to be able to perform."

Something in Joe's eyes told Isabella he was telling her the truth.

"Isabella, please believe me when I tell you I would have never hurt you—not purposely. I was in love with you. It started as infatuation the first day I lay eyes on you in high school. You were beautiful, genuine, and smart, nothing like the other girls. My infatuation grew into love, but you didn't even acknowledge I was alive." His quiet admission dazed her.

The tenderness she saw in the dark eyes as Joe said the words ambushed her. How had she never seen what he was telling her as clearly as she saw it now? How had she misinterpreted all his actions? Actions she now perceived as those of a young, awkward, foolish, lovesick teenager that drove her to fear him.

"I never knew," Isabella said, unsure of what to say or do.

"It's history. I'm saying it because..." Joe stopped when he saw an unqualified understanding and forgiveness fill her eyes.

"I understand, Joe. I do." Isabella's voice softened, and with it, her eyes.

With the words he'd waited so many years to hear, Joe felt a peace he'd searched for this entire time flood him.

A reflective silence hummed for a full fifteen seconds before Isabella said, "Why now, Joe? Why follow me to Italy to apologize? You could have done this back home long ago."

With a glint of confusion in his eyes, Joe said, "I live in Italy. I have for the past twenty-five years. I thought you knew."

"Why would I?"

Joe sighed. "And all these years, I thought it was your doing. I should have known better. As Michaela explained it to me, Maria and Sal offered her seventy-five thousand dollars to leave the country after that night. Michaela, of course, demanded more money. And she threatened she wasn't going anywhere unless her demand was met."

Isabella's brows arched high. "Which was?"

"One hundred thousand dollars, yearly, for life."

Isabella's heart stopped. "And they agreed to it?"

"Salvatore did. He didn't even flinch. He agreed to it on the spot as long as she and I signed the contract." Joe detailed for Isabella the clauses in the agreement.

"So, if my math is correct, the two of you have collected over two million dollars." Isabella's voice came out a shocked squeak

"Although Salvatore and Maria forcing us to leave Canada was the best thing that happened to me, it was Michaela who cashed out on the deal. When Michaela moved us to Venice—she fell hard for Venice on our honeymoon—soon after, she discarded me like an old dishrag. With you out of the picture and money in her pocket, Michaela didn't need me anymore. That's when I managed to break away from her clutches."

"A few months after our move to Italy, I met a wonderful Italian woman who helped me get clean and get my life back on track. Once I got sober, I launched my own construction business here in Milan. I married her once my business took off. We've been married for fifteen years and have three beautiful children." Joe fished his wallet out of his jacket pocket and pulled out two photographs.

Isabella set eyes on the picture of a beautiful rosy-cheeked girl, no more than ten, in a pink bathing suit, dark curls flowing in the breeze, a giddy smile on her face. On opposite sides stood two older boys resembling Joe matched her cheerful smile. Isabella saw the pride in Joe's eyes as he introduced them.

"They're beautiful, Joe."

Joe grinned, pleased by her comment. "This is my wife, Francesca." Joe lovingly stared at the photo before handing it to Isabella.

She was an Italian beauty. Olive skin, a spill of long, dark curls hung below her shoulders, and thick bangs sat above her large brown eyes. Standing next to Joe in her white wedding gown, her smile was luminous.

"She's lovely."

"Inside and out," Joe pointed out with a love that was hard to miss. "She's been my rock. She supported and stood by me through my difficult years. She taught me what real love is." Joe looked at the photograph as if taking the picture into his heart before returning it to his wallet. "I'd like you to give this to Sal." Joe drew a cheque out and handed it to Isabella.

Isabella's brows came together, stunned as she read the amount. "That covers the payments Sal's made to date."

"It's my way of apologizing for what Michaela did to you and my part in it, Isabella. It's a gesture of gratitude for giving me my life back."

Although Joe understood the experience was not something Isabella could easily erase from her life, he hoped the payment reinforced not only how sorry he was but that he was a new person—the man he was.

"Thank you, Joe." Isabella's voice was subdued, and Joe understood her words of gratitude had nothing to do with the money.

"It's me who should be thanking you, Isabella." In the ensuing silence, Joe braced himself to tell her the last piece of information, which, however hurtful, had to be said. "There's one more thing you're going to have to deal with. It's what Michaela's planning to come at you with." Although he saw the exasperation in Isabella's face, he went on to detail what to expect.

"The contents in this envelope will help to prove your case. I know it's going to be a tough decision to make, but if you want to fight Michaela and win this next round, you will have to do it. Keep in mind she doesn't know you know about me, so you're one step ahead of her. If you play your cards right, you'll be able to cut her off at the knees and in the same breath end Sal's payments to Michaela forever."

Isabella reluctantly took the offered envelope and tucked it into the folds of her purse, where Antonio wouldn't find it.

"I'm glad we had this talk today, Isabella. And I hope it's done you some good," Joe said, with a hopeful expression.

"It has. Thank you, Joe. I think I'll finally be able to put that ugly past behind me for good," she said, feeling a strange sense of relief at finally saying the words with conviction.

Isabella felt as if she'd finally regained complete control of her life and sensed Joe's guilt for his actions, for the pain he'd caused her, which had weighed him down all these years, faded away at her words.

"It was good seeing you, Isabella." Joe rose to his feet.

"You too, Joe." The eyes that stared back were free of pain. Joe was pleased by that.

Lapsing into silence, Joe offered Isabella his hand, held it out until she reached across the table, and took it. His fingers curled tightly around her hand. Joe held it for a moment longer than he should before releasing it. Knowing he'd never see her again, Joe gave Isabella one last look.

With that, he turned, and Isabella watched him make his way down the cobbled road, fading in the distance until he disappeared from her life forever.

Chapter 42

IT FELT LIKE an eternity since Isabella escaped her daughter's confrontation and been holed up in seclusion at the family's Muskoka home. After three days of introspection and soul searching, she was ready to face Bianca—her entire family. Isabella was ready to reveal her secret, which had run its course and had to be told.

Meeting Joe in Milan washed away many of the emotions she'd carried for years, but there was still residual to take care of. Facing her family was the last step to cleanse herself of the lie at the heart of her marriage and family.

True love always finds its way back. Angelo's words rang in Isabella's ears.

She needed him to be right. Telling her daughter and husband she'd harboured this secret all these years was bound to set off a firestorm of emotions: anger, confusion, disappointment, and God help her, hate.

Isabella poured wine into her glass, took a long swallow.

She prayed they understood she did it out of love. Isabella prayed once the truth came out, it wouldn't burden them as it had her. Secrets, when told at such a late stage from inception, are perceived as deliberate deceptions. It changed people, embittered them, filled them with resentment and anger. Isabella prayed that wasn't the case. She loved her family more than life itself, and she couldn't stand the thought of hurting them or, worse, losing them.

Her hand tightened on the wine glass.

For now, she had to shelve her worries. Firming her lips in determination, Isabella made her way to the kitchen and set her focus on making dinner. Her family was driving in from the city and due to arrive in one hour.

WITH CHRISTIAN BEHIND THE WHEEL, HE and Bianca made the two-hour drive in record time. Before they knew it, Christian wound the Porsche up the circular driveway of their Muskoka cottage.

Shifting the car to park, Christian looked over to Bianca. From the car radio, Stevie Nicks poignantly questioned whether she could sail through the changing ocean tides. Christian wondered if his sister could sail through this unscathed, seeing the churning emotions raging in Bianca's face.

For a long while, with Stevie Nick's voice drifting through the radio, Christian sat alongside his sister in silence, allowing her to channel her emotions into a calmer state.

Bianca was two years his senior and the stronger of the two. While Christian prided himself on being a lover like his father, Bianca was made of sterner stuff. She got that from their mother. However strong she was, she wasn't bearing well. He supposed he wouldn't either were he in her shoes. How did you deal with finding out the last twenty-four years of your life was a lie?

With the stir of emotions in her eyes, Bianca flicked her gaze toward the two-story chalet. Bianca's mood lifted some when she saw the house gleaming white in the moonlight. Tall windows blinked gold from every room.

Beyond the living room window, Bianca caught sight of the glossy, white Steinway where she'd spent so many Christmases playing carols for her family. She pictured the flames from a crackling fire curl and sway in the fireplace as the pine's lingering scent from the tree she and her mother spent hours decorating scented the air.

As memorable as the memory was, it was marred by the idea she may never have been a part of the family she loved.

"You're going to have to get out of the car sometime," Christian said, stepping out of the car. The sound of night creatures singing their mating songs flowed in night's silence. Tulips wavered in the soft wind that ruffled the red maple tree leaves in the front yard. "Come on." He gave her his hand.

Bianca's stomach stirring like a tornado, she stepped out. "We're the first here," she said, hearing the nerves in her voice.

"Dad should be here soon. He had to make a quick stop to pick up Grandma and Gramps." Christian leaned his six-foot frame against the hood of the car next to his sister. "We're not standing out here until they come. She heard us drive up, so we may as well head inside."

"All right, but don't leave me alone with her. Otherwise, it could get ugly."

"Fine," Christian said, leading the way up the flower-lined flagstone walk to the double oak doors.

"Mom, we're here," Christian announced, walking into the kitchen, and Isabella couldn't help notice how his smile instantly lit the room.

"Hi, baby." Isabella raised a cheek for him to peck. "Dinner is served as soon as your father, Mama, and Dad arrive."

"I hope you've made plenty, 'cause I'm starved. I haven't eaten for a couple of hours." Christian poked his head in the refrigerator.

Isabella turned smiling eyes at her son. The boy could always put a smile on her face. "The beer's behind the orange juice, and I've made more than enough food. How about you, Bianca, are you hungry?" Isabella asked, meeting the blue eyes that demanded distance.

"No. I'm tired from the drive. I'm going to go up to my room to freshen up. Call me when everyone gets here." Bianca fought the urge to delve into the topic there and then.

"All right, honey." Isabella watched her daughter bolt up the kitchen stairs.

At Isabella's sigh, Christian put a hand on her tense shoulder. "It'll be fine, Mom. She just needs some time to herself." Affection came through the blue eyes, and it warmed Isabella.

She could always count on her son's support. Christian was her sensitive child, easy to talk to, always there when she needed him. Her boy was his father's physical image, and like Antonio, he always had the perfect words for every occasion.

Isabella watched Christian twist the bottle cap. "She told you?"

"Yeah, she did." Christian took a pull of his beer.

"Is she okay?"

"Not really." Christian's hand curled on Isabella's arm. "You need to talk to her. The sooner, the better."

"You know there's an explanation."

Christian leaned back against the counter, crossed his feet at the ankles, and gazed into his mother's shadowed eyes. "I figured as much, but it's not me you need to convince. From the look of you, it would do you a wealth of good to get it off your chest."

"I don't care about me. I'm afraid of how she's going to react." Isabella added salt to boiling water.

"As temperamental as we both know Bianca can be, which by the way she gets from you, she loves you, and she'll forgive you once she's had time to digest whatever this is. But you need to tell her what this is, Mom."

Isabella felt her throat constrict at the thought. As she was about to open up, the sound of the front door opening echoed into the kitchen.

"Hello. The cavalry's arrived. Where's everybody?" Antonio called from the foyer.

"We're in the kitchen. You have just enough time to wash up. Dinner will be served in ten minutes." Isabella dropped fresh pasta into the boiling water.

Dinner was uneventful, quieter than usual. Bianca picked at her food and barely said a word. The tension between Isabella and her daughter was palpable, but no one dared to say a word, although Antonio vowed to interject soon. If the two most important women in his life didn't address whatever was building the rift between them, he'd forced them to do so.

"Let's head into the living room for dessert. Mrs. McCarthy, will you please bring in the coffee and the wonderful cheesecake you made this afternoon." Isabella told their long time maid as she rose from the dinner table to lead the march.

Everyone settled in the comfortable living room, surrounded by framed family photographs on the walls, fireplace mantel, and the baby grand. Maria turned to Isabella and asked the question on everyone's mind. "Is everything all right, honey?"

"Not really, but I'm hoping to make it so." Nerves jittering, Isabella looked over at her daughter when she spoke. Hesitating for a moment, she rubbed damp hands on her jeans and, for the last time, formulated the words she'd say in her head.

"There's no easy or right way to say this, so I'm just going to come out and say it." The room took an immediate tense tone, and Isabella prepared for the backlash her words were going to spawn. "When we were in Milan for fashion week four months ago, I was approached by Joe Smith."

Coffee cups clanged on dishes, and the gasps of shock were heard around the room. Maria's hand pressed to her throbbing chest, she wondered what possessed her daughter. Salvatore recoiled in horror at the thought of his daughter with Joe. Bianca and Christian eyed one another with furrowed brows. Neither knew who Joe Smith was, but both sensed it wasn't a welcomed name in their circle.

"All he wanted to do was talk, and I eventually relented," Isabella said.

Unable to contain himself, Antonio shot Isabella a look so heated it burned through her. "Are you crazy? Why would you do such a thing?" He lashed out with a seething anger that rippled in the shouted words, shocking Bianca and Christian in the process. They'd never heard their father raise his voice in anger at their mother. "Where were you when he approached you?"

Isabella swallowed on a dry throat. "At the cafe, I like to go to for my morning alone me-time."

Antonio felt every muscle tense. "You were by yourself?"

"I was in a public place. There were lots of people. Giorgio was there." Isabella's voice was mild in contrast to Antonio's temper.

Antonio's blazing gaze locked on Isabella. "Why, why would you give that lunatic the time of day? After everything he did to you. And why wouldn't you mention anything until now?"

In their father's words, the quivering rage sent a shiver through Christian and Bianca, and both wondered what Joe Smith had done to warrant such hate.

"I'm in complete agreement with Antonio, honey. Why would you, especially after…" Salvatore pressed his lips together to hold in the words he swore never to utter when Maria rested her hand on his.

Isabella broke in. "Please, calm down. Let me explain. All he wanted to do was talk."

Unable to come to grips with what she'd said, Maria, Salvatore, and Antonio stared at Isabella with a dumbfounded look.

Isabella's expression softened. "Antonio, I love you so very much. You're my life, my soulmate, and I'd never do anything to upset you or cause you pain."

"What's that got to do with anything?" Antonio murmured through clenched teeth.

"There's something I…" Isabella went silent, touched on her ringed finger to find the strength to go on. "There's something I've never told you if only because I was afraid of…"

Seeing the growing tension on her face, Antonio regretted snapping at her. "What is it, Isabella? You know you can tell me anything."

The strain clear as day on her face told Antonio that whatever was on her mind was about to change things forever, and he braced himself.

Isabella's insides churning, she met Antonio's eyes, held. "Joe assaulted me the night you left for Vancouver. The story I told you about falling down the stairs at Mama's was a lie I made up to cover for the bruising on my body and the gash on my face."

The staggering statement plunged the room into an instant silence as the shockwave her words set off filtered through Antonio, Bianca, and Christian.

"What do you mean by assault?" The breath of panic caught at the base of Antonio's throat.

The tension in the room pulsed with a life of its own, and everyone's eyes fixed on Isabella, who didn't answer Antonio, but her hunched shoulders, her guilty sidelong glance, her pursed lips, confirmed his worst fears.

Antonio's face changed from stunned to guilt, followed by outrage, and circled back to rage.

Antonio's eyes, nearly black, he shouted, "That fucking, bastard. I'm going to fucking kill him with my bare hands. I knew I should have killed him the day I had the chance. I should have beaten the life out of him." The wildness in Antonio's eyes told everyone in the room he'd do it in a heartbeat.

It was a side of him no one had seen. It was then Maria and Salvatore understood why Isabella begged them to keep the assault a secret.

"Please, Antonio, calm down," Isabella begged as he began to pace the room with the frantic energy that matched his temper. "Please, let me explain."

Antonio's face flushed red as he raked fingers through his hair. "Goddamnit, Isabella, why wouldn't you tell me when it happened? We're supposed to be a partnership." He shot Isabella a look of real pain.

The tears welled in Isabella's eyes. "I was scared you'd have…"

"Turned away from you?" Antonio jumped in. "I would never have done that." He sank to his knees beside Isabella. "It's me who's unworthy of you. I'm supposed to protect you, and I failed. It's my fault. Knowing what he did, I should never have left you that day. I'm sorry I put my business ahead of you. I'm sorry I let you down, Isabella."

Isabella framed his face with her hands. "It wasn't your fault. Never think that. I never once thought you'd turn away from me. To this day, I can always count on you to be by my side for better or worse. I was scared of what you'd do to Joe. I'd seen the anger in your eyes for him, and I figured you'd react erratically."

"Damn straight, I would have. No one touches my family and gets away with it."

"That's exactly why I didn't tell you. I figured you'd do something you'd regret for the rest of your life, our lives, and I wasn't going to allow you to end up…" Isabella's voice broke. "I didn't care that I was tarnished."

Antonio ran a hand over her hair. "Don't say that. You could never be. Not for me."

Love rolled through her in one fast unrelenting wave. "I could deal with that, the tarnished part, but I couldn't deal with the thought of losing you, the thought of you ending up locked up to avenge my honour. I wouldn't have been able to live without you. I'd have withered away if I lost you." Isabella's voice was so tender Antonio felt something catch in his throat.

Regret swimming into his eyes, Antonio brought her hand to his lips. "I'm sorry I made it so you couldn't turn to me during your darkest hour. I'm so sorry you had to deal with it on your own. I'm sorry I made it, so you felt you couldn't talk to me about such a difficult time in your life. I'm sorry I wasn't there for you." Antonio's voice was brittle. The torment inside him at the thought of what she must have dealt with on her own had guilt flaring up, choking him. "You're everything to me, and I should have been there for you. I'm sorry for failing you."

Isabella touched her hand to Antonio's cheek. "You never failed me. You never could." Throughout their marriage, Antonio had given Isabella nothing but unconditional love and support. From the onset, their relationship was based on understanding, on an all-consuming, enduring love. "I'm sorry I never told you, but I couldn't stand to lose you." Isabella fell into him, and Antonio stroked her hair as the long due tears of relief flowed, and with it, the guilt she'd harboured all those years faded away.

Watching Isabella's face, Antonio linked fingers with her. "You don't need to apologize or feel guilty for anything. I'm... we're your family, and we're here for you. We'll always be here for you."

Isabella buried her face in her hands as she burst into fresh tears. "I've felt so guilty for so long for not having told you. It's been eating me up inside all these years." Isabella's words were contrite. "I'm so sorry I need to bring this up for the family to deal with. It's not what I wanted, but it's something we need to deal with now."

Christian reached for Bianca's hand and tightened his grip around it. It hadn't taken him long to conclude his mother's reason for the DNA test. He looked over at his sister in the hope she hadn't come to the same conclusion. The tears welling in her eyes told him she had.

"Let her explain," Christian whispered, and Bianca remained silent, but only because raw nerves rendered her speechless as everything became clear—much too clear.

She was the product of an assault on her mother by a man she didn't know. Bianca shook her head, desperately trying to get the thought she couldn't come to terms with out of her head. She had questions, so many questions, but they'd have to wait, she decided, when Isabella, composed again, began to speak.

Isabella reiterated Joe's incredible story of how Michaela, along with her mother, orchestrated the sequence of the events that led to that awful day. Isabella described how adamant Joe was that nothing happened. That he believed Michaela and her mother staged the scene from beginning to end.

Isabella told the group, stunned with shock, that based on Joe's demeanour, his remorseful tone, and the guilt she'd seen in his eyes she believed him. Eyes pivoting from Antonio to Maria, and Salvatore, Isabella told them how Michaela fueled Joe's drinking and sabotaged his attempts to quit to manipulate him. She explained how Michaela manipulated Kat into giving her a copy of the door key.

"Kat was involved?" Maria's eyes fixed wide.

Isabella nodded. "She confirmed it when I spoke to her," Isabella explained Kat's lapse of judgment. "She told me Michaela blackmailed her into getting a copy of the key and, feeling guilty at her betrayal, immediately demanded that the key be returned. When Michaela refused to return it, Kat told her she was going to the police. It was then, Michaela relented and returned the key, but by then, she'd probably made a duplicate."

Rising, Isabella walked to the glass doors leading to the slate patio surrounded by spring colours. She listened to the night before turning to tell them about Michaela, and her mother became obsessed with her success and her relationship with Antonio they took to stalking them.

"Jesus, Nina, and Michaela were stalking you?" Maria shuddered at the violation of someone watching her daughter and son, and family no less.

"Mainly, Michaela." Isabella flicked eyes to Antonio. "They stalked us for months. They're mentally unstable. I never suspected. Michaela was always so supportive, but Joe told me it was all part of her plan. Joe even told me that when Michaela claimed to be helping me out with Mrs. Johnstone, she was sabotaging me. Luckily, she never succeeded."

Michaela, with her mother's support, Isabella told her family, concocted the plot to manipulate a broken Joe into stalking her to instill fear, and ultimately attacking her. Isabella told Antonio the reason for Joe and Michaela's sudden departure from their lives, which she knew nothing about until Joe raised it. She turned to Salvatore and her mother with a loving, grateful gaze.

Isabella relayed how Joe used Salvatore's money to pull himself out of the dark place in his life and launched a successful construction company in Europe. In detail, she described his children, his wife of fifteen years whom he adored. Isabella described the man Joe had become. The man he was now.

With each sentence, Maria, Salvatore, and Antonio's shock swelled at the fantastic story.

Isabella fished through her jeans pocket. "Joe gave me this cheque to give you, Dad. I've been holding on to it until the right moment." Salvatore and Maria gaped at the cheque in astonishment before passing it to Antonio. "Joe said that should cover the total amount you've paid Michaela to date. He felt the need to take responsibility, accountability for his part, and not stop their insanity. So, you see why I believe he's not the Joe we knew."

Isabella hoped she'd offered enough proof to convince them of Joe's innocence because now wasn't the time to mention Joe's professed love for her. The ultimate proof he never meant to harm her was a conversation she'd have with Antonio in private when the time felt right—if ever.

"And now that I've opened this Pandora's Box, your questions must be answered." Isabella turned pain-filled eyes to a teary-eyed Bianca. "Bianca, honey, everything I've said until now leads to the document you found." Remorse flooded Isabella when she looked into the eyes, swimming in tears, drowning in angst.

"I'm so sorry you had to find out as you did, but I was hoping to deal with it myself. It wasn't because I wanted to conceal anything from you, but because I didn't want to involve you in this ... ugliness. When you confronted me, I panicked. I shouldn't have, but I did, and for that, I'm so very sorry. I should have addressed all of your questions then, but I wasn't ready for you to find out about such an ugly time of my life, and I didn't want it to come out during a heated argument. Can you understand that? Can you understand that I never meant to hurt you? I never would."

Bianca lifted her head. Her eyes levelled to Isabella's she couldn't help but see the storm of emotions raging in them.

"You're my daughter, Bianca. Our daughter and I love you. I would go to the ends of the earth to protect you and keep you from harm's way. I dealt with this on my own, not to hide a truth from you, but to keep you from what I believed, was unnecessary pain. Can you understand that?" Isabella asked, knowing Bianca would only fully understand a mother's deep-seated need to do whatever necessary to protect her children when she had her own.

Bianca still hadn't fully processed everything, but she respected her mother's fierce determination and resolve to overcome such an awful, dark time. She could only admire how difficult it must have been to carry such a burden alone. The thought of just how alone her mother must have felt drove Bianca into tears. The anger, hate, and fear that had consumed her in the past three days faded, and at that instant, she let herself fall into her mother's arms.

"I'm so sorry, Mom."

Isabella pulled back far enough to look into Bianca's eyes. "You have nothing to apologize for, honey. I'm the one who's sorry for dragging you into this. I wanted my past to remain my past. I didn't want it touching you. I didn't want you seeing the world through damaged eyes."

"I'm so sorry for doubting you, for what I said. God, I said so many hateful things. I should have known better, but I was hurt and angry. I didn't mean any of it." There was a softness in Bianca's eyes.

Isabella brushed the hair from her daughter's face, wiped the wet cheeks dry. "I know, honey. I'm sorry for not being upfront with you. In my eyes, you're still the little girl who needs protecting. But these past few days, I've realized you're a strong, intelligent woman. I accept that now, and it's why I'm going to leave the decision to you as to whether you want to know everything. I won't keep anything from you, not if you don't want me to."

It took some time for Bianca to decide. Eventually, she nodded, and Isabella gathered the strength to go on.

"All right. This is difficult to say, but before we parted, Joe told me Michaela would be making contact with me in the coming weeks to question..." Isabella hesitated, "Bianca's paternity."

As difficult as the words were to say, Isabella knew they were more difficult for Bianca and Antonio to hear. Isabella let the stunned silence hang for a moment, allowing her outlandish statement to sink in.

"Goddamnit, when is this nightmare going to end?" Antonio exploded with anger as forceful as a blasted cannon. Antonio's abrupt outburst rattled everyone, but for Bianca's sake, Isabella maintained her composure.

"Joe told me Michaela found out Bianca was now on the board of directors of our companies, which automatically led her to believe Bianca has a stake in The Café and the Isabella Farfalla companies. Michaela's goal is to get her hands on Bianca's shares by claiming she's..." Isabella huffed a deep breath, "Joe's daughter." At the thought of the impact her words had on Bianca, Isabella felt the waves of exhaustion swamp her.

"Jesus." Antonio's head jerked around to face Isabella, spilling scotch on his hands and counter. "Why the hell would she think that when she and Joe are divorced?"

"Michaela's going on the assumption we believe they're together. It was why he made it a point to seek me out." Isabella and the group remained fearfully silent, listening to Antonio's long, colourful oath laced tirade before he took his drink in one gulp, wincing when the alcohol hit his system. "Joe hoped by telling me we could stay ahead of her."

Antonio stopped his drink mid-sip. "How the hell does Joe know all this?"

"Son, can you bring the bottle over," Salvatore called to Antonio.

Isabella's eyes followed Antonio, making his way back to the couch with the refilled snifter in one hand and the bottle of scotch in the other. "He's had her watched like a hawk since he remarried to protect his family and company interests."

"He could be making all this up, to absolve himself." Antonio protested, and Maria and Salvatore jointly nodded in agreement.

"He's not." Isabella searched through her shirt pocket for the photographs, handed them to Antonio. "The detective Joe hired to track Michaela's movements took them. Joe had him courier them to me on our return from Milan."

Reluctantly, Antonio took the photographs, eyed them dismissively at first. When recognition set in, he studied them more carefully. Antonio's brows slammed together in disbelief at the familiar face of the man pinned against the wall, Michaela's lips on his. Flipping through the prints, Antonio saw the man's hands kneading Michaela's buttocks before they walked into the hotel room. One of the photographs depicted them in a compromising position in the back seat of a black Mercedes.

"Joe's detective took those and told him Michaela has been getting all sorts of information about Bianca from the man in the photo. Do you recognize him?" Isabella's eyes never left the face expressing deep disbelief.

"It's David Strubb." Antonio passed the photos to Salvatore and Maria.

"That's David, all right," Maria confirmed.

"Note the date stamp. It's as recent as three months ago." Isabella pointed out.

"He's been our lawyer for almost thirty years. He's like family." Maria's downcast eyes fixed on the photographs.

"I know. I was as disappointed when I found out, but Joe did say Michaela's a master manipulator, particularly with men. She's been having an affair with David for some time. I'm guessing for the sole purpose of getting him to feed her the information she wants. I, therefore, decided to take advantage of David's loose lips. I called him after we got back from Milan."

Isabella explained she asked their longtime lawyer for legal advice about giving Bianca complete control of their companies. Isabella scanned Antonio's face to see his reaction and was surprised when she saw the thoughtful narrow-eyed look that told her he was considering the angles.

"My goal was to…"

"Dangle a carrot, entice Michaela out so you could confront her face to face." Antonio's eyebrows winged, he finished in a calmer tone. Isabella could see he looked calmer, steadier. "It's a smart move. Facing her head-on is the only way to deal with people like her. I hope you have a plan in mind." Antonio's sudden shift of support caught Isabella off guard, and for a moment, she was rendered speechless. "Isabella? Have you formulated a plan to deal with this conniving bitch?"

"I have. For one, I figure I'd play on her greedy nature. I believe she will easily dismiss Dad's payments for the larger windfall she stands to make by pursuing this ludicrous paternity suit. I think she'd be willing to sacrifice everything when I entice Mr. Strubb to inform her she has a good chance of winning the case, but that she has to return to Toronto to set the suit in motion." Inspired now, Isabella spoke with confidence.

Salvatore said, "And once she sets foot in Canada, she'll violate her agreement with me so that it will end the yearly payments."

Isabella swept a pleased gaze at Salvatore. "It's her only source of income, and I want to take it from her. I want to take all I can from her. I want her to regret touching my family. I want to send her a message of who she's dealing with," Isabella said, with the fierceness of an attack dog meant to cause serious harm.

"And how do you plan on dealing with this paternity suit?" Antonio asked, although he was sure he wasn't going to like the answer.

Isabella looked over to Bianca with a cautionary look, and mother and daughter shared a moment of complete understanding. "Go ahead, Mom. Tell him, tell us everything."

"Before we parted way, Joe dropped an envelope on the table and told me to use the contents when I found it necessary. He told me it would help me prove Michaela wrong. I threw the envelope in my purse and forgot all about it up until I began to set a trap for Michaela in motion. I dug it up, and when I opened it, I found hair follicles. Joe's hair follicles."

The blood drained from Antonio's face, and his shoulders tensed, as the implication was becoming much too clear. "Jesus. You ran a DNA test on Joe and our daughter?"

The surreal comment stunned Maria and Salvatore. "Jesus," both said in unison.

"I had to." Isabella fixed her gaze on Bianca. "It's not because of the money. You know that's the farthest thing from my mind. I did it because you're my daughter, and as much as I know Michaela doesn't have a leg to stand on, this woman has managed to do so much to me I wouldn't risk her hurting you. I need to get her out of your life. I need to get her out of our lives, and the only way I figured to do that was to provide concrete evidence she doesn't have any standing when it comes to this ludicrous paternity suit. I'd go to any lengths, do anything necessary to protect you." The ferocity of a protective mother ripped through Isabella's words.

Looking over to her mother, Bianca had nothing but love and admiration for her mother. Bianca hoped to one-day feel as loved by her daughter as she felt for Isabella then.

"You do what you feel is necessary to take that bitch down, Mom," Bianca said, quick enough to cut Antonio's oncoming outburst.

"I'm glad you said that because that's exactly what I aim to do." The eyes that stared back at her daughter were those of a brave woman resolute in fighting to the death. "Are you all right with this?" Isabella asked, turning to Antonio, who had fingers pressed firmly against his temple.

When Bianca directed an intense gaze at her father, he accepted defeat, and all he could do was sigh. "I guess I'm going to have to be. I can't go up against the two of you."

"That's right, Daddy, you can't go up against the Mesi women."

Isabella's lips curved as she went on to lay out her plan. "Honey, I'm going to leave the decision to you as to whether you'd like to know the DNA test results. I still haven't read the papers myself, so I don't know the results. I can tell you which of the two subjects in the report is Antonio," Isabella said, turning the envelope over to her daughter.

Eyeing the envelope in her hands, the muscles in Bianca's stomach tightened. The notion the results would indicate her father, the man who'd been a part of her life her entire life, wasn't was more than she could bear.

The image of him cuddling her when she ran to him, crying when she fell off her bike and scraped her knee came to her. She saw him sitting by her bedside when she was down with the chickenpox. The memory of the time he set everything aside to be with her at her first piano recital and how much he bragged about her performance even though she'd messed up Chopsticks came to her. The proud smile that followed her to the podium when she accepted her MBA degree flashed in her mind.

Bianca flicked eyes up from the envelope to her father and back to the envelope tightly clutched in her hands. Antonio's quick intake of breath, the jolt of emotion in his blue eyes, spoke to her, and Bianca felt her throat swell as she wondered whether she was doing the right thing.

In one easy leap, Bianca was in Antonio's arms. "You're my dad, always have been, always will be. You're stuck with me, Daddy."

Antonio's world snapped back on its perfect axis. Through the blur of tears, he took his daughter into a tight embrace. "I wouldn't want it any other way, peanut."

Taking a picture of Antonio and Bianca into her heart, Angelo's words came to Isabella. True love always did find its way back.

Epilogue

ISABELLA WALKED INTO David Strubb's office and spread the photographs on his desk like a colourful pictorial. She let him drift shocked eyes over the pictures awhile before threatening to have copies distributed to his clients and wife.

Pointedly, Isabella told David she wouldn't hesitate to turn them over to his father-in-law, the distinguished Sir Charles Templeton. As his employer and father to the cuckold daughter, he wouldn't look kindly to his extracurricular actives.

Sitting across from David, Isabella leisurely crossed a long, toned leg over another. "Both you and I know, David, that Charles will go to any lengths to keep Antonio's and my multi-million dollar accounts from walking out the door and into competitors' hands. Not to mention the lengths he'll go to avoid the blemish his reputation and firm will sustain with the exposure of your blatant breach of our attorney-client privilege were I brazen enough to tell him I'd put it out there for public consumption. You know how nasty your competition can be. Lawyers." Isabella tsked with feigned disgust.

"Now, this is what you're going to do." Isabella outlined in bullet form her requirements. "I expect my instructions to be carried out at the soonest and to the letter, David, otherwise Charles finds out about everything." She rose to her feet in one fluid motion, brushed the front of her impeccably cut pearl-white suit.

"And, David, Antonio and I want nothing to do with you from here on. I'll be calling Charles to let him know just that," she said, relishing in the satisfaction of how losing his only clients would affect him and his standing in the firm. "Remember." Isabella waved the snapshots over her shoulder as she walked out of his office.

The trap set it was a matter of waiting. It felt hugely satisfying to feel like the spider at the center of a well-knit web.

Days from their conversation, David notified Isabella that he'd talked to Michaela to return to Toronto to set the paternity lawsuit in motion.

The moment Michaela set foot on Canadian soil, Isabella's detective documented her every move. Just as Isabella demanded of David, the investigator was treated to the staged images of Michaela and him at various locales throughout the city, including the downtown condominium David bought her three years ago.

David's end of the bargain fulfilled, he thought it best to distance himself from Michaela. As expected, Michaela threw his ass out of the one million dollar apartment when he told her his father-in-law had taken over Isabella and Antonio's accounts. It was a write off David was more than willing to take.

Although Michaela had brought the sexual excitement his wife never did, David knew she was a spiteful, vindictive woman who'd go to any lengths to destroy anyone who crossed her. Now that retirement was in the cards, he couldn't stand to lose his wife's cushy trust fund.

Like a preying lion, Isabella patiently waited for the last phase of her plan to be executed.

Twenty-five years from the ugliest, darkest day in Isabella's life, she watched Michaela on her security monitor. Swaggering through the Isabella Farfalla Fashion Company's front doors—previously the Hart Designs design building Isabella purchased on auction— Michaela demanded to see her. Although Isabella kept Michaela waiting fifteen minutes, a little power flex, she was more than happy to set everything aside to meet with her darling cousin.

Michaela's eyes surveyed the vast office overlooking Lake Ontario. "You've done well, Isabella."

Michaela's honey-blonde hair was the same shade, and she'd changed little. Long, slim curves were draped in lavender Versace silk. Diamonds sparkled at her ears, neck, wrist, and fingers. As strikingly beautiful as Michaela looked, Isabella could see what she hadn't until now, ice under the polish and darkness in the blue eyes.

Isabella signalled Michaela to a guest chair and got right down to business. There was no better feeling than the one that swamped Isabella when she slid the envelope from the DNA Diagnostics across her desk and told Michaela the report conducted with Joe's consent proved Bianca was not his daughter.

"No, you're going to listen to me." Isabella walked around her desk and ripped the cigarette from Michaela's hand dropped it into her coffee cup. "For one, there's no smoking in my building." Isabella held her hand up to silence Michaela when she opened her mouth. "Two, your paternity case is a fictional story concocted in your tiny, diluted mind, Michaela," Isabella said, with the confidence brought on by the feeling she was in complete control of her life.

"Joe is more than willing to testify to you, and your mother being the instigators of my assault. To clarify, since I know you've likely done your research, I'm aware the statute of limitations on the assault has lapsed, but in the court of public opinion, there are no statutes of limitations. Juicy gossip is always welcomed, and I know you wouldn't want to be tried or judged. You know how capable gossipers like your mother are at broadcasting malicious news. They can cause so much damage." Isabella savoured the long-overdue moment.

"I will make sure your parent's friends, co-workers, butcher, barber, bag-boy, hell, anyone who'll listen, come to know what you and your mother are, what you've done. I'll make sure they know what vile, vindictive sociopaths you both are. I will make your life and that of your parents a living hell as you did to me. I will destroy you by any means necessary if you don't leave this country if you don't leave Bianca and my entire family alone." Isabella threatened with a fierceness that unhinged Michaela.

Stunned by Isabella's unsettling, murderous glare, Michaela didn't waver to say, "Fine. I'll do as you ask. I'll leave the city."

"The country, Michaela," Isabella injected with a forceful tone. "The country."

"Fine, and you won't hear from me again. I still have your daddy's yearly payments," Michaela hissed like a venomous cobra.

Isabella's lips curved into a smile. "Think again. The payments cease as of today. The agreement was they would continue as long as you didn't set foot in Canada, and last I checked, Toronto was still a part of Canada. And look at that, we've been filming you on our security system since you set foot in the building." Isabella pivoted her laptop screen toward Isabella and replayed the captured footage in a loop. "And," she spread the photographs taken by her private investigator and let Michaela's eyes drift over them awhile.

"Now, get out of my office, and crawl back into the hole you came from." Isabella bolted up, giving Michaela her full attention. "I don't ever want to see you come near my family or me again. If you do, Michaela," Isabella slammed hands down on her desk and fixed an intense gaze on Michaela, "You will deeply regret it, and I'll sue you for the last three payments my father made to you. That's what, three hundred thousand dollars? Because according to this deed," Isabella waved it at her, "you've owned the downtown condo for as long. So, it's safe to deduce you've been in and out of the country since then. Don't underestimate me digging up the proof if needed." With those words, Isabella buzzed her security guards and, with a triumphant look, watched them forcibly escort Michaela out of her building.

All the pieces neatly in place, Isabella swivelled toward the wall of glass. Bathed in serenity, she watched a gull skim the water, then bullet away in a sun-washed sky. For a long while, staring out of her tenth-floor office window as bright rays of sunlight danced over calm, blue waters that rolled forever, Isabella relished in the feeling of deliverance.

For the first time in years, Isabella felt settled.

It had been a long road she'd travelled, with a myriad of obstacles she'd overcome with the support of a loving family and a husband she knew would always be by her side come what may. With the helping hand from the man who filled her memories, the man who looked down on her with a proud smile, she was the woman she was today.

Turning her focus back to the manila envelope containing the DNA report, Isabella stared at it for some time, contemplated, debated. After much consideration, she picked it up and walked it to the shredder. Running the envelope together with its contents through the blades, she watched the last piece of a past she would put behind forever disappear, but not before reading the contents.

Sneak peek at M.L. Lexi's new novel
THE BLIND WOMAN

Prologue

Richmond Hill 1991

ONE-MINUTE BOB and Mary Taylor, with their thirteen-year-old daughter Celeste, were on their way home after a night of merry celebration with family and friends to welcome 1991, and the next...

Their world turned upside down.

The impact of metal against metal, the grating, and the screams came when the oncoming Mercedes slid on black ice and careened into Bob's Ford head-on. Celeste's ears pulsed under the agonizing volume. Nausea rose so fast so sharp it stole her breath. Celeste screamed as the wave of panic swelled inside her, pushed up into her throat, choking her. Then...

Bob lost control of the car.

The car spiraled, zigzagged across both lanes. Celeste saw her parents' body fling back and forth like a lifeless rag doll in the front seat. Mary's piercing screams filled the car as her husband's bloodied head bounced off the steering wheel. Blood spurted from the gash on his head, spraying his wife's face red.

"No, Mom, don't take your seatbelt off," Celeste shouted when a dazed Mary started to unbuckle herself to grab hold of her passed out husband. "Brace your head with your arms. Do it, Mom. Now." Celeste's words tinged with the terror choking her compelled Mary to do as told.

Next thing, the car cut across the banks of Lake Wilcox and became airborne. The high-pitched cracking sound that filled the silence when the front end of the car hit the smooth sheet of frozen lake water was as stunning as it was frightening. In one quick, ugly moment, Celeste drowned in fear so great that it numbed her body. Terror and fear punched Celeste in the stomach harder when the car's nose fell through the crack in the ice and began to sink to the muddy bottom of Lake Wilcox.

It was dark, so very dark. Sinister shadows lurked in its blackness. The coldness of the lake penetrated the walls of the car. Focused on surviving, neither woman felt it.

Celeste's headache was expanding inside her skull, and her vision was becoming blurred.

She tried to thrust the car door open, but the force of the water pressing against it made it impossible.

The front half of the car filled with water. Celeste could feel her chocked gasps wanting to rise into shouts, screams, and prayers she'd never prayed. Nothing came out.

Celeste heard her mother gasp for air then… Silence.

The silence was eerie.

A fear so sharp curled in Celeste's gut, snaked down to the soles of her feet. She called out to her mother but was sidetracked by the wall of water rising, filling the back half of the car. Struggling for air, Celeste frantically slammed fists against the window. Nothing happened. Then…

The darkness came.

CELESTE LAY ON THE COLD, SNOW-COVERED ground. A wind, cold enough to pierce bone, swept over her. Raw with wet, the chill dug deep into her. She was cold, so cold, and she began to shiver. The man covered her with his coat, and the warmth came over her.

Celeste thought she heard the muffled sound of a man's raspy voice come at her. Exhaling a breath of relief, she heard him thank God she was breathing. In the distance, she thought she heard the wail of an ambulance. Maybe it was the wind. She wasn't sure.

The man's raspy voice encouraged her to hang on. Just hang on, she heard him repeat and assure her she was going to be okay.

Celeste asked the raspy voice where she was, but he didn't answer. Celeste thought of her parents, asked where they were if they were okay.

The man she sensed was standing watchful over her said nothing.

Celeste shouted the question at the man again, but he wouldn't answer. Instead, he took his coat back, and she thought she heard the crunch of ice—one person, two, maybe three—underfoot as he walked away.

Coming Soon

The Complete Woman
The Conflicted Woman
The Spiteful Woman
The Tortured Woman

The Relentless Woman Duology

The Relentless Woman
The Vindictive Women

The Unbreakable Woman Trilogy

The Unbreakable Woman
The Brave Woman
The Valiant Woman

Visit or contact us at:

Visit us at www.mllexi.com to read excerpts of upcoming releases.

Email us at mllexiauthor@gmail.com

Click SIGN ME UP to receive emails whenever M.L. Lexi publishes a new book. There is no charge or obligation and your information will remain confidential.